FROM THE DEEP

A FICTION-ATLAS
PRESS ANTHOLOGY

FROM THE DEEP

A FICTION-ATLAS PRESS ANTHOLOGY

C.L. CANNON   KAT PARRISH   L.J. WYNN
MARGO BOND COLLINS   EMMA SHELFORD   K. MATT
MELISSA A. JOY   SABETHA DANES   LEANN MASON
L.B. CARTER   LISAH JAYNE WALDEN
ANTHEA SHARP   JC BROWN   LENA LANE
ROSA MARCHISELLA   JAMES RICKETT

FICTION-ATLAS
PRESS LLC

IN WATERS DARK AND DEEP
BY C.L. CANNON

KARIS

The ocean was unusually calm this night, more tranquil than it had any right to be when its mistress felt so tempestuous. She sat with her fins draped over the side of a small fishing boat, her back turned from her home, and eyes focused on the young man standing before her.

"But why must you go? Is the human world so devoid of fishermen only you can come to their aid? Only you can win this war for them? It is folly, my love."

"Karis, you know it is dishonorable to flee one's duty," Antreas admonished. He inspected the blade of his dagger carefully before securing it inside its sheath and placing the weapon into his tattered pack. He looked up from his task to meet the mermaid's gaze and gave her a small smile, though it didn't quite reach his eyes. "I must avail my kinsman, no matter how I wish it weren't so." He broached the distance between them in two long strides, reaching for her face with a familiar tenderness. His fingers brushed the line of Karis's jaw, his thumb wiping away a tear she'd never admit shedding.

"And will you answer the call of your beloved with as much

fervor?" she asked, turning her body from his view. She glared at the man she loved over her shoulder, trying to decide if her harsh words would make a difference. She was not playing fair, and she knew it. Perhaps she was selfish, perhaps all her kind were, but she was not ready to give up yet. The lantern light was growing weaker, illuminating only the barest hint of Antreas's face, but Karis could see through the darkness. She could see disappointment cross his features as the sharpness of her words cut into him, but disappointment was quickly replaced with steely determination, and it only made her love him more. He was a good man… in a world of horrible ones. And that is what she feared the most.

His hand caressed her shoulder as he spoke softly, sincerely. "I am yours, and I always will be. I will do what you will of me. I will protect you with my life," he assured her. His beautiful cerulean eyes fixed on hers, baring his soul for her to see. "I will bend to your whims, and I will strive every day to earn your affection… and your forgiveness. But you must let me do this, or I fear it will haunt me to the end of my days."

His eyes pleaded for permission, and she could not be the one to deny it. "Come back to me, Antreas. Promise you'll come back."

His lips met hers eagerly, and she returned the gesture with equal enthusiasm, both pouring every emotion and every fear into this last kiss.

"I promise. Not even death could keep me from your side."

EVANDER

The moon's pale-yellow reflection shimmered like a bright jewel upon the surface of the water. The *Neminia* cut through the waves with ease, most of its crew lost in the fitful sleep that comes before a battle. Evander did not feel as if rest would ever find him. Plenty of the other men had seen war before. Some even reveled in it. Though he was good with a blade, he had not yet run another man through with his sword, and he couldn't say he looked forward to doing so.

His new friend seemed to be having the same problem. He'd met Bastian just a fortnight ago at the training grounds. He was more severe than Evander, more focused on the task at hand for certain, but his mind always seemed far away.

Tonight, especially, he seemed distracted by something. He didn't acknowledge Evander until he was practically upon his heels.

"Couldn't sleep either, eh?"

"Something is not right. It's too quiet. The sea's never this calm." His friend searched the soft waves, his brow crumpled with unease.

"Oh, quit you're worrying, Bastian. Let's enjoy it while we can. We've a long day tomorrow, and I, for one, plan on living a little before I die," Evander said, plucking a bottle of port from the sleeping arms of one of his fellow soldiers.

Bastian gave a disapproving shake of his head.

Evander chuckled. "What? He's dead asleep. He'll never miss it. Probably figure he drunk it all, if he even realizes it's gone." He kicked the man's boot to prove his point, only for the soldier to let loose a large belch and roll to his side.

A genuine smile spread across Bastian's face, and he took the bottle from Evander's outstretched hand. "You're right. But don't tell anyone I said such a thing," he said, taking a long swig of the amber liquid.

"As if they'd believe me," Evander teased, snatching the port back and drowning his nerves with a fiery gulp. "You think we'll make it through this?"

Bastian bowed his head for a moment and sighed. "I hope so, my friend. And if not, may we meet again in Elysium."

"I'll drink to that. Though I'd rather not die if it's all the same to you."

Bastian smiled crookedly. "You should get some rest then. Hard to best a foe when you're half asleep."

"I think you should take your own advice, friend."

Evander offered the remaining port to Bastian, then slowly lowered himself into a sitting position against the ship's rigging. Bastian placed the bottle beside the sleeping soldier it had been stolen from and settled in a few feet away from his friend.

All was quiet for a few moments before Evander spoke once more, sleep coloring his voice. "Bas?"

"Hm?" Bastian murmured in response.

"If I don't make it, tell my father I fought bravely. That's all he ever wanted of me, to be a good soldier, like him."

"We'll make it through this, and you can tell him yourself," Bastian assured with utter sincerity in his tone.

Suddenly, the calmness of the night broke into chaos. There was a deafening crack followed by screams as men in the lower decks were plunged into the inky black water below. The ship had split from stern to bow. The wind whipped violently, and the briny spray of saltwater drenched the remaining soldiers and crew as they desperately clung to anything they could grab hold of to stay afloat.

Evander clutched the rigging he'd propped himself against, and Bastian had managed to latch himself to the deck's railing. Both men watched in horror as the now, fully awoken soldier they'd snatched their evening spirits from slid across the foredeck only to be snatched up by an enormous black tentacle. His screams permeated the air for only a moment before a sickening crunch put an end to his misery.

"It's the witch!" Bastian yelled over the madness. "The sea witch, she's come to take us all."

"Not this night," Evander bellowed, not sure where his courage had come from, only certain he was not yet ready to die. He unsheathed his sword and readied himself to attack.

With another loud crack, the mainmast splintered, sending bits of wood and rigging to rain chaotically below. A large plank slammed into Evander's shoulder, knocking loose his hold of both rigging and sword. He struggled to regain purchase somewhere, anywhere but found himself plunging into the raging water below.

KARIS

Grief can do terrible things to a person. It can twist you up and spit you out more violently than the most tumultuous storm. And the worst part is how desperate it makes you. Desperate enough to sacrifice it all—your freedom, your life, your very existence—for a glimpse of the past. For a piece of spent happiness.

Karis knew grief all too well. It had swallowed her whole and engulfed every facet of her being. But she refused to let it break her forever. It had been nearly ten moons since she'd lost Antreas and every day, a little more of him slipped away. She could barely recall the deep timbre of his voice or the rough feel of his hands, fisherman's hands. The least likely creature to fall for a mermaid, but fall he did and Karis soon after. Their love was forbidden, an affront to the very nature of the merfolk, and her kin were happy to tell her so, but it was impossible not to love the man. His jests were terrible, he was stubborn as a barnacle when he set his mind to something, and his heart, his heart was too pure for this savage world, too trusting. That trust had cost him his life, and Karis was not about to let his kind nature be trespassed upon. The guilty would pay for their sins, and if all went to plan, she would rescue her love, even if it meant fighting death himself.

First, she needed a witch, and of course, some legs. Death's gate was a far journey, traversing over both land and sea. These fins would only take her so far.

"My dear, Highness, what in all the realms brings you to my door?" The witch's voice was soft and charming, but Karis was no fool. Any bargain she made here was likely to come with a heavy price. Her words would need to be carefully chosen lest she fall into a trap.

"I wish for you to grant me legs, human legs, for as long as I have need of them."

"Whatever for? Not thinking of abandoning your people, I hope?"

The creature was digging, searching for a weakness in defenses. She would not find one.

"My people will be well looked after," Karis assured her. "I have no intention of deserting them. Andronia will rule in my stead. You need not fear."

A smirk slid into place as the witch busied herself with all manner of bottles and herbs.

"Of course, Highness. How foolish of me. This wouldn't have anything to do with the untimely demise of that fisher boy, would it? I was so saddened to hear."

"What is your price for this enchantment?" Karis spat, angry and impatient with the direction the conversation had taken. "I have gold aplenty. I'm sure something can be arranged."

"It is not gold that I desire, Regent, nothing as fickle, I assure you."

"Then speak plainly, witch. What is it that you want?"

"Merely one single tear from your own eye. That would be a fitting prize indeed."

"And what use is a tear?" Karis wondered aloud.

"Precisely," the witch declared, swooping a vial from her shelf before swimming closer to Karis. "Let me take your tears for the boy. They will do you no favors in the battle to come. If you wish to find him, to bring him home, you will need determination, perseverance, two legs, and a guide. I can help you with all of these."

"And what are you not telling me?" Karis hardly supposed the witch to be of a helpful nature, there was always an angle, and in her experience, the odds were against her.

"Well, of course, all magic must be balanced. You are a mermaid, bound to the sea, forever. Nothing can change that, but, for a time, I can make you human or as close to human as possible. But you must give freely a piece of yourself. A token, if you will."

"The tear." Karis understood now. Saltwater, a symbol of what she was leaving behind.

"Yes, and should you fail to return to the sea by the next moon, you forfeit that bond and will remain human, forevermore."

"But if I don't go, I'll never see him again, will I?" Karis knew the answer, but she couldn't keep the question from slipping past her lips.

"No, child. You will be parted for eternity."

"Then do it. Make me human. Help me find him."

A single tear dripped from the mermaid's eye down her cheek and into the witch's waiting vial.

EVANDER

Loss changes everything. It can cripple the strongest of spirit. But guilt, guilt leeches onto a man's life and sucks the very marrow from his bones. It feasts until there is nothing left but a shell of his former self. Evander didn't recognize the person he was now, but he could no more transform into his carefree past iteration than he could pluck the stars from the sky. He'd seen too much and done too little. And then there was the sea witch. If only he had been brave enough to die, he might have never struck such a foolish bargain. Better dead than a slave to that woman's whims. But soon, soon, everything would change. He'd win his freedom, even if it meant taking the damned creature down with him.

No sooner had Evander made his vow did he feel the familiar pull of the witch's magic. There was a slight jolt in his stomach, and his world went black for a moment, then gradually came back into focus. Before him stood the sea witch in all her terrible glory. Long hair, black as night, flowed down her back and curled around her supple thighs. Her bright green eyes sparkled like emeralds, and her cruel mouth twisted into a frown.

"Dreaming of escape again, mortal? Well, never fear, I may have a task momentous enough to buy your freedom. If you survive, that is."

"And what murderous request do you ask of me now?" Evander spat, disgusted at himself for being once again pointed at another of the sea witch's enemies as one would a dagger. If she was offering an end to his servitude, it was likely an impossible feat.

"One of the merfolk called upon me this morn, and not just any sea maiden, their regent. It seems she fell in love with the enemy. Tragically, he met his demise before they could be pledged. Now she's gotten it into her pretty little head to rescue her beloved from the underworld, and I want you to help her."

"And how should I do that? It's not as if I've ever journeyed there, and even if I had, how would I have made it back alive? Who would believe me?"

No one had ever made it back from the underworld alive. It was the realm of the dead, and only the dead trespassed there. This quest was madness.

"You leave that to me. All you need do is befriend the girl. Earn her trust. Then, when the time is right, I want you to make sure she never returns to the sea."

His father would have refused such a request. His father was an honorable man, a better man than Evander could ever hope to be, no matter their differences. Yet, if this girl was the key to his freedom, how could he refuse it? He'd dishonored his father moons ago, and there was no turning back now. Now, he could only survive.

"So, you want me to kill her?" he asked, swallowing the lump in his throat as he weighed the cost of the deed.

"Oh, no, not yet," the witch cautioned, absently stroking a small green vial she'd hung round her neck. "She must abandon the call of the sea, then and only then may she be disposed of. There are many perils of the world the young maid has yet to face. The world of men is harsh and unforgiving, as you well know. You have until the next moon to ensure her safety. Flirt with her, befriend her, rescue her if you must, and encourage her if her spirit should despair. Lead her to the very gates of death itself, but no further. She must go willing into the abyss if it is freedom you seek."

"And what will harming this girl buy you?" asked Evander.

"Why, her kingdom, of course. If the girl abandons her realm, so too will it abandon her in search of a new master. And I intend that to be me. Complete this task, and not only will you be free, you will be rewarded with wealth and power beyond your imagining. Refuse, and forfeit your life and that of your compatriot," the witch warned, waving her hand to reveal an image of Bastian. His friend looked thin and weak—a far cry from the man who had pulled him from the depths of the ocean that horrible night—the man who had changed his fate and paid an unspeakable price. If there was any soul he owed a life debt to, it was Bastian. He could not let his friend remain the vile plaything of this creature.

"No, I'll do it. I'll make sure she doesn't return, but then you will keep your end of the bargain. You will free us. We will no longer be swayed by your magic or your whims. Keep your blood-stained coin and leave us in peace."

"My dear, Evander, you have my word," the witch purred.

KARIS

The seaside market was rank with the aroma of rotting fish and sweaty humans alike. Every stall offered a new horror. Karis kept her eyes trained at her feet, her stomach lurching at the sight of so many creatures so ruthlessly slaughtered. She'd never liked the barbarity of men, though, she supposed they must sate their hunger with something.

Her human legs were long and awkward. It had taken her a fair amount of time to use them properly once she'd stepped from the sea. The melodic rhythm of a flapping fin was an entirely different song than that of these sticks poking the ground beneath her. Nor would these magical enchantments hide her true nature. Her eyes were still a pointedly non-human shade of violet, and the tangled strands of her blonde hair were tinged green with the salt of the deeps. But it was her gills, positioned squarely over her chest, that attracted the most attention. Merchants gasped, children pointed, and mothers held their babes closer as she passed.

She'd been instructed to make her way to the east side of the market. There, a man would be waiting for her, a guide. She trusted the witch's guide just about as far as she could throw him. If there was one thing Karis had learned, it was that trust was earned. It was bought and paid for with blood and tears. She would need to be on her guard.

There, a man in black just as the witch foretold. He certainly looked like a mercenary. A scar ran from one side of his cheek to just across his brow, and if the smell of him were any indication, he'd just made shore a short while ago.

"Oh, you don't want him," a voice from behind her called. "He doesn't know Tartarus from Troy."

"How did you-" Karis began.

"We have a mutual friend, it seems."

Karis spun around rather too quickly; she was still unstable on these newfound legs, and found herself plunging toward a slight man dressed in black from head to toe. He grabbed her arm, deftly setting her upright once more. This couldn't be right. The boy before her could barely be older than Karis herself.

"You are the guide the witch spoke of?" she asked in disbelief.

"I am."

"There must be some mistake. You're...you're not what I was expecting. You're-"

"Handsome? Fearless?" the boy boasted, stepping nearer Karis with each word.

"A boy," she supplied. "One I doubt has been further than this village, much less to the land of the dead. Do you know what awaits you, or has the sea witch hired you for my amusement?"

The man's jaw tensed, and his playful demeanor vanished. "You would do well not to judge on appearance alone. I have seen and done things that would make your skin crawl. I assure you, I am up to the task. Perhaps it is you who is not prepared for what must come next."

Karis could feel her blood boiling. How dare this boy speak to her in such a way. "Can you take me to death's gate or no, human?"

"I know the way, but it's not as simple as a stroll down to the underworld, Highness. You can't merely pluck someone's hand from the darkness and will them to life. It's a fair deal more complicated than that. Best go back to your castle and forget his name. You'll be happier for it."

It was a challenge. He was trying to get a rise out of her, and despite her best efforts, it was working.

"Don't presume to know me or what I'm capable of, human. A love such as ours is not so easily forgotten. I wouldn't expect you to understand." Her voice, so strong at first, faltered as memories of Antreas swam to the surface of her mind.

The man's face softened, and, for a moment, Karis thought she saw regret in his dark eyes. "I suppose you have a point. We don't know each other well enough to form such egregious opinions of one another, and we better learn to get along if we're to travel together. My name is Evander, not human. And what shall I call you?"

"Karis," she supplied begrudgingly.

"Well, Karis," said Evander, hoisting a large pack over one shoulder. "Are you ready to take on the lord of the underworld himself?"

"Can one ever be ready for such a task?" she asked.

"No, I suppose not, but we must try."

Together, the two made their way to the village's edge and a destiny only the fates could have foretold.

- To Be Continued -

I hope you've enjoyed getting to know Karis and Evander, they have a long journey to go on together and I can't wait to bring you every page of it when book one of the **In Waters Dark And Deep** duology releases in Summer 2022!

In the meantime, you can sign up for news, giveaways, character art, and updates here: bit.ly/clcannon

ABOUT C.L. CANNON

C.L. Cannon is a USA Today Bestselling Author, publisher, publicist, editor, designer, and lots of other occupations with the -er sound at the end! She is a woman of many talents who never gives up or stops improving. She enjoys writing about love and friendship. She loves it even more when she can add fantasy and science fiction aspects to those themes! She's a self-proclaimed Harry Potter freak (Slytherin Pride people), lover of anything Joss Whedon (Spuffy forever), Tolkien fiend (who enjoys second breakfast), and addict of classic literature

(Social class struggles turn me on... literally ;) yah see what I did there?) She spends her days trying to #bookstagram (and probably failing), helping other authors grow and succeed (I love my job), and loving on her two babes (velociraptors), Seth and Petey.

You can find her basically everywhere on the net (man I just aged myself). Visit her website, join her street team, or stalk her on her socials for more content!

Website
clcannon.net

Fan Group
facebook.com/groups/clcannon

Everything Else
lnk.bio/clcannon

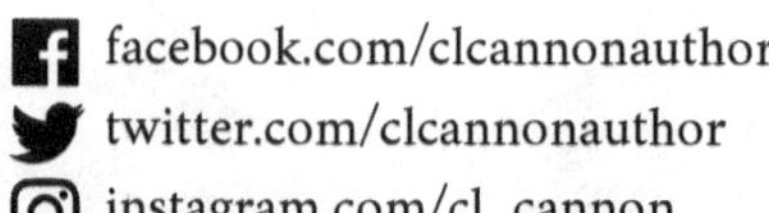

facebook.com/clcannonauthor
twitter.com/clcannonauthor
instagram.com/cl_cannon

OF LOVE AND LEVIATHANS
BY MARGO BOND COLLINS

"Oy! Watch where you're going!" The gearhead cuffs me upside the head, sending my braids flying out around me wildly. Tiny brass pieces woven through the strands make a cheerful tinkling sound at odds with my wince and the man's expression. His own gears are embedded into his body—a mechanical eyepiece, at least, and probably more, given his attitude toward me.

Nothing I could afford, even if I wanted it.

His companion, a blonde woman with one gear-driven arm, reaches out and touches him with her flesh hand, murmuring something to him. His expression smooths, and he turns his back on me, shoving past me to step onto the moving sidewalk. The woman holds back long enough to speak to me.

"Apologies, my dear. He had new eyeworks implanted recently, and he's still adjusting."

He's gear-cranked. Of course. I should have recognized the signs.

She reaches out and tilts my chin up, so I look her in the eye. "So pale," she says quietly. "You work in the underground?" When I nod, her mouth tightens, and it takes me a moment to realize she's not angry with me. "Will you be late for your shift?"

Again I nod, and this time I mutter something indecipherable, shifting my gaze away from her. She'll take it as begging her pardon if I keep the tone right.

Apparently, I do, too, because she reaches into her reticule and pulls out a complete sprocket. Steel. Probably worth more than all the brass bits in my braids put together.

"For your trouble. And to help make it up to you for your tardiness."

I waste a full second staring at the riches before me—then I reach out and snatch the sprocket, tucking it up into the sleeve of my faded shirtdress so fast it probably looks like it disappears. I bob my head in thanks, but the rich gearhead lady is already gathering her full skirts to scurry after her cranked friend.

The interchange will make me late for my shift, but I don't care.

Not with a shiny new steel sprocket hidden in my clothes.

They don't know it, but the 'heads have just helped fund their own destruction.

───────────

Even when I'm not being smacked around by gear-cranked 'heads, it takes me almost an hour to make it to my station every morning, moving from my tiny one-room apartment on the surface, down through the layers of the largest clockwork city in the world.

The gearheads think they run the city, that their expertise in levers and cogwheels and dials gives them dominion over the whole chronoscape. They're certain they're better than the rest of us—especially the underworkers, like me.

Oh, they're usually polite enough on the surface—more like the fine lady than her gear-cranked friend.

But surfaces don't tell the whole story. Not ever.

As I step onto the first elevator, I glance up at the morning sky one last time, memorizing the feel of its warmth on my face.

The gearheads have forgotten one thing: this is Clepsydra City, named after the great water clocks that started it all, and every layer of it literally rests on the past.

All the way down to the underground river that gave the city life—and is about to bring its death.

The farther underground I get, the less I have to watch out for gearheads and their ilk. Unless there's an inspection, the 'heads never make it down this far. Along my route, though, other underworkers call out to me.

"Hey, Moselle! Why you so late?"

I smile and wave but don't stop to talk, not even to old Cyrus on the gnomon level. The only shadows the sundials cast now come from the gaslamps, but Cyrus keeps it going.

He has to. The workings of every level are intertwined with the ones below it. The chronoscape is vast and interconnected. If Cyrus's sundials stopped telling time, eventually, all the gearheads' machinery would grind to a halt.

At the thought of it, a giggle escapes me—a light, airy sound, more at home on the surface than here.

For now, anyway.

Soon enough, everything hidden in the depths of Clepsydra City will be exposed.

Everything, and everyone.

The closer I get to my station, the more the sounds of the surface recede, overtaken by the rush of the river—at first nothing but a soothing murmur, but then rising, like the river herself.

Reaching a stone wall at the end of the gnomon level, I run my hand along an apparent crevice until I find the latch. With a slight grinding noise, a lever slides out of a crack in the wall, and I pull it to open the hidden door.

A damp, slick stone staircase descends into darkness. I could light a lantern or use a torch, but I know my way down, even in the pitch-black that swallows me as the door swings shut behind me. I'll light the gas lamps when I get to the bottom, but I don't need them to find my way around. This is my part of the city. My world.

There are only a few ways to the final level of the city, many of them forgotten by everyone but those of us who work here, like our parents before us and their parents before them. The 'heads call us the lower classes, but we've been here longest. We know things they couldn't dream of learning, no matter how many body parts they replace with mechanized bits.

Like right now?

I know how they're all going to die.

Most 'heads only know the waterworks stations as the source of running water for the upper levels. They don't pay attention to what goes on down here.

Even the other lowers, the workers from other levels, don't often bother to come down to the river level. Sometimes I think they're terrified by the sheer scale of the water clock, as big as any upper-level building, with its complicated system of tubes and tanks, siphoning water off the river to harness its power, then returning most of the water to its source.

People from up above don't understand it like they understand gears. I overheard an inspector one time, a 'head who'd replaced at least half himself with mechanicals, say that it was "too organic." Like his own body, I guess.

Anyway, that's why no one but me knows what happened two months ago.

Our world ripped apart, and She came through.

I'd spent the morning cleaning the river-clock, wiping down the metal holding tank, clearing away the moss growing on the hinges of the enormous vats that filled and spun and dumped, keeping time and sending power upwards.

That afternoon, I changed into my bathing dress—that's what Mama called it back when she was still alive, anyway. It was really an old chemise I wore on the days I dove into the holding tanks to clear the viewports and hour-markings from the inside. And on the days, I swam for nothing but the sheer joy of it.

That was most days, truth be told. Inside the tanks, underwater, the world disappears. The light from the gas lamps barely penetrates the water, even through the viewports. The sound of the water running into the tanks both recedes and magnifies. I can still hear the steady thumps of the vats spinning, the splash of the water dropping into the giant pipes, but when I'm in the water, the noises thrum through my entire being.

Sometimes I let the vats dump me through the pipes, too. Oh, I count it as a cleaning sweep—I keep rags in my hands and let them swish along the inside of the metal tubes as I'm swept along, spinning and swirling, until I can barely hold my breath anymore, and then I explode from the pipe to fly through the air, laughing maniacally as I dive down into the river itself.

But that day, when I rode the pipes, I burst out into a brilliant, painful, white light. That was all I had the chance to see before I hit the river and was underwater again.

When I surfaced once more, spluttering in a way I hadn't since I was a child, I blinked against the bright light shining like a sun after the cool, soothing darkness of the water. After a minute, though, my eyes adjusted, and the brightness toned down, resolving into a kind of gash in the air. It hovered over the river, leaking light, and I stared at it, frowning in consternation. Something electrical crackled around it, sending the smell of burnt ozone floating through the cavern.

And as I watched, She came through.

Only one tentacle at first, dipping down through that hole in the world and withdrawing just as quickly, so fast I wasn't sure what I had seen. Then two tentacles, tugging the tear, in reality, open just a little wider, until the third and fourth tentacle slithered through as well, curling up and down, feeling for some kind of purchase, something to hold onto with the giant suckers that lined the waving arms. Finally, one of those arms stretched out far enough to touch the pipe at the top of the water clock, the one that siphons water from the river and into the vats. She wrapped Her tentacle around it and pulled. The other arms followed suit, and She slithered out into the world, all tentacles and giant, bulbous head as if the world itself were giving birth to Her.

When She was completely through, the rift receded. It didn't really disappear, but what had been a bright, almost blinding light faded to a pale glow.

She balanced precariously on the pipe. With Her arms wrapped around it, it seemed tiny in comparison. She was huge. At least as big as some of the clockwork buildings upstairs—maybe bigger than any of them.

Her gaze settled on me, sending tiny electric jolts racing through my limbs.

Hello, little one.

Her voice echoed through my bones, settling in my mind rather than entering through my ears.

What place is this?

I answered aloud, though he wasn't sure She'd even be able to understand me.

"It's the water clock, ma'am." I don't know why added the ma'am—except that She was so enormous and beautiful that I knew She had to be important. Maybe even royalty. She acknowledged me—either the thought or the comment, I wasn't sure which—with a nod, a slight bob of Her head.

And from that moment, I was Hers.

She's both mother and child, savior and destroyer. I spend most of my days now communing with Her.

I've seen Her before. Parts of Her, anyway, all throughout Clepsydra City. I see them even more now. Up above, on the other levels, there are engravings everywhere I go. Old bits of metal repurposed to run the gearheads' clockworks still carry Her image, as do stone remnants from an older age, a time before any clockworks at all.

It's as if Her tentacles have already wound themselves through the city, peeking out in unexpected places.

Leviathan, Her voice whispers in my bones, in my heart and soul, and *Kraken* and *Lusca*—but I know She has no real name. She is a goddess, and I, Her only devotee.

For now.

Today, I lie on the floor of the cavern, near the edge, where the stone drops off sharply, falling away into the river.

She floats just under the water next to me, going over the important details yet again.

The lever on the riverbed below us—you are certain it will open all the floodgates harnessing the river's power?

I shrug. "As certain as I can be. That's what Mama told me—that it was placed there as part of the system that keeps the river moving, keeps it from flooding all of the city."

She caresses me with Her tentacles. The very smallest ends explore the skin of my stomach, my legs, my face, as delicate as fingers but more sensitive, not only giving the comfort of their cool touch but also taking knowledge as they leave. As She learns me, She learns all I know.

The 'head on the surface that morning had commented on my pallor, assuming it was due to working underground. But that wasn't the whole reason. She has been drawing from me for weeks. Everywhere She touches, She leaves blue-green and purple-black rings on my skin, bruises from the information transfer. At this point, She knows almost everything about the city that I do.

"Once the city is flooded, what will you do next?" I roll over to my stomach, guided by the delicate nudging of Her arms, the gentle lipping of Her tentacles' suckers.

I will invite my sisters, She tells me. *A world unknown to our enemies, all your people to worship us. It will be paradise.*

I nod, growing sleepier as She pulls from me, sapping my energy along with my thoughts. "Why do we need the money?"

You must use it to prepare a home at the highest level. We will need a space above the water for those who wish to commune with us.

"And those who do not?" My voice is desultory, as I barely care, but it seems like the right question to ask.

Those we shall consume entirely.

I accept Her answer, yawning as I turn toward Her. She rolls me up in Her tentacles, wrapping them around me, lifting me from the rock, and pulling me closer to Her. She holds me cradled gently against Her body, Her skin as cool as the river water itself.

I don't know how long I doze there. Since Her arrival, I've begun going back up to the surface only rarely. I wouldn't have gone to my apartment that morning had I not needed to bring down supplies. With Her ministrations, I find I eat much less, seeming to derive energy directly from Her. A glance in my mirror that morning had suggested I could do with more food, though. As I had changed out of one dress and into my only other one, I had noted my ribs showing through the bruises, turned to interlocking black and purple rings across my skin.

Some part of my memory suggests that it would be good to eat now, in fact. But I am comfortable in Her arms and do not want to disturb Her.

I drift off again to the internal sound of Her sing-song voice describing the world. She and Her sisters will create, soothing me with a sound like the river's rhythms.

Minutes—or possibly hours—later, I sense more than feel a stiffening of Her limbs, and a faltering in the water song She sings jolts me awake.

"What is it?" I ask. Her tentacles loosen their hold on me, and I realize my own body is stiff as She sets me on my feet on the top step of the embankment.

Someone is coming.

She slips farther out and down into the water, sliding away into the darkness. By the time the human coming to disturb us arrives, only one tentacle barely holding on to the rock shows She had been there at all, and I've shimmied back into my chemise and dress. I brush my hair back off my face with one hand and watch the lantern light bob down the stairway.

"Hello," the gearhead holding it in his mechanical hand calls out, glancing around the dark, open space as his voice echoes back to him. "Gods," he mutters. "What's that smell?"

He isn't close enough to see my expression yet, so I allow myself to scowl as I respond. "Begging your pardon, sir," I say, adopting my best underworker obsequiousness. "It's simply the smell of the river."

That isn't entirely true. With Her arrival, She brought a stronger scent to the cavern. The smell of something wild and free. Something of the water and not the land.

That's what She had said about me, too—that I don't belong on land. *Your name is from the Old language. It means one who is of the water. You do not belong to those above.* And She's right. I am one of Hers.

I am Her own.

This man is an interloper. But I smooth my expression as I step into the circle of light. He jerks back away from me in surprise.

"Can I help you, sir?" I ask, keeping my eyes downcast so he won't see the loathing in them.

"Maybe," he says, but he sounds doubtful. I realize I must've lost more time than I thought if the gearheads are already sending an inspector down. I thought that was not due for several months yet.

"I'm supposed to check for any anomalies," the gearhead inspector says. "There's something odd going on in all the upper levels, in the power output up top, and we're trying to figure out what's causing it. Something's draining it between here and there. So, I need to take a look around." I'm staring at him now, and something must show in my expression because he blinks and refocuses on me, his gaze turning sharp as he asks, "Is there anything new down here?"

I hold my gaze steadily on the inspector as he advances a few steps toward me. I don't dare glanced up at the still slightly glowing slash in the world, the hole She came through.

I want to ask Her if She's been draining power from the clockwork system as well as from me, but first, I have to deal with this intruder. As long as I keep him from moving any closer to me, though, the enormous river-water clock obscures his vision of the rift. I move toward him more boldly than I would have before She came into my life. "Nothing new down here at all," I say. "Just the usual. Clean the water clock, check the water clock, go home."

The agent makes noncommittal noises as he glances down at the check sheet he carries. "Aren't there supposed to be more of you working this level?"

"Yes, sir. But that hasn't been true since Mama died. There just aren't that many of us left who know how to run the water clocks. I have a brother who works three sections over, maintaining the river's course. But he's an engineer—much more important than I am. I just tend the clock."

I shouldn't be so forthcoming. Mama always told me that the inspectors notice any time things were out of the ordinary—like an underworker who talks too much.

"I guess you'd better show me around, then," he says. When he steps forward, I know that he won't be fobbed off with anything less than a complete inspection.

I'm not sure what I can do to keep him from reporting us to the gearheads in charge up top. And there's no way he won't notice the rift. I'm a little surprised he hasn't realized it's lighter down here than it should be.

It doesn't take him long, though. I see the moment he notices the extra light bleeding around the edges of the river clock rising above us. He gasps as he peers around the edge of the giant vats. The light still leaking from the rift in the air plays across his face, illuminating his bemused expression.

"What in Hades' name is that?"

I freeze, uncertain what to do, but then Her voice echoes through me. *Do not worry, little one. All is well. Bring him to the edge for me.*

"Well, sir," I begin, stepping closer to the edge of the embankment, toward the short staircase leading down into the water. I keep moving, down one step, then another until the water laps against my toes. I gesture toward the rift. "If you come over here, sir, you can see exactly what it is."

The inspector takes one hesitant step toward me, then another. He frowns. "It doesn't look at all different from here."

"No, sir, you have to be standing right here." I point at my feet for emphasis.

The man frowns but steps down onto the step above me, leaning out over the river below him. "What is it? I can't—"

With a sudden splashing roar, She rises from the water, Her enormous body held up by the whipping force of Her tentacles churning below, a true wonder to see.

I fall to my knees, tears of joy streaming from my eyes. The skirt of my dress grows heavy with the water it soaks up, and I absentmindedly strip it off as the inspector turns to try to run.

He doesn't have a chance.

His scream cuts short, changing to a gurgle as She throws out several of Her tentacled arms to wrap around him, squeezing him tight and pulling him toward Her. She opens Her jaws, and for the first time, I see how She will devour the world: with a mouth so wide and dark that it seems endless, edged with row upon row of teeth.

I shiver in anticipation, and my chemise follows my dress, both dropping into the river, carried away by the current.

She rolls the agent into a ball and shoves him into that gaping maw with a popping, crackling noise. As his skin shreds on the blades of Her teeth, blood runs out of Her mouth and down Her sides, dropping into the water below to swirl and mix with the darkness already there.

It's glorious.

When She's done, She sinks back into the water, and again, I feel more than hear Her satisfied sigh.

Thank you for bringing him to us, little one.

I smile and sit on the stone steps, dangling my feet into the water, where I lightly play with Her tentacles, rubbing the suckers with my feet. "Someone will come looking for him," I say.

Then it is time to begin.

I watch the last of the blood swirl away, sluicing off Her amazing, iridescent skin. "We will need to open the levers to let the river flow in sooner rather than later, then?"

Her assent echoes through me, tinged with Her satisfaction, Her joy.

"I haven't had time to take a room at the top of the world," I fret.

Would you rather join with me, Little Sister, become fully my own?

This time, it's my assent that throbs between us.

I would. I will. I do.

And so I stand on the edge of the river, arms stretched up toward the rift in the cavern air, my eyes closed and head dropping back, as She wraps me one last time in Her river-cool tentacles, lifting me and drawing me to Her as the suckers latch on to my delicate skin, draining me of everything I know and everything I am—and as I let go, finally, of all that I have been, I slide into Her.

I become Her.

I am Moselle, and I am She.

The world around Us glows in shades of purple and black, limned in the silver and gold lights of the rift, We travel through.

As We no longer need the shell of a body We hold in Our arms, We consume it, feeling its shivers of pain as ecstasy soaking through Us, until it is gone, its power depleted in the transfer from little sister to Goddess—from her to Us.

We dive down deep, toward the lever We know will give Us this world.

And Our laughter bubbles up behind Us to pop into the air through the bloodied water We leave behind.

This, We think. *This is love.*

THE END

Enjoy this story? Be sure to leave a review for the collection and mention it!

ABOUT MARGO BOND COLLINS

USA Today, Wall Street Journal, and New York Times bestselling author Margo Bond Collins is a former college English professor who, tired of explaining the difference between "hanged" and "hung," turned to writing romance novels instead. She now writes urban fantasy, paranormal romance, and science fiction romance. Sometimes her heroines kiss aliens, sometimes they kill monsters. But they always aim for the heart.

You can learn more about her books at
MargoBondCollins.net

f facebook.com/MargoBondCollins

🐦 twitter.com/MargoBondCollin

📷 instagram.com/margobondcollins

THE SELKIE'S KEEPER
BY JC BROWN AND LENA LANE

"I'm not a child, Lachlan," the young girl cried angrily. Hot tears burned her eyes and streaked along her pale, freckled cheeks. Inhaling sharply, Brynn squared her narrow shoulders and declared, "I'm fifteen." With an angry hand, she swiped her long, red hair away from her face and spun to walk away. She scrambled up the boulders, slick with ocean mist, with a carelessness that came from years of familiarity with her environment.

"But you are a child, Brynn," Lachlan countered to her retreating back, seeing not the teenager before him but the young one he used to play with on the beach they'd just left. He remembered making sandcastles with her and telling her about selkies and mermaids and creatures that lived not so far away. With the eagerness of an innocent girl, she'd interrupted him often to ask a thousand questions. It didn't seem so long ago.

Truly, he missed that girl. Lachlan had very little patience for this older version, who was, no doubt, livid at his words. She was storming across the shoreline, leaving him behind. He would have loved nothing more than to leave her and her petulant attitude on land, to go back to the sea where he could swim to his heart's content. Unfortunately, she was going in the same direction where his skin was hidden. He had no choice but to go along.

"Stop following me!" she shrieked over her shoulder.

He would have been happy to oblige, but he couldn't leave without his seal skin. Seeking to pacify her, he called out, "Please understand, Brynn, when I see you, I see only the babe I used to play with in the sand."

"Seven years have passed," she panted, climbing higher on the rocky cliff walk, the landscape slowly changing from boulders and rocks to rocks and gravel. "I am no longer the wee babe from your memories." She turned to face him, the rising landscape bringing her eyes level with his. "Look closer, Lachlan," she challenged. "I've grown." Hands on her hips, her emerald eyes raging at him, she continued, "Fiona is but a few years older than I. Why would you love her and not me?"

"Chi--" Lachlan began and cut himself short before he called her a child again. He cupped the side of her cheek, trying to soothe her, and she nuzzled into his hand. "Brynn... I love no one," he stated with a slight shake of his head, words he was quick to regret when she pulled away from him and began sobbing once more.

"Don't lie to me!" she cried, stamping her foot. The smaller rocks of the cliff wall began to slide out from beneath her. Lachlan reached out, catching her in his arms before she could fall. Oblivious to her environment and the loose gravel she stood upon, she began wailing anew. "I saw the two of you, together... making love..."

Lachlan stroked her hair and looked down at the top of her head as she curled against his chest, sobbing. Perhaps he should have listened to his kin when they told him he was a fool for playing with her as a child. But she'd been such a cute babe, running around the beach as if she owned the whole land. He'd been intrigued with her.

From the corner of his eye, Lachlan caught the sight of a small tuft of fur, silver, and grey, peeking out from the rubble beneath her feet, unearthed by her anger. His heart began to race, hammering in his chest. *She has climbed atop my hiding spot and knows not what she is doing,* he reassured himself. Taking in a deep breath, he let the salty brine that the sea air carried to calm him, lest he lose his patience and knock her over the head. He was ready to snatch his skin from under her and go from this place but knowing that a human should never witness the change, he had to send her away.

"May the Fae grant me patience," he whispered as he set her on the other side of the rocks. Holding her steady at her tiny waist, he informed her, "What you saw was not love, child." He saw her eyes flash fire and continued before she was able to argue. "You may have a woman's body, but your mind has not matured enough to know what you ask of me."

Furious at his words, she tried to pull herself away, slapping at him until he was forced to release her. She stumbled again, and Lachlan watched her bottom fall right atop his hiding place, her delicate hand just inches from the silken fur of his magical skin. A silent growl erupted through his body.

How do I get rid of this human?

Resolved that he was stuck on land until the brat went home, he sat on the ground beside her, his body concealing the fur from her view. Clenching his jaw, he offered, "In seven years' time, you will be older. More mature." He paused and took a deep, fortifying breath before continuing. "I will return and come to this very spot to see you."

Brynn gave him a suspicious sideways glance before asking, "What do you mean, you'll return?"

Lachlan could see no other way other than to give her what she wanted. Almost desperate enough to do anything. *Almost.* The others would only wait so long. If he didn't leave soon, he would be left behind, alone. "I will return to see you again."

That seemed to appease her. Instead of arguing, her eyes brightened as she asked, "Do you mean it? Do you promise?"

"Yes." He muttered reluctantly, glad that he had chosen his words carefully, promising his return and nothing more, regardless of how she may perceive or understand it.

Ecstatic, she jumped at him and threw her arms around his shoulders.

Tired of her, he pushed Brynn back and told her, "You should head home now before your Da comes looking." He wanted to hate her, but the bright light in her eyes reminded him of the youth he'd once known. Tucking a stray red curl behind her ear, he continued, "I must go, as well. I only have limited time here."

After an eye roll and a sigh, she stood and began her walk home, turning back only once to blow him a kiss over her shoulder. Lachlan waited until she was more than halfway to the small stone cottage on the cliffs before his desperation consumed him. Hastily, he tossed aside the rocks and swept away the dirt, leaves, and debris that nature had thrown upon his hiding place, revealing his magical skin. His one and only possession and his greatest weakness. After removing the sacred seal skin from the earth with great care, he used his human legs one last time to race to the shore.

Settling himself in the sand at the edge of the ocean, he hastily removed his itchy male clothes and carelessly threw them aside. He then stepped into the velvet seal skin, pulling, tugging it up over him with a swiftness and finesse that came only with many years of practice. The magic, with a swift surge of power, transformed his human form. He vaulted into the waves, past the seafoam, and into the open ocean.

———

Lachlan thought her only a child, but she was smarter than he gave her credit for. Each time they'd met, Brynn had listened to all his stories and drank down his words like her father drank down his whiskey every night since Mother left. His stories were full of the magic and adventures of fascinating beings she could only dream of. He'd taught her that sea folk were creatures not to be trifled with, but they were not without their faults and weaknesses.

Pleased with herself for having bested a sea-faring Fae, she smiled to herself and headed home with a skip in her step. She considered her win. By eliciting a promise from his lips, she had ensured his return.

But the elation was fleeting. He will return in seven years' time and be hers for only one night.

Her smile faded as she considered. Would their previous meetings allow him to see her as more special than the others he'd been with? Or would he leave her at dawn to sleep on the sandy shore, as he had done with countless others? Would he come back to be with her forever?

Needing clarification of his promise, Brynn turned and began to make her way back toward the beach, stumbling on the rocks. When she got her feet back under her, she looked to the shore and gasped in astonishment. For a moment, Lachlan was there, and then....

Seeing the Fae change from man to beast took her breath away. Confused, exhilarated, she could only stand and stare for long moments after he was gone, overwhelmed by the brush with true magic. There was no evidence of him ever being there, except for the clothes scattered along the sand. She collected the articles and held them while watching the waves, eagerly waiting for just a glimpse of the animal he'd become. After a while, she made her way home, her mind racing with a million thoughts, all on a collision course with seven years until a promise was fulfilled.

Throughout her childhood, Brynn knew that the only person she could rely on was herself. Her father often worked late into the night or sometimes didn't return for days. She was often on her own and had to be self-sufficient. Being the lady of an empty house was not as rewarding as some of the townsfolk would lead her to believe.

But when he visited, he made her feel loved and cared for in ways missing in her daily reality. She knew at that moment, as she witnessed Lachlan's transformation from man to animal, that she needed to have him for her own. She needed him in her life. She needed to find a way to make him stay with her and be hers and hers alone, forever.

It had been seven years since Lachlan had been in the warmth of his human skin. He had forgotten how the sand felt against his bare feet and missed the warm air on his unprotected skin. The beach had a distinct smell of salty ocean air, blended with the earthy smell of the trees that grew near the shoreline. Every time he came onto land, it was like his first time.

But it wasn't his first time.

A low growl of annoyance escaped from him as he recalled his last visit. He'd made a regrettable promise to a child. A promise he'd been forced to make because of an impetuous child's angry step. It was unfortunate that water Fae were no different from the others: a promise, once made, is binding and must be kept.

This time, he would have to find a much better place to hide his seal skin. He'd have to do it soon, before anything else.

His eyes returned to the glistening water, lit by the cool rays of the full moon. Considering what he knew about the land, he decided he would hide his magical skin in the caves beneath the cliffs on the south side. The path was narrow and steep, slick with the spray of the waves that crashed furiously against the rocks. It would be difficult enough for him to reach, nearly impossible for a human.

Gripping the skin, he jumped back into the water and swam until he found the perfect cave. He picked one halfway down the vertical wall. It was big enough for him to walk into, yet difficult to reach. Once inside, Lachlan took the extra precaution of burying his skin beneath a boulder, knowing with certainty that no human could move it because of its sheer size and weight.

With his most precious possession safely hidden away, he made his way to the cottage that rested on the north side of the shoreline. Intent on keeping his promise to Brynn, this would be his very first stop.

With each step, he berated himself for not listening to his family's warning about being discrete. *There are but twenty humans in the entire town. What harm could they cause?* he'd argued. Now, he knew.

It didn't take him long to get to the cottage, but when he arrived, he found it desolate and in ruins. Large holes in the roof let in bright shafts of moonlight that cut through the small interior. The bed was torn to tatters, and the table and chairs were lying on their sides, shattered. The dust had long settled, layers deep, onto the furniture. He didn't need his Fae vision, which allowed him to see within the darkest depths of the ocean, to show him that no human had inhabited the cottage in years. He contemplated the dark brown spatters on the walls and floor and surmised that an animal must have come through and torn the humans to shreds. A small part of him was saddened to think such violence took place here. But he quickly dismissed the emotion as he realized that their destruction meant his promise to Brynn was now void.

Without another thought, he turned on his heel and returned to the sands of the beach. He listened to the waves that carried the tears of unsatisfied women who cried into the ocean. Their loneliness called to him; an echo of their void that needed to be filled. It drew him to the land, to them.

In the early hours of the morning, the female he had spent the night with returned home. She hurried before her husband woke to find her gone. Alone, he rested on the beach, his back against a natural sand dune surrounded by tall grass and watched the sun rise. When his eyes grew heavy, he closed them and slept the day away.

The sun had long since set when Lachlan opened his eyes again. He expected to be alone but sensed an eerie gaze upon him. He turned to find a slightly older version of Brynn staring down at him from atop a boulder a few yards away. She sat upon it like a queen, her chin held high, her back straight. The long strands of her flame-colored waves streamed behind her like a luxurious red cape. She stared down her nose at him disdainfully, as if disgusted by what she saw.

For a moment, he wondered if seeing her should surprise him, considering what he'd suspected happened at the cottage. But she had always been a tenacious girl.

She'd been but eight years old the first time they met, a thin wisp of a girl with a threadbare dress and tiny bones covered in flesh that barely held it up. They'd sat on the sand, letting the salty water wash over their feet and legs while he'd told her stories of ocean creatures that no human should ever know. She'd told him of her solo adventures while he wondered where her parents were.

Brynn had been a survivor, even at such a young age, motherless and alone most of the time. When they'd first met, Lachlan wondered if she even had anyone to care for her at all.

"Still a survivor," he said in greeting.

"Me?" she asked, slipping herself off the rock with ease and grace. "You've no idea."

Lachlan lay unmoving in the sand, watching her as she came to stand above him, one leg on either side of his body. This time around, she also wore a dress, but this one was far from threadbare. The fabric was a rich green that matched her eyes, with elaborate designs and intricate stitching. It was of a silky material that he'd only seen in a country on the opposite side of the world. "You've married well, Brynn. Congratulations."

She threw her head back and laughed heartily. "Me? Married?" With hooded eyes full of secrets and suspicions, she squatted down and sat on his bare hips, her skirts bunching high around her. "I've married no one, Lachlan," she whispered. Settling down more comfortably, she rested her forearms along his chest and added, "I've been waiting for you."

His stomach churned at her words and at the flesh he felt against his own. Warning bells rang in his head as he remembered yet another piece of advice his family had given him: *As soon as your skin is safe, find human attire and blend in.* But it was too late. Struggling to put distance between her naked body and his own, he squirmed beneath her. It only made things worse. He felt the curls of her core rubbing against him and froze.

Seeking to stall what he knew she wanted, he focused on her words. Lachlan imagined a younger version of Brynn, sitting on the beach, day after day, growing older with each passing year, stalking the very ocean for him. The hair on his skin rose with unease. Rather than pursuing that line of conversation, he asked, "Then where did you come upon such finery?" His gaze drifted to the bodice, though when his eyes landed on the swelling of her breasts, he returned them to her face. "Such adornments do not come without substantial cost."

Brynn pushed on his chest to straighten her back, her lips curling into a veneer smile, one that never reached her eyes. "You believe my dress to be fine?"

A soft groan of misery escaped his lips as the center of their bodies came closer together. Spinning the sound into a word, he said, "Aye." He reached for the fabric, feeling the silky material between his fingers. "This isn't something one can find in just any town. How did you acquire it?"

"Enough with this nonsense chatter," she told him with a dismissive wave. "Unless you're looking for a seamstress to sew you a new dress, it doesn't matter how I acquired it." She lay back down along his chest, bringing her mouth close to his. "What matters is that you're here... And I'm here..." Brushing her lips against his in a kiss, she caressed his nipples with the palm of her hands.

At that point, Lachlan could take no more. Brynn didn't call to him. Her tears, her body, her soul didn't speak to him, didn't entice him. The more insistently she pressed against him, the more his body revolted, the further his manhood retreated from her touch. Gently, he shoved at her shoulders and scooted from beneath her, growling, "I can't."

He didn't get far.

Nails as sharp as knives pierced his flesh. By the time his movements stilled, four identical, inch-long cuts bled on the right side of his chest where her fingertips had once been. His left side was a mirror image. Astonished by her strength, he gripped her wrists, pulling at the claws that were still buried deep.

"Who are you...?" he whispered gruffly, studying her face. "What are you?!"

"During your sea-faring days, much has happened. Much has changed," Brynn answered, dismissing his question altogether as she pressed herself harder against him. "Can you not tell?" The last time they'd been together, he had called her a child. Brynn seethed in anger at the memory. But he couldn't call her that anymore. Her breasts had filled, her hips had rounded. Wanting to please him, she had learned everything she could about the marriage bed, even if she hadn't married. There was no way he could dismiss her now.

"Aye, you seem much different from the young girl I made my promise to," he said, pushing her further away from him. "If that question were easily answered, I would not have asked it."

She sighed and rolled her eyes. Tearing her wrists from his grasp abruptly, Brynn stood and perused the blood that stained her nails. Turning away from him, she licked the sweetness from each finger before asking, "Have I not aged well enough, Lachlan?" She turned gracefully to face him as she pulled at the strings of her bodice. He was standing, too, wiping at the red streaks on his chest. "Fiona was nineteen when you first laid with her." She grabbed his hands and pulled them to her hips, holding them in place with her own. "My body has matured one year past that."

"Brynn," he began, tugging his hands away and turning his face from her. "I can't--"

Ignoring him, she leaned up to lick a line over the pulse at his neck. Again, he stepped back. Frustrated, she gripped his chin hard, digging her nails into the flesh of his face, and forced him to look at her again. Her predatory gaze set upon him as she pulled him closer to press her lips to his. "Seven years I have waited patiently, but I shall wait no longer," she whispered against his lips.

"Enough!" he roared, shoving her away from him. Unprepared for the push, she stumbled and took several steps back. She forced herself to keep silent while he lectured her in a stern voice. "I've tried to be kind, Brynn, for the sake of the child I once knew," he continued. "But this cannot happen—*will not happen*," he quickly corrected. Shaking his head, he added, "My promise was to see you." He locked his gaze on her and took another step away from her. "I have now fulfilled my promise." With those smarting words, he turned his back on her and walked away.

She watched him leave, and a part of her wanted to yell at him to stop. But she didn't. "Not wise, Lachlan," Brynn whispered as she watched him retreat into the night. She knew he wouldn't go far. And certainly, not for long. A sardonic grin crossed her lips as she considered her backup plan.

As soon as he was out of sight, she began.

The cave was much harder to get to than she'd anticipated, but she'd seen him enter it with his seal skin and then leave without it. The full moon lit the cavern far more than she needed, but it didn't matter. The extra light didn't hurt her search, either. She hurried through the space, knowing the sun would soon rise, and he would most likely return, looking to ensure its safety.

Brynn hiked up her dress and dug where she thought it might be. She looked for patches of earth that had been disturbed or rocks that might have been moved. Despite her best efforts, Brynn, now filthy and wet, had turned up nothing. In her anger, anger that seemed to increase with the rising tide, she picked up a large rock and flung it into the ocean. Her chest heaving with welling emotions, she fought against the tears of frustration that were threatening to burst from her eyes.

Seven years of waiting. Seven years of planning. It must be here.

Seeing the first sign of dawn on the horizon, her desperation grew as. Her window of opportunity was shrinking. Her time was limited. Desperately trying to gather her thoughts, Brynn slapped dramatically against the largest boulder, the sting of pain against her palm satisfying. She allowed the side of her lip to rise when she saw the large crack along its center. The evidence of her strength ran down to its base. In her distress, she almost missed the tiny movement of the huge rock as it slid backward, away from her. But as she scrutinized the length of the crack, realization dawned. A sinister smile curled her lips. Pushing harder, the boulder revealed the hand-dug hole in the center of the cavern floor. Inside, she saw the silvery grey fur that had been hidden within it. Brynn bent, taking great care in brushing off the dirt and small pebbles before picking up the seal skin carefully, examining it.

Heavier than I expected. She grinned widely at her victory. *He can never deny me again.*

Brynn didn't bother putting things back the way she had found them, leaving the cave in complete disarray. She wanted him, and she wanted him to come to her panicked.

The sun was setting in beautiful shades of pink, purple, and orange as Lachlan slipped away from yet another woman, although this one was far from lonely and unsatisfied. As he took his leave, he admired the splendor of his surroundings. Like the woman herself, her home was beautiful and luxurious as far as homes were concerned. She had everything a woman could need, but still, she was filled with enough want, for something more, that her desire had called to him.

Their encounter had momentarily surprised Lachlan. When he'd come to her, he'd found her in her husband's embrace. Embarrassed, the man had taken his leave while avoiding any form of eye contact with the sea Fae. It was at that moment that Lachlan knew what was expected of him for the day. She hoped the special brand of faerie magic he provided would give her what her husband could not, a child. It was not the first time it was asked of him, and it would not be the last. Lachlan was sure that in the coming months, her belly would grow round with a halfling child.

As he climbed into the cave opening, he wondered if that was why Brynn was so set on having him in such an adult way.

The thought flew from his mind as his eyes scanned the ransacked cave.

"No!" Lachlan grit out between clenched teeth as he dug deeper into the hole the boulder had left behind. "Where is it?" he screamed, picking up the rocks that surrounded him and tossing them about the cave. "It—it can't be gone." He cried out in anguish, collapsing to his knees.

Cool hands ran down his shoulders from behind, sharp nails leaving slight scratches in their wake. "Hush," a familiar voice told him, trying to lull and pacify his rage, his sadness.

His body stiffened under the soft caress. Without turning, he hissed in rage. "What have you done?" he asked, not bothering to keep the anger from his voice.

"Lachlan, I'm sure I do not know what you mean. I only came when I heard your cries."

Reaching up, he brushed her hands away as he stood and turned to face her. She still looked so young; her eyes, deep emerald pools shining in the moonlight, conveyed nothing but a sweet innocence. An innocence he now doubted she'd ever actually possessed.

She reached for him, and he grabbed her by her wrists, stopping her before she could touch him again.

With wide eyes, she began, "Lachlan, I—"

"Stop!" he commanded. "I don't want your feigned innocence, Brynn." He gave her wrists a shake, wanting to shake her to her core. "Tell me what you have done with my skin." Without giving her a chance to speak, he demanded, "Tell me how you came to this place when even I had some difficulty getting here."

The fear he expected never came. She ripped her wrists from his grip abruptly and turned away from him. "Come home with me," she said with a bored sigh, "and I will tell you all you wish to know." She paused at the cave's entrance and added, "When you've provided some much-needed warmth for me."

Her words cut him like daggers. Laying with her was the very last thing he wanted to do, but he would not sacrifice his freedom for his morals. But then he watched her walk off the cliff, disappearing into the night. His heart thundered in his chest, wondering how she expected to survive the fall. He ran to the edge and looked down. His hope for her death shattered as he saw her in the water, swimming to shore.

Brynn stood at the edge of the shoreline, knowing that he would not leave her waiting long. The cool water washed over her feet, leaving only the soft foam the waves made as they churned. She watched him make his way out of the water. His clothes, no doubt stolen, slick, and plastered to his body. Her eyes lingered on the white fabric that clung to the lean muscles of his chest. The corners of her lip twitched, and her core pulsed with need as she watched him slick back the auburn waves of his hair.

"Come now, Lachlan. We've only the night to enjoy one another, and if we must spend some of it in conversation, then I do not want to waste a moment." She gave a small sideways smile when he scoffed, then turned to lead him into the woods.

It didn't take them long to get to the small cabin hidden just beyond the tree line. Far enough away where it would go unnoticed, yet close enough to hear the waves slapping against the rocky shore, it was her favorite place.

The door had not closed yet before Brynn hurried to pull on the strings of her corset, loosening it. Her clothing was suddenly too restrictive, making it difficult for her to breathe. But she wanted him more. She wanted to feel his strong body beneath her. Her fingers worked diligently, pulling and tugging at the buttons of his trousers. He remained frozen. She stared up at him, silent and unmoving before her, his face painted with disgust.

"You look at me with such disdain," Brynn stated calmly. "Do you look at the others like this, too?" she wondered aloud. Tugging at his now open trousers, she took a seat on the bed in front of him and pulled him closer before running her hands up to his chest.

"No, but I have never been enslaved by any of the others." He scowled and looked away from her.

"Lachlan," Brynn sighed, "I have waited my entire life for you." Her voice softened, and her fingers slowed, circling each button on his shirt for a few moments before pushing it through the hole when she said, "As a child..." She hesitated and chose her words carefully. The last thing she wanted was to frighten him away with heavy passion. "I remember feeling the flutter in my stomach when I saw you that first time. Too young to know what it meant but knowing that it was the only thing... that the thought of you was the only thing that brought me joy and comfort."

She could feel the muscles in his chest tighten under the gentlest of her touches. "As I grew, so did those feelings." With the buttons finally free of their trap, she opened the shirt and splayed her fingers wide on his bare chest. "It wasn't until I saw you again that it returned, with desire as its companion." Her voice grew husky when she admitted, "I have felt the swell in my heart grow with each visit from you." Brynn stood, reaching up to touch his cheek and adjust his face downward to meet her gaze. "Just as I have felt the cold ache of emptiness when you are gone."

"What do you know of these feelings? You, who have only lived a blink of an eye compared to my existence." Lachlan growled at her. "This is not love, child," he sneered, shoving her hard onto the bed. "It is nothing more than infatuation!"

Her body bounced on the bed. She covered her mouth with the back of her hand, attempting to stifle the giggle that, nevertheless, escaped. *Just where I want to be.* If he thought his anger would turn her away, he was wrong. She would lay claim to him this night and every night after.

"Enough of this!" he growled, climbing onto the bed with her. Brynn gave a small yelp as he grabbed her roughly by the knees, parting them before jerking her hips closer to his. "Just know, I will never love you the way I love the sea." She heard loathing from his voice as he added, "And because of this, you will never have what you desire, save for this night."

After much coaxing to get him prepared for the night she so desired, he watched as she gave up. Flopping back onto the mattress and rolling her eyes, Brynn let out a loud sigh. Side by side, they lay motionless, letting the silence speak volumes around them.

For just a moment, Lachlan's lip twitched as he fought the smile that threatened to bloom at his body's refusal of her advances. "Perhaps if things had been different..." He didn't understand his need to make her feel better but said, "If I had listened to my kin and not been as curious about you as you were of me, I might have just answered your call willingly, like all the rest."

"All the rest?" She scoffed, sitting upright quickly and without warning. "I have been told," she said over her shoulder in a frigid tone, "by many suitors that I am more desirable than most." When he didn't reply, she turned to glare at him.

Lachlan met her glare with an emotionless stare before letting out a heavy sigh. "Brynn, you have, indeed, grown into a beautiful woman." He reached up to push one of her lustrous red curls behind her ear with care. Sitting up, he laid a hand on her cheek. "The men who told you this were speaking truth." She closed her eyes and turned into his palm as if seeking warmth. "You have all charms men most appreciate and desire in a woman."

He didn't lie. She did have everything that he appreciated in the humans he visited.

"But I cannot appreciate them," he told her and infused his words with as much regret as he could, "because all I see when I look at you is the broken wisp of a girl with orange, tangled hair on the beach."

That earned him another brief glare before she laughed out loud, her teeth flashing. For the first time since coming ashore this time around, he looked at her—really looked at her and saw the dainty set of fangs resting in her mouth. Before he could react, she grinned wider and leaned in closer to him, pushing him down into the bed, reminding him she had more strength than she should.

"I have died and have been resurrected for you, Lachlan," she whispered in his ear. "In time, you will forget all about that child and be able to appreciate the woman that lies before you."

The sharp pain of her bite at his neck sent a jolt of panic through him.

In time? In time!

He fought against her, and she held him down almost effortlessly. When she pulled herself away, he saw his blood dripping from her mouth as she smiled.

"You are mine now, Lachlan," she said with triumphant conceit. "I have your skin, and I know all your secrets. I sold my soul and walked through the fires of hell just so I could spend an eternity with you." She wiped her lip with her thumb before licking it slowly. "I am a patient woman and have all the time in the world to wait. You will come around."

Brynn died every day at dawn. Every day, Lachlan used those precious hours alone to search. His skin, his escape, must be there, somewhere.

But time was cruel.

Each passing moment was excruciating for him. He could hear the sea, slapping at the shore, calling to him. He could return to it, but at what cost? Unable to survive the open ocean as a human, Lachlan had no other options.

She said she was patient. But am I?

Days became months, and months turned into years, each day accumulating at a snail's pace. Lachlan had hoped Brynn would grow tired of him, that she would grow tired of waiting for him to succumb to her carnal desires and finally release him. Hoped that he was strong enough to outlast her.

"I know what you do every day, Lachlan." Brynn's voice carried through the dim room to the window where he stood. In the small space of the cabin they'd shared, there was no place for either of them to hide. "You search and search, but to what avail?" She came up silently behind him, her arms snaking around his waist to caress his bare chest.

His gaze remained on the ocean he could see, so close and yet so far. "I want nothing more than to return to my home, Brynn. Does that not matter to you?" He didn't know why he bothered. She'd kept him trapped on land for so long, he knew the only way out was to force her hand.

"I have not taken you from your beloved sea," she whispered to him, her breath at his ear. "It is right there." Her wandering hands crept lower, her fingernails scratching his skin, leaving angry welts along the way. "You can hear it, can you not?" she continued. "You can smell it, touch it." A hand dipped lower and snuck inside his low-hanging breeches to toy with the auburn curls peeking out.

"It is not the same, and you know it," he growled, annoyed with her constant desire, annoyed with himself for allowing this captivity. His heart was filled with emptiness, unsure of who he was. Who was he, if not a selkie? He had no one. No seal folk to cuddle against in the cold nights, no family to swim with, to talk to.

Is this what loneliness is? Is this why the woman would cry into the sea for me?

His voice was as hoarse when he warned her, "You cannot hold me here forever, Brynn. I will never stop seeking my freedom." The light laughter that filled the room fueled his anger.

"I know that," she replied dismissively. "Is that not the nature of a selkie?"

"Then you already know that even if I bend, even if I were to fold and give into your desires, it changes nothing." Lachlan's words were soft even though he did not bother to turn and face her. His body had begun to betray him with each of her gentle touches, caresses. It was only a matter of time before his will would finally break.

"Yes," she admitted while cupping him, stroking him, "I have read the legends of selkie wives. They abandoned their husbands, their children once their skin is discovered."

"It is because those things are meaningless to us. We, selkie, are not meant to be away from the sea for long. We do not belong here." Finally turning, he met her gaze, the move forcing her to release his body from her grasp. Lachlan leaned forward until his lips hovered above hers for a moment before eventually closing the distance. His fingers tangled in her hair, pulling it back just enough to deepen the kiss. "Set me free," he pleaded. His lips ran a path of kisses down the cool flesh of her jawline, attempting to sway her decision the only way he knew how.

"Please," she begged, ignoring his request, her hands at his hips.

"Tell me, Brynn," he demanded against her ear. His hand slid beneath the thin fabric of her nightdress to caress the bottom curve of her rear. "Tell me, and I will be yours."

"I cannot..." she panted.

Lachlan slipped his hand between them, cupping her core, and she gasped. Unlike the rest of her skin, this part was warm, always so warm, just like her mouth. He could pretend that time had no effect on him, that she held no other power over him, save for his skin, but he would be branded a liar. Holding her steady with his free hand, his other dipped into that velvet warmth.

"Yes...!" she hissed before her lips found his again. This time, she kissed him with such a needy tenacity that her small fangs nicked his bottom lip.

Lachlan paused in his actions, frozen. Pulling his face back to see her wide, apologetic eyes before he matched her ferocity. His fingers caressed her wildly as she ground herself against the palm of his hand.

"Give me a clue," he murmured as he ran his lips along her neck, "a sign of where you've put it." His voice was hoarse with need.

Gripping his biceps, she bucked against his hand. "Yes! Lachlan, please!" she begged as her legs began to quiver. "I—"

Almost. Almost an answer.

"Tell me!" he growled. "Tell me, and I will take you to bed." Not a lie; a promise. He needed release just as badly.

"I—I can't! I—" she stuttered out, "I don't have it!" Her entire body shivered and shook with the power of her release, her core clamping down as she screamed her pleasure. Brynn nearly collapsed in his arms from the force of her release. Panting, she tried to slide to the floor, but his grip on her tightened.

"What do you mean you don't have it?" he growled at her.

The fury in his gaze would've been frightening if she wasn't a powerful being herself. She used force to pry his arms from around her. "You will not find it here, Lachlan," she stated flatly. Marveling at the size of him, she reached up to grab and stroke him. "No matter how hard you look," she finished, her voice just as calm and matter of fact as it had been.

Brynn leaned forward and pleasured him the only way he'd allow.

"You are a wicked woman, Brynn," he panted out before fisting his hands into her hair.

Raising her chin, she met the gaze of his beryl blue eyes, eyes that would forever reflect the sea that he'd come out of. His expression hardened as he used her mouth, taking control of his own pleasure. Brynn moaned when his roughness caused her fangs to scrape his delicate flesh.

He growled, fisting her hair harder, and she could feel her heat building again. She knew he would not take the news of his imminent capture well and could tell by the way he used her now, more vigorously, that he was upset. But at this moment, she didn't care. She was getting exactly what she wanted, him.

Knowing that he was nearing the end, she reveled in every single action. Lachlan let out a half moan, half growl as he held her head in place, finishing it. The taste of him, mixing with the sweet metallic flavor of blood, was intoxicating and nearly brought her to completion again.

He released her violently, throwing her head back while releasing her hair. She watched with sheer amusement as he backed away from her. A wide smile spread across her face as she wiped the remnants of him from the sides of her mouth. "In time, you will be more comfortable with our arrangement," she paused to lick her lips and fingers before adding, "now that you have no reason to spend your days searching for something that can never be found."

"You were right to say that, in time, I would see you as a woman, but in this," he waved his hand in the air and scoffed. "In this, you will be wrong. I will never come to revel in our time together the same way you do."

Unperturbed, she replied simply, "We shall see."

Brynn was wrong. At the very least, he had that small dignity. More time passed, and he had eventually stopped searching for his skin. But his longing for the sea never wavered. Brynn was no replacement for the joy it brought him. Lachlan had overturned every rock on the damn island. Searched every crevasse, of every house, to no avail.

He settled into his life, this life with Brynn. Their nights would be filled with hours of sex. Some of it kind and gentle, some of it angry and rough. His days, however, were taken up by naps at the beach and drinks at the pub in town. Home by dark was the only rule he needed to follow. He had all but given up on any form of freedom, of salvation.

Until they'd arrived.

At first, Lachlan paid them no mind. They entered the pub and went right to the barkeep, asking questions. Most of them ordered drinks, filling up the small place, uncomfortably so. Few of them, however, never let a drop touch their lips. The others seemed to fall in line when they entered, and, day after day, Lachlan was witness to them questioning the townspeople rather thoroughly.

He avoided them as best he could, even stopped going to the tavern altogether for a while. Instead, he found his contentment by floating in the waves near the shore and of longer naps on the beach.

"Excuse me, sir," an unfamiliar voice called out, a voice far nearer than he would have liked.

Opening one eye lazily, he looked for the speaker. A tall, stocky man with a head full of gray hair stood above him, making Lachlan have to stretch his neck back to get a better look. He was dressed primarily in black, the glint of a gold cross hanging from the man's neck catching Lachlan's eye.

"Fine day for a nap." Lachlan sat up in the sand, twisting to get a better look at the man in question.

"Yes, so it would seem." He pursed his lips together and examined Lachlan with his gaze. Not in the hungry way that Brynn looked at him, but in a calculating way. "I am Father Andrews. My associates and I believe that you can help us with our mission, and in turn, we can help you."

"Why do you assume that I am in need of your help?" he questioned, pulling himself to stand in front of the other man, not bothering to shake the sand from his body. "And what makes you believe I'd help?"

The old man squared his shoulders and raised his lips in a semblance of a smile. "Why? Because we are the Disciples of Mercy." He gripped the gold cross from his chest and kissed it before continuing. "And we have been sent here to rid this island of the accursed."

"Accursed?"

"Vampires, dear boy. The unholy. The undead." His hand held the lapel of his coat as he spoke, the other reaching to caress the gleaming cross around his neck. "We, few, are traveling men of God, and those marks on your body tell us all we need to know."

He pointed out Brynn's *love bites*, as she called them. Usually hidden from sight by the shirt he wore while he was in town, but while alone on the beach, he went shirtless. Lachlan tipped his head in thought.

They mean to kill her.

He would have to weigh his options on the matter quickly. If Brynn was dead, Lachlan would be stuck in this form, alone. Forever. Lachlan, however, still held some residual hope that one day, Brynn would eventually let her secret slip, and he would be able to gain his freedom from it.

"No," Lachlan denied flatly. "I am in no need of your assistance.

These markings," he stated as he pointed to the small bites, "are from animals, fishing lures, and anything else you can think of."

The older man's lips flattened. "Do not deny it, my boy. I've seen them plenty a time." He took a step closer and warned, "They are alluring and beautiful, as many of the sirens of the sea, but they will steal your soul and bleed you dry." In a gentle voice, he added, "They will never love you, my son."

"I am *not* your *son*." Lachlan sneered, finally realizing why Brynn hated when he referred to her as a child. "I am older than you think, and my *soul* is none of your concern." He settled himself back down into the sand, in nearly the exact position he had been in before Father Andrews had come to disturb him. Ignoring the man, he closed his eyes and declared, "If you wouldn't mind, I'd like to finish my nap."

Lachlan paced in front of the bed, his head constantly turning to look out the window, waiting for the sun to set. He'd never love Brynn, but he did care for her. Enough that he didn't want to see her die. Not yet anyway. The child he knew would always have a place in his heart, but she had turned herself into a monster, and Lachlan has made peace with it. And he didn't want to see her demise because it would mean the end of the line for him.

The sun began to set, and she stirred. He parted the heavy drapery that hung around the bed and shook her awake, alive.

"Brynn! Brynn!" he called. "We have to leave this place soon. Some men, they've come—"

"Let them come." She yawned, stretching her form across the sheets like a cat that had just woken from its nap. "You know that I cannot feed from you alone, Lachlan. It was only a matter of time before the Pirates of Mercy found me again." She said, crawling towards him with hungry eyes.

"Again?" He threw his hands up in disbelief. "Pirates?"

"Yes, the Disciples of Mercy. They are nothing more than pirates who accost my kind in the name of their God." Brynn gave an exacerbated sigh as she pulled on her dress. "They kill us and steal from us."

"That does not matter," he told her urgently. "They came to me and saw your markings. They are soon to find you." *And kill my chances of freedom, as well.* He looked to the window again, not seeing the ocean but looking at the swarm of men approaching. "It seems they already have." She looked at Lachlan, and for the first time in a long time, he recognized the panic she was desperately trying to mask. "You've only just woke, Brynn. And they know to strike when you are weak." Lachlan looked over his shoulder to see the flicker of torchlight approaching. "You must feed from me, right now," he offered, knowing the price would be his own weakness. He wouldn't die, but he would be unable to protect himself. Then again, he was not the intended target.

He didn't have to ask again. She pounced on him, sinking her fangs into his neck. Unlike Brynn's love bites, this pain was sharp, like a white-hot needle setting his veins on fire, and he could not help but struggle against her.

Three bangs are all it took. Three bangs and the door splintered and fell. Lachlan recognized the giant man that stood in the doorway from the tavern, always drinking. Pushing their way in, men flooded the room before finally, Father Andrews made his appearance, flanked by four others in similar dress.

Lachlan was pried from her grasp, held in place by the arms of the ogre that had broken the door down. Lachlan would be made to watch. He knew the moment he made eye contact with Father Andrews, saw the hint of a smile on his face. Lachlan struggled as the men surrounded Brynn, who looked just as innocent as the day he'd made his promise, save for the blood staining the front of her face.

That's when the screams began.

Even if he were blind, he would recognize the sound. The screams of men on land sound nearly identical to the screams of men at sea. Both cry out as they are slaughtered by monsters—beautiful monsters, but monsters nonetheless. The only significant difference was that the sirens of the deep worked together while Brynn was alone.

He was in awe of how skillfully she disposed of them, as he bore witness to her savagery for the first time. Bodies fell before her. Blood coated the floor. Lachlan's heart jumped in its chest as he watched Father Andrews lunge for her.

Brynn swiped at him, her nails leaving long jagged marks across his face, causing him to howl in pain. As she gloated, another came. He drove a long metal spike through her chest, riding her down to the floor.

Then, and only then, did they release him. He raced over to her side, pushing the blood-soaked hair from her face.

"No, no, no..." he whispered, "you cannot leave me like this, alone." He panicked.

"Search this place," one of the men spoke from above, his deep, uncaring voice filling the room with the satisfaction of a job well done. "Take anything and everything of value before we *cleanse* the area." This came from another like Father Andrews.

Brynn was right. They were pirates. Lachlan glared at him before Brynn's gentle touch captured his attention.

"You would have never truly loved me," she whispered, her voice faint and weak, "I know this." With a sad smile, she said, "Still, I had to try." Lachlan could feel the smile through her emerald eyes, even as their light faded. She coughed and spat the blood from her mouth before adding, "Your freedom lies with my Master, my maker."

Lachlan's heart lurched in his chest as if it was starting up for the first time. She will die, but he will finally be free. "Who, Brynn, who is it?" he urged softly, forcing himself to keep the excitement he felt weaving through him from coming out.

"Lord—"

Her words were cut off by the sharp clang of metal on metal, followed by the cracking of the floorboards beneath her.

"No!" he screamed, seeing his only shot of freedom dashed.

"Tis' okay, boy. You're free now," spoke the brute of a man that still held the enormous hammer he'd just used to drive the spike completely through Brynn's body. "She cannot hurt you no more."

"Free? I was so close!" He screamed. He stood with clenched fists, anger vibrating through his body as he watched the men clearing out of the house, arms full of loot as they made a hasty exit.

"Time to go home. They're bout to cleanse this place." An older seaman said, clapping him on the shoulder. "With fire." He waggled the eyebrow above his good eye to Lachlan.

"I can't go home," Lachlan growled as he was ushered from the house.

"Why's that?" the old man asked. "She—she took something from me, and I can't go home without it." He confessed.

"If it's worth anything, it's already on the ship." The man added, "Talk to the fathers to get it back."

But it's not on the ship, Lachlan knew. *It's in some other vampire's house.*

Lachlan walked towards the beach where he happened across Father Andrews. A young man was fussing over the wound on his face. "See? You were helpful after all," he said, looking at Lachlan with his uninjured eye.

"I wish to come with you," Lachlan told him. "To join you on your mission."

"Well, we have lost quite a few men, thanks to her." Her name need not be said. "But tell me, why I should allow it?"

Lachlan sighed heavily, bringing his hands to scrub along his face. The Fae cannot lie, but they can bend the truth to suit their purpose. Lachlan did just that. As he spoke, he willed the old man to believe that Brynn had taken a precious heirloom from him, one that he could not return home without. To do so would mean certain death.

All truth, yet not.

But it didn't matter. Believing his words, Father Andrews allowed Lachlan to join their group, and with a humorless laugh, he became a pirate of mercy.

With his freedom barely within reach, Lachlan had returned to the sea, just not how he had intended.

ABOUT JC BROWN

JC Brown lives in a world where magic is real and anything is possible, or at least she likes to pretend so. She has always held a fascination for the darker side of the paranormal, like evil witches, zombies, were-wolves, vampires and the fae. When her adult ADD allows, she's able to focus and carefully craft the intricate web of imagination onto paper.

JC is an avid reader and lover of education that's led her through many careers. From barista to graphic design, certified nursing assistant to school bus driver but weaving paranormal tales is what she enjoys the most.

As a Cuban American, family and culture are especially important to her. While writing is her absolute passion, her full-time job is Mistress of Minions to her four needy goblins. They definitely keep her on her toes. However, her hysterical husband makes everything easier with his wild, and sometimes inappropriate humor. She shares her Rhode Island home with her husband, children, and parents.

Find out more at: AuthorJCBrown.com

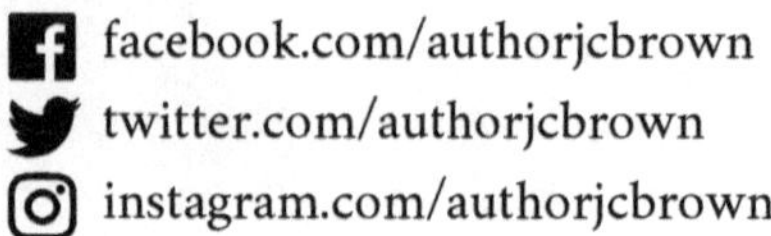

facebook.com/authorjcbrown
twitter.com/authorjcbrown
instagram.com/authorjcbrown

ABOUT LENA LANE

Lena has been writing since high school—though that first story will remain in the dark corners of her closet to protect everyone. After all, she writes romance, not horror. Just kidding! It's not really that bad, but her idea of romance and love has certainly changed through time, not to mention her writing skills.

Growing up in a traditional and strict family, Lena was protected—or maybe overprotected. Books became her escape, her only avenue to see the world beyond the walls of her shelter. It wasn't long before she realized that romance was the way to go. No matter how difficult the characters' circumstances were, by the time the book ended, everything was perfect. In romance, there is always a guaranteed happy ending.

Reality was unwelcomed and Lena devoured books like people eat chips. As soon as one was done, she was on the hunt for another. When reality intruded in her life—like work (ugh!)— and reading other people's work was impossible, she started daydreaming, creating her own stories. Now, she wants to share those daydreams and passion with the rest of the world.

After getting her own happy ending, Lena lives in a small town in Massachusetts with her husband, two girls, two dogs, and three cats, and if her eldest daughter has anything to do about it, maybe a bird in the future... She really hopes not, though. Birds are really, really loud.

Her stories have been described as cute and sweet with just enough humor to give the reader an occasional giggle.

Find out more at: LenaLaneNovels.com

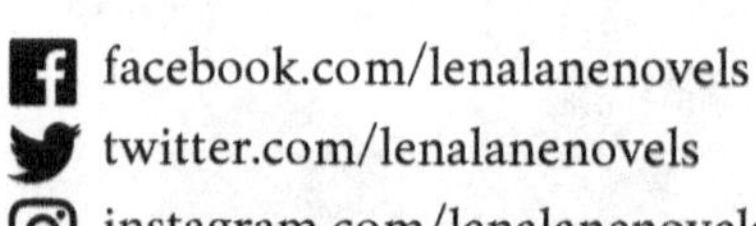

ISLAND OF MAGIC
BY KAT PARRISH

PROLOGUE

The island was not marked on any map nor depicted on any globe. Indeed, even travelers who had glimpsed its green mountains and white beaches from the decks of passing ships could not agree on where exactly it was located. Some swore it lay east of Italy, while others said it was the southernmost jewel in the necklace of islands that dangled from the southern tip of Greece. Others concluded it was off the coast of Africa, hidden by an everlasting bank of fog.

They were all wrong. The island occupied a place outside of space and time and was only accessible under certain conditions—when the moon was full in the daylight sky, and the tide was high, and the wind was fresh.

Born of the sea and ancient magic, the island was an enchanted place where sweet water flowed, and trees bore fruit year-round. Most fantastically, the air on the island was full of sweet sounds, tunes played by unseen musicians and sung by unseen voices for the benefit of the island's only inhabitants, a drove of feral pigs that were shy and hard to catch.

Such was the magic of the island that it was perpetually summer and even the night air was soft and warm. If more people had known about such a wonderful place, it would have been overrun decades ago, but such were the vagaries of magic that the only humans who came to the place came there unwillingly or by accident.

Those who had lived there in the past had called the place Aenea, but its name, along with the memory of its existence, have been lost to both history and myth. The four who live there now simply call it home. And only one of them is a native.

CHAPTER ONE: MISCHIEFS MANIFOLD AND SORCERIES TERRIBLE

She was the highborn daughter of a noble of ancient name and a seawitch he seduced one moonlit night redolent with the perfume of many flowers and pregnant with the promise of myriad delights to come.

Their union was brief and happy, but when the child, a girl they called Sycorax, was born, her mother took her back beneath the waves to raise, leaving the mortal world behind. But her mother's people could not accept the child's mixed parentage, and when she was thirteen, Sycorax returned to Al Jazain, the country of her birth, to live with her father.

He was overjoyed by the reunion and treated her like a rare gem, clothing her in silks and showering with both affection and jewelry. His home was among the greatest of the grand mansions in the city, and his extensive gardens were landscaped with lush greenery and lakes filled with lilies and fishes and graceful fountains.

Proud peacocks patrolled the grounds, including one that was pure black, with a tail like a delicate wrought iron design. Sycorax was delighted by the bird and named him Hasan, which means beautiful, and fed him nuts and morsels of cheese from her own hand. Hasan rewarded her affection by following her around like a pet dog, though he screeched loudly if anyone else in the household approached him.

Sycorax played among the mosaic paths and the towering fountains and often sat for hours on stone benches as she took lessons from a procession of tutors, both human and djinn. She had a quick and ready mind, and her teachers were pleased with how fast she learned and how eager she was for their instruction.

By the time she was eighteen, Sycorax spoke thirteen languages. She was learned in astronomy, mathematics, and art. She created art and played music and wrote poetry.

But for all her learning, she didn't really understand people all that well, and that would eventually prove her undoing.

Because she had been a privileged and pretty child whose every whim had been indulged, she had never learned that sometimes there are penalties for being a woman. She didn't know that being an individual and following one's own heart could be unwise—especially where marriage was concerned. And she was expected to marry. Her father had been entertaining suitors and rejecting offers for her hand since she first arrived, expecting her to make a fortunate match that would enrich him even more with dowry gifts and outright bribes. But Sycorax was uninterested in marriage. She was having too much fun to shut herself up in a household where she would have no more rights than a household pet except where domestic matters were concerned.

<hr>

Sycorax's beauty drew admiring glances but also engendered fear among some who saw the subtle scales on her skin as proof that she was not entirely a human and, therefore, to be shunned and avoided and despised. They were not so different from the sea people who had rejected her, though the humans hid their true feelings behind a dissembling mask, and Sycorax found it easy to ignore them as she went about her life.

But they watched.

And they took notice.

And they remembered what they saw and stored these observations away for future use.

Because she had inherited more than her beauty from her mother,

Sycorax practiced magic in many small and harmless ways. She could summon fire. She could heal small wounds. She could control the moon in its course across the sky. And perhaps most sinisterly, she could cast love charms.

Or so it was said when the son of a powerful Phoenician trader fell madly, deeply, hopelessly in love with her.

Hopelessly, for although Sycorax was fond of him and welcomed him into her bed, the dalliance was not serious for her, and she had no wish to make it either formal or permanent.

And when she discovered she was pregnant, she did not ask her lover to lend his name to the child she was certain would be a boy but instead announced her intention to raise him by herself. Her lover was heartbroken, and his mother, who was something of a witch herself, devised a cunning plan to both punish Sycorax and remove her from her son permanently.

All without raising a hand against her.

It was simply a matter of a few whispers here, certain insinuations there, and before long, her son's lover—the mother of her grandchild—was hauled before a tribunal of stern male judges who had all experienced romantic disappointments themselves. These men took only minutes to pass judgment on Sycorax, finding her guilty of manifold mischiefs and terrible sorceries.

The sentence was banishment, and it was carried out swiftly. Her father was distraught, for all his wealth and power could not save her from the fate they decreed.

But the announcement of her punishment was only meant for public consumption. The vengeful mother had come to a private accommodation with the captain of the ship that was to deliver the condemned to her final destination and had paid him in gold coins and silver to simply throw her over the side of the vessel and leave her to her fate, far from any hospitable shore.

The captain was privately appalled by this arrangement, but he owed gambling debts to a house of chance said to belong to a family of djinn, and so he ignored his considerable misgivings, paid off his debt, and executed his commission with an extra measure of cruelty born of his own self-loathing.

When the peaks of the island were first visible on the horizon, much too far for anyone to swim but tantalizing, tauntingly close, the captain pushed Sycorax overboard himself and then sailed away without a backward glance.

He would later be shipwrecked after his vessel was attacked by a kraken, and though he alone made it to the refuge of an island, it was an inhospitable place of rock and guano and no water at all. He died slowly of hunger and thirst and madness.

It was painful, and he was alone, and the dying took a long time. By the end, he was raving, confessing his guilt and begging imaginary demons for respite.

Or perhaps his demons were real. Who can say?

As for Sycorax...she stayed only for a little while under the sea. Her mother was long dead, and Sycorax was never truly welcomed, and after so many years, she no longer felt at home there.

She stayed long enough to give birth to her misbegotten child, and then she began the long swim toward the island which she claimed for her own. The only other inhabitant, an airy spirit named Ariel, welcomed her as a sister, and the three shared the island like a family, though one that was prone to squabbling for Ariel was a mercurial sort as all elementals are.

Sycorax's son Caliban grew up into a strong and fearless child, certain of his mother's affection and untroubled by their isolation. He was untutored but unfettered by others' expectations of him. Ariel treated him like a troublesome little brother, but they watched over him and kept him safe when his mother could not be with him. Their ability to turn invisible allowed Caliban the illusion that he was free to explore and ramble and examine without supervision.

He was happy. And then, like the serpent invading Eden, a mage named Prospero arrived with his young daughter in tow.

And everything changed after that.

Prospero had been a Duke in his native Milan and found it impossible to share his new home on equal terms. Stranded on the island by accomplices of his brother Antonio, his humiliation and anger knew no bounds. Within a month, he had murdered Sycorax, enslaved Ariel, and taken Caliban into his own dubious care to raise as a servant.

But he had not reckoned with his daughter's kind heart. And from the first time she saw Caliban, she became his companion and protector, keeping him safe from the worst of Prospero's temper, although she could not shield him from her father's sharp-edged tongue. Nor could she defend him from Prospero's whims and caprices, the monstrous entitlement that kept Caliban a virtual prisoner.

He could have swum away—he had his mother's ability to breathe water—but he stayed.

He stayed for love of Miranda.

CHAPTER TWO: THE SEA WILL GIVE UP THE DEAD

Caliban and Miranda had been on the beach for hours, gathering seaweed into baskets for drying later. He was relishing a rare day with no chores required for his master and basking in the time alone with Miranda. As usual, she was happily distracted, picking up more pretty rocks and shells than she was the strands of green and brown seaweed and that had washed up on the beach.

There were crabs and small fish trapped in little pockets in the sand, darting about madly, looking for escape. Caliban decided he would come back and gather them later.

Though Miranda ate such creatures with relish, it distressed her to think too much about how they came to be on her plate. Caliban was happy to maintain Prospero's fiction that he simply magicked them up and into the cookpot without any mess or pain.

Prospero. He'd seemed moody of late and more inclined than usual to vent his moods on Caliban, who'd learned to avoid his master when he was in the grip of an uncertain temper. It was those times when he seemed to feel his exile most keenly and would rail against the injustice of the world and how badly mistreated he had been.

It had been more than a decade since he'd come to the island, yet it still seemed a fresh and bleeding wound in his mind.

And as if thinking of him had conjured him, Prospero suddenly appeared on the cliff above them, dressed in his *stregone's* robe, the gilt embroidery along the hem catching the light of the brilliant, sunlit afternoon.

The ivory walking stick he used to focus his spells—carved from the single tusk of an elephant—was clutched in his right hand and pointed toward the sea.

Caliban nudged his companion. "Your father is making magic again," he said.

Miranda looked in the direction he pointed. Her father was gesturing grandly with both arms and muttering unseen words. She shrugged and went back to sorting sea wrack. She was so used to her father doing magic that it no longer seemed remarkable to her.

"What do you suppose he is doing?" Caliban asked.

"He and Ariel were closeted together for hours last night," Miranda replied, "but he didn't tell me what they were discussing." Miranda was untroubled by her father's surreptitious sorcery and understood it was bound up with his identity in a way she would never comprehend. She had been too young to remember his actions before they came to the island, and she chose to believe what he'd told her about the fate of Sycorax, the servitude of Ariel, and how Caliban had come into their household. Caliban *was* old enough to remember, but for the love of Miranda, he held his tongue about the horrors he had seen, and when he was alone with Prospero, he pretended to be the brutish simpleton the mage believed him to be.

Miranda knew that her father was endlessly fascinated by the images in a mirror he had brought with him into exile. "My Magic connected the mirror to my rooms in the *palazzo*, he said, and it still shows me what goes on within."

Sometimes he would study the mirror all day, watching people Miranda did not know, doing things she did not care about.

"Perhaps it has to do with something he saw in his mirror," she said, "and Ariel is helping him."

"Ariel is not to be trusted," Caliban said darkly, for the spirit often tormented him.

Miranda laughed. "That's exactly what they say about you." She mimicked Ariel's light voice. "You need to watch out for Caliban Miranda. One day you'll see what I mean."

"Ariel says such things to curry favor with your father," Caliban said, a shadow falling over his features. "They know how much he likes to sow discord."

Miranda frowned when Caliban said that but hurried to defend her father. "Perhaps he is summoning a ship to rescue us."

"It has been twelve years," Caliban reminded her.

"For him, it is as fresh an insult as if it only happened twelve seconds ago," she said.

Caliban said nothing, and after a moment, he realized Miranda was shivering slightly. It was growing cold on the beach. Loose sand had begun to blow across the sea strand as the wind quickly freshened from a breeze to a gale.

The woven baskets they had used to gather seaweed went tumbling across the sand, spilling their carefully collected bounty as it turned over and over. Miranda looked dismayed to see all her labor lost.

Dark clouds rushed in, blotting out the sun and making the afternoon darker. "You should go in," Caliban said, "before you get wet."

But his warning was too late. The storm was already upon them with raindrops so fat and heavy that they burst like ripe fruit against the skin. Caliban was unconcerned by the wild weather. The rain merely bounced off the armored carapace that protected his back and head.

Miranda, though, had no such protection, and she was soon soaked, her clothing clinging to her body like a second skin. And still, she made no move to flee for shelter, mesmerized as she was by the sight of her father conjuring the storm.

As she watched, the waves approaching the shore grew in height and slapped down on the beach like an invisible giant was swatting an invisible table with his hand. And still, Prospero shouted his spell into the teeth of the wind though it threatened to blow him from his perch. He seemed the center of his own personal tempest as wind whipped around him, lifting his garments and his hair and beard and scattering his words into the briny void.

Larger pebbles were swept up into the winds and began to circle in the air as if dancing. Lightning crackled in the distance where, if Miranda squinted, she could see a magnificent sailing ship just over the horizon.

Surely, she thought, *father sees the ship. He must know he is putting it in jeopardy.* She was right that he saw the ship and knew exactly what he was doing. Caliban knew it too. He knew exactly what Miranda's father was capable of.

———

Because Caliban stayed outside in the storm, Miranda stayed too. She found the violence of the wind and the water exhilarating, allowing her own wild nature to surface.

The first wreckage floated ashore an hour later, large pieces of splintered wood and fragments of torn linen and metal fittings that had come loose, and then another kind of debris altogether was vomited up from the sea.

Caliban was distracted and distressed by the sea creatures who'd been dredged up from the depths and flung onto the sand, and so it was that Miranda found the boy.

CHAPTER THREE: TO PLAY THE FOOL

The boy was splayed on the sand, pale and tangled in seaweed like some strange fleshy fish. *Or like an angel fallen to Earth*, Miranda thought, for she was sure she had never seen anyone so beautiful as he with his perfect face and curly russet hair falling in ringlets to his broad shoulders.

He was so still that at first, she thought he was dead, but as she watched from an arm's length away, he gulped a hitching breath, turned on his side, and vomited a measure of sea water. When he was emptied, he sat up weakly and blinked, his eyes blearily trying to focus on Miranda.

"Are you alive or a vision?" he said. "I cannot tell."

Miranda blushed at these words, but before she could reply, Caliban joined them, and when the boy saw him, he crabbed backward out of fear. "Get away," he yelled. "Get away, get away."

What on earth is wrong with him, wondered Miranda, but what she said was, "You have nothing to fear from us." The boy did not look reassured, and he grabbed at the waist of his tunic as if searching for a nonexistent weapon.

"What manner of monster is it?" he asked Miranda, looking past her and staring at her companion as if he assumed Caliban had neither feelings nor a voice.

"That's just Caliban," Miranda said carelessly. "He lives here."

Caliban turned to stare at Miranda, hurt and baffled by her easy dismissal of him. But she was not looking at him. All her attention was focused on the castaway.

"I'm Miranda," she said. "This is my father's domain."

Looking fearfully at Caliban, the boy said, 'I am Ferdinand. My father is the King of Naples."

"Oh," Miranda says. "Perhaps he knows my father? Prospero, the Duke of Milan?"

Ferdinand looked confused. "The Duke of Milan is named Antonio. He is great friends with my father."

"How fortunate for you," Caliban said. "I hope your father is not dead."

Ferdinand looked so alarmed by that possibility that Miranda hastened to assure him that if he managed to swim to shore, it was more than possible that his father did too.

"I didn't swim here," Ferdinand said. "I just floated on a piece of wood."

Caliban made a disgusted sound. "I will search for him," he said. With a glance at Miranda, he added, "and leave you to the ministrations of the fair Miranda."

"Thank you, Caliban," she said. "I'll take Ferdinand to my father. He'll help him."

Caliban privately doubted that Prospero would have any fondness for the son of a man who helped his brother betray him, but from the besotted look on Miranda's face, she was not going to listen to anyone gainsay the boy. The soft, beardless boy.

Feeling completely out of sorts, he stomped down the beach, pretending that he could not hear Ferdinand say to Miranda. "Is he your brother? He's quite ugly."

Pretending that he didn't hear Miranda's answer, "No, he is like my brother, but we are not kin."

The last thing Caliban wanted was for Miranda to see him as a sort of brother.

Caliban searched for an hour and never found Ferdinand's father, but he did come across another survivor, a boisterous fellow who claimed to be the King of Naples' butler.

"Then you know his son," Caliban said.

The butler, whose name was Stephano, spit on the sand in disgust. "That randy goat."

"He's a lecher then?" Caliban inquired.

"He never met the woman he couldn't lay," Stephano said, then burped. "Do you have anything to drink on this godforsaken piece of rock?"

"There's water," Caliban said, knowing he meant something stronger. "Or perhaps some bottles of wine will wash ashore. They do occasionally." Stephano brightened at that possibility. "In the meantime, could you take me to the king of this island? I would make his acquaintance."

Caliban bit his tongue to keep from saying *he* was the king of the island but was curious about the other man's plans.

"He's not a very pleasant man," Caliban said.

"Then I'll just kill him," Stephano said in an offhand way, "and take the island for myself." He looked blearily at Caliban. "I hope you don't mind."

"Take it if you can," Caliban said, "but leave me the tyrant's books."

"As you like," Stephano said. "I cannot read."

CHAPTER FOUR: I KNOW HOW TO CURSE

Meanwhile, Miranda took Ferdinand to her father, expecting him to welcome him with open arms. The meeting did not go as she had expected. Instead, he accused Ferdinand of merely pretending to be the prince of Naples and declared he had no use for him other than as a slave.

"But don't you already have a servant monster?" Ferdinand said in bewilderment before Miranda could protest.

"That thing of darkness belongs to my household," Prospero said, "but he has nothing to do with you." With a wave of his hand, he bound the boy in chains so heavy he bent beneath the weight of them. "Now fetch me a hundred logs for my fire."

Ferdinand looked around the cave that was Prospero's home and saw no obvious fire pit. "Where do you want me to put them?"

"Worry about that when you return," Prospero said. "If you return. There are dangers on this island. Cannibal monkeys and birds with teeth like blades."

Ferdinand was familiar with moneys, for his own mother kept a fettered ape as a pet and paraded him at court on a regular basis, but he had never heard of a sharp-toothed bird outside of myth.

"When my father finds me, you will be sorry," he promised. Prospero laughed.

"I knew your father when he was barely older than you are now. He was a weak-willed sot overfond of wine and women and not at all interested in siring an heir." He had looked at the boy critically. "In fact, you don't resemble him at all. I suspect that someone else was your father."

This slur upon his mother so enraged Ferdinand that he attempted to attack Prospero, but with a lazy wave of his hand, the magician caused the boy's chains to tighten with a jerk so that he found it hard to breathe.

"Father," Miranda cried, and Prospero relented, releasing the young lord so abruptly he fell to the floor of the cave.

"You will do my bidding little lordling," he said and, with another wave of his hand, propelled him out of the cave. Then he turned his attention to Miranda. "Stay away from the Napolitano," he said sternly. "All such men are scoundrels."

"He is not his father," Miranda said hotly and turned on her heel and followed Ferdinand out the door, not seeing the calculating look her father gave her.

"And so it begins," he said to the air, and Ariel flickered into existence right at shoulder level.

"She is besotted with him," Prospero said. "You've done well to bring him here, Ariel."

The spirit fluttered their wings excitedly. "Is there more toil, master? Will you free me now?"

Prospero looked at Ariel indulgently. "Soon," he promised. "The play is not yet done."

Miranda caught up with Ferdinand as he struggled to lift a smooth log of wood from a pile he had found in a clearing and hurried to help him. Taking the log from his grasp, she said, "When this burns, it will remember that it wearied you." Ferdinand smiled at that.

"You have a tender heart," he said, and then he reached out as much as his bonds would allow and laid his hand flat upon her chest. "And knowing it beats for me gladdens my heart. I could love you, Miranda, if only I were not in chains."

Miranda felt her heart speed up at his touch and felt an unfamiliar flutter in her loins. She was just about to say something when Caliban pushed her aside to grab Ferdinand and throw him halfway down the beach, where he landed with a clank and a thud. "Be glad that he is in chains and cannot love you," Caliban said.

"Are you mad?" Miranda said, beating at his shell with her fists.

"He's playing you false Miranda; can't you see that?"

"Why would he do that?" she asked. "Am I not fair of face?" Caliban had no rejoinder for that, so he lashed out in another direction.

"Did you like it when he touched your heart?" Caliban demanded, reaching out with his own rough hand.

"Stop it," she said, but her childhood companion was in a fury and refused to let go, taking her to the sandy ground and pinning her there.

"Stop it," he said again.

"Make me," he said and buried his face beneath her breasts, his hard carapace biting into her softness.

He began tearing at her clothes, and alarmed, Miranda tried to push him away, only to realize...she could not. He was much too strong.

"You beast," she said, "you are the savage my father always thought you."

At those words, Caliban pushed himself away, allowing Miranda to sit up. Wounded, he started to say something, but she overrode him with more angry words. "I pitied you," she said. "I taught you how to speak when you could do nothing but gabble like a thing most brutish."

"And in return, I brought you ripe berries and showed your father the purest springs," Caliban said.

"I gifted him all my riches. I gave him all I had, freely, but he took more. He took my birthright as your uncle stole yours." He gazed down upon her, his eyes—which had always been so full of loving warmth—cold and heartless. "And he killed my mother."

"She went away."

"She wouldn't have left me," Caliban said.

"You never valued me. So I will take from you that which you do value."

It took a moment for Miranda to grasp Caliban's meaning, but when she did, she struggled even harder and managed to wriggle free and stand up. For a moment, they stood there staring at each other, each of them breathing hard. waiting for the other to make the next move.

"You taught me language," he finally said. "And my profit on it is I know how to curse."

And with that, he turned and walked away, leaving Miranda both angry and bereft. And very, very confused. But rather than go after him, she went down the beach to check on Ferdinand, just as two men in sodden clothes were converging on him.

CHAPTER FIVE: FULL FATHOM FIVE THY LOVER LIES

One of the men was short and somewhat stout, dressed richly in silken garments now ruined by their salt water soaking. The other was the very image of her father, a man she had seen in his mirror and always assumed was some shade of Prospero trapped in the glass. She realized now this was the usurper. She stared at him as the other man fell upon the unconscious Ferdinand, kissing his pale face with joy. "He lives, Antonio," the man said, pulling at the chains that bound him. "I thought he was lost."

"There will be rejoicing in Spain," Antonio said dryly.

Spain? Miranda wondered, and as if she had asked the question aloud, Antonio turned to her. "We were en route to Valencia where Ferdinand is to marry the Infanta."

Marry? Miranda flushed with dismay at how badly she had misjudged the situation. Before she could say anything that would embarrass herself, Prospero arrived, face like a thundercloud and dressed for magic.

The King ignored him, all attention on his son, but Antonio heaved a resigned sigh and straightened up. "Brother," he said.

"Brother?" Prospero echoed. "You call me brother after all this time?"

Antonio looked around at the deserted beach and then back to his brother. "You've brought us here for your revenge. Do with us what you will."

For a long moment, Miranda held her breath, knowing that her father's soul hung in the balance and could come down on either side.

Finally, he sighed wearily. "I wish to go back to Milan," he said. "I want to go home." He looked out to sea, and there, with a wiggle of his fingers, a ship appeared with a full component of sails. "There's no harm done."

He looked at the unconscious Ferdinand in his chains, and suddenly the links dissolved like so much seafoam, and the boy groaned.

"Thank you," King Alonzo said, "I am in your debt."

"Then you will not object if my daughter and I take passage on your ship."

"We can leave immediately," the King said. "On the next tide. You have only to gather your possessions."

"There is nothing here I care to take with me."

"Not even your books?" Antonio asked.

"I renounce my dark magic," Prospero said. "I'll drown my books." He turned as if listening to some unseen conversation. "Yes," he said to the air. "You're free."

And for just a moment, Miranda saw the image of Ariel as they circled Prospero's head three times and then flew away. She felt a pang then that the spirit had not even bid farewell.

"I forgive you all," Prospero said to the men. "But I do not forget." He glared at his brother, who had the grace to look ashamed. "You will find your man Stephano passed out in front of my home. Why he is there, I cannot fathom, but I don't want him left behind."

"We will fetch him," the king said.

"Come, Miranda," Prospero said.

"No," she said sadly but resolutely, for her true feelings had come to her. "I cannot go with you," she said. "My heart is here, with Caliban."

"If he is not here, he has gone back to the sea that vomited him out," Prospero said.

"Yes," she said calmly. "And I will go there and find him."

She did not have to search for him. Since they were small, his refuge had been an underwater grotto that could be reached only by swimming through a narrow passageway that was so long, she was nearly out of breath before she arrived.

The grotto was lit with a soft, blue-green glow that came from the algae clinging to the walls. It was just bright enough for her to make out Caliban's figure as he sat hunched on a natural ledge of rock.

He barely acknowledged her as she swam into view and pulled herself up out of the water to sit next to him.

"You walked away from me," she said. "You've never done that before."

Caliban looked at her but did not say anything for a long moment. "I left so you could go to Ferdinand."

She blew out an impatient breath. "I don't want Ferdinand. I love you."

Miranda expected that he would return the sentiment, but instead, he moved away from her. "I don't want your love if it is the love of a child for her companion."

"I am not a child," she said, though she felt herself perilously near to childish tears. "I would not wish any companion in the world but you."

"Brutish Caliban. Savage Caliban," he said.

"I said hurtful things," Miranda admitted. "Please don't hate me, Caliban. I think I was under some dark enchantment that compelled me to reject you and favor Ferdinand,"

"An enchantment?" Caliban said skeptically. "Why would your father want you to fall in love with Ferdinand?"

"Why does my father want anything," Miranda said miserably. Caliban had drawn so far away from him that she could no longer see his features. "He has foresworn his magic and plans to leave here with his brother. Now. Right away."

That surprised Caliban, who turned back toward her, his expression still stern.

"Farewell then," he said and seemed to draw further into his shell.

"I am not leaving," she said and reached out to touch his face.

"What if I don't want you to stay?"

Miranda didn't know what to say to that, so she leaned forward and kissed him. And he kissed her back. Later, they swam back to the beach and sat together, watching the sunset and listening to the cry of the seabirds as they hunted.

There was no sign of the ship.

Miranda looked a little sad, but Caliban held her close, warming her, comforting her.

"Let us not burden our remembrance with a heaviness that's gone," he said, murmuring the words into her hair, which had dried into a mass of unruly curls.

The debris of the wreck that had been undone continued to wash ashore for months. Trade goods floated in on the tide, still packaged in crates with mildewed hay around them.

One day Caliban found a small treasure casket half-filled with mud.

When he poured out the contents, he found a hoard of jewelry, chains and necklaces, and other fine things. At the very bottom was a tiny gold ring with a shining red stone.

He brought it to Miranda, who was pleased.

She loved shiny things.

And that night, and every night after for the rest of their long lives, they drifted off to sleep wrapped in each other's arms, lulled by the sounds of the sea.

The End

If you enjoyed this story, please consider leaving a review.

ABOUT KAT PARRISH

Kat Parrish is an internationally bestselling author. A former reporter, she prefers making things up! An Army brat, her motto is "Have passport, will travel." She has lived in seven states and two foreign countries and would love to celebrate her 100th birthday with a trip into space. She lives in the Pacific Northwest near a haunted cemetery.

For information about new releases, special offers, giveaways, and
other goodies, sign up for her newsletter here:
http://kattomic-energy.blogspot.com/p/blog-page.html

facebook.com/eyeofthekat
twitter.com/eyeofthekat
amazon.com/Kat-Parrish/e/B0133WSZHG

DEATH SONG
BY L.B. CARTER AND LEANN MASON

CHAPTER 1

Jessica's voice grated on her ears worse than a pig squealin' at daybreak. To the surprised officer, though, it was like an angel singing.

Before he could call in the escape attempt, the wide eyes of Officer Tall-Dark-and-Armed glazed over. A soft smile spread across his whiskered face, and he subconsciously leaned dazedly toward her in complete adoration.

Poor little lamb didn't know any better.

It may sound like an operatic soprano, perfectly on pitch and alluring in a compelling melody. But it was a death knell.

And Jessica was getting tired of all the death. Every song she sang, albeit beautiful and compelling, sounded like a funeral dirge to the tired siren.

To shake the mucky thoughts from her mind and focus on the mission, she tossed her blonde curls and pasted on a bright-as-a-daisy smile, lifting her plump, red-tinted lips alluringly. As another so-called perk of her kind, a few weeks of prison showers and cot-induced bedhead couldn't even detract from her inescapable lure.

"I'd do anything for you."

The officer's baritone voice did pleasant things to her body. It was a dang shame to waste an opportunity for some fun between the sheets -- or a detention center hallway, as it were. A girl had to take advantage of the few benefits of her supernatural magnetism, didn't she?

Sadly, there was no time to play with her food this time. *Sigh.*

"God, I love you."

Jessica winked one of her large, blue eyes as Ricky pressed a kiss on her cheek and added a pat on the rear as she passed right by the mesmerized officer, waving on their group.

The Harbingers weren't supposed to show their powers to humans. But people always trusted what they wanted to believe. Ricky and the other girls just thought Jess was a smokin' singer who got caught selling drugs while working a gig at a speakeasy.

Watching Ricky's hips sway, the blonde bombshell almost regretted that she'd wooed the convict on day one with her unnatural pizzazz. The bitch was the best lover Jess had been with out of… Gods, she'd lost count of how many humans and supes she'd been with over the years. She rather suspected that, this time, it just may break her little heart if her play toy ended up being their target.

Seke never told his team exactly who their mark was -- something about not wanting them to be watching and waiting. It might make their target nervous and draw attention, like a young fella at a debutante ball. The captain gave just enough information to ensure his Harbingers of Death Prison Unit was there when it was time to do the job.

Technically, she didn't even know this was that time. They never knew the 'when' of their marks' deaths either. Even their leader, an Egyptian god of death, didn't know that. It was a right pain in the booty, having to be vigilant all the time.

This was one of HDPU's longest missions, at least that Jess could recall, and now that it was time to part ways and move on to the next mission, Jess found herself feeling… reluctant. The fun always ended. And it often ended in gore. She didn't always mourn the deceased, but she did mourn stability. She had her team, but her one rule was no dating colleagues. She hadn't met anyone she wanted to be with permanently yet, but… she wouldn't have the opportunity to seize it even if she did. She wouldn't be able to stay.

Not that she wanted to stay in the stinky detention center for one more moment. Gods, she missed her conditioner and hairbrush. She longed for a long soak in the tub or, better yet, in the bunker's tropical, salt water, indoor pool. A relaxing soak sounded fantastic right about now: the muting waters blocking everything out, the weightless feeling of the buoyant water taking away all stress, the warm temperature easing her muscles…

"Yo, dumb blonde. You coming, or you wanna stay in this shithole?"

Jessica snapped to the present, giving her teammate, Raven, a scathing glare. "You better watch who you're callin' stupid, sweetie. Your hair may be black as pitch -- just like your heart --, but I was there when you glued your fingers together. Bless your heart."

A snorted laugh came from the redhead walking backward down the hall to keep up with Ricky and the rest of their group.

"That was an accident," Raven gritted out, dark eyes flashing at both Jessica and Ember. "And you both know it. If you hadn't broken Cole's favorite coffee mug, like a clumsy fish out of water…"

"*That* was an accident." Jessica tweaked an eyebrow in challenge. "Now, if you hadn't…"

"Enough! Back to work, ladies. You two," Ember scoffed. "Day." She pointed at the siren's golden curls. "And night." Her finger moved toward the raven-shifter's long, sleek mane. "I swear."

Raven turned away from Jess, crossing her arms over her slender chest as she began walking again, her long legs catching up quickly to the short phoenix with the pixie haircut. "And what's that make you?"

Jessica shook her head as the other crazy women in her hodge-podge team carried on their inane banter. The officer caught Jessica's notice as she started after her friends.

Pausing, she elevator-eyed his toned physique, and desire sent heat zinging beneath her jumpsuit. Glancing down the hall, she bit her lip. Just a quick detour?

She prowled closer, backing him up against the wall. He went willingly. Her tongue flicked over her lips as she moved closer to his, and she wished she had some lip gloss. He was a fine gentleman who clearly worked out for his job, that oh-so-fine uniform hugging his muscles as if the fabric were painted on.

Jess's chest pressed up against the still-glazed officer, so she felt the vibrations when he let out a contented purr.

"Mmm," she echoed. "And what's your name, sugar?" Her chipped, gold-painted fingernail flicked the name badge pinned to his pec. "Dick?" She let out a sultry laugh. "Well, now. If that's not an invitation to--"

"Jess! Move that curvaceous booty!"

Sighing, Jess tapped the man's cheek. "Maybe someday... before you die." She winked.

"Whenever you want," he breathed, trapped in the weave of her preternatural spell.

Glancing over her shoulder to check that Raven and Ember weren't still watching, Jessica pressed up on her toes, wishing she had her fuck-me heels on. The power of her hormones was hard for her to resist, too. "One for luck." She planted a kiss on his mouth real quick-like. A goodbye kiss, a thank-you kiss, an apology kiss. It was the polite thing for a girl who'd manipulated a man's feelings to do. Right? That was all.

But, gods, he tasted like temptation and danger, and she found herself lingering, inhaling his cologne. People always thought she was a sweet southern girl, but she loved playing the bad girl. The prison guard and the prisoner. It was taboo. It was sinful. It was dark and delicious.

Her arms snaked around his neck, fingers wrapping in the chain of his dog tag. She nipped his lower lip and sucked in a heavy breath as the tang of blood hit her tongue, making lust shoot through her like a lightning storm. She tried to hold back the hunger that willed her to take a harder bite. Officer Dick was clearly strong, crushing her to him, but he was still human. She didn't want to kill him in the throes of passion and double their reapings. Maybe just a little taste...

Suddenly, Jessica was yanked away, the guard slipping through her fingers faster than a buttered pig at the county fair. Tripping down the hallway, Jessica watched the guard slump down the wall, a euphoric grin on his slackened face.

"I *said*, keep it in your pants, blondie. We've got a dead one."

That comment wrenched Jessica from her lascivious haze. "Well, butter my biscuit. We got our target?"

"That's right, *sweetie*," Raven replied with sarcastic emphasis on the borrowed term of endearment, still tugging on Jessica's upper arm. "And it's time to do our thing and then blow this popsicle stand."

Jessica perked up, wrenching her arm free before she bruised, and clapped her hands. "Oh, do I get a little nibble?" She was hankering after that unsatisfactory non-encounter with Dick.

"Not this time. Clean death."

The siren's lower lip pushed out in a pout. "Boo."

They rounded a corner and came to a pair of exit doors that were propped open. As Ricky had promised, her inside sources had pulled up a laundry truck to the loading dock and buzzed the doors open from the outside.

However, it was Cole who stood inside the van, its doors flung wide open. Slightly hunched over, the hellhound's massive frame taking up much of the vehicle's storage space. Only his abnormal amber eyes were visible in the shadowed interior, his dark skin and dreads blending with the shadows. It was fitting for the shifter who could visibly cloak their presence to be looming in the dark.

And because, at his feet, lay a body.

"Where'd everyone else get to?" Jessica asked, brow furrowing as she sought out her play toy.

"Another van," Ember said. She nodded past the loading bay. "They won't get far, though."

Heart dropping, though she tried not to let it, Jess asked, "Ricky left?"

"No." Raven stepped toward Cole. "Like I said, we got our target."

Jessica felt the blood drain from her face as she refocused on the body in front of Cole.

No. Damn it all to heck. Why did the good ones always get taken? Why couldn't it have been one of the shitty women who made fun of Ember's height and pushed Raven around? Not that Raven let that happen for long. Why did it have to be the one who'd befriended the new girls, who held no judgment over whatever reason anyone had gotten themselves on the wrong side of the law?

Eyes flashing to Cole, anger laced Jessica's normally peppy tone as she stepped forward. "What did you do? Did you do this? Did you kill her?"

"Jessica, no!" Ember pushed her back. "Cole got here after it happened. Her contacts backstabbed her. Said she didn't bring what she'd promised them in return for their help."

"You know we don't interfere in the natural cycle of things." Raven stepped between Jessica and Ricky, protecting Cole, who absolutely could hold his own against Jessica. Not that he would fight back. The hellhound's eyes were pitying, and that just made Jess madder than a wet hen.

"Jessica." It was Seke's voice that stopped her from continuing her struggle to get to Ricky. "Take a step back. You've become too emotionally involved. Let us handle this. Jessica. Look at me."

Heaving an aggravated grunt, she swung her head toward the man who'd stepped out of the driver's seat of the utility truck. Tall, dark, and handsome, Seke embodied the gorgeousness an Egyptian god would be expected to have. The hazel eyes pierced her, his tanned face hard and disapproving.

Shame immediately swamped her, and her eyes dropped.

It didn't matter. Even if Ricky hadn't been the one to die today, the one whose soul they were tasked with helping to the afterlife, they couldn't have been together. Jessica would move on to another prison, another mission, another fleeting lover. She would forever wonder if those she loved would be ripped from her by the cold grip of death or its assisting organization of harbingers.

"Step back. Please."

Obeying the order of her superior, with reluctance, she watched as the rest of her team worked to help Seke extract Ricky's soul from her deceased form.

When she realized what had happened, Ricky let out a wail of despair that sliced right through Jessica, filling her eyes with tears. The blurring of the siren's vision wasn't enough to block out the hurt expression on Ricky's face when their eyes met.

Jess turned away, catching only a glimpse of the scarlet glow as Seke used his magic to shift into his hawk form and escort the soul across the veil, both him and Ricky disappearing in a flash. A choked sob wormed from Jessica's throat like a mewling barn cat.

"Hey. You only knew her for a few weeks."

Blonde curls bounced as Jessica shook her head at Raven. "It's not Ricky. It's… I'm just so dang tired of everyone dying, leaving me."

"You're not alone," Ember protested.

"You have us," Cole agreed in a deep rumble. He always went a bit hellhound when his teammates, *his girls*, were upset.

The emotions were bubbling out, unstoppable. "I know, but… it's just not the same. I love y'all, but…"

"We can't give you what you need," Raven finished, surprisingly without any teasing in her tone as she spoke of Jessica's notoriously insatiable libido.

"And none of them give a hoot about losing me. Soon as my allure wears off, I'm nothing to them. No one *chooses* me. They're just helpless fish caught in the net I toss." *Self-pity, party of one.* Jess couldn't help it. She was worn slap out.

"I think you are long overdue for a vacation," Seker intoned as he rejoined the rag-tag band wrapped around Jessica in comfort, having taken care of the dead as was their purpose. "Go visit a beach. Take some time off." Her captain was gentle but firm. "That's an order."

"No deaths? The ocean?" She thought again of the muting water, the weightlessness, the warm temperature... "What about y'all?"

"We'll manage," Seke reassured.

"Psh. You think we can't function without you, sweetie? Bless your heart."

Raven's jibe cracked Jessica's blubbering exterior. The siren welcomed a break from using her powers, from luring in victims and then tossing them aside, often against her will.

Nodding, she wiped at her eyes and sucked all her hot mess back up. For now, they needed to move. She was slowing whatever escape Seke had orchestrated for them.

"That sounds..." Jessica took a deep, rejuvenating breath. "That sounds sweeter than peach tea on the porch on a hot summer Sunday." Her smile was wobbly but hopeful.

She just needed some alone time. That should do the trick.

CHAPTER 2

Bouncing tits, shaking hips, and gyrating bubble butts. That's what Stone needed.

He could do without the strobing lights, though. The atmosphere at the club was electric without his vision washing in an alternating spectrum of rainbow-colored lights. It made him want to close his eyes, to really focus on the thumping bass as it beat like a fist against his chest. Vibrations shimmying up through his legs from the floor reminded him, unpleasantly, of the rumbling motor of his team's sturdy, old vessel: The Ferry.

He'd be perfectly content never to step foot on another boat ever again, yet that was not his life. Music, dancing, women... They were a temporary balm, a way to release the tension that built to boiling while he and the rest of his crew were stuck trolling the seas, waiting for people to bite it. Fleeting companionship had become his comfort as of late, so he endured the nearly stroke-inducing bevy of flashing lights like the champ he was.

He couldn't tear his burning gaze from the cluster of female forms. If he weren't careful, his heated stare would begin to turn fiery crimson, washing his surroundings in a red glow no matter the actual color of the club lights overhead.

Giving in, he closed his eyes and tipped his head back, face lifted toward the iron-clad rafters as the circle of vivacious women tightened around him. Every brush of soft skin or flick of silky hair was heightened with the lack of vision. So, too, was the pungent amalgamation of odors that made up the cloud of scent engulfing every single body on the dance floor. Perfumes, whether woodsy, sultry, bright, floral, or clean independently, mingled with alcohol and sweat to create a heady mix. Add in lusty hormones, and Stone was in freaking heaven.

It was a good time, a great night, where inhibitions were forgotten, appetites were sated, and names forgotten. That's all he was good for anymore. He didn't know whether he should blame himself, the job, or *her*, but it really didn't matter. The facts didn't change. Such was life. At least such was *his* life.

A life of dealing in death.

Death was grueling, and he wanted to be done. Being born and bred to protect should mean that Stone saw a lot of life. But no, he only saw a whole lot of death. To balance the toll of his job as a Harbinger of Death, Stone made a point to live life to the fullest every moment he could.

Like now.

Assured that his eyes were their normal vibrant blue shade of his human and not the crimson of his hellhound, he popped open the orbs, hands clasping reflexively against the hips of the curvy blonde who'd shimmied into his sphere.

Her hair, curled in big, looping waves, shone like spun gold as it bounced nearly all the way down her back. Which only brought attention to the glorious ass barely hidden beneath the siren-red, nearly-painted-on dress.

"No touching," the woman said absently, removing Stone's hands from where they still clasped the dip of her waist. Her grip was strong and sure though not malicious. More matter-of-fact, like her words. Her voice was like honey, sweet, and a bit sticky. It lingered on his senses unnaturally.

"No problem, honey." Because the term was too fitting. "Keep that gorgeous ass out of my bubble, and I'm happy to watch like a good little boy." He smirked devilishly, his cheek twitching to pull at one side of his mouth. He had good lips, he knew. He'd been told countless times.

But Red Dress didn't see.

She hadn't so much as twitched her head in his direction, other than to toss her curls around with her gyrations. The woman faced away from him almost as if on purpose.

That wouldn't do.

Leaning in without touching a hair from that luscious mane or an inch of creamy skin, which was covered in a dewy sheen beneath the still pulsing lights, was difficult, but the riled hellhound wanted to say something clever. He wanted to be sexy, like he'd used to be before he'd been jaded by life. Or rather, death.

Opening his mouth to deliver a killer line, his suave intentions were thrown out the window as the blonde's perky ass bumped upward, knocking against him. The confines of his jeans became uncomfortably tight as a result. A low, strained growl emanated from his tightening throat, Stone's beast rising with the sensory overload.

"Down, boy. Someone else might mistake that kind of sound for something more sinister. Don't make me set you right on your sorry hiney."

Finally, with her sultry warning, the vixen deigned to show her face, flicking her eyes at him from over her shoulder only briefly before dismissing him again.

Though fleeting, the look had been enough to learn a few very important things.

First off, Stone had been right. She was drop-dead -- pardon the pun -- gorgeous. Deep ocean-blue eyes were filled with a boldness that matched the blood-red lipstick, which was perfectly applied to the most luscious, pillowed lips he'd ever laid eyes upon.

Second, those perfect lips were tipped in a knowing, nearly condescending grin that told him the booty-bump had been a perfectly aimed dick-knick.

"Well now, honey. That's not playing fair, is it?"

He tried to maneuver himself toward her front, so they could at least pretend the conversation was two-sided and so he could glimpse what he was sure would be flawless, *ample* breasts. They couldn't *not* be, not with the curvy shape of the rest of her.

His no-touch dance partner, however, stonewalled his attempts. Expertly matching him move-for-move, his quarry succeeded in keeping him behind her shoulder.

It was a game.

He wasn't one to be deterred by a challenge. In fact, a challenge would be welcome. All too often, this whole seduction thing seemed easy. The thought of actually needing to *win* this woman was heating his fireborne blood in a way he hadn't experienced since...

Well, how long didn't matter and wasn't worth thinking about.

"Have we met?" The way she teased him almost seemed familiar. Had his team made port in Boston in the near past? Had he forgotten a tryst with this glorious specimen? He didn't think so...

She wasn't the kind one forgot a damn thing about.

"Oh, honey," she tossed back at him. "I can hardly believe you actually just asked me that." The vixen laughed. At him. Though harsh in nature, the giggle was pure melody, and it tugged at his ears. His hellhound side perked up in response which meant only one thing.

Supernatural.

It was in his very nature to shield and protect their world, the *other*, from the sight of humans. This woman, tickling his senses, was something from his world. But what?

"What *are* you?" Stone breathed, still at her back. Maybe his other senses would clue him in, seeing that he couldn't stare into her eyes or peek at her teeth; those two facial features could give some big species hints.

Oh shit. Was it... her? It couldn't be but... *Could it?*

Forgetting his manners in his creeping worry, his hand reached out to wrench the bombshell around to face him. He needed to look at her face.

"Where are your manners? No means no."

The blonde's words hit him at the same time as her clenched fist. The force behind the blow would have surprised him if he hadn't known she wasn't human.

As it was, he hadn't anticipated that she might break his nose. She was a force, whatever she was, which raised his hackles.

With a ragged wipe of his forearm that sent another shock of pain through his nose, he smeared away the torrent of blood that flowed down his face and trickled off his chin. Glaring daggers, he saw the same anger aimed right back at him as the woman squared up to him, ready for round two.

But just as quickly as his instincts went on-guard, they stood down as he fully took her in. Stone relaxed his stance, blood dripping onto his shirt, turning the blue fabric purple in flowering blooms.

"Oh, thank the gods," he breathed, head tilting backward and hands planting onto his hips.

"What in Sam Hill are you on about? Why are you smiling like a cat that ate the canary? Are you touched?" Those gorgeous eyes would have incinerated him on the spot. However, on the plus side...

"Your eyes." He couldn't keep the cocky smile from his face even while his nose still throbbed and spit red like an angry volcano. Each jostle from a still-gyrating throng of partying bodies didn't help, but Stone couldn't care. "They're blue."

"No shit, Sherlock," she deadpanned, hip cocked at a boner-inducing angle, and her cheeks flushed a lovely shade of fire-engine red that reaffirmed his conclusion.

"You're not her."

Surprise filtered across her lovely, sculpted features, and her hands dropped from her combative stance. That wasn't what she'd expected him to say. "I take it that's a good thing? Buy me a drink, and I promise you'll forget all about *her*. But I suggest you get cleaned up a little. Can't have you bleeding everywhere like a stuck pig, hellhound." With a wink, she turned on the point of her ridiculously high stilettos and sauntered toward a bar tucked to the side of the cavernous room.

If he didn't know any better, Stone would think the timing of the strobe, the pulsing of the bass, the very heartbeat of the club was tuned to her, accentuating the long line of her enticing body.

What the hell was she? Aphrodite?

"Give me strength." He murmured the words like the prayer he'd meant them to be, taking a moment to gather his chin from the floor before swiping at his nose again and plowing after his unknown supernatural goddess with single-minded intention: to lose himself for just one more night.

One night of freedom before he had to leave again on that damn boat. Maybe, having found someone non-human, he could put a little something extra into his attentions. Maybe it could be more than one night...

He caught up to the alluring creature in time to hear her shout her order to the bartender--bourbon, neat. He growled, a visceral reaction of approval of her drink choice. Throwing up two fingers above the crowd, he doubled the order.

"Don't go drinking my whiskey while I'm making myself look less like a horror movie extra." Stone willed his best panty-dropping smile to do what he needed it to and worm its way into the heart, or at least, mind, of his new companion... whose name he needed to learn. Because if her smolder was any indication, Stone would be yelling it more than once if the night went well. "Don't go anywhere," he demanded with a scolding eyebrow quirk and a finger shake.

"Be careful what you wag in my face, or I just might bite it." Her smile was devilish and candy at the same time.

He blinked at her teeth, but the strobe light made him wonder if the quick flash of pearly whites was what he thought he'd seen. There were a number of supes with sharp mouths anyway, including himself, some very, very welcome. "Promise?"

It was nice not to have to yell above the music. Supernatural hearing, being superior, meant that he could speak normally and not have to get right up against her ear… though that would be fun, too.

Before he could distract himself further, he hurried toward the men's room. Luckily, the line was non-existent, and because he didn't need the facilities, he went straight to the sinks. Grabbing a fistful of brown paper towels, Stone ran the wad under the water then went to work clearing away the browning smears staining the lower half of his face.

The shirt he unbuttoned, shucking into the nearest trash bin, left him in his white tank top undershirt. Being supernatural and a hellhound, in particular, blessed him with large, shapely muscles that he wasn't sad would be on display with the loss of the outer layer.

His nose, however, was a different story. With a steadying breath, he pinched the bridge with one hand and the base with the other. Breathing out, once, twice, he yanked his nose back into alignment.

Damn, that hurt.

It wasn't the first time his nose had been broken. It wasn't even the first time a woman had done it. It was, however, the first time he still wanted to get down and dirty with his attacker.

With nose back in a semi-straight line and no longer bleeding, and the clues of its former state effectively removed from his body, he prepared to return to his mysterious date. Leaving the bathroom, he went back out into the hot box of sensory overload.

One drink. He'd take his one drink and get that knockout out the door and horizontal, ASAP. With luck, maybe even vertical a time or two.

CHAPTER 3

Jessica didn't consider herself a booty girl; she liked a full package rather than just one part. And even better, what one could do with it.

But tripping after her mighty-fine club snatch, she decided the view wasn't so bad. Then again, the rest of his body was hotter than a scorching desert.

And now, more of it was on display.

Most hellhounds were muscular, but there was something that made this one pop. He was coiled tight, a tension and fire bottled inside that made him... extra.

And boy howdy, was Jessica hoping he'd unleash it with her.

Seke had been right. A vacation was just what the doctor ordered.

Grinning to herself, Jessica let the hellhound, who'd said his name was Stone, tow her toward the beach. The sea breeze, that salty smell, seagulls calling in the night sky... it was a balm to her soul. And her body was singing. Jessica was so ready to have a chance to have some fun with no foreboding of incoming death.

Sliding her tongue across her sharp teeth, Jessica imagined taking a big chomp into Stone's bared bicep. Being supernatural, he could take it. He might even like it. The thought turned her on more, and she was grateful for the cooling breeze that skated across her exposed skin. Heck, her punch hadn't dissuaded his interest.

In fact, he'd returned from the powder room with confidence. And the wardrobe change had heated her core even more than the two drinks downed in his absence. The mint julep Jessica had ordered when he had to ask the bartender to replace his bourbon had not cooled her down a smidge.

"You got a tent on the beach, sugar?" Jessica called as the sound of waves reached her ears, pulling her senses away from the delicious hunk of man-meat ahead of her.

The siren was all for a skinny dip, but she doubted the hellhound could keep up. Doggy paddling wasn't conducive to the kind of underwater dance she hoped for.

When he sent her a sensual grin over his shoulder, heat more red-hot than the tube dress she wore radiated from her. Heck, if the hellhound wanted to shake and shimmy in the middle of a public beach sans tent, she wasn't going to say no. Sand in undesirable places would be worth it, and it was easy enough to get cleaned up when the water was mere feet away. Vacation meant no hesitating, no second-guessing.

Besides, she saw nothing wrong with a little exhibitionism.

"My place is a little more robust than that," he chuckled. "It has to be to keep up with me."

Bingo. Time for this girl to have some fun without the fear of harming anyone, revealing her secret supernatural nature, or losing Stone to the next mission. None of those worries pertained to this night which was… liberating.

Stone surprised her when he suddenly altered trajectory from the inviting moonlit ocean, pivoting left and dropping down a step onto a pier. Not ready for the abrupt redirection, Jessica momentarily stumbled as if she had fins instead of feet.

Proving that he was as smooth in his actions as his suave demeanor, Stone swung around and spun her as if they were at a swing dance. Then he scooped Jessica up, adding an extra spin to carry on the momentum.

Naturally, her arms wrapped around his neck and her body pressed against his, her minidress and his thin tank top the only pieces of clothing between them. Her headlights were undoubtedly on their high-beam setting. The friction was delicious torture. A gentle wind tousled her curls. The contrasting temperature raised goosebumps on her skin as she stared up at eyes that had turned a warm crimson, smoldering into her. The two were so close, she could see a faint smear of blood on his upper lip, and she longed to lean forward and lick it up.

When his head tipped forward, she swung her legs gracefully off his arm and playfully stepped back. Hand at his chest, she pushed off, trying to calm her raging libido.

"What did I tell you about touching, sugar?"

Stone's eyebrow quirked. "That will make what I have planned somewhat difficult."

She gave a sultry pout. "You gotta earn the privilege of this." She ran her hands down her body, and his attention followed. Trying not to sound too breathy and eager, she distracted herself by looking around at where he'd detoured to. "But if we have to take a dang boat to get to your place, I reckon you'll have plenty of time to woo me."

He grinned and gestured for her to follow him with a crooked finger. Then he stepped back, still smiling at her, and dropped out of sight.

Surging forward, heart in her throat, she watched him finish his slide down a metal ladder like a fireman and land on a wooden dock floating alongside the pier to which several boats were moored. Realizing she'd actually feared for him as he'd disappeared, she had to shake loose the remnants of her funk.

Everything about this situation, this partner, was different. The fears, the heartbreak she endured on a daily basis, would not intrude tonight. She felt a thrill whip through her. It was exciting, freeing… refreshing. She felt reinvigorated, ready to enjoy life.

And dang, did she need a fireman to put out the fire incinerating her from the inside out.

"You coming down? Or you want me to gaze adoringly up at you all night?"

So, they really were going on a boat? She'd rather swim, but she wasn't going to complain about being near her element. Although… Jessica didn't admit that she was hoping that his place wasn't far. The tension was rising the more they resisted, which was why she was enjoying her little game, but if they didn't get clothes off and mouths on soon, she was going to need to dive into the water to cool off.

"I rather like the adoring gaze option," she teased, cocking a hip and crossing her arms to push up her chest.

He tipped his head back and held his hands up to catch her.

She shook her head at him. "Uh-uh, sugar. Not yet."

Waiting until he stepped back and put his hand behind his back like a good boy, she turned and took slow, careful steps down the rungs in her sand-riddled heels, knowing he'd catch her if she slipped. She felt his eyes on her rear and hoped he couldn't see just how much she enjoyed it, but with him being a hellhound, she'd bet he could scent it. Still, he didn't touch her as she'd asked. A gentleman. For now. She hoped he didn't hold back in the bedroom. Because she sure as heck wouldn't.

Reaching the floating, wooden platform, she rotated to look up at him and saw in his expression that he'd enjoyed the show.

"Well," she prompted when he didn't move. "Sticking with the adoration option, then?"

Clearing his throat, he led her down to the end of the dock and helped her board an old vessel that seemed well-used but also cared-for. It was too dark to read the lovely lady's name.

Jessica pirouetted once, taking it in briefly. She was in a hurry, so she registered just enough, not too invested in scoping out the digs. She didn't really care about the level of luxury or not; he could lay her down in a dumpster, and she'd still be willing. Though the disinfectant after would be extreme. Maybe afterward, once she was sated, she would care a bit more about Stone's ride. For now, she just wanted to get a move on.

"Where are you charioting me to, oh ferryman?" she jested, referring to one of the harbingers on another team.

Stone grinned and said, "Nowhere. *This* is my place. And you can relax; Charon won't be around tonight. We have the place to ourselves." His hands spread to indicate the boat.

The smile slipped from Jessica's face, her skin paling.

Stone strode forward. "It's not much, but I promise you'll have a good time." When she didn't move, concern pinched his brows. "You don't get seasick, do you?"

Jessica snorted. "Hardly. I'm a siren."

He reared back. "My vixen is a siren? But the eyes..." Muttering to himself, he shook his head. "Ensnared." He backpedaled further. "Just like *her*." When his nose wrinkled, he looked more like a dog with a snout than a human. "Luring me in." His eyes narrowed, the red thinning. "Did I even have a choice?"

"Oh, that's a fine how do ya do," she shot back. "*You* brought *me* here, sweetheart."

"Under false pretenses."

Her hands lifted. "What false pretense?" Her chest heaved as she huffed. "I never said I wasn't a siren. You knew I wasn't human."

His nostrils flared. "I didn't know you were a harbinger."

"Yeah, well, me neither." Her hand swung up and down his fine form. "Not like you told me anything about yourself. I had to infer you were a hellhound all on my own." Her fingers poked toward his red-tinted eyes. "And what the heck is a hellhound doing on the water team?" Glossy curls swung as she shook her head. "Screw you. Or rather not." Jessica pivoted and stomped back toward the dock, then froze.

"Mother of pearl!" The dock wasn't there. Jess stared dumbly at the water, then lifted her chin and saw the lights on the dock like a beacon shrinking in the distance. She swung back around toward Stone. "You untied us? Take me back. Right now, you hear?"

Stone looked baffled, joining her at the boat's edge. "I didn't."

"Ah, Stone! Glad you're here. We just got an emergency call. Pirate attack on a commercial fishing vessel just off of -- Oh! Who's this?"

"Jessica," Stone answered as she gawked at the man who'd joined them, winding up the thick rope that was supposed to be anchoring them to the dock. "Jessica, meet my captain, Charon. Charon, Jessica. A siren." The word was spat bitterly. "You said you were going to be doing errands onshore tonight."

"Emergency mission. Just said, didn't I?" Charon replied gruffly, but he was studying Jessica. "A siren, eh? Good. You can help us. The others are still on land. And your skills will be helpful, especially after we lost--"

"Don't."

Jessica's eyebrows shot up at Stone's sharp bark, more houndlike than human. She would never dare speak like that to her captain, interrupting him. Charon must be referring to the nebulous "her" that had wounded Stone so severely.

Not that she gave a hoot. Jessica was supposed to be on break from missions. And she wanted to be as far from Stone as possible.

"Sorry. 'Fraid can't help you. I'm on vacation. No calls for this Harbinger."

Charon wasn't listening. He'd already moved to the helm and kicked on the engine. Another time she'd marvel at just how gosh-darn cliche the fella looked. He didn't have that Greek-god look about him. But he was every bit an honest-to-gods fisherman, a quintessential sailor. Long, wiry, gray, water-logged hair covered both his head and his face, and he wore waterproof overalls that made him look like some kinda sea farmer.

She guessed, technically, he sorta was…

Jessica chased him down, a woman on a mission, her heels clacking on the weathered deck like some kind of urgent Morse code missive. "Excuse me. Didn't ya hear? I don't want to be part of this. Shouldn't be. Can you drop me back at the dock first, please?"

"No time," Charon muttered through beard-shrouded lips as he pressed buttons and pulled levers and tweaked doohickies, reading all kinds of, well, readings. "We're almost… Ah. Here we are."

That was too quick to be unaided by the godliness of the man before her.

A bloodcurdling scream echoing across the water in the night made Jessica whip around. She smacked Stone's hand off her arm when she wobbled on her heels. Kicking them off in irritation, she heard her pumps clunk against a railing with only a tiny portion of her awareness. She gawked at the horrendous scene before them.

One boat had pulled up alongside another and latched on, flinging a rudimentary plank between the two. The commercial fishing boat was engulfed in flames that leapt from the bridge and along the length of the vessel, consuming the dry material as it fled the blanket of quenching water below it. Shadowed bodies, silhouetted by the flickering flames, dashed from one boat to the other, fighting and shouting. Others fell overboard with screams that cut off when they slid underwater.

"Go!" Charon shouted as he cut the engine. "Before anyone else arrives."

Sighing, both Jessica and Stone spoke at the same time. "Can't escape death."

Jessica was already shucking off her dress with a resigned reluctance. She had hoped the dress would come off that night, but she'd anticipated Stone pulling it off of her -- and a lot more slowly -- followed by a roll in the hay. Being nude in the line of duty was a wholly different experience. It was only an unavoidable feeling of compassion for the poor soul whose life had been ruthlessly ended that drove her to peel it off herself in a hurry before taking a dip with Davy Jones.

Next to her, Stone was also stripping. She could hardly enjoy the flash of skin, as he was already shifting into his hellhound form, hair thickening on his plump muscles, his reset nose elongating into a snout, and hands she'd wanted on her body contorted into paws.

Lifting her arms over her head, Jessica noticed Stone's red eyes caress her bared curves briefly before shaking his shaggy head.

They both dove in.

Plunging into the water, Jessica felt that sense of calming peace she'd been lusting for on her vacation. And when something brushed her hand, she smiled. Stone was continuing their game. She couldn't yell at him for touching underwater.

Then she opened her eyes and saw chaos raging on the ocean surface. There really was no escape from death.

CHAPTER 4

Thank the gods that only two were reaped even though there was fire, a sinking ship, and loads of flailing bodies.

Stone grabbed the rather large man who'd been floating face down in the water mere feet from where he'd been launched from the deck where he'd been stabbed. A warning to the rest of the crew. They'd all heeded it, except for one young man: Jessica's charge.

Stone wanted nothing more than to rewind the night back a couple of hours. To choose another spot. Hell, he'd gladly take the beach if it meant he could be rolling around naked with a gorgeous woman instead of dragging two-hundred and fifty pounds of bloating man-meat in his canine jaws and paddling through brined water. Just clamping down on the guy's leg was throwing water back in his face where he was forced to breathe it in, making him splutter and huff in that fun canine way.

Just another night with the HDWU.

Finally, Stone was close enough to Charon for his captain to snag the body and haul it onto the skiff with a gaff. Gruesome business when he used that overlarge hook, but sometimes, when there were too many witnesses, the actual reaping needed to take place on The Ferry.

Without his burden, swimming was infinitely easier, but there was no chance he'd be able to haul his canine ass out of the water. So, quick as lightning, he shifted back into his human form and launched himself high enough out of the water that he could grapple a handhold affixed strategically for just this purpose.

"Good of you to join us, Beasty," that honeyed, sultry voice cooed from overhead.

Stone's head fell forward, forehead thumping against the hull of his floating shitbox of a home. A siren. Why did Jessica have to be a siren? He thunked his head a couple times more before finally meeting her lovely gaze.

"So, you're a fast swimmer. Does that mean you do everything fast?"

Deflection with innuendo. That was his jam nowadays. *She* had been a phenomenal swimmer, too. She'd been great at everything. And he meant *everything*. She'd been *it* for him, the one -- ruined all other women for him.

And the loss of her ruined him for women.

He wasn't capable of loving again, so he didn't try. Now, he'd found someone else who tickled his emotions. But she was a freaking siren. Everything she elicited in him was fake. *Damn supernaturals*. He should have known better, but he'd let the stirring in his pants link to the beat of his heart.

Big ol' hell no.

"Why are you still naked?" he groused in deferred agitation as he looked away from her piercing blue eyes and even more enrapturing nakedness. He heaved himself the rest of the way over onto the sea-soaked deck, flopping like a beached fish.

Those water retrievals always took a lot out of him. Rolling onto his side, he came face-to-glassy-stare with his charge. Not a better view.

"Not long ago, you couldn't wait for my clothes to disappear," the buxom siren purred.

She couldn't help being so sexy. It's what she did, what she was. What they all were.

"Work has a fun way of shutting that shit down," Stone grumbled, choosing to bypass all his personal feelings attached.

"It sure does. Funny how, even on my vacation, I get roped into doing this mess. Was that the goal all along? Lure the siren with the promise of sex that could be a little... wild, then put her to work to replace the colleague you lost?" There was a distinct undertone of hurt lacing her words.

Had he misjudged her?

"Don't you bring her into this," Stone growled. "The way I see it, you have two choices. You can put on your clothes... or not. Busy work's over now. I wouldn't be opposed to continuing with the-- how did you put it? 'Sex that could be a little *wild*,'" Stone shot back, his lip kicking up into its characteristic smirk.

He was, surprisingly, getting back into the mood. Even if she was a siren. Stone's blood heated as he came to full height, his gaze raking across every inch of Jessica's exposed skin. Her legs strategically placed to keep herself covered for the most part only added to his anticipation. Droplets of water glistening in the moonlight rolled down her supple skin, and her wet hair hung long, plastered atop her ample breasts. He was glad not to be wearing restrictive pants.

"What… what's going on?"

The weepy question pulled both of their attention toward the two bodies they'd dragged aboard The Ferry. The younger one, in his late teens, it looked like, hovered over his wet, stiffening body with confusion that every soul that passed seemed to carry. Then he looked over at the much larger but equally dead man next to his own body.

"Dad?"

Oh, man. This just kept getting better and better. The kid that got popped was trying to save his father, the captain who'd been the example. *Awesome.* And his dad was rising now.

"We giving them a moment, Cap?" Stone asked Charon, sympathy creeping up on him.

Damn emotions.

"I will permit them their goodbyes before judgment," Charon replied, eyeing the duo as the father rose to join the son, looking upon their corporeal forms with disbelieving shock as their attentions flipped back and forth.

"Jimmy? What? Why?"

"I tried to get to you, Dad. I tried," Jimmy spluttered.

"No. Nononono. My boy! No!" The burly man attempted to hug his ghostly son only to find that he couldn't hold him. It didn't matter that they were both dead and their souls exposed. Not yet. Not until after judgment, when the soul was in its final resting place, could they resume life-like activities.

Which made the spectacle that much worse.

Stone closed his eyes, steeling himself against the emotions that wanted to leak back into his guardian soul. *Damn it all.* Without opening his eyes, he turned away from the men, waiting, praying that Charon would take them quickly.

"Look at me. That's right. It's okay. You're okay." The words floated on the sea breeze, Jessica's impromptu siren song, a melodic tune weaving around the souls, stalling their grief so that Charon could perform his duties without hysterics.

It was probably the only thing that could make Stone recall the positives of a siren's lure.

Multiple death situations could get hairy. There was only one Ferryman, after all, only one of their team who could actually take the souls they were charged with to their afterlife, and he could only do so one at a time.

Judgments weren't a generic cookie-cutter kinda thing. What was meant for one often was not meant for another. Tempers had been known to flare, some trying to fight, others flee. So, having a being who could sing a song so lovely it actually entranced those who heard it into accepting their fate calmly... Yeah, he missed that.

He missed *her*.

The song, though lulling, didn't dull him entirely, and he turned to watch the blonde beauty weave her spell. Looking at her pulled him further under, something he forgot would happen, but it didn't matter. He couldn't tear his gaze from her luscious lips, how they moved around the soulful melody she sang. Drifting forward, Stone felt his muscles loosen, his stride lengthening as his cares fled his mind, allowing his body the freedom to do what it wanted.

And what it wanted was the glorious creature standing before him.

Reaching her side, his hands lifted to drift across the curve of her neck where it met her shoulder. Though her drying light yellow strands covered the skin, he knew the flesh to be silky smooth beneath. If he just pulled the length away, he'd be right there. He could touch, kiss, lick...

"What in Hades do you think you're doing, dog?"

And just like that, the spell broke, and reality crashed back onto his shoulders.

"Nothing I would do if you weren't a damned siren," Stone muttered aggravatedly, pulling at the wet strands of his own dirty blonde hair to busy his hands.

He hated that he'd allowed himself to fall under the thrall. She'd made a fool of him. Suddenly, the realization that he'd lost his free will made him deflate, quite literally.

"I think it's time you left."

"You expect me to just walk the plank or something? A gentleman you are not. Forget it. You're right. It's time to go. I don't need this. Tell Charon it was nice meeting him," Jessica seethed, striding past the corpses still splayed on the deck. She bent and scooped up her dress and shoes. "And don't be a total jerk and make me seem like the bad guy here. Explain to your captain why I left. I'd hate for him to think badly of me." With a scathing look over her shoulder in his direction, Jessica flipped up a perfectly manicured, red-lacquered middle finger before swan diving with perfect form from the ferry into the dark sea below.

The tightness in his groin may have lessened, but it had kicked up to heart-attack levels in his chest. He gripped uselessly at the affected area, his fist closing around empty air. He didn't feel anything for her, not really. How could he? She was a siren. A woman he'd just met that night.

He needed to stick to humans. They were easier, less messy. Yeah. No more supernatural escapades from now on.

Now, if only he didn't instantly regret being alone on the dark, open sea, with two dead bodies at his feet.

"Where'd the pretty one go?"

"She left. Said it was nice to meet you, though." Stone relayed the words to Charon with little life in his voice. He was tired. So tired. Of all of it.

"Oh. Well, she was a nice one. Could use a siren on the team again. Forgot how handy they could be," the old, burly fisherman intoned thoughtfully.

Ancient as the Ferryman was, he didn't always catch on to moods or sarcasm, so Stone chose not to engage.

"Yeah. Me too," Stone said somberly as he strode across the deck and disappeared down the stairs to find his dingy cabin and sink into oblivion alone for… as long as his crappy life would let him.

CHAPTER 5

The siren didn't stop swimming until the sand rose to brush her toes. She crawled the last few feet onto the beach. Panting, on all fours like a tired dog with salt water dripping from her face, some of it from the ocean, some tears.

"You did well."

Raising her face, bedraggled and wet strands of gold slid off her shoulders and stuck to her cheeks. Fresh tears sprang to her eyes when she saw the hellhound standing there.

Cole held out a towel. There was no judgment in his light eyes, no pity in the angle of his full lips. He was just there to support her, be whatever she needed.

"Did Seke send you to follow me on my vacation?" she asked as grains of sand dug into her palms.

His dreads swung when he shook his head. Jerking his chin behind him, he explained, "Bartender is an old friend. Fellow hellhound. He recognized you." He was quiet for a moment. "Stone has a reputation among our kind. He hasn't been the same since… He lost someone close to him. Now, he's a womanizer," Cole said bluntly. "He would have used you and tossed you aside."

Jessica let out a bitter laugh. "That's what I was hopin'." Secretly, though, a part of her had considered more; a supernatural would have been someone she could keep. Now, she'd never know if it might have been more than one night. "I didn't expect him to use me for *work*." Sitting back on her haunches, her hands dropped to her knees, and she remained hunched over, hiding her nakedness from her colleague. She'd dropped the dress and shoes in favor of just… leaving it all behind. "I guess vacation is over."

The towel draped over Jessica's back, and the weight of Cole's arm landed on top, anchoring it against her shoulders. His voice was soft in her ear. "So, you're not going to teach me how to swim?"

Her eyes lifted to his. "Swim?"

He shrugged, the movement shifting his comforting presence

beside her. "It'll be a sad week at the beach if I can't enjoy the water, too."

Jessica gave a watery smile. "Really?"

Cole looked down at her with brows raised. "I can't let you have all the fun." Which meant that he wasn't going to hold her back. It also meant he was staying.

Like all hellhounds, he had a protective streak. In this case, though, he wasn't just guarding her heart from Stone, he was making sure that she got the vacation she needed.

"Death is the natural order of things," he told her somberly. "It will always be there. But it will always be there," he repeated. "We can't let it overwhelm us or become part of who we are. It is not *our* time yet. We cannot allow ourselves to get lost in the timeline of others."

Jessica accepted Cole's hand and rose to her feet, pulling the towel tighter around her body. Turning, she looked out at the water over her shoulder. She couldn't see The Ferry, but she knew Stone was out there somewhere.

"Well, then, sugar." Throwing her shoulders back, Jessica pasted a bright smile on her face. She was certain her mascara was streaked and her lipstick smudged. It didn't matter. She felt ready to try again, to embrace the night, the vacation… her life.

Leaving everything to do with Stone, and death, in the depths behind her, she led the way back toward the bumpin' nightlife.

"Give me an hour to freshen up and find a new outfit. Then let's hit the hotel bar. Maybe you can introduce me to that bartender friend of yours." Supernaturals may not be off the table; she still wanted the chance to let loose. But harbingers were work, and she was on vacation. Death could wait. "Night's still young."

Cole chuckled. "That's my siren."

*To dive deeper into the grueling world
of the Harbingers of Death,
check out book 1, Mortal Scream.*

ABOUT L.B. CARTER

L.B. Carter is a multi-award-winning, internationally bestselling author, bookworm, scientist, and cat-mom who loves hot chocolate, fairy lights, and foxes. Her books are a mix of haunting paranormal urban fantasy, gripping suspense, chilling horror, and dark humor with a dash of light romance. Expect unique contemporary twists on magical lore told by quirky anti-heroes.

Follow L.B. Carter on social media, join her reader groups, and subscribe to her newsletter at LBCarter.com to learn more about her books and download an exclusive free novella.

Find all L.B.'s links at:
https://linktr.ee/lbcarterauthor

facebook.com/lbcarterauthor
twitter.com/lbcarterauthor
instagram.com/lbcarterauthor

ABOUT LEANN MASON

LeAnn Mason writes YA/NA fantasy and paranormal stories, with some common themes to be found woven within: Strength. Attraction. Intrigue.

There is something for everyone. The Minefield Enforcers has a dystopian vibe, whereas the Grimm Hollow books are fairytale retellings with a modern paranormal twist. Harbingers of Death rings with mythology.

When she's not writing, she's hanging out with her hubs and two munchkins around our new Alabama home. Though currently horse-less, she has been riding since her teen years and adores the giant animals so much that she writes them into her stories. Hers is a family of music lovers who rock out just about all the time, so of course she had to put that muse onto the pages as well.

Oh, and Dean Winchester is her spirit animal.

Find out more at: LeAnnMason.com

facebook.com/LeAnnMasonAuthor
twitter.com/LeAnnMason01
instagram.com/leann.mason.author

VELANTIIR: CITY OF THE ANCIENTS
BY MELISSA A. JOY

CHAPTER 1

The booming sound of cannon-fire echoed across the rolling waves of the Athacas Ocean as two warships engaged one another in battle. Both ships braced their yards, switching tack to catch the swift easterly wind, slowly circling each other. They looked to be identical in design, save for their paintwork and figureheads. Black stripes cleverly obscured the gun ports, and beneath each of these was a colored stripe; one ship displayed royal blue, the other cardinal red with carved golden vines winding through them. At a distance, this paintwork made each man-o-war appear as though she sported three gun decks when there were, in fact, two, though one might argue the weather deck itself served as a third. They were elite class ships-of-the-line, hybrids bearing magi-engineering systems designed to surpass standard first rates in speed and maneuverability, though one of them mysteriously held an advantage in firepower.

The red ship completed her turn, her bow facing north, and her yards braced to port, sails filling out as they caught the wind blowing westward in the direction of the Lands of Elinda. The name *Gresh-*

endier was printed in capitals at the base of her sterncastle with the image of a phoenix flanked by two eagles positioned at its peak, matching the red and gold flag fluttering atop her mainmast. A young man's voice bellowed from the weather deck, "The mainmast is weakened; continue aiming for it with the chain shot! If nothing else, we'll cripple her rigging!"

On the upward roll of the next wave, *Greshendier* unleashed another broadside. Chained cannonballs erupted simultaneously from the central guns, thundering ruthlessly into her adversary, smashing through the rigging and cutting into the masts, sending shards of splintering wood exploding in all directions. There was a loud, groaning creak, and slowly the mainmast of the *Idrianos* leaned, twisted, and crashed into the sea in a fountain of spray. Larkh scanned the deck of the enemy ship as her crew tended their casualties. Smiling broadly, he lowered his spyglass, turning to face the helmsman.

"Well done," he said, patting the man on the shoulder as he passed, his smooth and cultured voice oozing with satisfaction. "Steer southwest by south to the Maidhrég. I'll navigate the stacks when we arrive. It isn't called the Maw of Elinda for nothin'." The helmsman tensed at the mention of the Maidhrég, though he forced himself to maintain composure.

Descending the steps down to the quarterdeck, Larkh removed his scarlet cavalier hat and smoothed out the thick white plumes pinned in place on its right side. He ran a hand through the layers of his shoulder-length sandy blond hair, brushing them away from his boyish good looks, and then placed it back on his head before dusting off his matching full-length coat. He had noticed the helmsman's fearful expression; and knew he wasn't the only one to wear such a look on his face. The Maidhrég was known for its tumultuous waters and vicious storms, but with proper navigation, a respect for the sea, and tentative maneuvers, it was possible to cross; he'd read the reports of the few who'd managed it. The many shipwrecks there had likely either sunk due to trying to sail through the tempests through the center, or been smashed against the stacks, which was a deterrent to most sailors who'd ever thought of seeking out the inner regions of Elinda. Many considered him far too young to captain a ship, much less navigate such treacherous waters, but he was a prodigy and had proven himself time and again in both swordsmanship and tactical skills, having learned from the best and with firsthand experience of the sea since his life was turned upside down as a child.

He watched as several of his men were hoisted and carried below deck for surgery. *Greshendier's* timbers had been reinforced, having been showered with a variant of the altirna found in the archana she carried, the crystal fluid refined through alchemical magi-technology that enhanced her ability to maneuver. It minimized damage to the ship, making the wood more resilient but not impervious. There was never a shortage of casualties after any sort of battle, but at the very least, it helped reduce them.

"Tha's one of 'em down at least," said Krallan as he approached, folding his thick, muscular arms across his chest. His mane of black hair was tied at the nape of his neck.He was the quartermaster, and though he stood just a few inches taller than Larkh, he certainly outmatched him in bulk. Larkh was six foot tall with the lean, wiry frame of a well-seasoned sailor, but Krallan looked like he might be capable of wrestling a fully grown python.

"Aye," said Larkh, leaning against the capping rail. "It won't be easy catchin' up with Vansq, though. *Greshendier* might be swift for her size, but she'll never run before the wind like a brig."

"Didn't think ye gave a shit 'bout speed Cap'n," Krallan grinned. The wry smile that crept on to Larkh's handsome, clean-shaven face told the quartermaster all he needed to know."Heh, yer a sly one, Savaldor," he added.

"That's part of the beauty of it," Larkh winked. "Many think speed over power is the answer, but all you really need is a healthy balance of both."

"Couldn't agree wi' ye more," said Krallan, chuckling and making his way up to the helm.

. . .

Larkh pored over clusters of charts strewn across the table on the port side of *Greshendier's* rather sophisticated-looking great cabin on her approach to the Maidhrég, the treacherous channel leading into the heart of Elinda. A great series of stacks lined the channel's gaping mouth along the northern and southern coastlines of the continent, earning it its nickname, the *Maw of Elinda*. It was a region well-known for its tropical cyclones, where the waters rapidly became tumultuous. Smashed against the stacks and under the waves were dozens of ship-wrecks, some clinging to the rocks like inconvenient bits of meat stuck in the teeth of some titanic monster. The ocean floor here was deep enough, according to the few reports available, for the mast's sunken ships to only grasp in vain for the hulls of vessels passing overhead, which should allow even *Greshendier's* keel to glide over them effort-lessly. It was the stacks that were the bane of every sailor who dared enter the Maidhrég, but Larkh was smiling assuredly to himself as he studied the Elindan charts, drawing navigation lines across a copy he'd had made, for he'd also chanced upon meeting someone from the region; one of the Thénya, the nomadic plains elves who dwelt upon Elinda's savannahs. She had given him all the information he needed to know about the region and its storms.

Most of the crew were terrified, but they had learned to trust his judgment in these kinds of endeavors. Hundreds of ships had lost their way over the centuries, not knowing where best to take shelter, or too often too late, which is how many of them ended up shattered against the stacks or swallowed by the sea. There was also the fact *Greshendier* was equipped with the crystalline fluid altirna System; her maneuver-ability was truly exemplary for her size, especially since she now had purer and more highly refined altirna running through her. It took less than half the time to raise the anchors than on a ship of her size without such a system installed. Her class was fitted with two helms; one consisting of two large wheels that had to be manned by between four to eight crewmen; the other a single smaller wheel positioned on the aft deck that connected to the altirna system. His grandfather's connections with the magicians of the Archaenen had proven to be ten times worth their salt when he'd designed her and her sister ships to form the Faltain Navy's truly expensive elite class ship-of-the-line, which required an extensive amount of altirna crystal to be mined for a single ship.

Larkh traced a line with his left hand between the positions of the stacks on the copied chart, his bright azure eyes scanning their contours and the gaps between each one individually. Committing every potential change in their heading to memory, he reminded himself of the average strength of Elinda's storms, with particular regard to the words of warning the Elindan native had given him. He'd experienced a few such storms on the Athacas Ocean before, but the Maidhrég's converging currents were what made the area particularly perilous.

A knock at the door jolted him from his methodical reverie, though he continued to gaze at the routes he'd mapped out, checking them repeatedly against the notes he'd been given on the tides. "Come in," he said, looking up. The door opened; it was Argwey, the bosun. The elf's eyebrows arched at the number of charts on the table.

"The Maidhrég will soon be in sight," Argwey informed him. "Can't say the lads are too happy though; there're a lot of stories 'bout this place that unsettle 'em."

"Aye, I can feel it," Larkh said, rising to his feet and sliding around the edge of the table. "An' those stories unsettle me too. Most of them are true, but we've a chance to seize. We have to fight for what we want, an' I know we can do this." The dark-haired elf smiled confidently in response as Larkh slipped his long red coat back over his shoulders and left the cabin, leaving his hat hanging on the peg and locking the door behind him.

CHAPTER 2

The first of the stacks rose like stone giants out of the sea as Larkh strode out on deck. *Greshendier's* approach to the Maidhrég was rapid; not only was she propelled by the wind filling the ivory canvas of her sails, but the surging ocean currents were sucking her in. Waves crashed into her hull, sending salt spray leaping over the bowsprit as she pitched and rolled in the tumult. And yet, despite a blanket of miserable grey clouds looming in the distance behind them, nothing ominous was stirring in the heavens just yet.

Larkh made his way aft, ascended the stairs, and came to stand by the altirna helm. He gauged their distance from the first series of stacks and moved to the starboard side to get a better view. "Steer west-south-west he instructed the helmsman, a tanned man with broad shoulders and shaggy chestnut brown hair. He'd recently taken over from the man who'd been steering earlier. "We're headin' through the two stacks straight ahead of us; we shouldn't need to brace an' trim sail until we close in on the second cluster."

"I'll start prayin' to the gods then," said the helmsman, a man named Laisner with a heavy tan, thick stubble, and chestnut hair tied back into a bushy ponytail. Larkh's brow arched as his eyes slid toward him, noticing the man was feigning nonchalance as he turned the wheel slightly to the left, steering the ship a little more to port. That was certainly the kind of attitude that kept a sailor alive longer, but he knew the man was joking. Laisner had known for a long time that he loathed the gods, and he knew why.

Larkh snorted in amusement. "I'm always up for temptin' their little game of fate. The fly is quick to flee, but still, he goads they who call him pest into tryin' to swat him anyway." Laisner glanced over his shoulder at his captain and grinned. Larkh returned the gesture with a confident smirk.

Somewhere on the quarterdeck, someone shouted, "Lovely weather, an' she's rollin' like a bitch! It don't make sense!"

Then a distinct voice rang out, "There're collidin' currents beneath us, Bennett! Just think of it like havin' a rough—" Argwey's voice was cut off as another wave crashed into the side of the ship, soaking him head to foot, "—on an open meadow under a blue sky, it might help!" he finished.

Larkh rolled his eyes at the comment. Anyone who understood the nature of Cerenyr society would be shocked, and anyone who'd never met elf of his kind before would be bemused by this behavior, having heard tales of their prudish nature. Argwey knew how to behave like a typical Cerenyr elf when needed, but he otherwise failed to fit the description other than in appearance.

"So," said Laisner, smirking despite himself, "what d'ye suppose that weasel Vansq is up to?"

Larkh folded his arms as he leaned with the roll of the ship. He licked his lips, considering the question. "He's probably halfway into this monster's throat by now if he's not sunk already, an' that'll be easier for him to navigate with his brig if he's got his wits about him given Dirn sold the same information to him, so he'll probably find Velantiir before us," Larkh mused. "Not that I really give a shit."

"What've ye got up yer sleeve Cap'n?" Laisner asked, turning the wheel. Larkh ran his fingers through the underside of his sandy hair and gave the man a sly smile.

"Antorian Vansq thinks he can outwit me," said Larkh, "an' that's fine for us so long as he thinks that. The difference between me an' him is that I know when somethin' is out of my reach. I take a step back to revise my plans if I need to. He doesn't; he goes in hell-bent for leather. He won't be goin' anywhere fast if *Greshendier* has anythin' to do with it, though. The man's got a bloody death wish if he wants to tackle her." When Laisner's brow arched, the corners of Larkh's mouth twitched upward. He didn't need to tell the man anything else; he'd given enough of a hint. Laisner understood him clearly. "Keep her steady," he added, turning and making his way back down to the quarterdeck.

"Aye, sir!" Laisner called out behind him.

Larkh strode toward the bow, ordering lookouts to be especially vigilant and to report anything looking remotely suspicious. He stepped up onto the forecastle and leaned over the port rail to get a better glimpse of the pair of stacks looming before them. More and more of them were slowly appearing on either side of the ship as they headed into the legendary Maw of Elinda.

"We're all gonna die, Daron, tha's what," one man grumbled, leaning against the foremast, glancing to where Larkh stood on the forecastle. "This hunt is suicide."

"Nah," said Daron, a dark-skinned man, following his gaze. He grinned. "The Captain knows what he is doing. Follow his lead, and the ship will be just fine, and we tie ourselves to somethin' if we must."

Navigation through the stacks was both a dangerous and arduous task, but Larkh took his time. Even when it was suggested to him that he break out more sail to squeeze a few more knots out of *Greshendier*, he shook his head. More speed meant more time would be required to slow the ship down, and that meant they might not be able to avoid crashing into the stacks or running aground. Whenever the skies darkened on the horizon, Larkh ordered the ship to be drawn to the coast where she was anchored in inlets and coves where the cliffs sheltered her from bearing the brunt of the violently surging waves.

"Slow an' steady," Larkh said to his men." Vansq might be ahead of us—if he's not dead—but he was a day ahead when we encountered the *Idrianos*. If he truly knows where the forgotten city is, he won't be able to explore it all in a few days.Besides, the storms won't be kind to him either."

Greshendier then spent two days at anchor in another sheltered cove where the ruins of an ancient whitestone watchtower overlooked the Maidhrég. Even if there had been a means to scale the cliff to explore it, the relentless howling of the wind, driving rain, and thunderous black skies were more than enough to put them off. Ill-humor spread like a disease, and Larkh's own mood was no exception. He never made promises he wasn't sure he could keep, so anyone who dared suggest otherwise received a swift reprimand and a reminder of the fact. The weather here was rapidly changeable, and though it slowed their progress, they nevertheless made good headway. They would reach Velantiir with their lives and the ship intact so long as they took their time, and any time they spent waiting out storms was filled with shanties and gambling. The drinking of spirits was permitted only in moderation, and as and when the weather was favorable, they would weigh anchor and set off again, so all crew were required to be sober.

So he'd been told by Dirn, the Lands of Elinda were known to be plentiful, so they certainly wouldn't starve and would be able to hold on to more of the preserved provisions in the hold. They would likely need to spend a few days hunting for provisions for the journey back to Enkaiyta. According to the Thényan informer, there was a hidden route out of Elinda, but it could only be opened from within the region, and it was a one-way channel. She had also said when he had asked that it was unlikely they would come across any Thényan settlements as few tribes chose to stay put for more than four to six months at a time in order to follow the herds with the changing of seasons.

Little more than a week into the journey, the wind turned against them for another two days, which was shortly followed by another violent storm, but when a strong easterly breeze swept in once it had cleared, they were carried into the channel known as the Throat of Elinda, where the cliffs rose high either side of the ship, and the tumult of the Maidhrég gradually died away. The shelter of the channel brought with it an eerie silence, save for the rush of the wind gently ushering the ship along her way. Eventually, they glided out of the channel and along the coast of the inner sea for a few more days until the half-sunken remnants of a large harbor came into view, and behind it stood the ruins of a great city, of which roughly a third had been claimed into the sea.

"Ruins!" someone shouted from the foremast." Three points off the port bow!"

Larkh was summoned from the great cabin, and in minutes he was standing back on the forecastle, spyglass in hand with a satisfied grin on his face.

"That's it!" he cried, "we've found it!" Argwey stood beside him, matching his grin.

"How'd ya know tha's it Cap'n?" someone called.

Larkh smiled knowingly. Having heard reliable information from the Elindan native as well as his mentor, who'd trained him how to dual-wield in the ancient style the Nays had used and honed his skills with deadly effect, there was no mistaking it. Relics from a place like this were sure to be invaluable. That, however, also depended upon how things went with Vansq; that man was sure to cause trouble.

"We haven't seen any other ruins of this size on our way in," he said, thrusting a thumb over his shoulder at the two masts poking up on the other side of the harbor as he turned to face the crew. "Much farther and we'll hit mountains, an' this is the exact location on the map Dirn pointed to. Vansq is also here. So, this lads, can only the forgotten city of the Nays; Velantiir."

The following morning, Larkh rolled up the sleeves of his shirt and stepped onto the quayside with a party of five. The weather in these parts was either extremely dry or humid, much like the islands of Enkaiyta and around parts of the Manlakhedran coast, and today, it was proving to be rather humid, and the wind was picking up. He glanced up to the eastern sky to see wisps of cirrus clouds drifting westward, which heralded the coming of another storm. Whether or not it would reach this far inland was the question. As they proceeded towards the ruins of an arch leading up into the city from the harbor entrance, abusive remarks were slung at them by a small number of Vansq's crew left to guard their brig, the *Seña Marcenia*. Raucous laughter erupted behind him, making him smirk and chuckle as he turned and made his way into the city with his shore party. When more caustic remarks and cursing reached their ears, he turned to his grinning crewmen and shook his head, sucking air through his teeth, making them snigger. In his experience, the crews of smaller ships did tend to have far more bark than bite.

As they passed under the arch and ascended the steps leading into the city proper, Larkh recalled every detail his mentor had instilled in him over the years. She always made a profound kind of sense, and it was she who'd informed him of these ruins. Those piercing aquamarine eyes of hers were always haunting, especially when she spoke of such legends; they stood out on her finely chiseled, porcelain face framed with layers of snowy white hair, the tips of her pointed ears poking through at the sides. Picturing her like that somehow allowed him to remember her every word.

More than three thousand years had passed since Velantiir was a flourishing Nays city. It was one of many Nays ruins across Aeldynn that had been suddenly abandoned as a result of an ancient war, with the Maidhrég having been formed as a result of a chain of cataclysmic events set in motion through seismic upheaval, as well as the use of unfathomable amounts of magica. There were many theories and legends floating around about these great cities, with their mottled sand-colored streets and grand whitestone structures sporting gleaming golden rooftops. The walls and towers were slowly fading to grey after hundreds of generations of neglect since Velantiir had fallen to ruin, but they still held much of their original grandeur, even after having been seized by vines and other forms of foliage. The silent, tarnished streets were also dappled with blotches of weeds and grass. Nothing, however, could compare to the truth of what lay before them as they reached the central plaza. At the end of a long boulevard, stood a great stately building that must have been a palace, and next to it, on the other side of the forked river, was a towering structure complete with a tall spire surrounded by crumbling turrets and flying buttresses which could only be a temple the Nays had called a kathaedra. These two appeared to be the only two buildings that remained mostly intact.

In the center of the plaza was an enormous fountain where seven winged statues wearing decorative armor stood facing outwards. The central figure was of a woman without wings, swathed in what could only have been the most exquisite kind of cloth. Each of the figures had been carefully chiseled in the finest detail, though it was hard to tell the faces of the winged beings apart, for the top halves of their faces were obscured by a helmet depicting the rear-curving horns of a dragon with a half mask covering the eyes and nose. Even their heights were different, and three of them were female. The tallest of the females was roughly six and a half feet tall and appeared to cut a more imposing figure than all the others, and the wings of each statue towered over their heads, the tips stretching all the way down to their ankles. The silent air stirred with wind at that moment, sending shivers shooting up Larkh's spine and along his shoulders and arms.

"Somethin' the matter, Captain?" Daron asked, following Larkh's gaze to the statues around the fountain.

Larkh realized he was frowning. "No," he replied. "Just thinkin' about what this place must've been like all those centuries ago."

"It is certainly a place to behold," Daron observed. "Do you know what you are lookin' for here, though?"

"Anythin' that might prove valuable," Larkh answered, "especially with collectors of ancient relics. I even heard there was an observatory somewhere in these lands, but I think it's inland on the northern half of the continent."

There was something else, of course, something his mentor had alluded to. She hadn't told him what it was, only that there was something of specific interest here and suited only to him. Where it was hidden was anyone's guess, and he could only hope that Vansq wasn't the first to find it – whatever it happened to be.

"Yahtyliir told you about somethin', didn't she?" Daron pressed. Of all his crew, he was undoubtedly one of the most observant.

"She did," he admitted. "However, she neglected to tell me what I'm supposed to be lookin' for."

"That does not mean Vansq will not be interested in takin' and sellin' it," Daron pointed out.

"Quite right," Larkh replied. "It would've helped if she'd at least given me an idea of where to look." He considered the area between the kathaedra and the palace and decided on a route, signaling to his men on descending the steps leading south across the square." Let's head to the palace an' see about the kathaedra afterward."

CHAPTER 3

The approach to the palace ruins opened out onto a vast plaza, where they crossed the remnants of a bridge across the river dividing the city proper into three major districts. Further downstream, along the western fork, parts of the city had sunk or entirely collapsed into the river, which had long ago widened and been claimed as part of the region known as the Throat of Elinda, cutting off direct access to the kathaedra. Even the plaza and steps leading up to it had been claimed by the inner sea.

"Well, that puts a knot in the plan," said Laisner.

"Aye," Larkh agreed, "for now at least. We made the right choice takin' this direction. We'll scout along the river on the way back to the ship an' figure out a means to cross."

The ancient whitestone palace, now dusty and overgrown with vines and weeds like the rest of the city, was silent save for the occasional call of a bird or the sound of a lizard skittering across the floor. The strong, musty scent of old stone permeated the cold air within its walls and sent a ghostly chill through any passerby whenever a gust of wind swept through its many broken corridors.

"Now's when we try to figure out what the hell, we're doin' first," Laisner grumbled, propping his back against a nearby wall. 'What d'ye think we oughta do Cap'n? This place looks like a bloody maze!" Looking up, he frowned. "An' I don't like the look of that," he observed, taking note of the fractures along the ceilings. "They don't look like they would take much weight." Larkh followed his gaze. There were several areas where the ceilings had already collapsed into the lower corridors, exposing the interior to the sky, and the fractures did indeed look like they were not far off giving out.

"Ssh!" Daron hissed, silencing them all. "We have company."

Larkh signaled for the party to hide. He tapped his right ear, looking at each of them in turn. They split into pairs, quickly hiding behind walls or heaps of fallen stone. He stood behind a vine-covered wall with Daron as Vansq, and his party stepped into what used to be the palace audience chamber.

"Looks like the bloody *Greshendier*'s here," shouted one member of Vansq's crew.

A sturdy looking man, perhaps in his late thirties, looked up at the large masts looming over the crumbling city walls, right where the *Seña Marcenia* was tied alongside the ancient quay. He was of medium height with dark hair and tan skin falling unkempt between his shoulders. A thin, neatly trimmed beard and mustache framed mouth and chin. His firm jaw clenched, and his brow furrowed deeply as he tapped the curved blade at his side.

"Is not surprising Capitán Savaldor made it here," said Vansq, his voice carrying a strong Alvántiz accent. "He is far too clever for his own good, and the Thénya bitch sold him the same information of how to navigate the Maidhrég."

"We'll lose out now," said one man.

"That is where you're wrong," said another. "They don't know about the Neiréyu; think about how much we'll make if we can catch just one of those!"

Vansq strode up to the man and threw a hard punch at the man's jaw, scowling. The rest of his shore party mimicked his expression. "Are you bloody stupid?" Vansq snarled. He pointed to *Greshendier*'s masts. "They are here, and they could be anywhere in the city. Fuck up again, and I'll have you keelhauled."

The man spat blood on the floor. "S-sorry," he spluttered, clutching his jaw.

Larkh and his team watched as the rival group ventured out of the palace, the scolded man lingering at the top of the steps several moments longer, shaking his head before he started following them.

"The Neiréyu?" asked Hakett, a lean and wiry fellow who was a rigger and one of the ship's top men.

"Merfolk; they are a type of fey," Daron explained. "There are many legends about them bein' fond of makin' their homes in sunken ruins.

Vansq invites bad luck to us all if he captures just one and intends to sell."

"How's that?" Laisner asked.

Daron shrugged. "So it is said, the fey races have many allies in each other, and all of them recognize Velhana, Goddess of the Stars, as the Mother of all fey. It can be like threatening a wasp close to its nest; do that, and the whole nest might swarm and attack. They could well use their unique gifts against you if you wrong them or callin aid of greater allies if they have them."

Larkh let out an exasperated sigh as he stood leaning against a crumbling wall. "So we keep an eye on them an' intervene, if necessary," he said, pushing off the wall and heading further into the palace. "I don't fancy gettin' caught up in the consequences of Vansq's stupidity if we don't. Let's have a look around here before we head to the river on our way back to the ship."

There wasn't much left in the palace ruins worth looting, but Larkh nevertheless found himself intrigued by the history left behind and spent a while observing the murals he found, including one depicting a leviathan painted slate blue with lightning bolts flashing around its draconic head and serpentine body, which widened below the neck to accommodate a torso with what appeared to be aquatic wings. They were distinctly different from any sort of fin he'd ever seen, and as such, could not truly be described as such. Legends claimed the seas close to major cities of the Nays were guarded by these beasts. It was no secret that the Nays still existed, but they had long ago withdrawn to their homeland and kept to themselves ever since—or so the stories told—so it was anyone's guess if any such guardians still patrolled the ruins left behind. It was something best not thought about.

After a time, the rest of the group moved on to follow the river to explore further places that might yield items or materials worth looting before returning to the ship, with the exception of Daron, who stayed behind in the palace with Larkh. Eventually, the two of them returned to the great audience chamber, with its huge braziers and an enormous statue of two dragons coiled around a great crystal dominating the space behind the throne.

"Are they the Dragons of Origin?" Daron asked as they approached the colossal statue.

"Must be," Larkh replied, "if any of the Nays scripts an' symbols I do know are anythin' to go by. They are usually depicted as clingin' to a huge crystal with their tails intertwined." He turned around and arched a brow when he found Daron sitting on the throne.

"What're you up to? Lookin' to be the next Atiathas?" Larkh observed with an amused quirk of his lips.

"Emperor Daron Án Ngares," said Daron. "I think it sounds good."

"You do have quite the regal name," Larkh agreed.

Daron laughed. "I think maybe I could pull it off for a heist in Manlakhedran or Enkaiyta if we could find some good robes," he suggested.

Larkh's brow lifted in interest, a glint in his azure eyes as he gave his crewman a knowing smile. "Givin' me ideas is a bad idea, Daron. You know that."

Daron snorted. "Bah! You give yourself bad ideas. We just sailed the Maidhrég on a bloody warship!" Larkh took a breath, opened his mouth to speak, then shrugged instead and smiled as Daron's laughter echoed throughout the chamber.

"Come on," said Larkh, looking up as rain started drumming on the palace roof; the water soon seeping through the cracks in the walls and ceilings. He glanced over his shoulder as Daron approached. "Let's explore the western wing until the rain stops, then detour past the kathaedra on the way back to the ship."

They ventured across the audience chamber and into the western wing. The route to their left was blocked, but much of the rest of the corridor seemed intact, with nothing of interest in any of the smaller rooms that were still accessible. Eventually, they came across a chamber with murals painted on every wall and a statue of four women at the far end behind an altar, one standing higher than the other three holding an orb in her hands. *'Must be Raiyah and the three Adels,'* Larkh surmised. He approached the statue and stood gazing at it for a time until Daron's voice rang out. "Hey, you should look at this."

Larkh snapped out of his reverie and turned to his right. Daron stood by the wall looking at a mural depicting an elaborate-looking longsword and a pair of scimitars crossed in the center. Beneath it were two figures seemingly using these blades against one another, with various winged beings at either side of the symbol in the center.

"Looks a bit like you and your scimitars, don't you think?" Daron asked him. Then noticing his captain had once again drifted into a daydream, he nudged Larkh on the shoulder. "Hey."

Jerked back to the present, Larkh considered the image. "Yeah, it does a bit. I was taught to dual-wield the Nays style scimitar by a Kensaiyr, though it's a style few know these days, an' fewer still know it well. I'm not surprised to see a depiction of it here."

A large shadow passing the adjacent hallway leading to the western wing of the palace made Daron stop in his tracks. "What is it?" Larkh asked him. He turned to face the doorway. "Did you see something?"

"Something quite large just passed us," said Daron, unsheathing his blade. "It looked like some sort of reptile."

Larkh pulled a flintlock from his belt and loaded it. "It can't be a wyvern or a dragon," he said, "they're too big to fit between these walls..."

"Whatever it was, Captain, it was still BIG!" Daron protested. "I did not sign up to become something's dinner."

"In any case, we're goin' to have to find out what it is if we stand any chance of figurin' out how to deal with it," Larkh warned him. He edged forward and peered around the doorway to see the tip of a scaly tail vanish down another corridor.

"What are you doin'?" Daron hissed.

"You were a hunter, weren't you?" Larkh queried.

Daron threw his hands up in the air. "Whatever that was, it is much bigger than anythin' I have ever hunted. As a hunter, I know when I should leave somethin' well alone."

"Stay there if you want," Larkh suggested, disappearing out of the door after the beast before Daron could answer. Exasperated, Daron hurried after him.

They both emerged at a destroyed portion of wall on the western side of the palace where a colossal waterfall plummeted down the mountainside, and an elaborate bridge bearing Drahknyr statues connecting the palace district with the kathaedra had all but been entirely claimed by the river. Above them, the sky darkened, and lightning flashed across the clouds as a booming thunderclap exploded across the heavens, reverberating beneath their feet as the rain turned from shower to deluge in an instant. The large creature they were following had all of a sudden vanished, leaving them to stare across the broken bridge under the shelter of the palace, wondering what to do next.

"What a day this has become," said Daron, dropping into a squatto pick at the weeds growing between the cracks in the mottled paving.

"What is—?" Larkh was staring at something emerging from the river. At first glance, it looked like some sort of fish, but on closer inspection, the fore-end of the creature appeared somewhat humanoid. "Is that one of the Neiréyu?"

Daron stood and peered through the driving rain at the aquatic being that had just emerged from the river next to the collapsed bridge. There were fins along its forearms, a dorsal fin with spines stretching from the nape of the neck all the way along its back, and there were gills along the ribs. A moment later, it turned its head towards them to reveal an otherworldly, yet beautiful feminine face framed with frills and large, golden-yellow eyes.

'Sivardazeiyansa, weiya yanei étu?' The words echoed around them as though they'd been spoken aloud, but the Neiréyu's mouth remained closed, and she was looking directly at Larkh.

"Did you understand that?" Daron asked him.

Larkh kept his attention on the otherworldly creature. "Not a word, but it sounded like a question."

"Aye," said Daron, "a question directed at *you*."

He was right, Larkh realized. The Neiréyu's eyes were indeed fixed on him. He took a deep breath and shrugged, shaking his head. "I'm afraid I don't understand," he said. The Neiréyu tilted her head and then dived back into the water and rose a moment later, beckoning with a webbed hand. Larkh arched a brow and looked up to the sky as the rainfall let up and sunlight broke through the clouds. Steeling himself, he cautiously approached the sea-maiden, wondering if this might be some sort of ruse. He recalled the tales he'd heard of sirens, merfolk who had been exiled or turned their backs on their tribes due to hatred and spite toward surface dwellers.

"Be careful, Captain," Daron warned him.

"I know," Larkh replied, glancing over his shoulder. Turning his attention back to the Neiréyu, he asked, "what is it you want?"

The sea-maiden brought both hands to her forehead, then lifted her arms up, extending them out towards him. Did she want him to come closer? He took another step forward and knelt by the water. Taking out a flintlock and loading it, Daron approached, aiming the weapon at the Neiréyu.

"What are you doin'?" Larkh snapped when she recoiled, "I thought you said not to upset them."

"I did, but if she tries to pull you in, I shoot her," said Daron.

Unable to fault that logic, Larkh shrugged. "Fine," he agreed, "but from what I could tell, she came out of the water to enjoy the rain without even knowin' we were here. Lower it."

Daron frowned. "They are still fey, Captain," he reminded him, lowering the pistol. "They are all capable of being tricksters."

"No more than we are," Larkh retorted, lifting a hand to calm the Neiréyu, the frills around her jawline vibrating; "Especially we pirates – an' let's not forget Vansq is after them; an' he'll be usin' tricks of his own... Daron?"

He turned his head to see his crewman staring blankly into space, who then turned and wandered off in the opposite direction, back into the palace and straight past the beast they'd been following only minutes ago. It was a drake, and it lay placid by the broken wall they'd emerged from, only sparing Daron a glance as he passed. He turned back to the Neiréyu. "What did you—"

She smiled, then placed her hands on either side of his head. Images flashed through Larkh's mind; the main entrance to the kathaedra was now an impassable mound of rubble, and there were more drakes wandering around the plaza leading up to it, but there was a route under the water where an ancient cataclysm had torn openings into the temple foundations. From what he could tell, it wasn't the depth that would be the problem; he was a reasonable swimmer–unlike many of his crew–but by no means the strongest. It would be the distance to the other side, and he had no idea where he would be able to surface for air. Sensing his apprehension, the Neiréyu spoke again; but this time, he understood her meaning, even though she still spoke in her native language.

'*Worry not. I give you air.*' Her melodic voice resonated in his mind.

"How is it that I can understand you now?" Larkh asked, staring into those deep, otherworldly eyes.

'*A connection mind to mind,*' she answered. '*This way, I bypass the barrier of language to the one I speak to.*'

"All right then, what did you do to Daron?" he demanded.

'*I sent him back to your ship,*' the sea-maiden replied. '*This does not concern him.*'

"And why does it concern me?"

'*Part of you knows the answer.*'

Larkh snorted. "An' most of me doesn't, love. I've no idea what you're up to, an' I don't even know your name."

'*I am Lenaia,*' she said.

"Larkh."

Lenaia smiled again. '*I know what you are thinking, Larkh. People of the surface distrust us; the dissenters among us made it so. I am here only to show you something.*'

"Why me specifically?" he pressed.

'*The blades you carry,*' Lenaia replied. '*There is a story left behind by the*

Ancient Ones called the Nays about their sword dancers who carried weapons like yours.'

Somehow Larkh knew she was telling the truth. It can only have been a result of the connection she had made with him, but there was still something about it he didn't like about it. It wasn't as though she was reading his mind, but she was able to sense his emotions, and it made him feel vulnerable; there was too much pain in his past, and this connection was treading far too close for comfort. Whatever it was she wanted him to see, he at least knew she was not there to drag him to his death.

'Come,' she said, *'it will not be long before they look for you.'* She released him and gestured toward the ruins of the kathaedra.

There was still something bothering him about all of this, but whatever it was, he wasn't able to put a finger on it. Could this have something to do with what his mentor had talked about? It wouldn't surprise him, knowing Yahtyliir was a Kensaiyr far older than anyone knew. Larkh removed his weapons and laid them on the ground, keeping only the daggers secured at his belt. He then took off his boots and shirt, revealing a lattice of silvering scars across his back and a tattoo of two eagles on either side of his neck with a phoenix between his shoulder blades, which appeared to pique Lenaia's interest. He arched a brow at her while hers narrowed, along with what might have been a sensual smile. Unable to help himself, he returned that smile and, steeling himself, took a deep breath and dived into the water.

CHAPTER 4

What happened between the moment Larkh hit the water and when he surfaced was almost a blur. Lenaia glided swiftly through the water, pulling him along so effortlessly that he didn't have time to register much of what was going on around him. With nothing to shield them, his eyes were useless down here; all he could see were the shapes of fish or other creatures flitting about; some small, some large, and he was sure he was able to make out other Neiréyu watching them; their shapes, though vague, were distinct. He was just able to see the opening of the passage as they approached it; it was likely only one of many crevices created during an ancient cataclysmic event.

When he was no longer able to hold his breath, he resisted her pull and fought for the surface as Lenaia seized him. *'Release your breath,'* she spoke into his mind, *'I renew it.'* Her touch, unusually reassuring though his heart raced with panic, allowed him to relax a little. He did as she bade, and in a fleeting moment, her lips were on his. He took in her breath gratefully and allowed her to take him down to the crevice and into the dark. The chill of deep water was setting in, tiring him, but it wasn't far to the surface.

They eventually emerged in what could only have been the inner courtyard of the kathaedra. Water from the recent downpour flooded down the steps from the entrance to the main building into the pool he climbed out of. The entire courtyard was overrun with plants, with moss and vines creeping up walls and columns dripping with moisture.

Lenaia caught hold of his hand. *'I wait,'* she said.

Larkh nodded, shivering. "Aye, I'll be back as soon as I've found whatever it is you brought me here for," he said, wiping water from his face and wringing it from the layers of his sandy hair. He touched the tips of his fingers to one side of his head and headed off barefoot across the sodden ancient courtyard, arms hugging his chest. That had certainly been quite an experience, though he couldn't say he was looking forward to the return journey back through that cold under-water tunnel. At least it wasn't far, though he wouldn't be surprised if he ended up catching the chills.

On entering the nave of the kathaedra, the first thing he noticed, other than the tilting structure and vaulted ceiling, was another variant of the same statues of the women he'd seen in the palace, and seven winged figures lined up in front of them behind an altar-like the foun-tain in the city's central plaza. All had sustained damage, though they had otherwise weathered the ages surprisingly well. He glanced around; the place was huge; how was he supposed to find anything here, half-naked, soaked, and shivering? Yahtyliir had told him he could always rely on his instincts, but he wasn't so sure they would help him in these circumstances. How did the Neiréyu even know there was anything here? Stories were one thing, but the existence of something contained above the surface? He pushed the thought aside; to call the Nays and all the elven and fey races enigmatic was an understatement. If anything of significant worth here still survived, it was likely to be in the treasury–wherever that was. He had no idea of ancient Nays floor plans, but if they were anything like human constructions, he had a good idea of where to start; he just hoped it wasn't completely flooded.

He picked his way across rubble and cracked, wet, slippery tiles that had once been a pristine mosaic floor, wishing he had been able to explore this place with his boots on. He'd already sustained a few cuts on his feet, but it was nothing compared to the years he'd spent aboard ship as a boy without shoes. Argwey, who doubled up as both the boatswain and the ship's physician, was going to be having words with him later; he was already rehearsing the conversation. This venture was going to be yet another notch of recklessness on his belt.

Behind the statues and the altar was an enormous arched door flanked by a sculpted frieze of a pair of the same winged beings, along with two dragons facing one another over the top of the arch. One side of the door was ajar where the building was leaning, with just enough space for him to squeeze through. On the other side was a chamber partially destroyed where chunks of the mountain behind the kathaedra had fallen and smashed through. At the far end of the area that survived was another altar surrounded by scattered debris, along with two tall archways in the walls on either side. The route to the left was blocked, having once led upward, but the one on the right led underground to the undercroft. He picked up a number of pale jade-colored gemstones that might well be worth a decent price on the black market.

The steps down into the undercroft were unusually wide, and the sconces on the wall appeared to require certain types of crystal to create light, many of which had been broken and long since lost their power. He selected one of the still working crystals and removed it to light his way. Unsure if there was anything living down here, he pulled a dagger from his belt and proceeded cautiously. Parts of the area were flooded or had been exposed to natural caves, but it looked like he would at least be able to keep his head above water–not that he fancied getting cold and wet again this soon–and at least there were more of the same glowing crystal sconces here. Trying to find wood in this place that wasn't damp and having no means to light it would have proven difficult and prevented him from even exploring this area.

He didn't know how long he spent searching the undercroft, but it felt like hours, and the mixed odors of damp, algae, and stagnation was becoming overpowering the longer he stayed. Eventually, he came across a larger chamber, half-drowned and filled with weapons and armor. *'An armory?'* he queried, *'in a temple?'* He admitted to himself that he didn't know much about the Aeva'Daeihn religion, in which the Nays had worshipped the sun goddess Raiyah, but it still seemed odd to have an armory in a place like this. From what he could tell, most of what was stored here was still in reasonable condition; it was another confirmation about the old legends that proved to be true; the materials the Nays had used could last indefinitely if properly maintained but still weathered the ages far better than anything humans had ever created.

Three metal chests, partially submerged, sat in a corner by the far wall. Something was drawing him towards the one on the right, leaning into the water where the room was tilting. Having only just begun to dry off, he groaned and waded into the water, which soon rose to chest height, and all of a sudden, he could find no purchase beneath his feet. The floor, he determined, had long given away, and he was going to have to swim to the other side, which he did so quickly. There were too many tales about things that lurked in dark places, especially underwater. When he reached the other side, he found the locks of all the chests had been bound with glyphs, so how was he going to open any of them? He tried each of them in turn, and while the first two resonated and repelled him, the glyph on the third and final chest he'd initially felt drawn to glowed briefly, then faded. There was a faint click, and the catch popped up.

On lifting the lid, there was a rumbling sound as a minor tremor made the kathaedra shudder. For a moment his heart seized at the thought of the ancient building collapsing on top of him, but it seemed no worse off – at least for now. Sucking in a deep breath, he pushed the lid open to find what could only have been what Yahtyliir intended him to find. In the chest sat a pair of Nays scimitars with their gentle curve and a widened tip, their condition only a little short of pristine. Had these once been hers? He wondered. A low groan from somewhere in the depths nearby suggested it was time he left this place and, truth be told, he would be all too happy to get out of here. As mesmerizing a place as this was, the odds were against him if he lingered much longer. Thinking quickly, he took off his belt and wrapped both blades together, and secured them with a knot before tying another to create a loop with which to carry them. He set off swimming back across the room and hastened his way back up to the nave.

When he reached the pool he and Lenaia had emerged from, he found her conversing with another of her kind, who turned to him, frowned, and dove back into the water. He gave her a questioning look as he stepped into the pool, but she shook her head, taking his hand. *'It is Zanjhatmas,'* she said. *'He stirs.'*

"Zanjha… who are you on about?" Larkh queried, confused.

'The leviathan guarding these waters,' Lenaia answered. *'We have to go. There is another storm coming.'*

Larkh's eyes widened. He remembered the mural from the palace depicting a leviathan, so it was still here. Not wanting to be near if it did fully wake, he pressed his lips and frowned, wrapping the end of his belt holding the scimitars around his hand. "All right," he said, "let's go." There was a knowing look in the sea maiden's eyes at that moment, and then once more was he dragged into the deep.

.   .   .

Argwey set out with three others to gather herbs around the outskirts of the ruins. When they returned, he split from the group and used glámar to camouflage himself against the foliage where Vansq and some of his men sat around a fire cooking freshly caught fish. He found a spot to sit and listen for shreds of information that might tell him about their plans. At the other end of the camp, he noticed their prisoner. He recognized the Elindan plains elf instantly. *'Dirn,'* he thought, frowning. *'Larkh isn't going to like this...'*

"So what's the plan wi' capturin' one o' these mermaids, or whatever they bloody are?" asked one man.

Vansq sat across from the fire, slowly tapping one foot. After a moment's thought, he leaned and glanced over his shoulder at the brown-skinned Thénya woman sitting behind them, tied to a tree with her arms bound to her sides. "From what our guide tells me," he said, "they are very curious creatures."

"But they are *not* stupid," the Thényan captive snapped. "You have heard tales of their voices before, luring sailors to their deaths."

"I never said we should not be cautious," Vansq replied, shrugging. "We must be far more cunning in how we approach this."

"You say they are curious," said a man sitting near the bush Argwey was hiding by. Vansq lifted his head. "Maybe we could set up camp on the flooded side o' the ruins near the water, have a few lookouts 'n keep watch for any of these *curious* Neiréyu."

Vansq clicked his fingers and pointed at the man. "I like your thinking," he said, "but we don't want to run the risk of them not surfacing at all, so we'll set up a camp near where we saw them but stay out of sight. That might be a place where they often surface to enjoy the sun or the rain. We will take our nets with us."

Dirn's attention shifted to the bush where Argwey was hidden and eavesdropping. She narrowed her amber eyes in his direction. Like him, she was an elf, so she would be able to sense another nearby using magica, even if she couldn't see him. A brief movement of her head and her eyes shifting to Vansq and his crew expressed it would be foolish to attempt a rescue at the moment. His jaw tightened; she knew it was him, probably recognized his energy from the times they'd previously met. She would know Larkh would want to see her freed. He gave her a knowing look and retreated back the way he came, having heard enough.

On his return to the *Greshendier*, he saw Daron wandering back alone. He had a glazed look in his eyes, appearing to be in some sort of trance. Argwey arched a brow and approached him. "Daron?" he called to him. "Hey, snap out of it!"

Daron blinked and shook his head. "What the—? What's goin' on?" He asked. "Why am I here? Where is the captain?" He then remembered the encounter with the Neiréyu, and then a strange, vibrating sound inside his mind. She hadn't been using her voice to mesmerize him but had still managed to compel him to return to the ship without Larkh. "Damn those tricksters!"

"Slow down," said Argwey, folding his arms. "What happened?"

"The rest of the group came back, scoutin' the city from the other side on the way while Larkh and I continued searchin' the palace," Daron explained. "We saw the shadow of a beast and followed it to the waterfall; the heavens broke, and in the middle of the storm, one of those merfolk came ashore to enjoy the rain. She took a shine to the captain, and—"

"Ah," said Argwey, "that doesn't surprise me, an' by now, it shouldn't surprise you either. Can you take me there?"

Daron blew out a long breath. "It is a fair walk, but yes, I remember the way," he said. "Give me a few minutes to catch my breath, and I will take you to where we saw her."

"Aye, I'll need a few minutes myself," said Argwey. "I need to report what I just saw to Krallan an' grab a few things before we set off."

CHAPTER 5

On his return to the surface, it came as no surprise to Larkh that he would not be making his way back to *Greshendier* alone. Waiting by the river where he'd left his belongings was Argwey, along with Daron and two others. The elven bosun stood with a blanket slung over one arm and a rather unimpressed expression on his face. Then his attention shifted to Lenaia, who regarded him with equal curiosity as he gave her. A split second later, she frowned, her lip curling. Her hand gripped his momentarily. *'Thank you, Larkh,'* she said. *'Take care.'* In a flash, she was gone, swimming back into the depths before he could say a word.

Larkh's attention snapped to Argwey. "What did you do?" he demanded, hoisting himself out of the water.

"We've got trouble," Argwey told him.

"I asked what you did just then," Larkh growled at him. "Why did she leave so suddenly?"

"I warned her of somethin'," Argwey replied. "I wasn't able to put it in words, but it seems she understood me well enough."

"What kind of warning?" Larkh pressed.

"You know what we heard earlier, Captain?" Daron asked him, "about Vansq and his crew intendin' on capturin' the Neiréyu?"

Larkh's jaw clenched. "Shit!" he muttered under his breath. *'I forgot to even mention it to her.'*

"They're goin' to find out where they surface most often an' try to capture them wi' nets," Argwey explained, handing him the blanket. "An' they've got Dirn."

"Damn that son of a bitch," Larkh growled, putting the blanket around his shoulders as he sat and pulled his boots on. He picked up the blades he'd found and gripped the strap tight. "I'll kill him."

Larkh found the trek back to the ship warmed him up enough, with the blanket and the sun shining over the enchanting ruins of Velantiir. Daron complained that his feet hurt after far too much walking, but it was understandable given that Lenaia had sent him back to *Greshendier,* unbeknownst to him. Once back on the ship, Daron flopped onto the deck and made it clear he was more than done for the day.

Once in the welcome familiarity of the great cabin, he changed his clothes and left his feet bare, sitting on the edge of his wood and canvas cot. Argwey soon arrived and handed him a cup of herbal tea. "You're probably goin' to catch a chill after that, you know," the bosun pointed out.

"Aye, I'm aware," Larkh grumbled, "though I'm sure these are what Yahtyliir intended me to find." He pointed at the pair of Nays-forged scimitars sitting on the chart table.

"And the Neiréyu knew where to take you?" the bosun queried, eyeing the blades with interest as he knelt and began applying salve to the cuts Larkh had acquired during his daring adventure into the ruins of the kathaedra.

"Aye, somehow," Larkh replied, wondering why Argwey wasn't throwing a barrage of sarcastic, mothering comments at him. "She mentioned stories passed down about the Nays sword dancers who used those kinds of blades; the very same style an' techniques Yahtyliir taught me. I even wonder if these were once hers."

Argwey snorted. "Sounds probable; you'll 'ave to ask her. You've a habit of gettin' yourself caught up in all kinds of shit. You know that?"

Larkh pulled a face. "Blame Yahty for puttin' me up to this one."

"Aye," said Argwey, "I'll be havin' words wi' her an' all."

"Good luck survivin' that one," Larkh retorted with a smirk.

"I'll take my chances," Argwey said with a grin. "I'll be fine, though; she likes me too much."

"I think you might be getting' ahead of yourself there," Larkh chuckled, "but seriously, I'm concerned about what we're goin' to do about Vansq. I had a worryin' experience while I was in those ruins."

Argwey finished bandaging the cuts and stood up, frowning at him. "What's that then?"

"There was a tremor," said Larkh. "Did you not feel it?"

"Aye, we felt somethin'," Argwey replied, "but this area's known for havin' a few earthquakes here an' there. How'd you know this one's different?"

"Lenaia, the Neiréyu, she told me it was the leviathan that guards the waters around here," Larkh told him. "She said he stirs."

"That can't be good," Argwey said, pushing up and leaning against one of the locked book cabinets on either side of the door. "We'll have to sabotage their quest for capturin' Neiréyu in any case, an' we'll have to get on board the *Seña Marcenia* to release Dirn."

"I think I'll leave that one to you," said Larkh.

Argwey arched a brow. "Me? Wh— oh you clever bastard; you want me to use the glámar again. It's not as easy as it looks, y'know; blendin' into nature is one thing for we Cerenyr, but this is a ship; it's a manmade construction."

"It's wood," Larkh argued, pulling his boots back on. At the unimpressed expression Argwey gave him, he burst out laughing. "I'm sorry, Argwey. We'll figure somethin' out later. We should get another party or two ashore to comb more of these ruins. It's too big not to investigate more thoroughly."

A sudden gunshot put an abrupt end to the conversation as the two of them exchanged glances and leapt to their feet, rushing out on to the deck. Lying on the deck clutching his shoulder was one of the men keeping watch on the gangway. The shot was mere inches away from having been fatal. The shooter stood at the bottom of the gangway, a murderous glint in his eyes – Vansq, and he was surrounded by several of his crew.

"That's for messing with me, *Capitán* Savaldor!" Vansq spat. "Get in my way again, and I'll feed you to the fish personally."

"Such a lofty threat, that one," Larkh growled back. "That the best you can come up with?"

"Call it a promise to the spoiled brat of a rich man," Vansq sneered. "Better keep a good watch over your ship, Savaldor. If I catch sight of you or your men near the flooded side of the city, I will not hesitate."

Argwey's hand caught Larkh by the arm as he reached for a flintlock of his own. "Calm down," he urged him. "We'll pick our time; now's not it unless you want to risk Dirn's life."

Larkh growled, his hands balling into fists. He yanked his arm away from Argwey and made his way over to his injured crewman, a bald man with a sun tattoo on his head named Anvor. "He just came over an' pulled the trigger," he told Larkh, pressing a rag to the wound.

"Get below to Thurne," said Larkh. "He'll sort you out, an' we'll think of how to deal with that pissant." Anvor nodded, allowing his captain to help him to his feet.

CHAPTER 6

With all the preparations having been put in place overnight two days later, Vansq was confident they were in the right place. He'd sent scouts to watch the area by the sunken district they'd agreed upon on a rotational basis, and sure enough, the Neiréyu frequently came ashore there for recreational purposes. Today he was going to be there when he caught one, or maybe two or three. He didn't need to worry about keeping them hydrated; they could stay in the nets in the longliners, and his men would sling buckets of seawater over them regularly. That would have to do.

He was surprised that Savaldor hadn't made more of a nuisance of himself. He'd been certain the all-too-clever young man would have tried something stupid by now, but then he'd been forced to avoid a fight as the crew of the *Greshendier* greatly outmatched his own. How had a youth like him been able to win over so many? It didn't make sense. He was indeed a prodigy, and it made him seethe. It had taken Vansq years to build up his pirating career, and this cocky brat waltzes in and does it all as though he's had a lifetime's worth of experience.

"All's in position cap'n," said Gren, one of his riggers. "If we've the need of it, we can see about drivin' 'em in the direction we want."

Vansq patted the man on the shoulder as he followed the man back to the site. "Good work," he said, lighting a cigar and staring out across the sunken ruins. "Now we wait."

Once most of the crew of the *Seña Marcenia* had gone ashore, Argwey made his move, climbing up the brig's sterncastle and edging his way across the deck to and blending in where he could to remain hidden. There were likely too few of the crew onboard to cause him any significant hassle, but he preferred to remain undetected – and this he did with ease as he slipped below deck and into the brig's hold and swiftly knocked out the man charged with watching Dirn.

"I thought you were not going to come," she said, angling her amber eyes in his direction as he removed her gag and untied her arms from around the ship's foremast.

"I must've read you wrong the other day then," Argwey retorted. "It came across to me like you were suggestin' there would be an appropriate time to come rescue the princess."

"Princess! Bah!" Dirn snorted, flexing her wrists and tossing her jet-black braid over her shoulder. "I should cut off your balls for that."

Argwey's eyes widened, then he laughed. "But you won't, though I probably deserve it with how much I make fun of my captain," he said with a shrug. "Anyway, we should hurry."

"Just a moment," said Dirn as she searched the hold. In the corner in an otherwise empty barrel, she picked up a pair of long daggers, a quiver full of arrows, and a bow. "There is no way I would leave without these."

"Aye," said Argwey. "I expect we'll need them soon."

At this, Dirn gave him a wicked smile. "I look forward to it."

At the top of *Greshendier's* mainmast, Larkh stood braced against the royal yard with his spyglass, watching the movements of Vansq and his crew while Argwey headed across to the *Seña Marcenia* to free Dirn. Most of the enemy crew were engaged in their plan to capture Neiréyu, leaving only a handful on board, and Vansq had told *him* to keep a good watch over *his* ship? He had more than enough crew to keep an eye on several ships, where that hypocrite clearly wasn't bright enough to keep more of his own men back to keep watch of his own. Did he truly think he was going to listen and not intervene? He lowered the spyglass and rubbed his eyes, taking a short break. He might not want to miss anything, but he needed to give his eyes and arms a rest once in a while. Glancing across the ancient city, the ruins looked, even more vast and beautiful from up here, and at least the weather that morning was clear and pleasant enough to appreciate it.

"Captain!" Daron yelled. Larkh looked down to see his crewman waving at him from the quarterdeck. "You have a visitor!"

'A visitor?' He glanced around; nobody was waiting by the gangway, and Argwey's team hadn't returned yet with Dirn. "I'm on my way down!" he called. Pocketing his spyglass, he stepped off the yard onto the mast's standing rigging, swung himself across onto the ratlines, and made his way back down to the deck.

Once back on the quarterdeck, Daron approached. "It's the Neiréyu," he said. "She wants to see you."

"She didn't say why?" Larkh asked.

Daron rolled his eyes. "I don't speak Neiréyu!" he protested. "The only word I recognized was your name. And if you get the chance, tell her I resent what she did to me. My feet still hurt."

"You'd understand if you let her make a mind connection with you," Larkh said with a shrug. He smiled to himself, thinking of how easily Lenaia had got the better of Daron.

Daron's eyes widened. "Are you mad— wait, do not answer that!" He sighed. Larkh could only grin back at him in amusement. "She is under the sterncastle."

Sure enough, Lenaia was waiting for him beneath the ship's sterncastle in front of the rudder. There was panic in her eyes. It could only be about Vansq. He threw down a rope and pulled her up onto the quay; he had no intention of risking getting thoroughly soaked again. "Tell me," he said, allowing her to make another connection with him, knowing it was a spell that only worked through touch.

'The elf, he warned me,' she said. 'I warned my people, but many did not listen. They say I am hypocrite to help you. I think—'

"I know what could happen," he sighed. "I've no intention of puttin' my crew at that kind of risk, so I'll do what I can."

'No, please listen,' she pleaded. 'They do not intend to avoid this.'

Larkh's eyes widened. "What do you mean?"

'Some will lure the enemy, some will sing, and others will try to awaken the leviathan. They say I should not have helped you.'

"Bloody hell," Larkh breathed. "Even had you not helped me, it would not have stopped Vansq! I'll do what I can."

Lenaia bowed her head. *'Yaiena,'* she said, planting a kiss on his lips. *'As will I. Good luck.'* She released him, then dived back into the water and was gone. Blinking in surprise, Larkh pushed to his feet and turned around to see Argwey standing next to Dirn by the gangway. The bosun wore an amused smirk, while Dirn's brow was arched, and her lips were pursed. He felt his cheeks color as he approached.

"Wipe that stupid look off your face Argwey," he muttered, coughing. "Good to see you alive an' well, Dirn. Come aboard; we've got a few things to discuss before we make a move against Vansq."

"What was that about?" Dirn asked, following him up the gangway onto the ship.

"What was what?" Larkh asked, picking a spot on the quarterdeck and leaning against the capping rail. "We can discuss that later if we must, but for now, we have more immediate concerns. Lenaia tells me her people are goin' on the defensive *now* before Vansq has even done anythin' to lure him into a trap, an' whatever the Neiréyu do to defend themselves will undoubtedly include us an' Gresh 'cause they don't see a difference between us an' that bloody moron!" Next to him, Argwey began swearing profusely.

Dirn planted her hands on her hips where her long daggers now sat at either side, with her quiver and bow on her back. "Our best option is to leave right now," she said, "I can get you into the channel at the back of Elinda's Throat, but I think we are of the same mind when I say I believe we should put a stop to this before it begins."

"Aye, you've the right of it," Larkh agreed. "Argwey, muster a group of our best fighters an' meet on the quayside immediately."

"Aye, Captain," said the bosun tapping the side of his head as he made a move to gather the shore party. "After this, consider takin' a break, eh?"

Larkh stifled a smirk. "I'll think about it," he said, heading for the great cabin.

Dirn smiled and ran a hand over top of her head and down the length of her braid before making her way back onto the crumbling quayside.

CHAPTER 7

The shore party made their way through the cracked and desolate streets, keeping watch for anyone who might be looking out for them. They split into three groups, while Dirn made her own way there, doing the same, quickly picking off anyone who might get in their way or alert Vansq. By the time they reached the sunken district, there were Neiréyu already there, appearing to be minding their own business while Vansq's thugs slowly crept up on them, thinking their quarry none the wiser. Larkh tapped the top of his head twice to signal they were permitted to engage the enemy when discovered.

It was Dirn who was the first to take action. Two of Vansq's crewmen made a move to net one of the Neiréyu. The first man screamed as an arrow hit him square in the chest, causing the other to falter, with no time to react before another arrow thudded into his back from a different direction. Stunned, the Neiréiyu onshore leapt back into the water, and a furious Vansq roared at the top of his voice, "I warned you, Savaldor!"

Larkh already had his new scimitars drawn as he stepped out onto the remains of a plaza, where half of it had toppled into the sea and left a sheer cliff behind. "Aye, you did," he answered with a half-smile, "but I don't take threats or orders too well; that's why I tend to be the one givin' them." He glanced to either side as three of Vansq's men approached brandishing cutlasses and sabers. "Damn coward," he growled, sinking into a ready stance.

He danced aside as the first of his assailants struck, parrying with one blade while slashing with the other, felling the man instantly. Turning right on his heel, he cross-blocked a downward strike and kicked his next attacker in the kneecap before bringing both blades slashing down diagonally across the back of his neck and shoulders. Back-stepping, he continued turning, using both his momentum and that of his blades to slash across his opponent's throat. With all three dead, Larkh paused and glanced around to see Vansq was nowhere to be seen as another group of attackers charged at him. Argwey and Daron took down two of them, then a third, leaving him with three more, who he struck down in another flurry of strikes. Upon the final stroke, as the last of the attackers fell, a gunshot sent him staggering back. He dropped both blades and sank to the floor, pressing one hand to the lower left side of his belly.

"Don't say I did not warn you, rich brat!" Vansq's voice echoed across the ruins. "I'll be leaving with my prize now!"

Argwey rushed to Larkh's side, propping him up. "Damn it, Argwey," Larkh groaned, wincing. "I've really gone an' done it this time, eh?"

"You're an idiot is what you are," Argwey replied through clenched teeth, pulling out a rag from his pocket. He lifted Larkh's bloodied shirt and pressed it to the wound between his navel and left hip. "A fight is a fight, though. Daron and Dirn've gone after Vansq. We need to get you to Thurne." The bosun looked up as Laisner ran over to them.

"What's left o' those cowards've run back to their ship," said Laisner, "an' there's a dark shape out on the inner sea I don't like the look of."

'The leviathan...' Argwey realized. "We can't worry about itat the moment; we're within the harbor wall inside the cliffs at least. Help me get him up; we've no time to go back for a stretcher."

"I'll carry 'im," said Laisner. "I'm no brute like Krallan, but I can manage 'im."

Argwey nodded. "Larkh, keep that rag pressed down, y'hear me?"

"Aye, mum," Larkh murmured, replacing Argwey's hand with his own as the elf wiped sweat from his brow. He picked up the scimitars as well as his own sword as they hurried back in the direction of the harbor.

Larkh was rushed to the ship's sickbay and laid on the wooden operating table, where Krallan and other crewmen held his arms and legs down, and Argwey set a circular piece of wood wrapped with gauze between his teeth. All in the room fought to maintain composure as Thurne set to work. Larkh screamed vehemently into the gauze, fighting against the men holding him down. There had been sedatives strong enough in stock in the ship's hold to knock him out and relieve him of the pain.

"The ball is quite deep," said the Thurne, "he'll be extremely lucky if his gut isn't perforated."

It wasn't long after those words had been spoken that Larkh passed out from the agony. Eventually, Thurne was able to retrieve the flint-lock ball; he stitched the wound and had Larkh moved to the great cabin, where Argwey sat at his captain's bedside, focussing his Cerenyr healing energies to ease and hopefully speed up the process. It was well-known to any healer using magica that the body needed to register its own trauma and heal itself; it was never wise for an outside force to close a wound entirely.

Larkh drifted in and out of consciousness for some time, though late during the evening, he called out fitfully in his sleep, woke suddenly and seized Argwey by the wrist. "On the wind an' sea they come," he said. "Elinda's guardian wakes."

"What in the hells do you mean?" Argwey asked. Then he thought a moment, realizing precisely what it meant. Vansq had departed during the afternoon, and he had stated he would be leaving with his prize. Had he captured one of the Neiréyu after all, or had he been lying? Or did the Neiréyu still intend on ending what Vansq had started in the first place? A moment later, there was an ear-splitting, gurgling roar from the direction of the Throat of Elinda, followed by an intense flash of lightning and crashing thunder.

"The *Seña Marcenia* is destroyed," said Larkh, his eyes fluttering open and staring at the ceiling.

"How do you know?" Argwey asked him.

"I saw it," Larkh replied. "In my mind's eye, at least. I think Lenaia tried to show me. Dirn was on the cliff watchin' it too."

Argwey looked at him curiously. "What happened?"

Larkh turned his head towards his bosun and drowsily arched a brow. "You know, I'm not sure. It might have even been a dream," he mumbled and drifted off back to sleep.

The next morning Larkh awoke to a ruckus coming from the quarterdeck. Wincing, he turned his head to see Argwey lying on the folddown bed next to his own fixed cot, one arm dangling off the side. The noise had also stirred him, for he groaned and blinked away the sleep from his eyes.

"What the—?" he muttered. His eyes lifted to look at him. "Oh, you're awake."

"Hard to sleep through that racket," Larkh muttered. His jaw tightened at the ugly ache in his gut. "Go an' see what it's about, would you?"

"Aye," said Argwey, heaving himself up off the canvas and making his way out on to the deck. He hadn't taken two steps out onto the quarterdeck before he saw what was causing the uproar. "What in the hells is goin' on out 'ere?"

A large group of the crew was mustered by the gangway, with Krallan standing in front of whatever they were shouting and cursing at. The quartermaster looked over his shoulder. "Hey Argwey, how's the captain doin'?"

"Better than expected," the bosun replied. Then he asked again, "what's goin' on?"

Krallan wrinkled his nose in disgust. "Brace yourself, Argwey," he said, stepping aside to reveal a damp and disheveled Vansq with his arms tied tightly around his back. Argwey's eyes widened. "He survived? How'd he get 'ere?"

"He jumped ship in an attempt at escaping his fate," said Dirn, leaning against the mainmast. "The Neiréyu caught him and dragged him back to shore; I then dragged him here. I thought the captain might want to deal with him personally, if he's up to it."

"I do," said Larkh, approaching with Daron's assistance, his right arm pressed gently to his wound. There was a cold darkness in his azure eyes that spoke of bitter hatred, though the beads of sweat on his brow were enough of an indicator that his pain was making it an effort to remain standing. Vansq's eyes widened. "Happy to see me alive?" he added with a sneer. "Punish him accordingly, Krallan; if he survives, we'll set a course for the Prison Isle of Macea." Vansq struggled against his bonds, spluttering into the gag in his mouth. "Or perhaps I should throw you back to the Neiréyu an' let them deal with you? I can't decide."

"What's it to be, Captain?" Krallan queried.

"The Neiréyu returned him to shore," said Dirn. "I think they want you to deal with him in a way befitting of surface customs."

Larkh's eyes narrowed. "You know what to do, Krallan. If he lives, lock him in the brig." His balance faltered, but Argwey and Daron quickly steadied him.

"Come on," said Argwey, "back to bed with you. I swear you're not quite human."

"Aye, mum," Larkh grumbled as the both of them assisted him back to the great cabin. "I sometimes wonder myself."

That night, between bouts of sleep and sleeplessness, he lay wondering what became of Lenaia and whether or not she had been the voice of reason in convincing her people to leave him and his crew out of their conflict with Vansq. He glanced out of the window at the waning moon and then heard a soft, melodic song carried across the harbor on the northern wind. He was now certain he had his answer.

EPILOGUE

The crew of the *Greshendier* spent the next few days hunting what provisions they could find to add to the stores for the journey back, as well as exploring other accessible parts of the city. It appeared they had also picked up a few defectors from Vansq's crew who'd made them-selves scarce during the skirmish. When able, Larkh went out on to the deck for fresh air, and he sat for a time, waiting, but Lenaia did not return. They left three days later, sailing west toward the Soreiden and Elindas ridges, towering mountain ranges dividing the southern Inèts Channel from the Aeurenial Ocean. When they reached a hidden arch large enough for a ship to pass through, Dirn recited an incantation to open it. The glamour fell away, and they passed into the narrow channel with relative ease. Larkh sat leaning against the sterncastle enjoying the breeze, and in glancing over his shoulder, he saw the silhouette of a figure in the calm water. He squinted into the sunlight and asked for his spyglass to be passed over. When he looked through it, he saw her. She lifted a hand out of the water, closed her fingers over her palm, and smiled. Unable to help himself, he smiled back, touched a hand to his forehead, and waved as the ship disappeared behind the mountains.

It was three weeks before they reached the southern coast of Armaran, where they anchored nearby to the port of Caerelln to go ashore and restock, and then sailed another two weeks back to the tropical island of Naredau, not far from Enkaiyta. Larkh was well on the mend, though he'd been wondering what else Velantiir might have been able to offer. He stepped off the ship in Naredau with a bag in one hand and was greeted on the shore by none other than his mentor and combat instructor, Yahtyliir. Her porcelain skin and shoulder-length snowy white hair shone like a beacon in the sunlight; she would never be hard to miss. Her bright aquamarine eyes regarded him eagerly.

"So," she said, "tell me all about it."

Larkh gingerly rubbed the site of the gunshot and sighed. "Maybe later. All I want to do right now is lie on a beach and get drunk. Besides, I've got a bone to pick with you."

Her brow rose, ears twitching. "What did I do?" she asked.

Larkh groaned and pushed past her. "Later!" he reminded her and set off along the beach.

ABOUT MELISSA A. JOY

Melissa A. Joy is a new fantasy author from The United Kingdom with Autism who challenges the conventional expectations of fantasy and takes them to a whole new level. It is no secret that she believes in the existence of all things fantastical, and that anything is possible.

She began building the world of Aeldynn and started writing seriously aged approximately 13, and has since developed it into something truly magical worth sharing. From the glorious winged Drahknyr and wise and fearsome dragons to pirates of the high seas and a world rich with history and lore, her imagination could be said to be limitless.

When she isn't locked in a reverie about what's going on in the world of Aeldynn, she's probably out sailing the high seas on a tall ship, training at Kung Fu, gaming, or perhaps dressed up in costume at an anime convention.

Find out more at: AeldynnLore.com

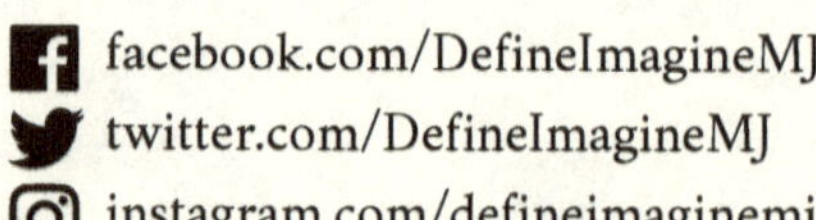

THE BRINY DEEP
BY L.J. WYNN

The soft sand of the dune clung to my feet as I sat one-hundred feet above the water. From here, I could see more than ten miles out over the deep, sapphire expanse. The gray clouds overhead blocked the intense sun, thankfully sparing my pale skin the worst of the radiation. Waves were beginning to churn the surface of the massive lake–so large as to be a sea in its own right. And for some unknown reason, the giant lake system which carved out the mitten of my home state had been changing.

The first wave of freshwater die-off had been horrific. Millions upon millions of fish carcasses had washed ashore as the water turned brackish. Scientists were still baffled and scrambling to explain. The extremists were blaming anything and everything they could; conspiracy theories abounded.

Even more astonishing had been the second wave of die-off when the brackish water converted fully to salt water. This far inland, this far removed from the sea, there was no explanation for the phenomenon. Scientists had hoped that Lakes Superior and Michigan would be spared the horrible fate of the other three lakes, given that they were the furthest inland. But they had fallen victim just the same.

I pulled my thoughts from my beloved lake's recent change in water climate and returned to my visual study. The sapphire water was the same deep blue I had always loved. Lake Michigan called to me on a deep, primal level. I felt at peace in a way I experienced nowhere else. The stinging wind whipping the waves brought tears to my eyes, and though it was summer, the long sleeves I wore to ward off the chill wind served well to mop up my wind-pulled tears.

I raised my notepad and jotted observations of the lake. With the die-offs, I had decided to change my major from English to marine biology. I had a lot of catching up to do, having previously avoided all the science classes that were now my ticket to success. This short summer semester, I was doing an independent study with my advisor to accrue the necessary credits faster. Not exactly the smartest move I've ever made, changing majors in the middle of my junior year. And from Arts to Sciences, too.

I spent the first weeks of May driving to the lakeshore every day to observe the state of the water and the climate and whether any further effects had been wrought on this chunk of shoreline. So far, the dunes seemed safe, but only time would tell. After weeks of observation, my advisor felt that I was ready to begin diving in the dark water of the big lake. The depths we were exploring were too cold for traditional wetsuits, so it would be my first time using a dry suit.

Just thinking about diving made my skin tingle. An excited smile danced across my face as I neatly filled in the columns of my chart. I was interrupted by an electric awareness dancing along my nerves, and my head jerked up from my notes. I stood, scanning behind me, searching the beach grasses and dune tops, finding no one. Paranoid about malefactors at the best of times, my mind ran wild with imagined evils thanks to my obsession with true crime shows and podcasts. When nothing happened, my heart started to slow, and I laughed at myself. Maybe dropping the English major was for the best: no more creative encouragement.

I stooped to pick up the worn backpack at my feet and took long, sliding steps down the dune to the shore. I waded into the water and noted the difference in how it felt on my skin. When it was fresh water, the lake had always felt smooth, silky, as it caressed my calves. With the salt water, I could swear it felt nourishing. It surprised me every time. I knew salt water dried out your skin and hair from magazine articles and blog posts I read, but it would seem they had lied. I had never swum in salt water before, as I had never been out of state. Never took a vacation that wasn't within the confines of the lower peninsula, even. Not after that dreadful attempt to visit St. Ignace across the Mighty Mac.

My only trip from Michigan's lower peninsula had been when I was about five. I begged my mom to take me to see the giant statue of Paul Bunyan and Babe the Blue Ox after we had learned about them in school. She capitulated, and off we went. Once we started to cross the bridge, however, a freak storm began to swirl. The big lakes would sometimes spawn gigantic storms, almost like hurricanes. They would form suddenly, with little warning, making waves so high and dangerous that they could sink massive cargo ships, like the Edmund Fitzgerald.

By the time we had crossed the five-mile bridge to the Upper Peninsula, my mom had been so anxious that she'd turned the car around and immediately crossed back. From then on, she had only been willing to go on vacations within the lower confines of our state.

I finished jotting down the last of my observations and then returned to shore. I laid my towel on the sand, letting my feet air-dry before strapping my sandals back on and making my trek back through the dunes to the car. Tomorrow was dive day, and excitement vibrated through me.

The waves lapped against the side of the boat, gently rocking my advisor and me. As waves crested against the hull, droplets of water broke free and dive-bombed my face. I licked the salty brine from my lips. Definitely not a freshwater lake anymore. What life would we find below the waves, if any? Would new plant life take hold, like salt water seaweeds? Maybe kelp since the water was so cold in these large basins? Plant life exploration would have to wait, as we were too far out for traditional sea flora to have really taken hold. The second die-off, when the hardiest species that had survived the brackish transition gave up and succumbed to the full salinity of the newly minted seas, had been a mere two weeks ago.

I struggled to pull the dry suit up over my shorts and t-shirt. It was thick and unruly, as only a diving suit can truly be. My advisor, Glen, zipped up the back, waiting for me to lift my long hair from my back before pulling the zip to the top. He pounded on my shoulder to let me know he was finished. There weren't too many female marine biology students at the university–they tended to choose other schools, usually, the ones located in a warmer climate with a salt water program of study. My advisor seemed to default to treating me like I was a fellow player on an adult weeknight softball team–lots of shoulder pounding and gentle punches. It was both disorienting, as I'd never really been the team-sports type, and comforting, as I knew he was trying to make sure that I felt welcome the best way he knew how.

We strapped on our tanks, checked our regulators one last time, and reviewed our hand communication signals. He used the same signs I'd learned in my diving lessons, and we completed our final pre-dive check. He moved to the back of the boat and climbed down to the swim platform. He gave me a thumbs up and pitched backward into the water. I gave him a count of 30. Then I followed suit.

Once ensconced below the waves, I followed Glen to the guide rope, and we began our descent. The deep blue of the water quickly swallowed us. We switched on the lights attached to our helmets. The beams pierced through the darkness. No fish, no plants–nothing greeted the beacons shining before us as we continued our descent. Lake Michigan was big enough that this in and of itself wasn't such an anomaly, but I was compelled to scan the waters around us constantly. Glen tapped my shoulder, and we paused along the guide rope. He tapped his ears, indicating that I should equalize the pressure of the water. I moved my ears a few times, a quaint trick I'd picked up in childhood. With the resulting cracks, I felt the pressure in my head ease. I took a few slow, controlled deep breaths and blew through my nose to ease the increased suction on my face.

Breathing underwater was something I'd struggled with when I first started diving lessons. It felt unnatural to breathe while submerged, even with a ready supply of oxygen. As a result, I needed to spend conscious energy focusing on breathing at the beginning of each dive. Before long, Glen tapped my ankle. He wanted to continue our descent, but before I could follow him, I thought I saw the shadows shifting far in front of me. Pulse-pounding and breathing harder, I took an extra moment or two to search the deep blue expanse in front of me, but I couldn't see any reason for the sudden awareness I felt. I swallowed hard, the respirator clanking against my teeth with the pronounced motion and pushed the sensation to the back of my mind.

After another hundred feet, the lake bottom came into view. We had chosen our dive site to coincide with one of the many shipwrecks lining the bottom of the Great Lakes. The dark mass of a corroded ship's hull loomed threateningly. The intense cold bleeding through the dry suit combined with the empty darkness made the underwater world look more alien than ever.

We both slid the diver's lights from our belts and swam to the yawning black shape of what was once a doorway. The porthole glass reflected the glare back into my face. Instinctively, I turned my head, waiting for the retina flare to subside. I blinked furiously, trying to hasten the process. In my field of vision, a long, dark shape lazily writhed back and forth, cutting through the water. I squinted, but whatever it was had gone.

Inside the wreck, the zebra mussels that plagued the lakes coated every available surface, but instead of hundreds of siphons being pulled back into the striped shells with our intrusion, the empty shells remained motionless in the deep, current-less water. The foreign atmosphere of complete isolation was almost stifling in its intensity.

Glen moved to my side to retrieve the test kit we were using to gather more data and freed the stopper. An air bubble rose from the tube, and we watched the water rush in to take its place. I handed him the aqua pencil. He made his notations, then passed it back to me. He tapped the stopper, drawing my attention to the label, then pointed to the GPS on his wrist. Message received: from here, I would do the sampling, making my labels match Glen's example. I nodded. Glen removed his small diver's notebook from his own belt and began to sketch a crude layout of our position and notated the same coordinates he'd recorded on the test tube.

We took samples both in and out of the wreck. Once we emerged from the battered mass of rust and detritus, we swam north, continuing our samples. One part of my mind stayed focused on data collection, but a growing portion of my concentration seemed to be drawn to the enveloping darkness, trying to see further through the inky black of truly deep water.

I yelped through the regulator when I felt a weight land on my shoulder. Glen's other hand came to rest on my other shoulder. He slowly turned me to face him. He tilted his head to the side in a quizzical posture, looking comically canine in his dry suit. I tapped my head with my fingers, then floated my hand up and out: *my mind is drifting*. He tapped my forehead twice and shook his head. He was right - being inattentive as a diver was a good way to wind up dead. As my grandfather always said, mountains and water will both happily kill you if you don't treat them with due respect and caution.

I told myself to take one last, long glance around the darkness and then focus fully on my task. If I wanted to come back out and marvel at the sheer emptiness underwater, I'd have to do it on my own time. I swear I could see a shape blacker than the rest of the water undulating, but the harder I looked, the less corporeal it seemed to be. Just as I was ready to signal Glen to draw his attention to it, it disappeared entirely.

Insistent vibrating echoed through the surface of my table. Dinner dishes done, I quickly dried my hands and grabbed my phone, Glen's name flashing on the screen. "Hey, did you get any of the test results back yet?"

"It's not good, Cal. The plankton we used to find in the Lakes are completely dead. In their place, we now have salt water plankton populations blooming. The salinity levels look stable, too. The Great Lakes aren't freshwater anymore."

His news stunned me. I couldn't begin to process the magnitude of that revelation. The state tourism board liked to boast that we had all the great parts of the sea without the salt. But how in the world did the largest freshwater supply in the western hemisphere turn to salt water? Could it be reversed? Glen's voice continued to buzz in my ear, but very little of what he said registered with me. Instead, visions of undulating darkness under the waves absorbed me. Maybe that darkness, whatever it was, was responsible for the drastic state of my beloved lake.

When Glen finished talking, I hung up the phone without saying anything more. My thoughts were consumed with getting back into the water and pursuing that dark, nebulous shape.

———

The early morning sun illuminated a crimson sky. I ignored the voice at the back of my head whispering sailing superstitions about the inherent warning. With one thing and another, maybe a nasty nautical natural disaster could reset the lakes. The waves lapped at the side of the boat as I went completed an equipment check. I was about to break the first diving rule I learned: never dive alone as a novice. It wouldn't be such a big deal if I were more experienced or had a greater familiarity with my diving environment. I mentally shrugged my shoulders: I had spent my whole life staying safe whenever chance had tempted me. I figured the time was now or never.

I pulled on my tank, settled the straps, and situated the regulator in the guide strap on my shoulder. Flipping my mask down over my eyes, I wrapped my lips around the mouthpiece and stepped from the swim platform. The dark water immediately enveloped me. It seemed even darker in the early morning sunshine than it had the previous day. I strained against my own lack of patience and forced myself to slow my descent. I had enough dive experience to remember to equalize my ears, suit, and mask. For my first solo dive in open water, I wasn't very relaxed, nor did I have a dive buddy above to keep an eye out for danger.

I closed my eyes and breathed deeply before resuming my descent again. I scanned the water. The darkness seemed uniform, so I focused on the space below me. I absently wondered how long it would take before more salt water lifeforms began to take over the former lakes. I was so absorbed in my speculation about repopulation that the sudden appearance of a large appendage didn't register at first. My instinctive thought was that the seaweed was out of control before I recalled the total die-off of all plant and animal species in the lakes. When the appendage wrapped around my waist and tugged, however, all conscious thought fled.

I sped painfully downward through the water, my ears, eyes, and lungs protesting the extreme and sudden change in pressure. The more I tried to equalize the pressure of the lake, the harder I was squeezed and the faster I was tugged asunder. My head was going to explode, my eyes bulging out, my lungs on the verge of collapsing. My arms flailed, trying in vain to grab onto something. I barely registered speeding past shipwrecks before I lost consciousness.

My first thought was that the crushing pressure around my waist was gone. I took stock: my head ached, my lungs felt raw, and my body felt as though I had broken every inch of bone and was newly mended. In short, I hurt every place I had nerve endings and then some. A rhythmic lapping echoed around me. I tried to figure out why that would be out of place, but it took me a disturbingly long time: the sound was echoing around a dry space. The last thing I remembered was being dragged deep down in the lake. Underwater.

I raised a hand to my head. Nope, very much not in water anymore. I wasn't even in my dry suit. What in Hades was going on? My hand fell back down, landing on a rough, rocky surface. I slowed my breathing, braced myself, and opened my eyes. It was pitch black. I tried to open my eyes again, thinking maybe I hadn't managed it the first time. I pressed my open palm against the tip of my nose. My sweaty hand smelled musty from the dive gloves, but I couldn't see it. Great. I lowered it back to the damp, rocky floor. The smell of salt water overpowered my other senses.

I heard movement as something crossed the stone floor. A soft, blue-green light appeared around a jagged rock edge. The creature carrying the light source looked like a cosplay homage to the Creature from the Black Lagoon. I couldn't tell if the skin was green or if that was thanks to the watery light emitted by the lantern it held aloft in its hand. Vertically-slit pupils studied me, clearly able to see better in the dim light than my poor human eyes. A small mouth positioned below the wide-set, over-large eyes opened, and a gurgling sound emitted. It was as though thousands of bubbles were fighting to escape the mouth of a very narrow bottle.

I let my head fall back to the rock. *This must be what a concussion feels like*, I thought. Maybe I was delusional. The being came closer and knelt beside me. An orb in its grasp emitted the wan light. It extended a slimy appendage, touched my forehead, then pulled down the lower edge of my eye. It tried to lean closer, but I rolled away. My head spun.

"What are you doing?" I croaked, trying to ignore the vertigo caused by my hasty retreat.

More bubble sounds.

"If you asked if I'm awake, yes, I'm awake." I tried to look around what I decided was a cave in the dim light. "Unless I'm concussed," I added in an aside. "In which case, I'm not awake." I leaned against the rock wall I had found in my evasive maneuver and looked back at the thing studying me. "What am I doing here?" Surprisingly, I wasn't afraid to find myself in this submarine cave. I was just bewildered.

Bubble sounds with a bit of squealing this time.

"Look, I can't understand you," I stated baldly. "Is there anyone else here? I've got questions." I pulled my knees to my chest and dropped my head to my crossed arms. "Like what in the world am I doing down here," I mumbled into my chest.

More movement. I raised my head again after a moment to find myself alone. At least I had a lantern now. The orb appeared to be bioluminescent algae encased in thick membrane, a touchable bubble. I poked it with a finger, and it began to roll away with slow, uneven plops across the rough floor. I looked up at the sound of someone approaching, failing to grasp the orb before it rolled out of reach.

Where the first creature had disappeared, another light source approached. A second being accompanied the first creature, and they stood looking down at me. I rose to my feet, my hand holding my forehead where I felt a pounding ache. My fingers prodded the sticky gash and came away covered in a dark substance. Even as I stared, bewildered, the second creature bubbled at me in an interrogative tone, though this bubbling sounded slightly different.

The first stopped the second with a touch. They bubbled at each other, then looked back at me. Just when I began to wonder if they would dissect bits of me to study under a microscope, the second one approached me. It moved slowly, reaching out toward me. I thought of every sci-fi movie ever, where the friendly human approaches the alien. A surprised chuckle escaped me. The lifeform stopped short, waiting to see what I would do. When I stayed still and silent, it came closer yet. Two tentacles wrapped around my upper arms, stopping any retreat I might attempt. Another appendage, this one ending in what resembled a hand, rose to my forehead. Its eyes traced over my features, bubble noises sounding the whole time.

"Do you speak English?" I blurted when they both continued to bubble on around me.

The one holding my arms stopped and turned its attention back to me. It emitted more inquisitive bubble noises, complete with head cocked to the side. My shoulders slumped in its grasp. "I'm pretty sure I can't speak in bubbles," I bemoaned out loud. It raised a second hand to pat my shoulder, the tentacles releasing my arms. A fifth tentacle surrounded my waist and tugged me alongside Thing 2, as I had come to think of it, who led me from the cave.

"Where are you taking me? I don't know you. It's one of the first lessons you learn as a kid," I continued in what I thought of as a real-life soliloquy. "'Never go anywhere with a stranger.'" I thought for a second. "And 'Stop, drop, and roll,'" I tacked on as I halted. I could see eyes looking at me from the side, feel them on my back. I shrugged. Thing 1 tugged me onward.

We made our way through a few corridors of a natural cave system, the small algae-lanterns lighting our way. The lanterns began to grow larger and more plentiful as we got closer to a large, yawning cavern entrance. I could still hear the dripping of water, but it was muted, and the salt smell had greatly diminished. Two more of the creatures stood to either side of the looming passage. My eyes dropped to the floor, where I noticed several tentacles arranged like feet. My brain helpfully supplied an image of Squidward. I bit my cheek to stifle another deranged chuckle. I was surer than ever that I was concussed.

Ushered between the two guards, I was led into what I could only classify as a throne room. My jaw dropped. My eyes raked over the scene in front of me. I had to be in bed, asleep. I turned to look at Thing 2. It avoided my gaze and released my waist, propelling me with a slight push forward.

The rest of the creatures in the cavern were facing a stone dais at the end of the elongated space. A large, glowing throne sat atop stacked stone slabs. A massive form sat, skin darker than that of my escorts, with long, dark filaments waving in an unseen breeze from its head. An enormous trident was clasped in one hand. My brows climbed my forehead, then sank between my eyes.

"Poseidon?" I blurted. I was deep into reading Greek myths to unwind from my studies.

"No," the ruler intoned. "Though I am flattered."

I gaped.

"Daughter of the sea," the deep voice continued. It was underscored by a sound of bubbles popping, and I wondered whether he was really speaking English or whether I had descended that far into my concussed dreamscape. "We watched you swim with the human. We tried to intercept you before you returned to the surface, but we could not reveal ourselves to the rest of your kind. We were glad to see you return alone."

"The…" I stopped. "I'm not…" Stymied, I gathered my thoughts. I settled on an elegant, "What?"

"You did not come to seek us out?"

"I don't know who you are."

The ruler's forehead creased in thought.

I interrupted before it could respond. "Did you call me 'Daughter of the Sea?' What is going on?"

It raised a tentacle to its face, massaging at the forehead. One of its hands made an imperious gesture. "Leave us!" it commanded.

The throng of onlookers shuffled from the room. In just a few minutes, I was alone with the ruler of an underground kingdom. I swallowed with difficulty. "Your, uhm, Majesty," I soothed. I tried to curtsey, but the king cut me off with a sharp look.

"Come. Sit," the deep voice commanded. He threw out an arm toward a small seating area nestled in an alcove I had missed when I entered.

I went.

I sat.

"My son, Abermere, was never happy being confined to the sea. He wanted nothing more than to explore the land. He roamed waters far and wide. He especially enjoyed tropical waters with vibrant coral reefs and brightly colored fish, but it was too hard to conceal himself during the day. His indigo skin was too conspicuous in the daylight and cerulean waters. So, he returned home to the darker waters of the North Atlantic. I thought he had finally listened to his old father, heeded my wisdom." The tentacled man shifted in his seat, eyes staring off into space as he reminisced.

"Sullen and discontent to learn his role as heir, he moped. Eventually, he began to spend more and more time away." He glanced back at me and held my gaze. "He was looking for a ship's bell that had not been damaged after the vessel sank."

I spoke before I could think better of it. "Why would he want a bell?"

"Among our people, an unblemished ship's bell, still shiny from the surface, will buy one wish from Daevrey Junnes, the King of the Deep."

I laughed. "Davy Jones?"

"No, Daevrey Junnes." He waved away my question. "Abermere found a ship's bell, intact and unblemished, shiny as the sun. His wish was granted." He paused.

When he didn't speak again, I asked. "What was his wish?"

"To walk on land. I never saw my son again. But years after he had disappeared to the sands above, I received a message tied to a ship's anchor, cut free, and dropped into the sea. He had been granted a human form. He was happy in his life on land. He had found love, and they had made their home surrounded by water, though it was not the salt water of our people." When he continued, his voice was like sandpaper. "They had a child. But the deal he struck with Junnes had limits. If a child were to be born of a union with a land-dweller, either Abermere's or the child's life would be forfeit. In his message, he begged me to find some way to break the curse. But there is no changing a deal struck with Junnes."

I studied the squid-man in front of me. Sorrow etched his features as he stared off into the distance. "How long," my voice cracked. I cleared my throat, tried again, as he turned his attention to me. "How long ago was that?"

He considered me for a long moment. "It has been almost twenty-one years."

I took a deep breath and let it out, stomach churning. "Why did you think I was coming to you?"

His shoulders sagged, his posture deflating. "I sent Abermere a missive in return. I instructed him to tell his beloved the truth of his appearance on land. She was to instruct their child to come to me before its twenty-first year. I could protect the child from Daevrey Junnes' retaliation, but not if he or she were to remain on land. We had no way to know what traits a child from a union between a human and a meian would have." He rose, offering me a hand. I let him pull me from the table, and he tucked my hand around his arm, patting it as we walked.

"Daevrey Junnes is not satisfied with my son's sacrifice. He demands the sacrifice of the child as well. We had to bring you to my kingdom so I can protect you."

I stopped mid-stride. "You killed the Lakes to come and get me?"

"It was not my doing." He swiped his hand across the air in front of us. "They will recover." My mouth worked while I tried to find words. I was shaking my head when he continued. "We will retreat back to the ocean. The freshwater will return in time."

"You destroyed an entire ecosystem. How can you be so cavalier about this?"

He scowled. "You misunderstand. We did not kill off the life in your lakes. We pursued Daevrey Junnes. It was only by following his lead that we were able to finally discover your location. Your lakes were already dying by the time we followed him. They would have died with or without us."

My brain was still spinning. "Wait. He was already here? HE killed the lakes?"

"Yes. We were able to stop him from grabbing you when you were with the other human. When you came back below the waves, we had to fight him off. It was a very near thing that we were able to get you safely to the caves before his kraken could steal you away to Junnes' lair."

"A kraken? Those aren't real," I dismissed.

"They are real. You have the marks from its tentacles to prove it. Or would you prefer I let you be taken next time?" His voice had turned cold and hard.

I didn't relish the thought of death by kraken. As I contemplated how horrific that must be, he waved me forward into a smaller cave. "This is where you will sleep. I will be down the passage. My quarters are in the first large pool you come to. Rest awhile. When we wake, we will abandon these caves and return to my home in the ocean." His tone had softened.

"Wait! That's it? 'Sleep here, then you're leaving forever'?" My voice rose, my hands waving wildly in panic.

"You cannot stay here," he intoned. "You will die if you try to remain in your life as it was." His tone was hard, brooking no argument. The bubbling sound I had tuned out crested in his vehemence, making itself known again.

My brows scrunched up. "Why can I understand you but no one else? I mean, I still hear the bubbles, but you're speaking English."

"Your father must have passed on to you an understanding of our language. Our line uses a different dialect of Meritlan. Once you learn it well, you will find communicating with others to be easier."

Not ready to be alone yet, I blurted out more questions to stop his departure. "Where am I going to sleep? What will I use for lights? What is your name?" I punctuated each question by thrusting my arm into the cave behind me. "Do you even know my name?" I shrieked in the end.

"You will sleep," he moved past me into the cave and gestured to what looked like a blanket draped across a boulder, "on this pallet." Moving to another part of the cave, he lifted two orbs in each hand, giving first a squeeze, then a shake to both, activating them. "You can use these lanterns for light." He set them back on the rock ledge that, to me, resembled a rocky desktop. "You may call me Grandfather. And your name is Calliope."

As I stood gaping at his audacity, he nodded his head, turned, and left me in the cave. I looked at the pallet - woven seaweed formed a rudimentary mat. Like all things I had seen so far, it was wet. Sleeping on that would land me with a cold at the very least. Great, spend a few hours in a damp, dark cave, trying to entertain myself while waiting to be moved to a new home. I wondered if he had any kind of accommodations there for me. Ones that wouldn't result in a case of pneumonia.

Of course, my other choice was to stay in my regular life and be hunted by some deep-sea legend. Oh, the choices.

By the time my grandfather came back to my chambers, I felt the sharp nails of madness clawing at me. The low light level had me seeing shadows and shifting shapes in my periphery. Each time I turned my head, the shapes resolved back into murky gloom. I was thoroughly unnerved.

His rich voice preceded him. "Calliope," he called, "we are leaving." When I didn't answer him immediately, he moved fully into my sight. He peered closely at me. "Whatever is the matter with you?"

My teeth chattered, despite my tightly clenched jaw. I stayed where I was, backed up against a rock wall, my knees pulled to my chest. I had settled in the driest part of the cave that I could find, but I must have listed sideways when I eventually fell asleep. I awoke shivering and soaked. My hair was damp, in matted ropes alongside my face. I could feel the drips through my shirt. My muscles hurt from the trembling. At that moment, I couldn't have cared less if they left me there for Junnes to find. It would have been a welcome relief.

My eyes strayed to the shadows behind him and back again. I couldn't keep my focus on him. His features contorted in concern. Two tentacles wrapped around me and helped me to my feet. His cold-blooded body leached more of my own body heat, and I felt icy tendrils begin to unfurl inside from where he gripped me. The longer he held me, the colder I felt. The trembling intensified even as I felt my heart start to slow. He raised another tentacle to my face and turned my head to look into my eyes.

"You are unwell," he muttered in a low voice. I couldn't detect the bubbling sounds behind his speech any longer.

"C-c-c-cold," I forced out through my teeth, clenched against the worst of the chattering.

He let me sink back to the floor of the cave again and left. When he returned, he was no longer alone. The second creature looked the same as the rest, innumerable tentacles, upright bearing, though its skin was darker, like my grandfather's. It approached me slowly, crouching low to meet me where I vibrated on the rocky floor.

One of its tentacles extended toward my face. I closed my eyes, unable to keep them open any longer. I was exhausted. I didn't care what they did to me anymore. I just wanted to sleep. The tentacle withdrew, and they began to bubble at each other. I must have drifted in and out of consciousness because I imagined that the cold continued to permeate my limbs, moving into my chest.

When next I came to, I heard voices arguing above me as I lay sprawled on the floor. Blessedly, the trembling had ceased. It felt like too much effort to open my eyes, but I began to pay attention to the voices. My grandfather was arguing with someone else, a man, from the sounds of it.

"Humans cannot survive in wet conditions. They are warm-blooded, and the constant cold and damp damages their bodies!" the mystery man argued. I wondered if it was wise to argue with a monarch.

"This is dry. We put her in the cave with no water access," the king interjected pointedly.

"Nothing down here is dry! Not by human standards! If she were to lay on the woven pallet, she would be deathly ill. She may be too sick as it is." The voice paused, and movement ensued. I sensed a presence next to me. "Calliope," it murmured.

I struggled to open my eyes. This new face—dark blue skin and amber, vertically-slit eyes—monopolized my field of vision. I looked behind his head to see the rocky ceiling and noticed, for the first time, great detail in the surface: pockmarks, cracks, even some anchored abandoned shells. A tentacle gently touched my cheek and moved my head slowly side to side. "This is not good, King Dagon. Her temperature is much lower than when you brought her to the caves, and her color has faded dramatically."

"What does that mean?" my grandfather demanded.

The squid-man examining me turned to look over his shoulder at him. "I do not know, Majesty."

"At least I'm not cold anymore," I croaked, my throat burning.

Both men looked at me. "Calliope," my grandfather asked, "what do you mean you are not cold?"

I braced myself on my elbows. "Before, I was so cold. I'm not now." My thoughts drifted to an article I once read, written by an avalanche survivor. He had said that the trembling had become almost violent in its intensity before ceasing completely not long before rescuers found him. He had been near death, and doctors had determined he would have died quietly in his "sleep" if they'd been even fifteen minutes longer in finding him. "I'm probably going to die now."

Both men blanched. "You will not die," my grandfather ordered.

"I do not believe she will die," my grandfather's companion said. "But she is unwell for a human. She is far too cold."

"Hypothermia," I supplied.

He continued, "She cannot be moved. Not yet. I need to find some answers." He spoke to my grandfather, but his eyes never left me. Then, the stranger rose and moved toward the king. They conferred quietly while I strained my ears to listen in. Why would they have been arguing in English while I was out cold?

When he left, my grandfather approached and knelt by me before turning and resting his back against the wall. "Who was that?" I asked.

"Learo. He has the most knowledge about humans among our kind, but he resented leaving his studies." He halted before sharing further. "I do not know much about humans, Granddaughter."

"He's not wrong. Humans can't be cold and wet, or we get very sick. We can die from it."

"You will not die."

My lips pursed together. "You may have saved me from Junnes, but I don't think it's going to matter," I told him, resigned. "Why were you arguing in English?"

"We were not arguing in English," he told me. "We were speaking in Meritlan."

I screwed my face up. "But I could understand you."

His face softened. Before he could answer, Learo was back.

"Majesty," he began. "The hypothermia your granddaughter suggested. She has shown all of the symptoms. Her temperature is far lower than it should be. If she were fully human, she would be dead."

"I'm sorry. Fully human?" I butted in.

His gaze moved to me. "You are not fully human. King Dagon explained this to you."

My mouth set mulishly. "I've seen pictures of my father. He was human."

"He may have looked human, but he was not."

My grandfather laid a tentacle on my shoulder to stop further argument. "We do not know the extent of Junnes' transformation on him."

Learo interjected. "Humans and meians are genetically related. We are what humanity would have become had they returned to the oceans." He studied me. "If I were to guess, the hypothermia initiated your transformation."

I looked down at my hands. A tinge of blue, darker on the backs of my hands, lighter on my palms, seemed to prove Learo's theory. "What does that mean?" I asked.

"We cannot know for sure," Dagon said.

Learo nodded. "We will conduct tests after we return."

"How am I going to come with you? I can't breathe underwater, and I don't have enough air left in my tanks to travel anywhere."

"I did worry about that," Learo admitted. "I had a few theories on how we might accomplish it, but your transformation may be a boon. I want you to swim before we depart. I have a theory I want to test."

My neck was sore from looking up at Learo where he stood. I turned to my grandfather. "I don't know what you expect to have changed, but I breathe air the same now as I did when I woke up in my bed this morning." I shrugged.

"Yesterday," Learo interrupted. "The sun both set and rose again while you have been with us."

My head dropped. "I didn't get to say goodbye to my mom."

My grandfather wrapped a tentacle around my shoulders. "Come, you will swim, and we will see what changes have been wrought."

Less than five minutes later, I was stripped down to my tank top and some shorts, my long sleeve shirt, and pants discarded on the floor of the cave. I lowered myself into the water and kicked toward where my grandfather waited in the middle of the pool.

He wrapped tentacles over my shoulders and around my waist. Looking over my shoulder at Learo, he nodded, then turned his focus to me. "Deep breath," Learo instructed from his rocky ledge, and Dagon applied a light pressure to my shoulders.

I filled my lungs and ducked below the water. Slowly, bubbles rose from my nose as I exhaled. When I felt my lungs emptying, I pushed my arms down to rise to the surface, but the tentacles securing me tightened, holding me underwater. My chest began to burn as I struggled to get back to the surface of the subterranean pool. It was in vain. The tentacles held me fast.

My brain fought the instinct of my body to breathe in. My diaphragm spasmed, and I sucked in a huge lungful of water. I panicked, thrashing against my grandfather, and I managed to dislodge his tentacles, kicking away from him toward the edge of the pool. Learo's tentacles wrapped around my arms and dragged me onto the rocks. I kneeled, hacking up water, fighting the urge to throw up. Learo's tentacles braced my shoulders, patted my back, and smoothed hair from my face.

"What was that?" I shouted between hacking sobs.

"A test, Princess," Learo answered, calm.

"Don't call me princess," I spat. "What kind of test?"

"To see if your lungs have begun to transform as well. Human babies begin life in fluid. Your lungs become air-sensitive as you age.

Our lungs," he explained, "never dry out. We are able to breathe in both air and water." I mulled that over in the silence after his explanation. When I looked up at him, he asked, "Think back, Princess. Did you cough the water out because you had to or because you have been trained to through your human experiences?"

I scowled at the nickname, but I sat up straight, my shoulders still heaving. I looked over at my grandfather. He merely floated in the pool, studying me. I looked back to Learo. Both waited on me. I finally edged back to the pool and slid into the water. I treaded water while I watched my grandfather, then glided over to him. He lifted two tentacles out of the water and waited until I nodded at him before securing me in his grasp once more. I took a smaller breath and placed my face in the water, opting for a smaller motion rather than full submersion.

I exhaled, then began to draw some water in through my nose. Unlike the burning sensation I expected, the water felt cool and soothing. I breathed deeper, then coughed. I tried to raise my head out of the water, but my grandfather's tentacles tightened around me and pushed me under. I drew on my dive training and schooled myself to breathe slowly and steadily, just as I had on my descent into the lake.

It worked. I was breathing underwater. The tentacles supporting me, loosened, and Dagon joined me. "You are doing very well, Granddaughter." My eyes widened. I could understand him perfectly, even below the surface.

Transformed though I was, I couldn't swim as well as the full-meians, so several of them took turns swimming with me, pulling me along as we traveled to the meian kingdom. I felt like a child on training wheels. I had the motions down, but I was nowhere near as skilled a swimmer as they were. I also couldn't see as well underwater, though the change in my eyesight was a vast improvement. When it was Learo's turn to tow me along with him, he explained to me that our destination was the continental shelf off the coast of the northeastern United States.

As we swam along, the meians showed me how to utilize the water currents so I could conserve energy. I could understand what they were saying to me, but I couldn't answer in Meritlan, my still-human vocal cords not quite able to form the sounds of their language. It seemed only Learo and my grandfather were able to understand me. They were all friendly, but I couldn't blame them for not wanting to keep up a one-sided conversation. While we swam, I thought about my mom. I never went longer than two or three days without calling her, but we texted each other daily. My heart lurched thinking of her.

The closer we got to the open ocean, the more lost I felt. What would my life be like now? Would I ever be safe from Daevrey Junnes? Would I spend the rest of my life hiding from the deep-sea legend? I could feel my fears and worries stack one on top of the other the further we went down the Saint Lawrence Seaway.

For all my worries and concerns, there was another part of me that was amazed by the changes in my life. I had a grandfather! The only family I've ever had was my mother. And as we went, I saw multitudes of sea life: turtles, crabs, sharks, even whales. I felt torn between the two halves of myself.

I was sunk so far in my thoughts as I mechanically swam along that Learo had to grasp me around the waist to keep me from swimming right into the meian in front of me. We had arrived at the castle, for lack of a better word, that was to be my new home. It was situated in an underwater fjord carved into the continental shelf. The castle itself matched the slate color of the sloping terrain. Tucked into the fold of fjord, little blue-green orbs speckled the rock wall, reminding me of visits to the planetarium as a child. The darker blue water in the shadow of the fjord behind it helped to camouflage the castle's presence.

A formidable line of creatures of indistinguishable origin rose up suddenly, blocking our way. Many looked to be straight out of the old Greek myths I had consumed back in my former life on land. In the middle of the line, an enormous being floated. The rest of the creatures seemed to wait for some signal from him. He lifted his arms straight in front of him, then moved them out to the sides before moving forward several strokes. His skin was obsidian dark, and I knew it was only my newly enhanced eyesight that allowed me to see him. Black eyes surrounded by blue fixated on me before Learo positioned himself in front of me.

"Don't make eye contact with Junnes," he ordered over his shoulder.

Junnes? The same Junnes that wanted me for a sacrifice? My thoughts raced. I let myself sink a bit in the water so I could see through a gap in Learo's tentacles to the sea demon beyond. Junnes held a harpoon in one tentacle, like a staff, and gesticulated wildly in argument with my grandfather. I watched as King Dagon began to inflate in size. Junnes followed his example, and for the first time, I noticed behind him a giant octopus. *No,* I corrected myself. *That must be Junnes' kraken.*

The kraken looked so similar to an octopus that I would have been hard-pressed to call it anything else had my grandfather and Learo not told me about the vile beast. Apparently, it was a deep-sea equivalent to a guard dog. Junnes doted on it and treated it well, and in return, the kraken did all of Junnes' most despicable tasks. *Like snatching a half-human girl to drag her to her death, I guessed.*

As I watched the marine beast, my eye followed the lines of its roiling tentacles. Deep crimson flesh flashed with spots of changing color, the effect like looking up through sun-dappled autumn leaves. I felt mesmerized. I began to strike out to swim past Learo toward it, but he gripped me hard.

"Calliope," he spoke firmly. His face was less than six inches from mine. "Do not look at the kraken." He gave me a little shake to reinforce the order.

I shook my head, dazed. "I'm sorry," I murmured, ashamed. "I won't let it happen again."

He studied my face for a long while. "There are many dangers when it comes to Junnes. Have you studied sea life?"

"A little, not very much yet. This was supposed to be my catch-up semester. I was cramming to switch majors to marine biology." Confusion colored his face. "My studies," I clarified.

"Do you know how deep-sea predators hunt?" he asked instead.

"Oh," I said, chagrined that I had almost succumbed to such a primitive and base creature's hunting tactics. I thought back to some of my favorite deep-sea documentaries featuring the anglerfish. Creatures like these relied on bioluminescent skin features to lure in their prey. The prey animals would be mesmerized by the lights or patterns, and the hunter could snatch them up before they were the wiser.

While I was being chastised, Dagon and Junnes must have concluded their confrontation. Movement over Learo's shoulder caught my eye as I watched the creature-barricade disassemble. My grandfather swam over to us. I dropped my eyes again, embarrassed of my mistake in falling for the oscillating pattern on the kraken's skin and nearly swimming right into Junnes' grasp.

Dagon called another meian over to stay with me while he and Learo conferred quietly some distance away. The rest of the meian contingent that had followed my grandfather to retrieve me began to break up as well, each going off to do his or her own thing. At a loss, I waited in mute company with my companion. This meian seemed to have no use for me, ignoring me completely to survey the area around us, no doubt looking for one of Junnes' lackeys who may have stayed behind. Learo swam back toward me with a carefully blank face. He dismissed the meian, who swam off after other pursuits, then motioned for me to follow him.

Learo led me toward the massive structure of the castle. The visual effect was like that of stalagmites on the floor of a cave or large cairns set up in a field. It abutted the drop-off of the continental shelf, built into the side like old cliff dwellings I had seen in pictures. As we continued inside, I felt comforted by the blue-green lanterns, their soothing light helping to regulate my nerves after the confrontation with Junnes. We turned corner after corner. I had no worries about falling prey to the kraken's tactics again because there was no way I'd ever be able to navigate my way through this place without a guide.

Everything looked the same. A feeling of despair took root in my stomach. I felt so alone.

Learo took his leave after he deposited me in a space that resembled a ship's bunk. The room was small and spartan, with simple ledges hewn in the rock. I made my way over to the seaweed pallet, which would serve as my bed. Now that I didn't have to worry about catching my death of a cold, I laid down and found it surprisingly cushy against the rock. I rested down on my side, pulled my legs into my chest, and wrapped my arms around them. At least underwater, I could cry by myself without anyone being the wiser.

After my pity party and a short nap, I felt much better. I had no idea how to make my way around the castle, so I tried to busy myself in the room, but aside from a few stray shells, there was nothing to do to pass the time. Back home, I would have read a book, or scrolled mindlessly on my phone, or called my mom. Here, there was nothing to pass the time. I gave myself a mental pep talk and decided to brave the labyrinth and hope that if I got sufficiently lost, one of the meians would take pity on me and bring me to my grandfather.

I didn't make it far before a frantic meian darted up to me, wrapping tentacles around my arm and dragging me along behind it. It babbled as I struggled to keep up, the speech cadence so quick I completely missed what it was saying. After the confusing mad dash through the corridors and passages, I found myself in yet another large cavern. A firm push in the middle of my back propelled me into the chamber before I heard the meian take off. Once again, I made an awkward entrance in front of my grandfather.

This time, the hall was empty, aside from Learo, who motioned me forward as my grandfather studied me. His eyes narrowed on my face. I wished I could tell what he was thinking; I wasn't left waiting for long.

His deep voice broke into my thoughts. "Junnes demanded that you serve his kingdom for two years. After that time, he will release you and allow you to return to your life on land."

My mouth dropped open. "What if I don't?" I demanded.

Learo broke in after a lengthy, silent exchange with my grandfather. "He will wage war against us."

My eyes narrowed. "Why does he care about me? Why do *you* care about me?" I challenged my grandfather. "I'm a college student who is woefully behind on her studies and who will be in significant debt by the time I earn my degree." I looked back and forth between Dagon and Learo. "I was average as a human. I'm less than average down here." I waved my hands over myself to indicate just how below average I was in meian terms - zero tentacles, minimal speech capability, poor swimming skills, poor eyesight, among other things.

"You are my granddaughter," Dagon answered in a fierce tone. "You will not disparage yourself."

I turned helplessly to Learo. Seeing no help from that quarter, I turned back to my grandfather. "What value do I have to Junnes? What could he possibly need from me that he is willing to war against you?"

"We do not know, Princess." Learo offered.

"Don't call me that," I snapped at him, keeping my eyes on my grandfather. I crossed my arms. "Fine," I changed tactics. "Say I do serve Junnes for two years. Then what? I just get released to go on my way? I can't go back to school, not like this." My skin, which had been tinged a slight blue when I succumbed to hypothermia in the cave back in the lake, had turned more and more blue the longer I was submerged. I was nearly as dark in tone as my grandfather. I thought back to those old sci-fi B movies. If I went back to my life on land, I would be the alien that scientists wanted to dissect. I shuddered at the thought.

Mind made up, I uncrossed my arms. "I want to talk to Junnes."

"No," my grandfather cut in. "Absolutely not."

"Well, I'm not going to be the cause of any war," I argued.

He scowled at me. "You're not going to talk to him." His royal decree rang around the chamber.

I filled my lungs and emptied them three times before I felt calm enough to speak. "Will your people fight a war for a human most of them have never met?"

"They will fight because I tell them to."

"I'm no Helen of Troy," I dismissed. "No one will thank you for ordering them to fight on my behalf."

Dagon seethed. "You are not going to speak to Junnes!"

"Your Majesty," Learo interceded. "She makes a point that war is unnecessary. If we can meet with Junnes and set forth strictures, we can try to control the situation. We do not need to make a decision yet," he soothed. "We strictly explore our options more."

The back and forth seemed to be over after Learo made his point. I waited while my grandfather fumed. Finally, he ground out that he would demand Junnes appear for an audience before he departed the chamber.

"You make fair points, Calliope," Learo complimented me. "We will have to wait to see what Junnes intends for you." He looked like he tried to smile, but it seemed very much forced for my benefit. He shook himself from his thoughts and refocused on me. "Would you like a tour?"

"Yes, please," I agreed.

Learo explained the castle structure as we made our way around. It resembled no human castle I had ever seen, being that it consisted largely of naturally occurring caves and passages. At one intersection, Learo paused and pointed to the roof of the passage. There, I saw a curious formation of shells wedged into the rocks. It reminded me of the Greek alphabet in a way, somehow familiar yet foreign at the same time. With his coaching, I began to recognize some of the symbols as we continued on. He promised to help me study so I would be better able to navigate without a constant guide before his sentence broke off. He pushed on.

I wouldn't need to study the symbols if I wouldn't be around to read them.

Soon we reached the outer terminus of the passages, and Learo led me through a large opening out to the shelf break. There, we made our way up to the ledge. Above the castle, a cold-water coral reef provided habitat for fish, crab, and mollusks, while sharks and turtles could be seen swimming among the coral fronds, no doubt hunting for their lunch. The corals weren't the resplendent colors of a tropical reef, but it was beautiful, nonetheless. I marveled at witnessing this slice of marine life. Learo seemed content to trail alongside me, answering questions I had along the way.

Before long, a small meian approached with a message. Unlike the previous messenger, this one spoke carefully, and I had no trouble understanding. We were being summoned. My heart kicked up a notch. My breathing, such as it was underwater, hitched, but I squared my shoulders and braced myself for what was next.

When we entered the chamber, Junnes' figure nearly concealed my grandfather on his throne completely. He had seemed large when we first approached my grandfather's castle and encountered the blockade. Now, in close quarters, he was far more massive. I clenched my hands into fists, digging my nails into my palms to steady myself. Junnes turned and faced the two of us, and Learo cupped my elbow to bring me around to Dagon's side.

Mindful of Learo's earlier advice, I avoided eye contact with Junnes. I figured it might give the illusion of deference, which I hoped would give a good impression. Lord knows I certainly didn't feel like deferring to anyone, least of all two undersea rulers who'd upended my life, regardless of the fact that, without both of them, I wouldn't exist. I scowled down at the floor, my head bowed.

"You must be Abermere's child," a low, mellifluous voice issued from the massive Junnes.

Surprised, I looked up, mindful enough to keep my eyes focused on his chin. The cerulean surrounding his eyes was carried over to his lips as well. He looked far more human than my grandfather, having a man's torso but octopus tentacles in place of legs. His tentacles pushed him forward, like a tank's treads, and he approached me. I kept my gaze locked on the hollow at his throat.

"What is your name, Child?"

I chanced a glance out of the corner of my eye at Learo, who had dropped my elbow but remained at my side. He gave a slight inclination of his head, so I answered. "Calliope."

"Come, Calliope, you do not need this meian's permission to answer my questions. As my servant, you should seek *my* permission," he corrected. His tone was firm. This guy was far more likely to be a Poseidon proto-type than my grandfather. One of Junnes' tentacles reached out and grasped my chin, forcing my gaze higher. I fought to keep from making direct eye contact. A wicked smile spread across his lips. "I see they cautioned you." His voice deepened, and he leaned in closer. "I do not need to mesmerize you. You will do as you are told, or there will be a war." His tentacle released my chin, shoving me back slightly.

"I didn't agree to go with you," I spat at him.

"You have no choice," he rejoined.

My grandfather cut in. "Enough! Calliope wanted this meeting to discuss your terms. As it is her future, I will allow her to take part as well."

Score one for Grandpa, I thought to myself.

Junnes studied me at length before he finally nodded his head. At that, my grandfather rose, and we followed him into an adjoining chamber, one much smaller than the throne room. The four of us settled into positions on the floor. Junnes opened the discussion with his expectations: I would serve as his advisor on human-related issues, going so far as to observe human sites to explain what was going on and help him understand the humans' logic behind the various marine endeavors they undertook.

Silently, I wondered to myself. I had been sure he was going to degrade me, visions of a repulsive alien slug monster lord and a stupid metal bikini having come to mind. Instead, he wanted me for my "expertise." Once he finished his explanation, I interjected. "I am no expert. Especially on what humans are doing in the ocean. I just started my studies," I explained.

"You have more expertise than anyone else here," Junnes countered. My grandfather scowled.

All things considered, Junnes' demands seemed pretty reasonable. I would serve as an advisor for two years, and then I would be released to my grandfather. Dagon ended the meeting by telling Junnes that he would have an answer in two days once I had time to consider all the angles.

I had other thoughts. I stopped Junnes, Dagon, and Learo with a single question. "What happens after two years are up?" Three heads swiveled toward me. My grandfather looked exasperated. Learo looked cautious. Junnes looked amused.

"After two years, Calliope," he answered, a strange tone to his voice. "You can return here to your grandfather." A pregnant pause. "Or you can go back to your life on dry land."

A tiny spark kindled to life in my chest. Keeping my face as blank as I could, I nodded, holding his gaze. His brows rose. "You will come with me and be my human advisor?" He glanced at Dagon.

"Yes, but I want three days with my grandfather before that."

Junnes considered that. "So be it," his deep voice rolled through the room, and then he took his leave. My grandfather's vehemence toward Junnes seemed markedly out of place. Our negotiations went well. He was calm and pleasant throughout my verbal poking and prodding.

My grandfather rounded on me. "You have not taken any time to consider the hidden traps in Junnes' words!" He turned then and shouted after his adversary. "I refuse to allow her word to be binding without further consideration."

"Grandfather, there could be any number of loopholes in Junnes' words. But I have no life on land while I am transformed as I am now. And if I refuse, he will wage war against you." I crossed my arms. "The way I see it, I made my own demands, and the terms seem clear to me. When this is all done, I can go back to my life."

His jaw hardened. He left without another word. Learo left with a parting shot. "I hope you know what you're doing, Princess."

"Stop calling me that!" I shouted to his retreating back.

The three days I had bargained for were useless. My grandfather spent little time with me, claiming that he had matters to settle for his people. I thought he was just mad that I made my own decision on the matter. Learo appealed to my sense by pointing out that my grandfather had risked war merely by coming to get me before Junnes could. I had weakened his position as a negotiator and as a ruler by cutting into the discussion. I felt a twinge in my conscience when Learo pointed that out.

The three days passed by so slowly, with my grandfather busy and Learo back to his own tasks. I should have just gone with Junnes that same day. I gave myself a shake and a mental pep talk. Surely, I could still communicate with my grandfather while I lived in Junnes' kingdom. I didn't know him well yet, but if we could correspond, we could build a relationship. Junnes seemed rather rational while we were discussing my terms.

My guide, yet another small meian, showed me to the large entrance of the castle on the third morning. Instead of Junnes collecting me, though, his pet kraken met me in the archway of my temporary home. I blanched. This was surely the same thing that had snatched me that fateful day in Lake Michigan. I scowled, thinking about it. It approached me, extending three of its tentacles to wrap around me. I looked around to say goodbye to my grandfather and Learo, certain they must be coming to see me off, but neither appeared to bid me farewell. A sour feeling took root in my chest.

Unlike last time, the tentacles were gentle as they gripped me. It looked at me through one giant, amber eye, its markings flashing in muted pastel colors in a gentle, soothing pattern. I relaxed into its grip as much as I was able. Taking my cue, it began to slowly move away from the platform. My eyes traced over the castle hidden in the marine fjord. I thought I saw movement on one of the large exterior ledges. I was too far away to be certain, but it looked like Dagon and Learo. I raised my hand in farewell. As our distance from the castle increased, so did the kraken's pace until we were racing through the ocean at unbelievable speeds. Even so, the journey seemed interminable.

The further we went from the continental shelf and the deeper the kraken dove, the less there was to see. I spotted some whales, sharks, and turtles in the beginning part of our journey, but we soon hit the midnight zone, then dropped further to the abyssal plains. My eyes struggled against the dark so far below the surface, and I could discern no other creatures in our race through the waters. The temperature dropped, but it wasn't long before I ceased to note the cold. I lost track of time. My mind began to wander.

With some surprise, I realized I could see light in the distance. Unlike the blue-green light at Dagon's castle, these lights were at the red end of the spectrum. I traced the shape of them and decided they looked like mountains. My eyebrows rose—we must have traveled quite a way indeed, as I guessed that we were now at the Mid-Atlantic Ridge. I shuddered to think how long it would have taken me had the kraken not done the hard work in transporting me. At my involuntary movement, the rest of its tentacles flailed outward, halting our forward momentum. I was maneuvered to the side so the giant eye could once again peruse me. Long moments passed before it started forward again at a much more sedate pace.

I was baffled that it seemed to be so mindful of me. Maybe this wasn't the same beast that had snatched me in Lake Michigan. My thoughts turned then toward my new home, at least for the next two years. The basalt rock face was pockmarked with caves, volcanic-looking lanterns dotting the terrain. The kraken made its way toward the base of the tallest basalt spire, which would have made the California redwoods look like saplings. Inside, the dark rock radiated a warmth that I assumed must be geologic in nature. I wondered if we were close to any volcanoes or fault lines. Pushing that concern aside, I focused on the room ahead.

It had a large opening, with two creatures I recognized from the roadblock at Dagon's castle standing guard on either side, wicked-looking spears held firmly across the opening. As the kraken approached, the guards raised the spears and allowed us to pass. I looked behind to see several creatures held back. We must have accumulated some curious spectators once we'd passed into Junnes' territory. The curiosity seekers all looked like a massive jumble of parts, the result of a zoologic mix-and-match game. I was reminded of the book of Greek myths sitting on my bedside table back home. One of my brows rose. *Maybe the Greeks weren't as mixed up about things as modern science likes to think.*

By the time I turned back around, the kraken had stopped. It was gently disengaging from my person as I stood to face Junnes. His massive throne was sculpted from basalt as well, with engravings along the front-facing edges. While studying me, he raised his arms. The guards allowed the crowd to flood into the hall, and they surrounded me, though they kept a respectful distance from my personal ferryman. The kraken stretched its long tentacles alongside me to keep the crowd at bay. Concerned I wouldn't be able to hide my reactions to the faces around me, I kept my eyes focused on Junnes.

He rose from his throne, standing tall on the dais, and raised his arms higher still. The crowd hushed. "I present to you the human-hybrid, Calliope."

A roar went up after the brief proclamation. I couldn't tell if it was from approval or disgust. Junnes lowered his arms, and the crowd began to disperse, though many remained to gawk at me. I stayed where I was, unsure of my next move. The problem was solved for me when a tentacle pushed the center of my back, propelling me toward Junnes as he moved around his throne to an archway concealed in shadows behind the dais. "Come along," he instructed.

I followed him through several rooms and down a few passageways before we arrived at a secluded part of the fortress. It was significantly warmer here. We must have moved closer toward the vents or volcano that supplied Junnes with heat and light. Junnes' fortress resembled many human fortresses - thick walls, high and narrow windows, and easily defensible. The room into which Junnes deposited me even had basalt furniture. My eyebrows rose yet again.

"Surprised, Calliope?"

"It's just so much different than Dagon's castle," I explained.

Junnes looked around. "I fashioned much of my kingdom on human architecture and building. The shipwrecks we have encountered have proven rich in detail about how humans live and work." He waved a hand, dismissing the subject. "These are your quarters. You will find another chamber beyond here that is strictly for your private use. You will restrict yourself to these two rooms. My people will bring their human problems to you here. You will determine how to solve those problems and set those plans in motion."

"Directing projects?" I shook my head. "You said I was going to be an advisor."

He turned to face me more fully. "You will advise by directing projects. We need to stop the damage humans are causing in the oceans. You are human. You know more about why and how they do these things than anyone else here."

I puffed up my cheeks as I blew out my breath. "No pressure."

His brows beetled. "No, the pressure here should not affect you, not with your hybrid nature now in effect. Do you feel ill?"

I felt absurd. "Ah, no. It's just a phrase."

He abruptly turned and moved further into the chamber to a passage that was hardly visible given the angle at which it had been carved into the wall. In it, there was a large pallet of seaweed. An underwater corollary of a bedroom, complete with bed, table, and chair. "You must be tired after your journey and your goodbyes. I will leave you to get settled in and rest."

"There were no goodbyes," I replied absently.

He said nothing more, and after a minute, he continued from the room. Exhausted, I made my way over to the pallet. The oblivion of sleep greeted me with a warm embrace.

My first day on the job was hectic. Several groups of what I came to know as generals and builders demanded my attention. I spent hours listening to their pitches before I could categorize and prioritize them. Junnes had supplied me with a diver's notebook and aqua pencil, so I was able to make plenty of notes. After each petition, I dismissed the creature from the crowded chamber. Eventually, I found myself alone at last. Junnes clearly didn't believe in easing someone into a new position.

When I returned to my bedroom, I found Junnes' hard countenance. He demanded to know what I had accomplished. I explained that I was still trying to sort out what problems I was facing. He said nothing, then left after several beats. I scowled at his back.

By the third day, many of the generals and builders were circling back through my chambers, begging for a chance to plead their case yet again. I managed to grab one of the small creatures that seemed to fulfill a servant role and asked how to gain an audience with Junnes. Hours later, Junnes appeared in the doorway to my bedroom as I was settling in to sleep. I sat up on the pallet when I saw him.

"What do you need?" he growled.

"An assistant. I can't coordinate all of these meetings AND prioritize projects AND educate on human factors."

"I see," he said cryptically. I waited for him to ask more questions, but when I had nothing further to say, he turned and left.

"Wow. Rude," I muttered under my breath. I had no idea what to make of his response. I wondered if he would send someone to help me or not.

"Do not insult me, Calliope," his voice carried back into my bedroom. My eyes widened. I was still not used to how well sound carried through water. Before I knew it, his large form filled the archway again. Flames danced in his eyes. "You will make your choice of project and begin resolving it tomorrow. That will be day one."

"What do you mean, 'day one?'" I shrieked. "I've been here four days! That's 726 days left!"

"No, Princess," he sneered. "Tomorrow is the first day where you will work to fix these problems. I said 'work' for two years. Not 'live here' for two years. The days you do not progress these projects will not be deducted from your agreement. You get no royal privilege here."

I stood on my pallet. "I *have* been working," I protested.

"No, you have been thinking and planning."

"You wanted solutions!" I shouted.

His jaw clamped, and the muscles along his face twitched. "You would do well to remember to whom you are speaking," he ground through clenched teeth, the flames in his eyes dancing higher and brighter. "You are a child."

"Yes, I am a child. I'm twenty-one years old!" Some of my anger dissolved. "I just decided what I was going to do with my human life. And now, thanks to you, it's not an issue," I tossed out.

His eyes narrowed. He suddenly invaded my space, gripping my arms with his human hands and squeezing in warning. "You know nothing of which you speak. You will *work* tomorrow. I will tally every day where you make progress. That will be the record of the days you will spend under my rule."

Angry and resigned, I groused. "Learo was right. I didn't take the time to consider the loopholes in your words."

"If you were given advice and chose to ignore it, that is no problem of mine." He gave me a small shake and released me.

Filled with despair, I threw myself down on my back on the pallet. *Make a deal with the Devil*, I counseled myself.

A month of Sundays, I thought. I felt that phrase very deeply in my soul now. I was ninety days into my stay at Junnes', yet only forty days of my servitude had passed. Junnes helpfully kept a tally on the wall in my bedroom. I found no sympathetic quarter in this realm. The closest I had to pleasant encounters was when I finally granted a general or builder permission to move on whichever plan we had charted. I chafed at the nitpicking terms of my agreement with Junnes, but he was right, as was Learo. I hadn't paid close enough attention to the details in my negotiations.

Junnes was taciturn at best. I was grateful to have my interactions with him restricted to his nightly counting of my markers, so to speak. The thought of spending nearly four years serving him, if my current pace held, galled me. The hatred I had seen blazing in both Dagon's and Learo's eyes for Junnes had kindled in my own chest.

After devising a way to dispose of old naval mines littering the Atlantic, Junnes once again violated my private chamber. I glared at him. He made his slash on my wall. "I want to send a message," I stated.

"No."

I counted to three in my head. "You can't stop me," I parried.

"You will find no one here willing to take your message. Not over the distance, and not to my enemy's province."

I ground my teeth to keep from calling him all sorts of names.

"When you can be useful and address the biggest issues we have, then maybe I would consider letting you send one message," he goaded me.

"Biggest issues?" My voice rose an octave. "I sealed leaking pipes from Russian oil rigs," I began to tick off with my fingers. "I dismantled the captivity pens the Russians use to hijack orcas. I figured out how to help seed coral colonies along the continental shelf in the Sargasso Sea!"

"Human problems," he dismissed.

"That's what you want me to solve!"

He advanced on me. "No, I want you to solve the problems that are important to *my* kingdom, *my* people. You would do well to check your temper. The last creature who dared show anger with me died a slow and painful death in the output from a volcanic vent. Do not tempt me. You have been more trouble than you are worth, all the way back to your useless father."

I took a beat before answering him. "I never asked to come here," I pointed out.

"No, you didn't. I took you." His look turned considering. "Maybe you need a point for comparison." With that, he wrapped a massive hand around my upper arm and dragged me along behind him. I tried to stop our forward progress any way I could, but I was no match for him. "I have been very lenient with you. Clearly far more than I should have been," he lectured. "It is time you see why your ancient ancestors whispered my name on the seas in fear."

"Your name?" I had a flash of insight to my first conversation with my grandfather. "Davy Jones," I breathed.

He rounded on me. "Yes, you have no life if not for me. I granted your father his greatest wish, to forsake his heritage and go among mortals on the sand. He went against our agreement and begat a bastard hybrid," he roared in my face. "He paid his end of the bargain, but if your worthless mortal life cannot benefit me, I will not hesitate to reap your life as well."

We had reached the infernal vents at the edges of Junnes' fortress. My entire body felt singed from the effects of the volcanic debris spewing into the surrounding water. While I was consumed with panic and pain, Junnes lashed me to a nearby anchor with a seaweed rope so thick and fibrous it resembled a jungle vine. He swam away without giving me a further chance to plead my case. I realized how much leeway he had shown me to this point. Swimming as far from the vent as the tether would allow, I gulped in the slightly fresher water. The dark depths of the abyssal plains abutting the Mid-Atlantic Ridge had encouraged my eyesight to grow more and more keen, and as my breathing slowed again, I looked around. Beyond where the anchor was mired, I saw a ridge crusted with mussels. Some fish appeared to be resting on the floor. Curious, I swam closer.

On the other side of the ridge, the water looked markedly different. I saw the shape of several bodies, some of them exotic beasts like those that served Junnes. Some were just ordinary sea life. All were frozen, completely intact. Horror washed over me. A brine pool. Maybe that was Davy Jones' Locker. Once something went into a brine pool, it never came back out again, just like the old sailor's legends about the Locker.

A second realization washed over me. Junnes may have agreed to only two years' service, but now that I had seen the way he would count those two years, I knew I would never be leaving Daevrey Junnes' kingdom. A numbness spread through me as I stared down the coming years of my life and the anoxic alternative.

From the corner of my eye, I saw a small, blue-green light bobbing. It winked out of sight. My entire being went on alert, and I kept my eyes trained on where it had been. It looked so much like the lanterns from Dagon's castle that my heart began to beat a staccato tattoo. *Had a meian followed me here?* I looked at Junnes' fortress before turning back to where I had seen the blue-green light. Maybe there was a third option after all.

ABOUT L.J. WYNN

L.J. Wynn is an emerging author with wide-ranging genre interests. She's dabbled in several genres and is recently feeling at home with speculative fiction, light horror, and fantasy. She is currently in Colorado, where she lives with her husband, kids, and cat.

Find out more at: LJWynnAuthor.wordpress.com

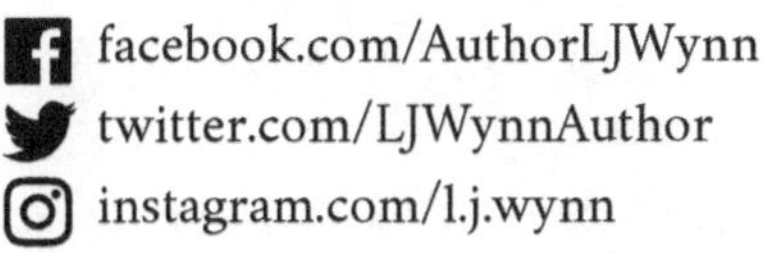

facebook.com/AuthorLJWynn
twitter.com/LJWynnAuthor
instagram.com/l.j.wynn

SIREN'S REVENGE
BY SABETHA DANES

CHAPTER ONE

This wasn't happening. It wasn't real life. I had to be stuck in a dream, or maybe one of the other factions had cursed me. We were at war with Lykaios, and anything was fair game during war—not that any of them knew I existed. *How would they?* The last time I made a public appearance with my family was during my mother's pregnancy announcement—pregnant with me, that is—thirty-six years ago.

Oh, Mom. Images of her mutilated body draped over her bed flashed across my mind. Half transformed, rib cage ripped open, heart missing. My father's head across the room from his own corpse, as if the killer had slit his throat, then hit one out of the park with his dismembered head. The dried blood splatters on the wall, and horrific facial expressions were frozen in my mind for eternity. I let my thoughts grasp hold of my being, my chest tightening the longer I lingered in the space that had been their healthy lives.

No, get it together, Cordelia. You'll be back in the water soon enough.

I couldn't go down this road, not again. The walls of the dressing room closed in around me. Panic rose in my chest. I looked around for someone to comfort me, but I was alone. The white room, with only a clothing rack, a vanity, and a full-length mirror, echoed my lonely sobs.

Our faction needed me to be a pillar of strength, but I didn't know how to be one. The only thing I was a pillar for was Nicole, the other half of my soul. *Where was she? She said she'd be here.* I pulled a tissue out of the box on the vanity, wiping my eyes, attempting to clean up the damage done to my makeup. Deep breath in, deep breath out. I could do this. I just had to get through this ceremony, then I could fall apart and mourn.

A light knock sounded at the small dressing room. "Come in."

Alice, my mom's—no, *my*—assistant, poked her head in the door. "We're almost ready for yo—oh no, you've been crying again?"

I looked through her, barely registering her words. They were always nonsense anyway. Do this, Cordelia, sit here, blah, blah, no one wants you to be queen, but you're what we got. She had a faux stroke when she saw what she was working with earlier this afternoon. My silver, chest-length, thin, damaged locks and sunken eyes from a sleepless night swimming around the coves did nothing to impress her. I didn't help matters by spending the first few hours crying. It took miracles to revive my pale face, though makeup couldn't fix my drawn expression.

She hurried over, shutting the door behind her to fix my face again. "You're going to have to stop this. Tears are not for royalty." Over the next thirty minutes, as she refreshed my makeover, she said the words "worst nightmare" and "how can this be Derya's daughter?" multiple times.

While my family had spent their days attending to the court and duties of siren royalty, I had focused on simple pleasures in life. Friendship, exploration, living life knowing I would never ascend to the throne. But here we were, getting ready to walk into my coronation. My body wanted nothing more but to be out of these clothes and to be swimming carefree through the coves surrounding Lake Marble Falls.

"Snap out of it, Cordelia!" Alice slapped both of my cheeks simultaneously.

I looked up at her, shock written across my face—the nerve of this woman! A million things crossed my mind to say to her, but I could only mumble something that had nothing to do with anything she spoke of. "Where's Nicole?"

"Who?" she asked as she pulled me to my feet, adjusting the wretched dress that had been forced on me. Someone had used at least five of their twenty-four-hour human-leg allotment driving into Austin and searching for a dress worthy of a coronation, and it made my heart hurt. Somewhere in my family's estate, there had to be a suitable dress. It didn't need to be hunted down. I winced at the memory of Alice's cackle when I told her to find something in the closet for me to wear.

"Nicole. Where is she? I told the guards to let her through when she arrived."

I squirmed as she adjusted the capped sleeves of the purple dress. The sequins itched my shoulders, and I couldn't wait to get it off. How humans lived restricted to their modest mindset, I never understood. The thought of not having to worry about clothes or being embarrassed about the naked body left me longing for the lake.

Though I had to admit, as much as I hated it, the dress suited me perfectly. Floor-length, with sequins starbursting from the bottom of the lace top layer, thinning out as it reached my knees. Purple strips of ribbon ran from the waist to the floor, glimmering blue as the light hit them right. The base of the dress offered tribute to our watery home through the sequins and ribbon, as it resembled many of my favorite things in the lake: various fish and shell shapes with small pearls to accent throughout.

"Oh right, that must be the trollop I sent on her way." Alice stepped back and gave me a once-over. "You'll have no time for that foolery. You're a queen now. It's time you start acting like one."

Without giving it a second thought, I raised my hand and slapped her across the face, backing up out of her reach once the connection caused her to stumble back. If I was truly queen, then I deserved respect. *Who did this servant think she was, speaking to me that way?*

I was the one who'd lost my entire family in one gruesome murder. *I* was the one being forced into a life I didn't ask for. Me. Not her, not the guards, not any other person in our faction.

Alice looked at me with disdain, touching her face where a red welt spread across her cheek. I'd never resorted to violence before, but I'd also never had a reason to. *My entire family dies, and this woman is stuck on what will the sirens think?* I don't give a shit what the sirens think. I am who I am.

"This is the last time you will speak to me in such a manner," I said. "I am not your charge, nor am I a child. This is my coronation and my faction. Is that clear?"

She stared at me for an agonizing minute, blinking, but I didn't relent. For the first time, I looked her over, taking in her disgruntled appearance, and wondered just how much time she spent out of the water. Did she only stay wet the required forty-eight hours, just long enough to get her legs back and continue to dictate the law around the estate? Her gray hair needed tender loving care from the lake instead of the tight bun she kept it in. I'd never seen such a dark and empty stare as hers. But I held eye contact for as long as it took her to let out an exacerbated sigh and agree to my terms.

"Good," I said. "See to it that Nicole is located and brought to me before the ceremony begins."

"Yes." She turned and headed to the door.

"Yes, what?" I asked, just to spite her.

"Yes, Your Majesty." She gave a curt bow and exited the room.

I let out a sigh and went back to the full-length mirror to admire myself. I was Queen of Drakos, of over one hundred sirens, spanning from the Gataki Dam to the Drakos Dam. I could do this.

As I paced the small room, I could hear the banquet hall filling up with members of our faction. With the ceremony being the only last-minute coronation our faction had ever performed, I did not expect that much of a turnout, but it sounded as if everyone had come out of the water to witness who exactly planned to take over.

Growing up royalty had been a different experience for me compared to my brother and sister. With two older siblings on their way to the throne, there was no need for my surprise arrival to change their lives. Thinking of them didn't bring the gruesome memories bubbling to the surface, as it did with my parents. The guards had spared me from seeing their bodies and those of their children. *Who would take out our entire lineage?* If this was the direction the factions were moving to rid themselves of each other, I did not want to partake.

A knock at the door brought me out of my thoughts. I glanced over to see Alice step into the room. "Your Majesty, may I present Nicole of Drakos." She spoke and bowed her head with more pomp and ceremony than I'd seen in my entire life.

What a farce, the absolute nerve of her. It took everything in me not to take my festering anger out on her by grabbing her bun and showing her exactly what that type of behavior would get her in the future.

As visions of slamming her head into the vanity toyed with my emotions, I said, "Send her in," keeping my tone and face neutral.

Since discovering my new lot in life, Alice had been nothing but overbearing, from organizing the ceremony to dictating my schedule for the next few days to me. I thought she only ever dressed my mother, but it seemed like she ran more of the show than I realized.

Nicole walked through the door and froze upon meeting my eyes. Instead of stepping forward, she gasped, raising her hand to her mouth in pure shock.

"That will be all, Alice." I spoke without taking my eyes off Nicole, her giddy disposition close to explosion.

"Yes, Your Majesty." Alice bowed again before leaving us. "Ten minutes."

We stood there frozen in the moment, waiting for Alice to close the door behind her. The pain of the day lessened the longer I took in Nicole's appearance. She was a sight for tired eyes. I had missed her lavender locks that curled when they were out of water, and where had she been hiding this beautiful seafoam-green formal dress? It complimented her body perfectly.

"Cordelia," she whispered, tears staining her eyes.

I ran over to her and embraced her. While less than six hours had passed since the intrusion of royal guards demanding I come with them, my heart said it was a lifetime ago. I longed for her comfort and supportive words.

"I'm so glad she found you," I whispered in her ear. "I worried you went back into the water without me."

She pushed away from me, giving my full body a once over. "And miss this? Never." After another quick embrace, she continued, "After that witch tried to send me away, I parked myself in the seat closest to this door, so I would be the first to see you come out. She tried to tell me my services were no longer needed. Like she even knows you."

I let out a sigh for the millionth time since meeting Alice. It was more than I'd sighed in my entire life, but words escaped me, my emotions were numb, and I just wanted to go back to the previous day when everyone was alive and thriving in their own lives. The many firsts for me overwhelmed my mind, creating too many threads of thought. Tears welled up in my eyes, and Nicole wiped them away.

"It's going to be okay," she said. "Don't smudge your face before you have to face the faction."

"Don't remind me," I groaned, attempting to blink away the tears threatening to push through. "I don't know if I can do this."

"Well, I know you, and I say you can. It's in your blood. You're Cordelia Drakos, Queen of the Drakos Faction, and you're going to kick ass at it."

"As long as you're by my side." I gave her a light smile and took her hands into mine, pulling her closer. She returned the smile and leaned her forehead against mine, whispering a barely audible *"always,"* allowing me to continue my train of thought: "Would you consider moving into the estate with me?"

She looked up at me in shocked excitement. "Is that allowed?"

"I'm Queen. Doesn't that mean I can do what I want?"

"I'd say so, but what do I know. I don't have the first clue about the laws of our faction."

"Me either," I said, laughing for the first time that day. "We can discover them together. If you'll have me, that is?"

"A thousand times, yes," she said, picking me up and spinning me around as I braced my arms on her shoulders. Once she slid me back down, and my feet touched the floor, I kissed her, letting the entire shitty day melt away from my bones, sinking into her embrace, and return kiss.

In our moment of ecstasy, we did not hear the door open or the few times Alice attempted to clear her throat. Finally, she half yelled, "Cordelia," before I glanced over at her, and removed myself from Nicole's arms, and smoothed my dress out. "It is time."

I glanced back at Nicole, whose face had turned a bright shade of red, and we shared a smirk before I walked forward to follow Alice into the banquet hall. Because of the uncertainty of the killer and the current war we were in, Alice rented the event center along the lakeside of Marble Falls. No faction could use their magic outside of water, and there were extreme laws against displaying any type of aggression in front of the humans. While she was about the most unpleasant person I'd met yet, she knew a thing or two about keeping our people out of harm's way.

Once I reached her, she whispered, "That is the exact behavior we will address this week. As the only royal, you will need to pick a male spouse from one faction we are not currently at war with. Unless your kiss can end five years of bloodshed? Your sisters couldn't."

Before I could respond, she opened the doors wide, and the rows of sirens turned back to see their new Queen. Many gasped and whispered as I walked the aisle, head held high, not letting them get to me.

Their lack of knowledge only helped me, no prejudgment, and more time to better figure out my place in the lake.

CHAPTER TWO

To my horror, Alice informed me on our ride back to the estate after the ceremony that the guards had cleaned none of the estate from the massacre. She had delegated the royal staff to coronation duties, leaving the blood coating from the rooms and grotto for later in the week.

I stepped in the front door to an eerie silence. No laughter of children at play, no people bustling through the house with a faction to run. Just the wind howling from a looming storm and silence. It chilled me to my core as Alice pushed past me to get on with whatever else she had to micromanage. With Nicole gone to our bungalow—miles away from the estate—I could only stand awkwardly in the entryway.

"Well, don't just stand there," Alice said, coming back into view. "Let's get that dress hung up."

I followed her obediently, unsure where to push back or go along with her guidance. Many things she said to me in the last twelve hours were out of line with my standards, but I wondered if she had spoken to my mother that way. I needed more information before dealing with her and a clearer state of mind.

The estate sprawled across five-thousand-plus square feet. Two main levels held the human living quarters and entertainment areas. Two more levels were sunken into the cliffside, the bottom level a grotto that fed back into the lake. The family had spared no expense when constructing the place, and from a boat's view, humans would never know the home held sirens. Since all sirens slept in the water, the house only featured two beds—a master and a guest—plus a bedroom-sized walk-in closet for the family. The other three rooms upstairs held offices for the family and staff.

We walked in silence from the entryway through the large room for entertaining, with floor-to-ceiling windows along the far wall and lush lounge chairs with side tables for eating in leisure as they discussed business or hosted parties. I followed her through the formal dining room, then into the industrial kitchen with a more intimate table. These rooms offered breath-taking views of the lake and woodlands across the way. It was still hard to grasp that I owned the house. Once on the other side of the kitchen, we went up the secret stairwell to the first room at the top of the stairs.

I thanked my lucky shells it was only the closet. The visions of blood splattered across my parents' room crept back into my thoughts. A shiver ran through my spine, and I hurried into the room. I didn't want to see it in person again, though pushing the images out of my mind proved to be more taxing than I could handle. I took deep breaths and stood still while Alice disrobed me, hanging the elegant dress in with the others. She placed the shell necklace worn by my mother at her coronation in the vault at the far end of the room, along with the matching earrings. Only having seen the jewelry in photos, having the pearl-filled pieces on my body added to the day's dream state.

Would Mom have been proud of how I handled today? Did she even think of me in her final thoughts?

"You may go," Alice said, not bothering to make eye contact with me. "Please stay in the grotto this evening. I will retrieve you early to start your lessons."

"Lessons?" I asked through tear-stained eyes.

"Unless you think you're informed enough to run the faction without assistance?"

I remained silent, unsure of how to respond or what lessons entailed. My school days focused more on math and language than on running the faction. Life skills, not negotiation skills, were my specialty. Lessons couldn't hurt, especially if they shed light on whether I could find a new Alice.

"I thought not," she said. She continued to organize around the closet as if my family would return from a long vacation any day now.

I turned and left her to it, giving a single glance to the end of the hall, to the master bedroom that held a king-size bed and bathtub almost as large. What were they even doing up here? We all had our own areas below the grotto, which was where the rest of my family's blood was soaked, but my parents—someone had walked upstairs and searched them out to murder them. Did the other factions know of our estate?

Too many questions ran through my mind. I raced through the four levels to the grotto and fell into the water the instant I reached the rock's edge. The faux human legs faded as they submerged, relaxing into a silver tail, with scales glistening in purples and greens throughout. I adored my colorings and felt lucky to have complementary tones. Not all sirens received the same luck, and I'd met a few who would give a right fin to change something about their features. The vibrant hues continued to my tail, side fins, and scales along my chest. Scales on each siren's body were unique to them. Mine started at my right armpit, under my breasts, and flowed across my ribs, then down my left side, stopping before my belly button, with a few patches on my back and arms.

Gills behind my ears sang at being introduced to water instead of air. I pushed forward through the current, swimming to the other side of the lake and back, enjoying the simple act of moving my tail in a rhythmic pattern to get to each shoreline. I didn't stop swimming until my chest hurt more from exhaustion than heartbreak. I reached my alcove under the grotto, a place I rarely ventured anymore. I sank onto the slab of rock my father had carved for me many years ago, during my enilikíosi ceremony, the time when siren children become adults, spread their fins and leave the protection of the family.

Each alcove offered an opening towards the base of the lake where we could swim up into a private sleeping slab. Most sirens didn't hoard possessions, and only prominent families within the lake had the human status to build into the cliffside. The rest of the faction slept wherever they fell asleep on the lakebed. With the guard patrolling the border between factions, there was little to fear while sleeping. As a young adult, I felt special for having a space to myself. It became the place I'd retreat to during a nasty breakup or to leave my favorite rocks. Thoughts of someone invading my siblings' alcoves to murder them as they slept seeped back into my mind. The pain of losing everyone I cared for in a single swoop crashed into me. With no reason to stay strong, I let go of the dam, completely falling apart for the second time that day.

I cried heavy sobs, each laborious gill-full in hurt more as I pushed through the pain to expunge my anguish until a hand touching my shoulder startled me into sitting up. Nicole took me into a deep embrace, and a fresh wave of tears came forward.

"Let it out," she transmitted. "I've got you."

"I'm beyond lost," I transmitted. "This wasn't supposed to happen. We had our whole lives planned out. Me becoming queen wasn't in the cards."

"Sometimes, life shuffles the deck and slips in a few new cards. We'll get through this."

We laid down together, her big spoon to my little, and she held me until I fell asleep.

Each dream that night had me moving through each alcove and room, experiencing the death of my family one by one, screaming out for the person cloaked in darkness to stop. *I need them. Please don't take them from me.* A sharp pain spread throughout my body, as if the person killed me instead, causing me to wake with a startle, only to fall back into the dream once Nicole calmed my panicked state.

"Noooo!" I screamed, choking on the unexpected influx of water into my mouth.

I blinked in confusion, looking around the alcove but only seeing muck. Any given day, sirens had perfect vision in the depths of the lake. Our second eyelids added clarity to our vision and kept our eyes clean of debris, but mine were failing me. The pain of my latest experience of my sister's death stayed heavy in my heart, and I shook myself out of the dream.

Pain continued to radiate from my tail. I tried to flip it to get the feeling back in it, but I let out an agonizing wail as soon as I attempted to move the muscles.

Was I still dreaming? Or . . .

I felt around for Nicole, and she wasn't on the rock with me. My heart seized up and panic set in as I continued to search for her body. No, no, no, not again. I slipped from the rock onto the floor of the alcove, unable to stop myself. Between the pain in my lower tail and the confusion of my dream-riddled mind, I surrendered to the horrifying notion that someone had hurt me. Maybe kidnapped Nicole while they were at it? I couldn't lose her too.

"Nicole?" I transmitted in full panic mode.

"On my way back, are you okay? Someone was in the alcove with us. I tried to catch them, but they got away. They threw something in the water, like a ton of grime from the bottom of the lake. Made it impossible to pick out their features."

"My tail," I whimpered. "I don't think I can swim. It feels like something's in it."

She swooped in, startling me all over again, and scooped me up to take me to the grotto. We broke the surface, and she lifted my waist, shoving me as far as she could onto the slide-like incline out of the semi-circle lake opening. Once she moved herself up next to me, she pulled my tail onto hers, keeping both in contact with the lake.

"What's happening?" I cried as we emerged from the water. "I thought you died."

"I'm right here. We'll get through this," she said. Her voice remained calm, but the panic in her eyes spoke volumes. "Can you contact Alice?"

I looked around the grotto, unsure of how my family contacted her when they needed her. The rock bed held six smooth lounge chair crevasses carved into the floor along the back wall, facing an inset pool for the kids to swim without fear of the lake or adults to sit shoulder-deep and relax. The room sat a foot below the lake level to keep the floor under water with a single stone staircase leading up to the next level, where a full-size pond-swimming pool and outdoor kitchen, and plush seating sat. I attempted to transmit, not seeing any other obvious way to get staff attention.

"Alice, I need in you the grotto, emergency."

There was a long pause as Nicole examined the wound in my tail.

"I don't know how to tell you this, don't freak out on me, okay?"

"I'm not sure I could freak out more than my current state," I said.

"Someone slammed a nail with a note into your tail."

"Someone what?! Can you pull it out? What does it say?" I asked. "The pain is excruciating. I don't know how much longer I can take it."

"I'd rather wait for a healer. Take a deep breath," she said as she scraped something along my scales. "It says 'Relinquish your rights to the throne or die.'"

"Pull it out," I cried, realizing for the first time that our faction lost its healer with the death of my father. Instead of reminding her of this, I took a deep breath and reassured her, "I'll figure it out. Just pull it out."

"Okay, okay." She took in a deep breath, and I felt her hand close around the spot on my tail that hurt the worst. Her other hand braced my fin. "If you're sure?"

"Do it." I sucked in a deep breath, and as soon as my lungs were full, she pulled, wiggling gently as she went.

A wave of relief washed over me, followed by the sting of the water filling the space where the nail had been. I reached to my tail. Nicole realized I wanted to put my hands on the wound and used the hand not holding the nail and note to push me forward.

"θεραπεύω," I whispered as soon as my palm connected with the blood-filled scales.

Nothing happened, and I cursed under my breath. Not having practiced a single incantation, I shouldn't have been surprised, but it hurt more to know that I either had to figure this out or ask a fellow faction for assistance. I had witnessed my father heal dozens of wounds as a child. It was in my blood. I took a deep breath and focused my mind, clearing out the pain. I could do this. Verifying I had my hand and the wound submerged under the water, I tried again.

"θεραπεύω."

Nicole gasped as the scales under my hand illuminated with bioluminescence and the wound closed with a blue glow.

"You did it," she whispered.

"I did it," I agreed, letting out a long sigh of relief.

As the pain subsided, we scooted ourselves into the lounge chairs, and I passed out from exhaustion, my last vision that of Nicole settling into the chair next to me and her light orange scales with smatterings of greens and pinks flowing throughout her tail. She'd never know how much comfort being near her gave me.

CHAPTER THREE

While Alice never responded to my plea for assistance the previous night, she was the only siren in the room when I awoke screaming the next morning.

"Oh, you're alive," she snipped as she flipped through paperwork atop a low table next to me.

"No thanks to you," I replied. I gathered my bearings and took stock of my location and the lack of Nicole.

"Before your plaything left, she mentioned something about an attack."

"My mate is hardly a plaything, and it would behoove you to stop addressing her as such."

Alice cackled. "Mate? Unlikely. It would behoove *you* to cut ties with bottom feeders before the other factions find out about your weakness."

This woman truly believed she knew the history of the royal family. I turned my body to face her, and as I did, I realized my tail felt fully healed. "Do you honestly think I, the daughter of Derya, would use the term 'mate' incorrectly?"

"That is yet to be determined." She continued whatever she was working on, giving little effort or emotion to the conversation at hand.

"Being as you weren't present when my mother performed the rituals, it's more likely that you're clueless about my life."

"No royal heir in the history of the Lower Colorado River Gerousía has ever mated without the ability to produce heirs. You would know that if you would have been taking lessons instead of gallivanting around as a child."

"You would know I never received the onomasía rituals if you weren't little more than a dressing maid."

She didn't flinch at the insult, to my dismay. A guard walked into the room carrying a low table identical to Alice's and placed it in front of me, cutting our conversation short.

"After you sign these documents, Noah will bring your breakfast. Eat fast. We have a busy day ahead of us. You do know how to write your name?"

She handed me the folder and a pen. I wanted to rip them from her and toss them in the lake, just to prove my rank over her. But more than that, I wanted to read them. I took the documents with more force than necessary.

"Yes," I sneered. "I have a signature."

"Good, I'll summarize them for you before I depart to check on the barrier."

"I'll read them myself, thank you."

"Right. . ." She smirked. "If you want to sign them without comprehending them, that's fine as well. They just need to be signed before I get back."

Oh shit, she believed I couldn't read or write. Did she think my parents threw me to the commoners after I became of age to handle myself? The more she pushed for me to sign them, the more I wanted to read every word of each document.

While most sirens did not know how to read or write—it didn't matter to the average siren's way of life—I took basic lessons throughout my youth. Though I would never see an office or official duties, my father wanted me to be a step ahead, just in case. Like he predicted, this day would come. I needed to play the situation right and not give her too much knowledge of just how capable I was.

"Fine, enlighten me," I said.

"The first one is verifying that you are of sound mind and body and are taking over the faction as its queen. The next couple are death certificates for each of the fallen, and the last few are regarding ownership of bank accounts, property, and stocks."

"Simple enough," I said, examining the pages before me.

"I will return in an hours' time, and we will begin the overview of the factions' current standings."

"How do I get in touch with the guards, or you for that matter, when I need you?"

"Transmission is fine."

"Why didn't it work last night?"

"I am not here to comfort your nightmares."

"Someone attacked me, you imbecile!" As I spoke, my face transformed.

Never had I been angry enough to trigger the root of all sirens. The reason we were at war. It was another path not in my original cards, but Alice took it too far. My single row of incisors grew, elongating to an impossible length that wouldn't allow for closing my mouth completely. By the look of shock on her face, I figured my lilac irises had turned black, and the tone in my voice as I spoke scared even me. It echoed yet sounded hollow.

"I am your Queen. You must meet my plea for assistance with prompt response. If you cannot do your duties, tell me now. If this happens again, you will not live for a third chance."

"Yes, Your Majesty." She bowed her head and kept it lowered until I dismissed her.

Once she swam from the grotto, I sank back into my lounge chair, and my face relaxed back into place. The horror on her face was worth the pain of the transformation, though I didn't know what it meant for my future.

Would I crave the rush of anger, as they said Lykaios did? Would I develop the taste for human flesh? Were those rumors even true? What was I becoming? This wasn't me.

Repulsion filled my bones, and it took everything in me not to vomit. I didn't know how to process any of it, and I lacked a mentor to guide me through this new life. Everything was happening too quickly. I needed time to understand the past twenty-four hours. But there wasn't time. It would have to wait until I had the lessons or time to comb the library. I looked at the documents. Maybe they would be a decent distraction from the shitshow of a morning. They weren't going to read and sign themselves, anyway.

I let out a deep breath and reached out to Nicole, unsure if I should let her know about the transformation. "Are you okay?"

"Yes," she transmitted instantly. "I didn't want to wake you nor argue with Alice. I left to check our traps. Would you like me to bring you breakfast?"

"She is becoming quite the pain in the ass," I transmitted, still lost in thought on my lashing out. I shook myself out of the funk I was falling into and continued, "They're bringing me breakfast here. Just wanted to make sure you were okay."

"Sounds good. You have nothing to worry about. Also, I took the note to our spot. Try to have a good day, okay?"

"You too, my perch. Thank you for taking it with you. Glad one of us is of sound mind."

"I got you."

I flipped through the pages to find all the death certificates. Each one was, as Alice stated, a simple certificate with dates, cause, and other official notations. I signed them all and placed them back in the folder, not letting my gaze stop on the cause of death for more than a second. Murder. Each time I saw the word, the red from the bedroom walls flashed through my mind.

The last three documents written in legalese listed more fascinating information. Alice had led me astray in her assessment of what these documents stated. The first did have me taking over power from my mother, but with the bonus of a five-year probation period overseen by Alice herself. At the end of the period, if I did not meet her standards, all power would transfer to a ruler of her choosing. To top it off, they would require me to perform the onomasía ritual for this unknown person. After that, the bank, stock, and asset documents led to more of the same doublespeak of me agreeing to relinquish my birthright in the event that I did not meet Alice's standards of a queen.

This woman was something else. I looked up to the ceiling of the grotto and thanked my father for forcing me to sit through mind-numbing education all those years ago. My life could have only gotten worse from here without them. I piled the pages back into the folder and set it aside, calling Noah to bring me breakfast.

He brought in a serving tray moments after my transmission and quietly placed a plate and glass on my table. After he left me, I went to take a drink of what I assumed was water but second-guessed myself. Any time my parents ate, they said something over their food. With the notion that Alice was up to something, it wouldn't hurt to be a bit more cautious around all the staff.

But would the incantation work for me? What was it they said? Think, Cordelia, think.

I dipped my right hand in the lake and touched the glass with my left. Concentrating on the drive to discover if my food was poisonous, I whispered, "δηλητήριο."

Bioluminescence sprung to life around my submerged right hand, while the glass on my left glowed red. I let go of it in a flash, breaking the connection. Red had to mean the liquid inside contained poison. My parents' food always glowed green after they performed the incantation over it.

Tears threatened to push through, but I shook myself. I couldn't keep falling apart every time something happened. At this rate, I would spend my days crying while someone got closer to killing me. There wasn't time for it, and I would die before letting my family's life work go to waste over me being too sad to get it together.

"Noah, you and the person who prepared this food are needed in the grotto immediately."

"Yes, your majesty."

Within minutes, two men appeared before me. They stepped into the submerged grotto, water lapping their ankles. It took a considerable amount of concentration to remain in human legs when a siren touched the lake. Them standing to my left in wait of instruction impressed me more than I let on. I adjusted my tail in my lounge chair as I let the silence stretch on.

The healthy body of the second man screamed he was the chef, as he looked to enjoy eating as much as I did. Noah's chiseled form was a stark difference. The man had muscles for days, from his shoulders to his calves. After giving them a moment to sweat it out, I broke the silence.

"Who prepared this meal?" I asked, calm and collected.

"I did, Your Majesty," said the man I took to be the chef, with his head bowed.

"What is your name?"

"Ben, Your Majesty."

"Ben, would you mind drinking this?"

"Of course, Your Majesty." He picked up the glass without hesitation.

"And Noah, please, eat this plate of food."

"Yes, Your Majesty." He picked up the plate, eyeing it with more caution than the chef.

I eyed them both. As one raised the glass to his mouth and the other a fork, neither man looked shaken. Perplexing, to say the least. Ben took a sip, and Noah ate. Neither broke a sweat. We turned at a splash from the front of the grotto to see Alice emerge from the water.

She took in the scene with utter indifference and situated herself next to me again. After the chef finished the glass, he placed it back on my tray, and we waited. Noah ate the last piece of fresh catfish and returned the plate as well. No one saying a word. They waited for my next order. But I didn't give either man the satisfaction of an answer. We just needed to wait and see if my incantation rang true.

Within minutes of finishing, both men showed problems staying at attention. I let them fall to the grotto floor, curious if Alice would put a stop to it, but she didn't. She picked at her nails like murder was just another day of the week.

Could I heal both men, or would I have to choose?

Once the convulsions set in, it was time. Since no one was going to speak, I scooted forward in my lounge chair until I could slip into the kiddie pool and pushed myself towards the men lying between the pool and the grotto opening, threatening to fall in.

Both transformed out of their human form before I reached them, their tails twitching with each scream of agony. The muted blue with flakes of lighter blues in Noah's tail, and black with flakes of muted greens and yellows in Ben's, flashed before me as I hurried over to them.

I placed one hand on each stomach and concentrated on removing the toxin from their bodies as I whispered, "θεραπεύω."

Bioluminescence surrounded my hands, and Alice let out an audible gasp behind me. Instead of acknowledging her, I kept my focus on each stomach glowing blue. The convulsions stopped, and they quieted to a light whimper. After each displayed signs of being on the other side of the poison, I returned to my seat, pondering my next move.

The silence stretched between us for more than thirty minutes. Eventually, each man sat up at the edge of the grotto, breathing deeply but not making eye contact with anyone. Once everyone recovered enough to discuss the situation, I broke the silence.

"Would anyone care to explain how my food came to be poisoned?"

No one answered me. Not surprising. Alice had more going on than she wanted to let me in on, and I was pretty sure neither of the men knew they would be poisoned by consuming the food.

"No worries," I smiled, meeting Alice's eyes. "I relieve you two of duty until your next shift. Please get some rest."

"Yes, Your Majesty," they said in unison and dropped off the edge of the grotto, swimming out of sight.

I turned to Alice, who was still picking at her nails, and asked, "Who created these documents?" I held up the folder.

"The family lawyer, among the humans." She didn't look up from her fascinating cuticles.

"Great," I said.

It would be easy enough to meet with this person once I could get my legs back and formulate new documents without Alice's oversight. I couldn't wait to discover what she'd told them was the reason for the clauses.

"If you signed them, I can have one of the other guards file them away?"

"It would be lovely if someone could place them on my desk," I said.

"Will you be requesting a second breakfast tray?"

"No, thank you. It seems it would be best if I sourced my own food for the time being."

"Very well," she said as another man walked into the room to retrieve the folder. "Are you ready for the faction overview?"

His scaleless body mimicked Noah's in the tone department, leaving me curious about their workout routines. I repeated where I wanted the folder to go, then thanked him before returning my attention to the question at hand.

"Yes," I said.

"Since you missed out on your entire education, I'm only going to give you quick notes to get you up to speed. Over the next few years, you will have to make time to get acquainted with the inner workings of the factions and Gerousía."

I gave a slight nod and stayed silent as she spoke, figuring it would be better for her to continue to think I was clueless about our culture and structure.

"Over the past century, the humans reworked our rivers to create basins of water to fuel their expansive nature. Sirens took advantage of these creations, using them as borders instead of constantly battling over territory. Our Gerousia oversees five factions: Aetos, Matsouka, Lykaios, Drakos, and Gataki. The two you will have the most interaction with are Lykaios and Gataki due to them sharing borders with our faction. The humans have their own names for these areas. You will be required to know them. Any questions?"

I shook my head no, and she continued.

"The current war with Lykaios boils down to a difference of opinion on how sirens should behave, regarding the humans, and in how to preserve the lakes best. You will have to analyze both sides of this disagreement and make the choice to either continue to follow the road your parents paved or revert to sirens' past ways of life."

"What are your thoughts on the arguments?" I asked, genuinely curious.

"Sirens are creatures of the river. Governments, laws, and forcing adults to follow rules is a disgusting human theme that should not taint the waters of our lakes. Factions were formed to give sirens the freedom to live their lives without having to worry about the dangers of humans or petty territory disputes."

"Fascinating." She wasn't wrong. Too much government oversight meant sirens in charge were pushing their personal beliefs onto other sirens for the sake of forcing them to conform to beliefs that weren't their own. Any siren could apply to transfer to a faction that held views aligned with their own. If each faction upheld its own views, like-minded sirens would seek them out.

"Any other questions?"

"Oh, umm, yes." I gathered my thoughts before continuing. "Are the Lykaios the monsters the rumors make them out to be?"

"That was your first time transforming?" She smirked to herself and cleared her throat before answering. "It is a shame your parents didn't feel the need to teach you the basics of siren physiology."

I shrugged, and she continued speaking.

"All sirens have the ability to become a seiréna. It takes a moment of pure anger and emotional overload to trigger the first transformation. Then the siren can practice doing it at will. Your personal song emerges shortly after the first time. It will lure humans and prey alike to you. I assume your question is more wondering if you are now one of those evil Lykaios?"

I continued giving her a blank stare instead of rising to the trap she laid out.

"Well, you can sleep tonight knowing no siren is evil just because they can become a seiréna at will. One could call you evil because you almost killed Noah and Seth today. Did you do that because of the transformation, or would you have tested your food on the staff, regardless? Evil is in the eye of the beholder, and you, little mermaid, are far from evil."

Ouch—the deepest insult to a siren. Mermaid. A bunch of seafaring hippies, not a single fin of assertiveness in the lot of them. Was she trying to rile me up? I was no mermaid, and I'd prove it one way or another.

At that, she scooted to the grotto's edge. "I'll be doing my lunchtime border check, please be back in the grotto in two hours, and we will continue discussing the fate of your faction."

CHAPTER FOUR

I laid against the rock of the underwater falls, scoping out the exit to our grotto from afar. I beat Nicole to the meetup location, as Alice did not have as much dirt to tell me regarding our own faction as I had predicted. My thoughts went over the day as I awaited her arrival.

The rest of the day dragged on for me, aside from lunch with Nicole, where I spilled my transformation woes and what Alice told me before breaking the news about the almost poisoning. Nicole took it better than expected, but a glimmer of rage boiled in her eyes.

We decided tailing Alice for the evening might prove enlightening or at least give us a better glimpse into who she hung out with during her off-hours. She held the only spot on our list of suspects, though I did not think her writing matched the note slammed into my tail.

"Coming up behind you," Nicole transmitted.

I smiled in relief. Laying alone in a sea of mated sirens was my least favorite activity. The underwater falls in the middle of the lake were a favorite spot of all, as they offered lounge-like relaxation and ample place to spread out or tuck away. It gave everyone a place to socialize without having to reveal their secret lurking places along the lake.

"No movement yet," I transmitted as she snuggled up beside me.

"Wonder what time she usually leaves."

"Not sure, maybe she lives near the house? I left when Simon brought her a plate of food."

"Guess you're not going to be eating at the estate for a while?"

"Not until we can figure out who poisoned me."

"Why don't you just fire her?"

"I considered it, but she may prove valuable if she isn't the one trying to kill me. I'm not against her ideas for our faction's future peace, and she's knowledgeable. Though it comes at the cost of her speaking down to me."

"Spoken like a true queen." She leaned her head against my shoulder.

"Tomorrow, I'm going into the human town to speak to our lawyer."

"We have a lawyer?"

"You do realize the estate is your home now, right?"

"Still surreal, mostly because I keep getting chased out."

I sighed and leaned my head on hers. Alice and I still had not addressed the catfish in the room in regards to Nicole and heirs. We both had the capability of having children, and with the onomasía ritual, blood didn't matter. The children Nicole birthed would have the same lineage as my own flesh and blood.

"Hey," she transmitted, lifting to make eye contact with me. "I'm only teasing. I know it will all get sorted out. Don't stress about me. I have our spots to go to when the witch is on guard."

I gave her a smile that turned into a concentrated grimace as I saw movement at the grotto base from the corner of my eye.

"She's leaving," I transmitted, keeping my eyes locked on Alice's gray and green tail.

"Looks like she's on a mission. Better try to stay close."

Nicole took lead, and we swam through the bed of sirens too busy in their own conversations to notice their queen swimming among them. Alice headed downriver towards the river split. Many sirens steered clear of the river channel because the lake shallowed up quickly, and if we weren't on guard, a human could spot us from shore.

"Wonder what she'd do if she caught us following her?" I transmitted.

"Lecture you on how unbecoming it is for a queen to follow her staff?"

I laughed at the idea, but it was likely true. According to her, Alice spent an obscene amount of time telling me exactly how to be a queen. I didn't want to believe my mother allowed her to speak with such authority. Either Alice always spoke her mind, or she planned to control the daft little queen that couldn't read or write, making herself the real voice of the faction.

Nicole stopped and abruptly darted inside a robust crop of giant cutgrass. I was lost in thought, and she grabbed my arm before I swam past her. Alice, a yard in front of us, swam into the mouth of the split but didn't go out of sight. A few feet from the entrance, she disappeared under the eave of the bank.

"Let's get closer," Nicole transmitted.

I nodded and followed behind her, keeping my eyes on the entrance. We wove between other sirens as Nicole looked for the best spot to rest and wait. After circling the bank four times, she settled on nestling into a bed of giant cutgrass across from the eave. I hoped the thick vegetation hid our colors enough not to draw attention.

"Look." Nicole pointed to the corner across from us. "That guy is up to something."

I brushed a few silver strands of hair out of my way as I peered through the thick blue-green blades of grass. Someone swam towards us, hugging the bank and glancing around. The man did a few loops in and out of the channel as if his goal was to catch dinner. But once assured no one watched, he swooped into the same eave as Alice.

"Does he look vaguely familiar to you?" I transmitted.

"Now that you say that, he does. Kind of like that prince from Lykaios, you know, the one that lost his wife in the last raiding party they sent over Lykaios dam."

"That's right. He was present at the vigil my parents held. You should be the one that is queen. You know all the dirt."

She nudged me while transmitting, "That's why I'll make a good right hand to your leadership."

"How these factions can kill each other, then pretend to be friends for the sake of mourning, I will never get."

"It's just gross. Either hate us or don't."

Sounds of water moving around us lingered in the silence. I didn't want to continue my parents' war. Alice made valid points about letting the sirens vote with their allegiance to which faction they wanted to represent. Who were we to judge another's way of life? That was, assuming she spoke the truth on transforming, not altering sirens' mental state and make them deranged."

"Should we get closer?" Nicole transmitted, pulling me out of my thoughts.

I blinked a few times, realizing she wanted to cross the channel, then agreed. She led the way as we crossed the entrance to the split-off, then swam into the brush of the bank, inching closer to the opening of the eave. We ended up having to get right next to the entrance to peer into the eave. They had scooped the dirt out, making a perfect cave. We could barely make out the two figures in the back of the cave lying atop each other.

"Do you see those chests?" I transmitted.

"They must have weighted them to stay on the lakebed like that."

"Wonder what's in them?"

"I swear the longer we're here, the more questions I have."

"The real question is, do I have enough to confront her?" I transmitted.

"Not really. As much as I don't like the witch, this is her downtime. She can do whatever she wants."

"True enough."

We watched them cuddle for an hour before movement snapped us both to attention. The two sirens swam towards the entrance, hand in hand. They paused to kiss before exiting, and I looked around, wondering if someone could spot us. Nicole had the same idea as she pulled me back, and we made a break for the open lake before the two lovebirds left their hideaway.

As soon as we were back in the middle of the lake, we both stopped and let our weight sink us to the lakebed. Plumes of grime exploded around us as we landed. I rolled to face Nicole, barely able to see her form as the dust held in the current.

"That was close," I transmitted.

"Nah," She transmitted. "They were pretty strung up in each other. We probably could have swum across the front of the eave without them noticing."

"Alice and Prince Struan, who'd of thought."

"Can't be sanctioned by King Malik. I mean, they wouldn't be hiding if it was, right?"

"Definitely not," I transmitted. "From what I've heard of the Lykaios faction, he runs a strict household when it comes to bloodlines. My parents had to submit a full lineage panel when Chantara married Monroe."

Thoughts of my siblings swarmed my mind, taking over the conversation. Loch could never see his children grow up, and Chantara never got the chance to birth her first child. She shouldn't have even been at the grotto. Why was she visiting from the Lykaios Faction? Tears formed at the corners of my eyes, mixing with the lake water. I closed my eyes and rolled onto my back, letting my tail stretch out.

It'd been months since I'd spoken to either of them, not that we were close during childhood. Them with their lessons, and taking on responsibilities, and me with learning the way of the non-royal members of our faction. I never felt unwanted or unloved—I followed my path, and they theirs. If I would have died instead of them, would they have missed me?

A light kiss brushed my cheek, and I opened my eyes to see Nicole leaning over me, concern across her features.

"Sorry," I transmitted with an embarrassed smile. "It hit me again. They're gone. They're really gone."

Sobs broke through my attempts to keep my calm, and Nicole scooped me up into a hug.

"Don't be sorry. The unthinkable has happened, and it's okay not to be okay about it."

I leaned into her embrace. "Thank you for being here."

"Always, my perch."

She lay with me on the lakebed until my heart slowed and my thoughts calmed. I didn't want to think about how I would have survived this ordeal without her by my side.

"How am I even going to sleep tonight?" I transmitted.

"Not to worry." She kissed my forehead. "I've napped throughout the day. You will get a full night's rest. Just tell me if you want the cove or the grotto."

"Grotto," I transmitted immediately. "I'd rather not go near the coves for a bit. At least not until we figure out who's after me."

"I was thinking about that. I wonder if you should reach out to King Malik and let him know about his son? Are you still planning on seeing the lawyer tomorrow?"

"I am. I don't want to make waves with Alice until I speak to them. Just in case they have more evidence for or against her."

"Smart thinking," Nicole transmitted as we swam through the schools of minnows and other sirens. "See, you're already thinking like a queen."

I couldn't help but roll my eyes. I was the last person in this lake to be considered queen material.

CHAPTER FIVE

The night went off with no attempts on my life, and I thanked the shells for a full night's sleep. After a quick breakfast of white bass with Nicole, we parted ways so she could get some sleep and I could prepare for an adventure in the human community.

For the first time since my coronation, I ventured into the estate, pausing in the kitchen to decide if I was truly alone. Did the guards only occupy the home when Alice was present?

I loved my parents' elegant style. Each room had a touch of the sea, with modern human comforts. Blues, light browns, and white filled the color palette of the home. Running my hand along the banister, I climbed the stairs to the top level. My heart slowed as I reached the landing, looking down the hall to the now closed door of my parents' bedroom. One day, I'd have to deal with that room, but it would not be any time soon. Especially, not alone.

The sea-blue hallway led to the walk-in closet, guest bedroom, and office on the right wall, with the left wall holding two other offices and a guest bedroom. My parents had shared the last office on the right side, and I beelined for it, hoping with all my might that the adjoining door to their room had been closed by the staff. As I rounded the doorway, I let out a sigh.

On my mother's—my—desk, sat the folder of legal documents. Perfect, now I just needed to figure out human clothes and how to get to the office. The lack of assistance Alice provided in navigating communication with the staff and picking up where my mother left off expanded with each day. Regardless of whether she was behind the threats against my life, it seemed less and less likely that I would keep her on.

I lifted random papers on the desk, looking for something that resembled a contact list. After opening a few desk drawers, I discovered a small leather binder filled with names, locations, and phone numbers. Now I just needed the person's name. I flipped to the L's, no luck.

Maybe it was written on the contract?

Looking through the folder, I found the lawyer's name at the bottom of the first page. Vivian Davis. Next to her name in the contacts, my mother's handwriting left a note in capital letters: "MAKE AN APPOINTMENT." *Thank you, Mother.* I picked up the wireless phone on her desk and dialed the number listed.

"Thank you for calling the office of Vivian Davis. How can I assist you?"

"I'd like to make an appointment for today if possible."

"May I ask who's calling?"

"Cordelia Drakos."

Muffled conversation came through the line as I waited for her reply.

"Yes, ma'am, we can fit you in at one-thirty. Will that be okay?"

"It'll be perfect."

"Great, we'll see you then, have a good afternoon."

That was easy enough.

I set the device back in its charger while my stomach fluttered with anticipation and nerves from using it. Now to figure out how to get there and what to wear. I grabbed the folder and headed to the closet. Since the meeting would be in an office, I opted for black slacks and a professional-looking purple top. I had to take everything back off, having forgotten to put on undergarments the first time around. Humans. How did they live this way?

Unsure of what time it was, once I was dressed, I walked back to the office. The clock read almost twelve-thirty. Just an hour until I needed to be there, wherever "there" was. I picked the leather book up and noted the address under Vivian's name. Too bad I didn't know the name of the siren that drove us to the ceremony.

I sat in the chair in front of the desk, and my eyes caught the signature on a white card atop the desk. I picked it up, curious why King Malik would send my mother anything.

Derya,

We thank you for holding a memorial within your Faction for Amaya.

To most, she displayed the strength and heart of a true warrior, but to us, her family, we will miss the softer side not known to most.

I can only hope you meant your display as an olive branch to peace between our factions.

Let's meet soon to discuss,

Malik Lykaios

I set it back down exactly as it was, feeling like I shouldn't have been snooping, but shook the idea out of my mind. The desk, and its contents, belonged to me. I would have to snoop through the entire office at some point. I looked around the room, starting at the door. I scanned over the bookshelf-filled wall that wrapped around the first corner of the room and stopped at my father's desk. The next wall held floor-to-ceiling windows displaying a magnificent view of Lake Marble Falls. My desk sat against the last wall, which also held the adjoining door to the master bedroom.

Should I reach out to King Malik? Would he be willing to talk peace with me instead?

Alice interrupted my thoughts by walking into the office as if she owned it, stopping short when she noticed me sitting at the desk.

"What are you doing in here?" she asked, with a touch of disgust in her voice.

"It's my office," I said, with a pause before adding, "Please stay off the second floor until I have time to go over everything."

She made a face and turned to leave without giving a response, but I stopped her before she could cross the threshold.

"I need the driver," I said. "And it's 'Yes, Your Majesty,' when you are given a direct order."

She spun around, anger boiling behind her eyes, "Yes, Your Majesty. I will call him now."

I followed her downstairs and closed the door to the stairs behind me. My parents only used the door during parties, but I figured it would help solidify my seriousness. Maybe the driver could also take me to a place to buy a doorknob to replace this one. Asking Alice for the key would prove hilarious, but it was more likely she already had copies of all keys for the estate. There had to be a person in town that could come and change them out for me. I put it on my list to ask the lawyer.

We reached the front door, and the guard from the previous day waited for us, fully clothed in khaki pants and a blue polo with sandy blond hair, shaggy.

"Good afternoon, Your Majesty." He bowed slightly. "I'd be happy to drive you into town."

"Thank you," I smiled. "Your name?"

"James."

"I have an appointment at one-thirty," I said.

He looked at the clock next to the front door and grimaced. "We should be on our way."

He opened the door for me, and I met Alice's eyes before walking through it to the front porch. We stepped out onto the wrap-around front porch, shaded by trees, and I took in the fresh air. The house sat nestled into the cliffside but did not light up correctly with the land holding the garage. I loved how the lush greenery hid the house. As we walked across the suspended bridge to get to the driveway, I wondered if she would search through the house while I was gone.

***

James parked in front of a building along main street, with Vivian Davis, Attorney at Law, written across the single glass window in gold lettering.

He looked back at me and said, "I'll wait here for you."

"Thank you." I smiled before exiting the car.

How did my parents convince some sirens to learn human traits, such as driving and shopping? Such a strange thing to aspire to be, compared to the lackadaisical life most of us led. I paused before opening the door to take a breath and gather my thoughts. This would be as easy as hunting.

"Welcome," an elderly lady behind a desk said as I entered the small office. I took her for the person I made an appointment with and matched her smile. Her bright white hair and floral skirt suit didn't fit with the browns that filled the space.

"Hi, I have an appointment under Cordelia."

"Oh." A look of confusion crossed her face. "Give me just a sec, hun."

"No problem." I sat in one of the waiting chairs as she walked through an opening in the wall behind her desk.

After nearly a minute, she came back around the corner and said, "Vivian is ready for you."

"Great, thank you." I followed her back.

We passed through the doorway and made a left. The back room had three spaces, an office, a break area, then another office. Once inside the small office, I sat in front of a wooden desk that felt like it was compensating for something. The desk took up most of the room, and the wall behind it was lined with matching dark wood shelves. Overall, the space felt stuffy and unwelcoming. I could crumble under the heavy colors and overbearing furniture.

"I'm glad to meet you," Vivian said, reaching over her desk to shake my hand. I leaned forward to meet her grasp. Her facial features mimicked that of the receptionist, leaving me to believe they were related, though Vivian appeared to be in her early fifties with a dark brown bob cut and black pantsuit. The only bright color in the office shone from under her jacket, a blue button-up shirt.

"Same to you," I smiled, uneasy sitting in the stiff chair. I moved my legs around, trying to find a comfortable position.

Was Alice rummaging through the offices while I was here?

"Before we began," I said, "Do you happen to know someone that can go to the estate and change out the door handles, so I have a single set of keys?"

"Definitely, let me give Terry a call. He could probably get it done before we're finished here. How many doors is it?" She picked up a small phone on her desk, pushed on the screen then raised it to her ears. As I replied, she took notes.

"The front door for sure, then the door leading upstairs, and the door leading outside from the kitchen. The patios off the two floors can't be reached from the outside, so I think they are fine."

She smiled and nodded.

"Hey Terry, you busy? Not here. I have a client that needs a few doorknobs changed out this afternoon. Oh, perfect, it's just two exteriors and one interior."

She gave him the address and locations of the doors. As she spoke, I transmitted to Alice, letting her know the estate needed to be vacated for the human's arrival, and no one would be allowed in until I returned. Surprising no one, she responded with her snarkiest, "Yes, Your Majesty.

Once Vivian finished up on the phone, she set it down and made eye contact with me. "He's heading over now, and will stop by here to give you the keys before you leave."

"Great." I was unsure of what else to say or where to take the conversation. Thankfully, she broke the awkwardness.

"I have to say." She paused before continuing to look over the papers on her desk. "I expected you to be younger?"

"May I ask why?" I said, still clutching the folder with the documents Alice had created with her.

"Alice spoke of you as if you were a child. How are you related to Derya? Alice only said a distant relative."

"Fascinating," I said aloud, mostly by mistake. I cleared my throat and continued. "Derya is my mother. I am the third child of the house of Drakos."

Her facial expression spoke volumes to the shock of the news. She folded her hands under her chin and thought in silence before speaking again.

"I'm sorry, Derya never told me. You weren't mentioned as an heir?"

"Honestly, I never thought I'd find myself here either." I smiled and let the silence fall between us again. Before speaking, I blinked away the tears forming in my eyes as the blood-covered room attempted to overtake my thoughts. "I'm not sure how much you know of our family..."

"Well." She cleared her throat, rose from her chair, and shut the door behind me before continuing. "I've been your mother's lawyer for many years. I am aware of the sirens living in our lake and have pledged an oath to keep her secrets. As I will do with you today. It seems we have a lot to talk about regarding Alice and the discrepancies. I guess we should start at the beginning."

"Sounds good." I gave her an uneasy smile, unsure of where to start. Telling my true story to a human felt weird enough, much less knowing I never spoke of my family to others. "While I was raised and educated on the human world alongside my siblings, once it came time for their onomasía ceremony, as a family, we decided I did not need to be put through the royal education. It seemed unlikely they would call on me. With two siblings planning for large families. I'd have been very low on the list. Going through the pain of being royalty when I could just as easily slip into the faction waters as an average siren, well, as my dad said, would be a new level of torture."

She smiled but didn't speak, so I continued.

"Back then, when we were kids, my parents had very little staff. After I turned thirteen, they let me explore the lake and take care of myself. As the years went by, they performed my sýntrofos ceremony at my request and let me live my life. Anytime I hung around the house, no one introduced me as a daughter of Derya, and since my appearances were usually for family events, most probably assumed I was some distant cousin or something. I wasn't the first child of a royal to be given a chance to be average."

"Makes sense. Did Alice know about any of this?"

"I'm unsure of how much Alice knew of my history or when she came to work for my parents. I'm still trying to figure out exactly what her role is at the estate."

"Well, I can tell you when she came here, she introduced herself as Derya's right hand. Though I'd never met her before, nor is she listed in any of the legal paperwork."

"I'm glad you cleared that up." I looked at my feet, then met her gaze again. "She was under the impression that I couldn't read or write, like most sirens. So, I assume she knows very little of me. When my family died, my father had a contingency plan for it. There was an emergency alert that signaled the guards to find me at all costs."

"Thank goodness, your parents were more prepared for life and death than most of my clients."

I smiled, knowing she was right. Their organization would be missed by all. I didn't know if I could ever fill their fins, but I had to try.

"When they first started coming to me," she reminisced, "We hit it off right away. They invited me to a few of their soirees. The atmosphere at the estate left me feeling as though everyone there was comfortable and truly happy with their lives. The nudity was a bit much for me. I only made it to a few before I came to terms with it being something I was not comfortable partaking in."

She smiled, embarrassed yet dreamy. I could only smile back. Humans and their self-guilt. Bodies were bodies. They all had them, strange that seeing one that isn't their own without clothes would cause such a reaction. It's just a meat sack. Even sirens have one. Who cares what it looks like?

I let the silence stretch before speaking to give pause to the memories.

"Alice requested I sign these papers," I handed her the folder. "But I have discrepancies with their contents. I was hoping you could help me reword them?"

"Yes, I'd imagine so. I'd be glad to."

She flipped through them, pulling out what I assumed to be the death certificates and filing them into a drawer in her desk.

"This will only take me a few minutes. I have the previous contracts from when your mother took over from your grandmother."

"Great." I smiled.

As she typed away, I looked around her office. The shelves had many books, most looking to be legal-related volumes. She did have a few shelves of fiction titles. Mostly classics from long-dead human authors. Had she actually read them all, or were they just shelf décor?

A loud noise brought me back to her desk, and she pulled pages from a machine behind her.

"All right, feel free to read over these, and then we can sign them together."

I took the warm pages and read through each one. Perfect. No trial periods and nothing in the documents mentioned Alice's name. Just me and myself. The sole member of the house of Drakos. She pointed to each place needing my signature and then took the pages and signed them herself.

After filing them in her desk drawer, she asked, "What is the name of your mate? I want to make sure I have her on your family list. I'd like to avoid this happening again in the future. While I understand your parents' desire for you to be average, it's best to let at least one person know the worst-case scenario options."

"I agree. While I'm nowhere near okay with everything that's happened in the past three days, it would have been smoother had Alice not been weaving her own story into it all. Nicole is her name."

"Perfect." She typed into her computer as a light knock sounded on her door. "Enter."

The woman from the front poked her head in, "Terry's here. He said you're waiting for him?"

"Oh yes, send him back."

A few seconds later, a gruff older man walked through the door, tipping his hat to me.

"Good afternoon, ladies," Terry said.

"Did everything go okay?" Vivian asked.

"Yes, ma'am. Y'all got a really beautiful place out there. Changed out the three knobs. Did you want the previous ones?"

"Thank you. Living lakeside is the only way to live. You can discard them or keep them if you don't mind."

"Not at all. Here's the keys to the new handles."

"Thank you," I took them from him, offering a smile.

"If that will be all, I'll be on my way?"

"Thanks again, Terry."

"Y'all have a good one." He said, tipping his head again and leaving us.

I stood and offered my hand to Vivian, "I'll be heading out as well, thank you for all your assistance today."

"Of course, if you need anything else, just let me know."

I followed Terry through the office and out the front door to find James sitting on a bench outside the business. As soon as he spotted me, he jumped up and opened the car door.

"Anywhere else, Your Majesty?" he asked once inside his own seat.

"Just home, thank you."

He gave a nodded and pulled out of the parking lot. As he drove, I human-watched from the window. Most were in cars, hurrying to their own destinations. A few walked the sidewalk, entering different businesses and coming out with bags. To have so many belongings and constantly having to be places. What a stressful way to live one's life.

Downtown Marble Falls had a quaint antique feel to it. The three-block strip featured brick buildings dating back to the town's humble beginnings. I'd only ventured into human stores once, vowing never to attempt it again. The chaos behind each enticing door was not worth the pain of being packed in like sardines just to admire someone else's belongings.

The car revved, and we jolted forward as James yelled, "What the fuck, asshole?"

I looked around to find the car behind us unusually close, almost on our back bumper.

"Everything okay?" I asked.

"Not to worry, Your Majesty. These humans drive like they own the road most days."

As he spoke, we jolted forward, this time from the car hitting us. We were now in the neighborhood across the highway, and there wasn't a way James could pull over and let the guy pass. He turned off Third Street and onto Avenue F. But it didn't matter. The person followed him onto the next street, tapping our bumper again. With the advantage of a Wednesday—the roads clear of cars and humans—James sped up.

"What's this guy's problem?" James said, speeding up, then taking a sharp right on Fourth Street, then a left on Avenue E.

I turned around to see if I could tell who was in the car, but the person wore a cap with large sunglasses. Basic features were the most I could make out. He was a man with a five o'clock shadow and wore a white tank top. I didn't recognize the car, though I knew just about nothing regarding vehicles, and the emblem on the front looked like a funky capital H.

As James drove down Avenue E, he passed our turn onto Sixth Street, and the guy sped up beside us, jerking his wheel to scrape along the side of our vehicle as we drove. I screamed and put my safety belt on. It was a rare day I road in a vehicle and never thought I needed it, but at the moment, my heart panicked with what was going to happen to us. The strap gave me reassurance. We'd at least live through this moment.

"Don't worry, Your Majesty. We're going to get out of this. I've had professional training."

"That's reassuring," I whispered, holding my chest and closing my eyes as the guy rammed us again.

James slammed on the breaks while turning the wheel to go the other direction on Avenue E before we hit the highway ahead of us. I peeked over the seat behind us and realized the guy hadn't been able to mimic our movement. He missed the stop sign at the highway and barreled into traffic, though once on the other side, he turned around and raced back across.

"He's turning around," I panicked.

As I spoke, James made a sharp turn at Ninth Street, causing us to be stuck on the road for two blocks before he could turn left again, taking us deeper into the neighborhood.

"Are you okay?" He didn't take his eyes off the road.

"I'm fine." I winced, my knuckles turning white around the oh-shit bar.

The rev of the car attempting to catch us made my stomach turn. I braced myself as James took a few more quick left and right turns. The final was onto East Avenue.

"I think we're in the clear," he said.

The car slowed to a normal speed, and with our house, in view, I released my grip to look behind me. Not a silver car in sight. I let out a sigh in relief, letting the pressure in my chest go with it.

He hit the garage opener as soon as we were in range and squealed into it, closing it before we were clear. Once the door finished, we sat in silence, breathing deep.

"It's time for a swim," I said.

"Couldn't have said it better myself." He leaned forward and wiped his face with his shirt before resting his head on the steering wheel.

I closed my eyes, relaxing into the plush seats. My body tingled as the adrenaline left my system, turning it into a mush of exhaustion.

"Take the rest of your shift off."

"Yes, Your Majesty."

We clamored out of the car, and James opened the garage door a crack before opening it all the way for me to pass through. My human legs had trouble holding my weight, and I hobbled to him, grateful for his foresight. All my thoughts pointed to the lake, not the continued threat against my life.

"Had to make sure."

"I appreciate it." I smiled at him as I passed through the doorway.

"Just doing my job."

CHAPTER SIX

I double-checked all the keys worked before heading to the grotto, stripping the human clothes, and dropping into the lake, calling for Nicole as I swam. Each flip of my fins recharged my body and mind from the ordeal in the car. If I didn't have to get into another car for a year, it would be too soon.

She agreed to meet me along the falls. As I waited for her arrival, I thought through the events of the past forty-eight hours. Attempts on my life, lies, and sneaking around. I needed to know what was in the chests. Too bad I let Alice go for the day. It didn't matter. I couldn't have been sure she'd be in the house. I had no clue how she spent her work hours.

The founders of Marble Falls named it for the falls, now nestled at the base of the lake. Before the dams, local humans would frequent the area to lounge or slide down rapids created by the Colorado River as it passed through Marble Falls. While the lake still made for a hot spot for humans, now they sped their boats across it, none the wiser to the sirens enjoying the hidden rocks.

Catfish lay hidden in the crevices of the falls as largemouth bass swam above us. The sight from below often left me enchanted, from the sun streaming through the waves to the schools of smaller fish dipping in and out of the undercurrents.

Why would any siren want to spend more time on land than under the lake?

Alice didn't know the first thing about what the average siren desired.

"A minnow for your thoughts?" Nicole transmitted.

"You're not going to like it." I rolled off my belly to look at her lying beside me.

"I'll hold my opinions if you'd like."

"I want to see what's in the chests in Alice's room."

"Didn't you just get run off the road?"

"Hey, you said you'd hold commentary."

"Matters of your safety are exempt to all statements."

I gave her a light smile, then rolled back onto my belly to continue to watch the sirens swimming throughout the lake.

"I just need more information," I transmitted after she stayed silent.

"I know, but what if she catches you?"

"What is she going to do? Kill the Queen?"

Nicole remained silent. I glanced back at her to see a face riddled with worry.

"It's not like I'm going alone," I transmitted. "You'll be there, right?"

"All right," she relented. "Where's Alice now?"

"No idea." I transmitted. "I locked her out of the estate. Not sure what she does all day."

"Well." She paused for a moment, then continued. "Let's at least swim by. If the coast is clear, we can peek. But only to satisfy your fears, then we need to get the hell out of there. Curiosity kills, you know."

I smiled. "Yeah, I know, you're the best."

"Damn right I am. Going into the mouth of the crocodile. Like we're some kind of guard."

She swam ahead, leaving me to launch myself forward to catch up. We did a few circles, looping into the split-off, then back out into the lake using the currents from the boats above us to propel us around the area. To an outside siren, we were playing in the undercurrents. After verifying we were alone and not being watched, we nestled into the weeds from the previous evening. I scooted as close as I could to the edge of the eave and peered inside the cove. No movement, and more importantly, no silhouettes.

"Looks clear," I transmitted. "Going in."

"If you must, but I'm stating for future us, this is a bad idea."

"Noted." I pushed off the wall edge and swam deeper in to look around.

Like most coves inhabited by sirens, someone had spent hours tunneling into the cliffside to create a secluded spot to call their own. Overall, I only knew of a few sirens with coves, as we did not feel the need for privacy the way the humans did. Sleeping wherever we were was a common occurrence among our species. The smooth walls, and attention to getting all the excess dirt out of this cove, spoke volumes of the love someone put in creating it.

How long had this romance been going on between Alice and Prince

Struan? Since before the raid? It was what? Six months, maybe a year ago at most?

I ran my hand against the wall. Carving this in a short amount of time would have taken dedication. I glanced back to make sure Nicole swam in behind me. She faced the exit, slowly propelling herself backward as if we were going to be discovered any minute.

I turned back to the chests. Two sat in front of the bed. For them to stay submerged, they had to have stones in the bottom. Or—well, the more obvious answer—incantations I had yet to learn kept them sunk. I attempted to lift one, but it didn't budge. Both were wooden with golden clasps and ornate corner molding. The clasp had a spot for a padlock to slide into, but both slots were empty. I gave it a lift and found that no incantation held the lid down.

"They aren't locked," I transmitted.

"Well, fling it open already," she replied. Her tone bordered panic, and I looked over my shoulder to see her hovering between me and the door.

Without a second thought, I lifted the first lid, gasping as the contents came into view. My hand flew to my mouth, and I backed away an inch, not taking my eyes off the display. The interior featured silk cloth coating the base and sides, with an air pocket holding down three siren hearts.

"No, no, no, no," I transmitted panic setting in as my chest tightened and my breath grew shallow.

The second chest held one large, with two small, and a fetal size heart surrounding it. Nicole shot beside me, holding onto my shoulders. She peered into the open chests.

"That two-timing witch," she transmitted.

I turned into her embrace, closing my eyes in an attempt to wipe the sight from my mind.

"There's no way they're not. . ." I transmitted in a drawn-out whisper.

"I'm afraid that'd be quite the coincidence if they weren't. I'm sorry, love."

She hugged me tighter as my thoughts raced with what this meant. Minutes passed with us huddled together in the cove. Never in my wildest assumptions of Alice did I expect her to be harboring pieces of my relatives.

Did she kill them? Had she been the one out to kill me? Why? Why in the sea would she do something like this?

"We can't leave them here," I transmitted.

Nicole let go of me and tried to move the chests, but neither budged. She poked the air pocket, and it reacted to the movement of her finger, not letting her past the barrier nor popping. Alice couldn't have been working alone. She didn't have the blood to cast.

"I don't think we have a choice," she transmitted. "We need to get out of here. Then we can come up with a plan."

She glanced back towards the entrance, and her face dropped, color draining from it as she glanced to me, then the entrance. I ripped my gaze from the chests to see Prince Struan swimming towards us.

"Well, well, well," he transmitted. "Finally came to your senses and delivered yourself to me, eh?"

"What did you do to my family?" I transmitted, straightening my torso to show him I wasn't afraid. Nicole grabbed my hand, preventing me from swimming up to meet him.

"Nothing they didn't deserve. You'll be with them soon enough."

"Hardly." I lifted my chin in defiance.

"How are you, a little minnow from nowhere, going to defend yourself? What can you do, like two incantations? Doubt they are the attack variety." He let out a deep chuckle that reverberated through our transmission link, making my stomach sink. No way a heal would get me out of this mess.

"Do what you want with me," I transmitted. "Just let Nicole go, and tell me why?"

He smirked and looked to the ceiling as if he was talking to someone, not in the room. "Fine, get the fuck out of here. We have no use for a mermaid, anyway." He laughed at his own insult.

I let go of Nicole's hand and transmitted to her, "Go. Find guards, find King Malik, whatever, just get out of the cove. I can handle myself."

"I'm not leaving you."

"You are my only hope. Go."

She looked me in the eye, then launched herself forward, hugging the wall until she reached the lake. Tears threatened to break, but I let the pain of the week flow through me and fuel my need to stay calm.

"Well." I crossed my arms to keep them from shaking as Alice swooped in behind him. Her face unreadable as always, she stopped at his shoulder.

He looked back towards her, glanced at me for a second, and let out a sigh, shaking his head.

If only they'd projected those transmissions aloud.

"We don't owe you shit," he transmitted, swimming within inches of me as he brandished his blade. A jewel-encrusted hilt, with a short metal blade, no longer than two hands length. "But you . . . you'll be parting with your heart today."

I looked to Alice, who had not moved closer but watched us with vague interest. Our eyes met, and hers stayed hollow as ever. She let out a yawn.

Thanks for letting me know my existence bores you that much.

"What's wrong with you?" I transmitted to them both but focused my gaze on her alone. "How could you do this to our family? He can't tell me because he doesn't know the reason, right? Only someone of your caliber could have set all this up. I just want to know why. You owe my family that much."

"She doesn't owe you shit," Prince Struan transmitted. "This is my doing, not hers. How'd a dressing maid orchestrate something this epic? Coordinating the killings of six adults and two kids, plus getting a bonus kid out of it. I bet you didn't even know your sister was pregnant. Did you? That was a fun one to discover. Made sure the blade went deep into her abdomen."

Internally, I reeled as he spoke but tried not to react externally. I couldn't let him see he was getting to me. None of this explained why.

"But why, what's the point? Revenge for your wife?"

At that, his smirk turned into manic laughter. I retreated in fear, unsure of his next move but not wanting to be within reach. He noticed my movement and abruptly silenced himself as he grabbed my arm.

"Oh no, you don't, *Your Majesty*." As transmitted, he dragged the blade across my abdomen, slicing into the flesh enough for blood to trickle out. Fear and adrenaline kept me quiet as I waited for him to continue speaking.

"Right here." He looked me in the eye. "That's where I sliced her open. Like this, any of this would be for that psycho wife dear old Dad forced on me. She deserved what she got. Going into battle, like she didn't have a place in my bed, bearing my children. I lost my place in line because of that ungrateful bitch. But none of that matters now, right Alice?"

He looked back at her as she picked at her nails. She rolled her eyes and transmitted something to him that he scoffed at.

"Why?" I transmitted in a whisper, hoping he'd take the bait and continue speaking. I looked away from Alice, wanting nothing more than to rip her nails off her hand. Each one she cleaned drove home another 'fuck you' to me.

"Well, little lost princess, I'll tell you why. Because once I have your heart, I'll be able to take over your family's estate. A few incantations, a dinner of hearts, and BAM!" He made another slice along my right side. "Drakos will be no more. The rise of Vitalis will signify a new era in sirens."

"Just kill her already," Alice transmitted. "Stop playing with your food. I want to get back into the estate before sundown."

"Keep your mouth shut," he growled, looking behind his shoulder at her. "Or I'll be finding me a new second."

Alice transmitting to me as well was clearly a dig, but his slip left me looking around the cave for a way to defend myself. I didn't want to see his transformation and transmission slipping spoke volumes to his current state of control.

No stone or stick within reached. Fuck. I wiggled against his tightening arm as he kept his focus on Alice, who threw her back and cackled at his last statement.

"You can't take over the estate without the documents, and I still have to figure out where the bitch hid them."

It was my turn to giggle. I covered my mouth, but the bubbles gave me away. Prince Struan shot his eyes back towards me and shook my arm hard enough to cause my shoulder to ache. "What? What's so funny? You laughing about how close to death you are?"

"No," I transmitted to both of them. "I'm laughing because Alice is an idiot. The documents are with Vivian, and we have corrected them to leave Alice out of the loop."

"You fucking what?" Alice lit up with emotion for the first time since knowing her as she charged at me, grappling my throat with both of her hands, cutting off my airway as she shook me back and forth. Her face transformed, incisors terrifyingly long. I slammed my lids shut, struggling to shake out of her grasp. "I'm going to kill you myself, you little bitch."

Prince Struan backed up, letting Alice have her way with me. "That's gold, we went through all of this, and you couldn't get the minnow to sign a few fucking documents. Just forge them, I said. But no, you had to do it legal. Like you're some kind of Queen or something."

"Fuck you, Struan," she transmitted.

My vision blurred as she held my gills shut.

Come on, Nicole. "I love you," I transmitted as a final thought before everything went black.

CHAPTER SEVEN

My head ached from heavy fog and exhaustion. Someone held me. The familiar caress lulled me into a sense of comfort, as if I floated in our secluded cove, just Nicole and I. Visions of the dream I'd been having seeped into my mind, and I shuddered, only to hear a voice in my head telling me to come back to them, that it would be okay. I shook out of the sleepy fog and fluttered my eyes open to see Nicole's worried face looking down at me. Tears stained her cheeks as they mixed with the freshwater.

"What's—" I transmitted, realizing it wasn't a dream. Alice had tried to kill me.

I sat up in a panic, looking around to see that they had moved me out of the cave, and many guards surrounded us, along with the Lykaios royal family.

"It's okay. Slow down. I'm right here." Nicole pulled me back into her arms.

"What's going on?" I looked around at the odd gathering of sirens, all but the guards deep in conversation. Alice and Prince Struan were in custody between a group of our own legion.

"King Malik suspected for a long while that his son would betray him, and when I called out to him at the Lykaios dam, he instantly agreed to come with me to the cove. We arrived right as you passed out. His son hasn't said a word since being apprehended. Did he tell you why?"

As she finished her sentence, the king noticed I was awake and swam over to me.

"Queen Cordelia." He bowed. "I'm thankful to see you still with us."

"Your Majesty." I bowed my head, swimming out of Nicole's lap to meet him eye to eye.

"I am ashamed to say. This murderer is my flesh and blood. Did he give you any indications as to why he shamed our family in this manner?"

"Yes." I nodded. "They both let me know their reasoning."

"I went into the cove," he transmitted. "I can't imagine what you're feeling right now, but if you would, recount their words for me so I can go forward with punishment."

Over the next ten minutes, I repeated the events over the past few days, plus filled in the information they gave me in the cove. The king's face went from concerned, to shocked, to horrified. Fitting for the actions of his own son. Once I finished, all remained silent, looking at each other as they transmitted between one another.

Prince Struan broke the silence in a lake-wide transmission by the looks on every siren's face.

"The lot of you are worthless parasites, holding onto artificial power like it's your lifeline. Kill me. Let my death lull you into a false comfort. But know, an uprising is coming. My death will be the marker. Sirens everywhere are waking up to see you for your true selves. Just a bunch of overbearing mer—"

Before he could finish the sentence, King Malik shot a trail of bioluminescence towards the prince, hitting him in the chest. He seethed in pain, his arms and tail stiffened in front of our eyes, and convulsions tremored through his body, making it flop at the will of the king.

Everyone looked on in silence. My chest hurt at the sight of it. Murdering his own son. I wasn't sure I could offer the same sentence for Alice, and the fallen were my flesh and blood.

"You dare to defy me?" King Malik transmitted. "After all, I've given you. An honorable wife that you couldn't even be bothered to produce an heir with. But you defile her name with your treason and a maid? She died for our faction, a genuine hero, and you have the audacity to spit in our face—ungrateful, sludge, unworthy of the name Lykaios. I find you guilty of treason against the siren species and sentence you to the most excruciating death. I hope it was worth it, son. Enjoying this agony yet? Not half as much pain as you deserve for killing your own brother."

With one last push, he forced more power into the spell, keeping the incantation to himself as he worked. Once the body sunk to the lakebed, whispered murmurs rose around us. King Malik put a stop to them. "I speak on behalf of the Lykaios Faction and hope Queen Cordelia will join me in the sentiment. We are not your overlords. By swearing allegiances to a faction, you are committing yourself to the ways of that faction for as long as you live in their waters. You are not beholden to us. We offer you a safe haven."

As he spoke, the surrounding area continued to fill with curious sirens. Many unfamiliar faces made me question from how far they swam. Only two factions were in close proximity via lake, unless by human transportation. I remembered my education when my mother informed me that a siren's top speed compared to a human car at fifteen mph. Not enough time had passed for the Aetos and Matsouka factions to have reached us by lake.

"If you don't like the way a faction operates, find another. But know, as far as the Lower Colorado River Gerousía goes, you won't find a faction in these waters that tolerates siren on siren unjust violence. You might wonder about the current war between myself and Queen Derya, but I stand here before you today, a humbled king, asking Queen Cordelia to accept my hand in truce."

He looked to me, fake smile and all, hand outstretched expectantly. I couldn't judge if this was a show or if he really felt this way, but since I still didn't understand the logistics of our war, I grasped his wrist, and we shook.

"We will recognize this day forward as the day each faction agreed to not resort to violence and to allow all sirens to live in peace according to their own customs."

The royal sirens circled around us, raising a fist in solidarity to the words he spoke. In a wave, the sea of sirens mimicked the gesture, holding their heads high. After the hype in the common sirens dissipated, the surrounding sirens introduced themselves to me, as various members of the Gerousía and other siren royalty from different factions.

I looked to the king, who hugged a woman I assumed to be his wife. "Thank you. I owe you a life debt."

"For the sake of the unity forged here today, I say we're even. My son was a vengeful soul unfit to rule, and I never realized it. Had Nicole not come to me, we'd be fighting a different war. It only feels appropriate to thank you for uncovering their plan."

"How did you realize they were up to something?" Gerousiastís Kyros asked.

I looked over to Alice, who lay behind the fallen prince, crying over his corpse, and looked back to the expectant group.

"She made a few assumptions about me that laid the groundwork for discovering her true motives. I couldn't figure out why she would put a trial period over my head, all while trying to kill me. But her romance with Prince Struan, plus my office being trashed when I arrived home today, made the pieces fall into place. Though I had it wrong by a mile, mostly because of my ignorance in incantation capabilities."

"And we would have got away with it too," Alice transmitted to all of us. "If it weren't for your little trollop. Why he had to gloat and let her go. Could have killed you both, the dolt." Her gaze fell from me to Prince Struan. She ran her hand through his hair, cuddling him in her lap. "My beautiful dolt. Look what they've done to you."

"What is your judgment regarding Alice?" Gerousiastís Brontes asked.

"Kill me already," she transmitted, yelling with a rage thick enough to cause my head to ache. "But you're too weak for that. Aren't you? You couldn't kill me if you wanted to. Just a docile little mermaid, unable to do a bit of dirty work. Well, give me a blade, and I'll do it myself."

"Banishment." I transmitted.

"From the Lower Colorado River Gerousía." Gerousiastís Nikolaos transmitted.

With that, the Gerousía joined hands, forming a circle around Alice.

"No," Alice transmitted. "You can't do this, just kill me, don't do this."

The Gerousía chanted incantations around her, raising their joined hands to the sky as their words sped up. I'd never seen spell work like it before, and I backed up towards Nicole. Within a few minutes, Alice ceased to exist in the space between them.

In the same moment, she would reappear in Greece, home of the Gerousía all others bowed to. The Gulf of Corinth would strip her of all siren abilities over the course of many painful months unless she could plea her way into another freshwater Gerousía. Once fully transformed, she would be nothing more than a mermaid in search of a tribe to call home.

EPILOGUE

For the first time since becoming Queen, Nicole and I relaxed in the grotto's shallow pool with zero stress or obligation.

"Did you ever figure out what the war was actually about?" she asked.

"Oh yeah," I said. "The Lykaios faction is still practicing luring humans to their death in the lake waters, and my parents demanded they stop or be stopped."

"That's barbaric of them."

"Honestly, after speaking with the Gerousía, I'm staying as far away from all their drama as I can. If the Gerousía wants them to stop, they can deal with it. Our people shouldn't fight for a cause of my deciding."

"Look at you, making queen decisions. Told you, you'd be good at it."

I smiled at her, and we relaxed into the silence.

"Do you think there really are Vitalis supporters out there, planning an uprising?" I asked.

"Doubt it. They'd have made themselves known at his execution."

"Guess that's true. I hope so anyway. I think I've had just about enough vengeful sirens to last me a lifetime."

I snuggled into her chest as she kissed my forehead.

ABOUT SABETHA DANES

Sabetha Danes is an eccentric introvert located in Central Texas, in a Stars Hollow-esque small town. Her default language is sarcasm, and is fueled by coffee. As a lifelong bibliophile, she reads all genres but her writing specializes in fantasy and cozy mysteries.

Her degree in interpersonal communication helps her over-analyze characters that are only found in stories. She spends her days with her daughter and dude walking trails and drinking coffee. Did we mention she enjoys a great cup of coffee?

Find out more at: aconitecafe.com/sabethadanes

facebook.com/TheCaffeinatedNecromancer
twitter.com/aconitecafe
instagram.com/aconitecafe

ONE STRANGE FISHING TRIP
BY K. MATT

Somewhere In The Atlantic Ocean

If Travis was being honest with himself, this wasn't the first time he'd woken up wondering where he was. No, this was a sensation that came to him far too often for his liking. In his teens, there was a point where he was unnerved by it, but he became used to it by his mid-twenties. And now, in his early thirties, he had shifted from "getting used to" to "All right, whose fault is it *this* time?".

Most of the time this had happened, there would be a cold metal table against his bare back, leather straps holding him down. But this time, he felt weirdly free...for the most part. His legs felt like they were stuck together, and he couldn't feel his prehensile tail. He tried to grab at his arm with it but couldn't feel it respond. He reached to grab ahold of the tail and nothing.

He waited for his vision to return, as everything had been dark even after his consciousness kicked in again. And that was when he saw it.

A school of fish passed him. Well, this was new. He was entirely underwater. It wasn't his first time being underwater, but for some reason, he didn't feel any sense of urgency to get above the surface. He scratched at his neck, finding a few slits that weren't there before.

"...When'd I get gills?" he muttered to himself.

Well, that certainly explained the lack of drowning on his part. He looked down to see what his leg situation was, his green eyes becoming even wider than their usual. He no longer had legs as he knew them. Rather, it was a huge, scaled fish-like tail with a fin at the end, all of it the same red as his hair.

Well, damn...

This certainly explained why he couldn't feel his usual monkey tail. Of course, he still lacked an explanation as to how, exactly, he became a merman. He had some idea. There was likely a scientist involved in this whole thing.

But that was just the thing: he was from the city of Hell Bent, PA. If one were to throw a rock in that city, they'd likely hit either a lab or someone that worked in one. So just to say that there was a scientist at fault in his current predicament did absolutely nothing to narrow things down.

With a sigh, he decided to start moving. His natural inclination was to walk, but with the current lack of legs, that wasn't going to happen. He did manage to move himself forward a bit with the new tail, though.

Something he noticed right away was that he was able to move quicker underwater than he ever could on land. Running on both legs could be a hassle sometimes. Running on all-fours, perhaps a bit less so. But down here, he was able to cut through the water like butter.

Travis may have been curious about why he was the way he was now and where he'd ended up. But even more than that, he was wondering what capabilities this new form would give him.

Hell Bent, PA
    Abbot Residence

Today was supposed to be a low-stress day off for one, Dr. Spencer Abbot. The plan was going to be to spend the day with his young son Daniel. So far, things were progressing according to this plan. They'd brought out an old copy of *Candyland* that Daniel's mother had picked up at a thrift store (along with a few stacks of books). They would play together for the morning, then meet up with Travis for lunch.

Lunch was planned for noon. The time was currently one-thirty. Daniel might not have been great with telling time yet, but Spencer knew for sure that Travis could figure out if he was late for the arrangement. Maybe he'd just gotten lost again. That was what the doctor hoped for. But there was a feeling he couldn't shake. His brother-in-law had always been a magnet for trouble. So, chances were, he'd run into another problem and probably needed to be bailed out.

Even Daniel could tell that something was wrong, his little tail curling around his father's wrist and squeezing somewhat. Spencer looked at him.

"Everything okay, there?" he asked.

"Is Uncle Trav okay?"

"He does seem to be running a bit late," Spencer sighed. "So, what we can do is call him and see if he's safe."

The boy nodded, watching as his father walked to stand near the door where their home phone was. Spencer put in the number and waited. But the phone on the other end never even rang. It went straight to voicemail. He glanced over to Daniel, seeing a somewhat expectant look on the child's face. Well, this was going to be a disappointment to him.

He hung up, running a hand through his short light brown hair. "Welp, he didn't pick up…Which means it's time for Plan B."

"What's 'Plan B'?"

"Plan B," as Spencer called it, was to use magic. The doctor had been a somewhat strong mage for the past few years. Part of his reasons for learning it had been to better defend himself against various threats. Another part was just because it sounded neat to him.

And yet another aspect, perhaps, was that he felt (in some small way) inferior to the rest of his family. His wife and brother-in-law were both monkey-human hybrids (the former possessing enhanced speed, the latter having an immensely powerful regenerative ability). His son had inherited his mother's light green eyes, prehensile tail, and hand-like feet. And from his father, the boy had gotten his light brown hair and poor eyesight. Nobody knew quite where the little tooth-gap came from, but they didn't quite question it, either.

Spencer made his way over to the couch, rummaging beneath it for a moment. Travis slept on this couch most nights and kept his hair-brush underneath the couch when he wasn't using it. Given that Travis didn't always clean out the brush, there was a good chance he could find what he would need for a tracking spell.

Sure enough, he was able to pluck a few strands of red hair from the bristles. Daniel watched with curiosity, and Spencer noticed his expression. He shifted a bit so the boy could watch what he was doing.

The doctor carefully (and quickly) wove the strands together as he explained it.

"You see, Danny, I'm going to use a tracking spell. For that, I need either your uncle's hair or blood. If it doesn't help me find where he is right now, it will at least give me a lead on somewhere he was not too long ago."

He soon had a long thread made from his friend's hair, which he wrapped around his wrist a few times and tied off. With that situated, it was on to the next step: gathering his magical element. Everyone that bothered to learn magic was connected to some element of nature. Spencer's element happened to be water, and so he needed to bring a vial of water to power his spells. The vial in question was in the kitchen, at the end of the bar.

Spencer picked that up, looping the leather cord around his neck and tucking the vial underneath his shirt. Okay, so he had the two main things he needed for the tracking spell. It was just down to grabbing his shoes and figuring out what to do with Daniel.

He could drop him off at his mother's studio. After all, he'd sat in on her classes before. But then she might start to worry about her brother, and he wouldn't feel comfortable about not telling her the real reason Daniel was there. His grandmother? No, she had that genetics symposium going on. His grandmother's sister was busy, and he didn't quite trust Trav's girlfriend with kids. She seemed like the type to happily corrupt a child.

But Spencer had promised to spend the day with his son. And he felt confident enough in his own magical abilities that he could keep him safe.

"All right, Daniel. How about we go track down your uncle?" he asked with a smile.

His son nodded, his small tail twitching with excitement at the idea.

"Walking or piggyback ride?"

"Hm...RIDE!"

Spencer crouched down, letting his son climb up onto his back. As he stood up again, he glanced toward the game on the floor. Eh, that could be picked up when they got home later. They weren't done with that yet.

The doctor walked to the door, taking a moment to pull his shoes on, before stepping outside. Standing on the front steps of his house, Spencer held up the wrist that had the makeshift hair-bracelet. He closed his eyes, letting his thoughts focus on Travis. The fact that he had this tracking spell down pat by now was, perhaps, mildly disconcerting. But it was better than being mired in confusion anytime something happened.

As he focused on his target and the spell to track him down, he could hear someone passing by, along with a not-very-subtle grumbling about "Frickin' magic-using weirdos." But he didn't let himself get distracted by that (as many around Hell Bent just saw magic as a weird hobby) as he opened his eyes. A glowing teal arrow appeared in front of him, ready for him to follow it.

Daniel's eyes widened as he looked at the arrow. Since he was in such close proximity to the mage using this spell, he could also see it.

Spencer chuckled a little as he heard the surprised gasp from the kid on his back.

The doctor began walking along, following the path created by his spell.

Somewhere In The Atlantic Ocean

"Okay, so I started somewhere around home, probably. So, I'd be in...the Pacific?" Travis wondered to himself. "Wait, no, no, that's not right..."

The monkey-human-hybrid-turned-merman cursed himself for not being better at the whole "geography" thing. Though being dropped off by the other coast wouldn't have been that much of a surprise. After all, he had no idea how much time had passed. For all he knew, he could have lost an entire day from this.

But which scientist might have caused it in the first place? Well, he could easily rule out Dr. Taylor. For one thing, she was his mother and would have asked before tweaking his DNA again. There were a few labs he'd been to, but they weren't related to genetics so much as ballistics. Unless someone had crafted a bullet specifically designed to change someone into a half-fish, he highly doubted one of the weapons labs had anything to do with his current situation. But then again, could he *really* rule that out, either?

So focused was he on trying to piece together his predicament, he didn't notice that something was barreling at him at top speed. He didn't notice until the teeth sank into his tail. With a screech, he whipped around to see what bit him.

Pulling away from his assailant, he saw it: a juvenile hammerhead shark. The pup ate the chunk of meat it ripped away as Travis watched the wound stop bleeding. The spot built itself back up within seconds, and he let out a sigh of relief. Okay, so his regeneration had not been negatively impacted. That was good news, at least.

But the hammerhead pup looked a bit more confused.

"...Why did...didn't I just..."

And now it was Travis's turn to be confused. He could understand a freaking shark now? He saw the shark come toward his tail again, pushing at its head before it could sink its teeth in again. Just because he could heal from a bite like that, it didn't mean he wanted to experience it again.

"Could you not? That shit hurts, y'know?"

"But why did--"

"Because I'm not food?"

"...But you taste like a fish..."

Well, Travis could see where one might make that mistake. The merman crossed his arms.

"Hm... would you have any idea where we are? Like, where the closest land is?"

"Nope."

He sighed. It was worth a shot, at least. "What about the time?"

Another negative. "Hm... well, what about food?"

The young hammerhead glanced at him with one eye, then the other, as if to ask if he was sure that *he* wasn't food.

"If you're not food, then what are you, exactly?"

Travis had to think about that one. He was human for a good fourteen or fifteen years before becoming a genetic experiment with monkey-like feet and a prehensile tail and that freakish regenerative ability. And as of recently, he gained the fishy tail and gills. Which left him with only one reasonable response to the juvenile shark.

"Hell if I know, kid."

He resumed swimming, the pup following him. He blinked, craning his neck to look at it. He let out another sigh.

"I thought we went through this: I'm not food."

"I know. I'm just...I'm just alone."

Trav turned fully to face his pursuer, his head tilted. Being alone was one of those things he hated, himself. He wondered if the pup was lost or just what had happened. He swam back over to it.

"Do you need help? Like, do you have a mom or dad out there? Older sibling?"

There wasn't a response for a moment, but the young shark eventually gave one.

"No. At least, not anymore...I had a sister, but then *they* got to her..."

The hybrid swam closer to the shark pup. "Who's *they*, here?" he asked, carefully placing a hand on its back.

"The whales. They're black and white and have sharp teeth."

Travis had to think about that one. Black and white whales. Surely this kid couldn't mean *orcas*, could they? If anything, the movies had always shown him that orcas were adorable. That they couldn't hurt a fly!

"Are you sure? I've heard of whales that look like that, and I don't think they'd attack a shark..."

"Tell that to my sister. Whole pod of them...Started ripping her to pieces right in front of me."

Travis could see that the pup was shaking, and he reached out to give it a hug. It was confused at the gesture but somehow found it oddly comforting.

"Sorry to hear, um...got a name?"

"No."

Well, now he had to think about it. He tapped his chin a bit, his tail flicking. "Sharky" sounded too on-the-nose. And he didn't want to go with "Finn" for that same reason.

"Hm...what about Roly?" he asked.

The pup thought about it. "Huh...has kind of a nice sound. But what about you? What do I call you?"

"Travis. Or just, Trav. How about we stick together until I can find a way back home, all right?"

"Sounds good to me!"

And so, Travis and Roly resumed their swim.

Hell Bent, PA

Badgerdragon Labs

The arrow conjured by Spencer's tracking spell had come to an end outside of one of the city's labs. Spencer remembered this one well. It was where he'd gotten that internship back in high school. He was so elated to have gotten the internship that he'd forgotten to reschedule the date he and Gemmy had together. But overall, his time there had been most educational. He'd learned a bit about the physiology of genetically altered people, all for the sake of being the best doctor he could possibly be. Though the fact that someone there had also likely helped themselves to his best friend's DNA didn't entirely shock him.

Spencer approached the main entrance, hitting a button near the door. An intercom crackled to life.

"State your name and your business."

"Dr. Spencer Abbot," he replied. "I'm here with my son, and we have reason to believe that my brother-in-law was here recently. Would we be able to come in and ask around?"

A quiet beep and the doors slid open for Spencer and Daniel to enter. He strode inside, moving across the black and white linoleum floor. The place still looked about the same as when Spencer was in his late teens. The walls were still the same light gray as back then, and it still had that same robot at the reception desk. He wondered if his old ID number would still work, as well.

"Identification?" the robot's mechanized voice asked.

"Abbot, Spencer. ID number: 42-14051804."

"Welcome back, intern."

He bristled a bit at being addressed as *intern*. He didn't put himself through medical school just to retain that title. But he could worry about that later. Currently, he had other business.

"Have any experiments been brought in recently?"

"If you are looking for an experiment, I will need its ID number as well."

Spencer muttered to himself. "Can I just give a name?"

"ID number."

The doctor took a few deep breaths, trying to keep himself from going ballistic on a robot. He didn't really want to show that sort of anger around his son, no matter how frustrated he may have been by now.

"Is there a problem here?" asked a somewhat chirpy voice.

Looking toward the elevator doors, Spencer and Daniel could see a slim woman. Her long light brown hair was pulled back in a ponytail. She held a clipboard, and Spencer couldn't help but glare. He knew who this woman was.

"Dr. Burke," he greeted, voice firm.

She smiled at him. "Ah, Spencer, it's been a while!"

Spencer didn't return the smile. He recalled Dr. Mara Burke and her sister Lila from his internship. Said internship was mostly wonderful. He'd learned so much during that time. But the Burke sisters had always made him uncomfortable. Lila had this knack for crafting creatures that had no place in polite society. It was one thing to combine human and animal DNA, but what she created went beyond that. Entirely too many teeth, hands where there should not have been hands, stripping the victims of her experiments of all sapience…Spencer may not have seen any of this happen on his own, but a couple of the other interns had worked directly under her and her sister, and that was why they left. He mainly stayed because the guy he worked under was their best boss.

"Yeah, yeah, I know…you seen a friend of mine, by any chance? Long red hair, monkey tail…"

Spencer's tolerance for bullshit was pretty low right now, as Mara could see in his brown eyes. And she nodded.

"Yes, as a matter of fact, we have," she admitted. "Lila picked him up on her way here this morning. Why do you ask?"

"We were planning to meet up. So, if you could release him to us, that would be appreciated."

Remembering that Daniel was right there on his back and wanting to be the best possible influence he could on the boy, he added a "Please."

Mara had to think about that one. "Well, we get a bunch of experiments, so he might not have been here."

He crossed his arms. "So, here's the thing," he began. "I've been studying magic for a few years now. One of the spells I know? It's a tracking spell. And it brought me here."

She shrugged. "Well, maybe it's mistaken?"

Spencer's eyes began to glow. "Daniel, I'm sorry. It's about to get cold in here…"

Before Mara could demand to know what he meant by this, she could feel the temperature in the room lower. Ice began to form on the floor, the walls, and her lab coat.

"Where. Is. He?" the doctor asked his tone as icy as the lobby.

Mara started backing away, only to slip on a patch of ice behind her. She landed on her backside with a yelp. When she looked up, she could see Spencer's unimpressed expression bearing down on her. She cleared her throat.

"Hey, Lila!" she called at the top of her lungs.

Nobody showed for a few moments (though Daniel flinched at the high volume at which Mara had shouted). Eventually, the other Burke sister made her appearance, stepping out of one of the ground floor offices. Her hair was the same light brown as Mara's but significantly shorter. It didn't go far past her chin. Her frame was a bit heavier than that of her sister's. Her hands were shoved into the pockets of her lab coat, and it was clear she'd been woken from a nap.

"There a problem here, Mar?" she yawned. "I was in the middle of something important."

"I told you to sleep last night," Mara sighed.

"I was too excited about the experiment. Anyway, what's the problem? Why's it so cold in here?"

Spencer waited for an answer, taking a moment to check in on Daniel. The boy was also looking at the two scientists for an explanation, his little tail lashing about. Spence could feel it slapping against his back.

"Well, Sister, this guy's looking for our most recent experiment…"

Lila grinned, going to grab onto Spencer's hand so she could pull him along. He sighed but figured she was leading him to Travis's location. Or at least he hoped that was the case. If it came down to teleporting an unconscious hybrid home, he could live with that.

They entered the elevator, Lila hitting a button for the second floor. On the way up, Mara's attention turned toward Daniel, who she cooed at and tried to pinch his tail. He swatted at her hand with said tail, causing her to pout.

"Didn't your parents ever tell you not to hit a grown-up?"

"Actually," said Spencer, "we've been teaching him the importance of consent. Maybe you could learn from him."

She rolled her eyes as they reached the second floor. A blindingly white hallway led to a huge room. There was a massive tank of water against one wall, with a rather expensive-looking computer next to it. There were charts and notes pinned to the opposite wall. Spencer could almost imagine those all being connected by red string, much like a conspiracy theorist's classic decor.

But as he looked over what was on the wall, he began to piece together what might have happened. There were a few photos of Travis in the mix. Some of the notes were clearly formulas. One chart was a haphazardly-rendered picture of Travis, with a plus sign, and another rushed drawing of a fish. There were a few possibilities of what such a hybrid might look like, ranging from a fish with ridiculously long hair to him having scales all over his body, to...well, he wasn't quite able to wrap his head around the last one, but there were huge sharp teeth where there should not have been, and there may have been a second head in there somewhere.

"...I think I'm gonna need you to walk me through this," said Spencer.

Spencer had an idea of what happened but wanted to hear just how they would explain it.

Lila bounded toward the charts, a wide grin on her face.

"Okay, so you see, we'd heard all about how this guy's," She pointed to one of the photos of Travis, "DNA was, like, *really* weird. Everyone else has tried testing how long it takes for him to recover from stuff, right? Well, I started thinking: 'Know what could be neat? Making him a fish-man!'. Mara's the one that picked him up. Her and a bunch of buddies of ours. But the good van was already in use, so we used Gary's old station wagon for that."

The doctor sighed. Somehow, none of this surprised him.

"And where is he now?"

If it turned out that Trav was also invisible...well, that also wouldn't be much of a shock. By this point in his life, it was a bit more difficult to surprise Dr. Spencer Abbot.

Mara crossed her arms. "Welp, we needed to send him on a test run in the ocean, so he's somewhere off the Atlantic coast. If you hold on a sec, I should be able to get his exact coordinates."

She strode toward the computer, pushing a few buttons. There was a soft beep from the corner. In said corner was a small device. One that looked almost like the sort of anklet one might wear if they were under house arrest.

"...Lila, wasn't that supposed to go on his arm before we took him out there?" Mara asked, squinting.

Lila chuckled. "Ah, right, right...ever get so excited about an experiment that you forget to *tag* it?"

Mara laughed, understanding entirely. "Ah, yeah. It happens to the best of us."

Spencer, meanwhile, was considerably less amused at this turn of events. Daniel blinked.

"...What happened?" the boy asked, trying to process this whole string of events.

"Well," Spencer replied. "These two dropped your uncle off in the ocean and forgot to track him. The ocean's a huge place, so he could be anywhere. So, they're gonna come help us look for him."

Mara scoffed. "Like we would...besides, you wouldn't force it. You're the one that's been teaching your kid about *consent*. Wouldn't that make you a hypocrite?"

"Dad, what's a hippo-cat?" Daniel asked.

"Hypocrite," Spencer told him. "And there are times where forcing someone is acceptable. Like when they need to take responsibility for what they've done wrong."

On that last part, he glared right at Mara and Lila.

Lila, for her part, shrugged. "Going with him would be a good idea," she said. "I kinda want to see how he's doing out there in the wild."

"Fine," Mara sighed. "I can rent a boat for us."

Somewhere In The Atlantic Ocean

Travis's sense of direction in a terrestrial setting was bad enough. But underwater, he had an even harder time getting his bearings. He was sure he and Roly had passed by that small cavern a few times, but he wasn't sure. The young shark probably had a better idea of where they were by now, being a native of the ocean...but then again, they were young. Young and only slightly more experienced with the sea than himself.

The two had been swimming for a while before Roly asked their next question.

"You mentioned getting home...what's your home like? It's on land, isn't it?"

Trav nodded. "Yeah, it is. I live in this city where you get a bunch of scientists running around. Sometimes they run experiments on people. Sometimes it's me they happen to. But my family's pretty great, and that makes it all worth it."

"What's your family like?"

Travis's fin flicked a bit as he thought of them. "Welp, my mom's a really talented scientist. Part-cat, good with machines, helped me and my sister out of a bad situation...my sister's an absolute sweetheart, loves to read, hates violence, and she married my best friend, Spence. I don't think I've ever been as close to someone as him. He uses magic, always there for me, and if anyone ever tries to hurt him, I'll kick their ass. He and my sister have a son. He's a good kid. Likes spending time with my mom. She teaches him about fixing stuff…"

To be honest, Trav wasn't sure how much of this Roly comprehended. The pup had lived underwater for all of their short life, so there was probably not a huge frame of reference for such things as *machines*. But to be able to tell *someone* what was going on in his head, what he wanted to return to…it comforted him, in a way.

"What'll happen if you don't get home?"

Now that was a question he wasn't quite prepared to answer. He'd gone through a thirteen-month span where he'd been separated from them. It was hellish for everyone involved. Though at least this time, he wasn't dealing with the twisted whims of a vengeful serial killer. No, he was just contending with being in an unfamiliar form in unfamiliar territory. Compared to what one Jesse Lynn Belle had put him through, this was far preferable.

That said, he still hoped to return to his loved ones.

"Not sure," he replied. "No offense, but I'm hoping it doesn't come to that."

As the pair swam about, Travis's mind was going to food. Where could he find something…

There were crabs around. But he couldn't conceive of eating one of those without it being fully boiled first. And the lack of melted butter would make it a bit harder to imagine, not to mention the lack of some way to crack the shell in the first place. A fish would probably be a better option, but wouldn't that be closer to cannibalism, given his current half-fish status?

He wasn't sure how well raw fish would work with him, either. Though given what he was now, it probably wouldn't make him sick. If he could find any clams or oysters, those might also be a viable option. But the plan, for now, was to go looking for a fish.

There was a small school of fish within view. Looking at Roly, Travis grinned. "So, since I wouldn't let you eat me…that look good?" he asked, pointing toward the fish.

The young shark was ready to do this, the pair stalking their way toward their target. They didn't need to obliterate all of them...just snag enough to sustain themselves for now. So focused were the pair, they didn't notice another, larger figure entering that region.

Travis was just about to grab one of the fish when a set of sharp teeth came dangerously close to depriving him of a hand. Despite his current half-fish status, he still couldn't help but let out a monkey-like screech. There in front of him, having devoured what Trav and Roly had hoped would be a meal for them in one bite, was a massive great white shark.

This one had a huge scar on its face, running from just by its left eye to beneath its lower jaw. Travis had to wonder if that was from an altercation with people, another sea creature, or what was going on. Either way, it seemed to regard him with curiosity.

"...Smells like a fish, but at the same time, doesn't?"

The merman chuckled. "Yeah, kind of a weird day for me too," he said. "Would you know how far it is to land? I ask because that's where I'm actually from, and I'm lost. Like, to a point I've never been lost before..."

The larger shark circled around the pair, and Travis could see that this shark was a bit on the chunky side. Or rather, its left side; the right looked like it'd been attacked by something with teeth, some heavy scarring in that region. There were also a few slight scars on its fins.

"So...things get kinda rough down here, hm?" Trav asked as the big shark swam around him and Roly.

"Damn whales wiped out half of my litter before they were even born," it--or rather, she--replied.

Another instance of orcas attacking. Were they also responsible for the face scarring and the scars on her fins?

"And what about that scar, and the ones on your..." He tried to remember the word but had spaced on it entirely and just pointed to his arm, given that that was the closest approximation he could think of to a fin.

"The face scar was another shark. One of the striped ones tried getting at the same meal as me, and...well, you should have seen *her* afterward. As for the fins? Ah, just a little side effect of mating."

He blushed a bit upon hearing that one. Travis wasn't exactly a prude, but he had literally just met this shark, and here she was, casually telling him about shark sex. He didn't even know her damn name yet!

"So, um...couple more questions: first off, what can I call you? Second, could you help me get to some land?"

"I'm known as *Requin*, and yeah, I could probably do that," she replied.

Well, that was a relief. He might have some help with getting a bit closer to home. He wasn't sure if he'd end up in, say, Florida or on another continent...but at least he could get to a phone after a while. Unless, of course, he didn't resume his normal form. He shivered at the thought of being unable to breathe upon reaching shore. He'd dealt with asphyxiation a few times before, and it was not an experience he wished to repeat anytime soon.

With the duo now upgraded to a trio, they resumed the trek to search for land.

***

Off The East Coast Somewhere
On A Boat
Spencer had hoped that when Mara brought up the idea of renting a boat, it would be somewhat bigger. It didn't have to be a fancy yacht, just something large enough to give him a little bit of distance from the Burke sisters. What they had instead was perhaps the saddest little rowboat imaginable. It was made of an acrylic material, concerningly held together with tape. He'd made sure to conjure a few lifejackets, of course. His son and himself were the priority, but if something happened and either of the Burkes drowned, he'd feel guilty over it. Plus, his son would see this, and he didn't want the boy to be traumatized.

"You couldn't have gotten a bigger boat…" he sighed.

"I wanted to, but lab equipment's expensive," Mara pouted, arms crossed.

"Please, you just wanted that new microscope because it was the shiniest one there," Lila scoffed.

"Like you're not attracted to the shine, too!"

"Heh, yeah, you got me…"

As the sisters bantered, Spencer ran his fingers along the hair-bracelet he'd used for the tracking spell. Daniel was seated on his lap, turning to watch as he used the spell once again. This time, however, the spell sort of fizzled out. Still out of range, it seemed. He let out a sigh.

He was out fishing with his son, essentially. But most of the time, one would do that with just their son, a couple of poles, and they'd start in the morning. Fishing trips were meant to be peaceful. Relaxing. A time to connect with nature…

This fishing trip was anything but peaceful, given that it was in a tiny, cheap-ass boat with three fully-grown adults and a child crammed into it. Two of those fully-grown adults were mad scientist sisters that kept bickering as siblings do. They were looking for one specific fish (well, *merman*)… None of this fishing trip felt like what he'd ever imagined one would be like, and yet here they were.

They had no more room aboard the boat for one more occupant, and so they had a harness for whenever they happened to find Travis, along with a tether for it that they intended to attach to the back of the boat.

"So, no luck finding him yet, hm?" Mara asked.

Spencer rolled his eyes. "Does it *look* like I've had any luck? Trust me, if I have, I probably would've accidentally thrown you off the boat by now in celebration."

Well, accidentally-on-purpose. He knew they'd survive with the lifejackets, anyway. But he would still be happy to get some form of revenge on those two for putting him through this search in the first place.

"Hoping we find him soon, though," said Spencer after a pause. "I would rather not have to place a call back home, but if I need to, I'm more than willing."

But really, he really would rather not have to; it felt wrong to have his son out there for too long. He had no intention of giving up before they located his brother-in-law.

They were several miles from shore now, and he tried the tracking spell again. This time, however, he got something. The glow was faint, barely visible against the light of the sun. But it was there.

He could feel it.

"...I think I have something!"

<hr>

Somewhere In The Atlantic

Today had been going too well, Travis reasoned. That was the only way to explain why he was seeing what he was right now. Roly had warned him about the orcas. Requin had also brought up how vicious they could be. But he wasn't sure if he believed them. They'd always seemed so sweet and lovable in movies!

And yet there, in front of him and his two new shark friends, was a small pod of them, all chowing down on a gray whale. Neither of them seemed particularly fazed, but Travis was still processing things. Plus, the sight of a partially eaten whale was a bit surreal to him.

"Well, that *could* have made for a decent snack..." Requin grumbled.

"Oh, it is!" one of the orcas called, tone almost sort of mocking. "Too bad we already got the best parts!"

Travis blinked. It was one thing for them to be predators, but this one was just being a *dick*. Seriously, why would anyone rub something in like that? Requin watched the orcas as if trying to keep from attacking. There were five of them, whereas her own group was much smaller. Five orcas of about equal strength versus one adult great white, a young hammerhead, and one whatever-the-hell-this-Travis-guy-was did not seem like particularly great odds. Roly had backed away, wishing to avoid a confrontation from a few larger creatures. And as for Travis, he was hardly qualified to fight a killer whale, let alone five.

But this was Travis Isaac Malone, who was not always what one might call a bastion of common sense. The merman swam forward, his human-like teeth bared. Hardly the sort of fangs that might intimidate someone else, let alone someone larger than himself.

"The fuck is your problem?" he growled. "Why do you have to be like that, huh? I mean, it's one thing to eat something in front of someone, but to rub that fact in? Total dick move…"

If a shark could facepalm, Requin would have done so right then and there. Roly just looked confused as to how he could possibly think this was a good plan. And one of the orcas advanced on the merman, eyes narrowed.

"Who or *what* do you think you are?" he asked, his much-sharper-than-Trav's teeth bared.

Travis scoffed. "Name's Travis, and I'm not sure what I am. What I'm sure of, though, is that my friends here want some food. Hell, *I'm* hungry, too! And here you are, all 'Yeah, it's good. Tough shit if you want some, though!'…"

His opponent pushed him back with his nose. It wasn't what one would call a gentle push, either—more of a violent shove that sent him slamming into Requin's face.

"Well, we need to eat, too," the lead orca replied. "You can get your own. So how about you try doing that now? Because we've still got room, and ever eat a great white's liver? Good stuff, right there… The little one? Probably a decent snack. And as for you? Well, we're willing to experiment, aren't we, guys?"

Three of the other four showed their agreement to the statement, but the fifth one was more hesitant. Travis was still ready to give them a piece of his mind, but a set of teeth closed on one of his arms, urging him to move back. He glanced back to see Roly trying to pull him away.

On the one hand, he wasn't done with this spat yet. On the other, he didn't want to disappoint a kid. And so, he backed away. Requin got between them and the orcas.

"Sorry about the half-breed," she told them. "He's not from around here."

There was a long stretch of silence before the orcas turned and swam off. Well, most of them did. One stayed behind, moving closer to the trio.

"Sorry about him," this one sighed. "That's my brother, and he has a few issues with sharks. Did you see the scar on his tail?"

Come to think of it, Travis did sort of notice that.

"That was from a run-in with a mako. Little bastard was an aggressive one... Granted, he's always been something of a jerk, but that pushed him over the edge. Is it true you're not from here?"

Travis nodded. "Yeah...home is somewhere on land. Been trying to get there."

"Hm...have you tried finding a boat?" she asked. "In my experience, there're usually a few around. Sometimes people go whale-watching, sometimes they're out fishing...sometimes just playing out in the water."

"You mean like when the humans do those weird imitations of seals?" Requin asked. "I've fallen for that a couple times...kind of an unpleasant flavor."

Travis had to think about that one. And then he recalled seeing something about surfers getting bitten by sharks. Okay, yes, he could see how that might happen.

"Humans do seal imitations?" Roly asked.

"Not on purpose," Travis said.

"Anyway," the orca continued, "it is a bit like that, yes. What I'm thinking is that if you reach the surface, you can eventually find a boat, follow it to a dock..."

He had to admit, that wasn't a bad idea. Yeah, if he could get to a boat...

Aboard A Boat

Atlantic Ocean

He had the trace, but now it was gone. Spencer was a bit frustrated over that. This spell had a three-mile radius, and the trace he'd had before was minimal. He couldn't have gone that far in a few minutes, could he? And that was without factoring in depth. The boat was fairly far from the shore by now, so it was just him, Daniel, and the Burkes surrounded by water. Unlike the vial of water around his neck, however, this water had not been gathered with the intention of using it for magic. Also, he wasn't sure if he even *could* utilize the entire ocean (or even just a patch of it) for his purposes. It might make him more powerful, but it might be the magical equivalent of using the wrong wattage lightbulb for a lamp.

"So, we gonna start heading back?" Mara asked. "I mean, it's getting kind of late…"

Spencer looked out at the horizon. Yes, for once, Dr. Mara Burke had a point. The sun was starting to set, and he was sure Gemmy had to be worried by now. Daniel had dozed off in his lap, Lila having similarly fallen asleep and using her sister's shoulder as a pillow.

"I can't just yet," he sighed. "I wouldn't feel right about leaving him, y'know?"

Mara nodded. "Yeah, I get that…kinda like if it were Lila I was looking for, I take it?"

"Exactly like that," Spencer replied. "I never had any siblings growing up. Closest I've ever had has been Travis. I know it's likely he'd outlive me, but the thought of losing him in any capacity… Why did you do it?"

She chuckled. "I couldn't help it. First of his kind…do you really think I could resist playing with his genetic material?"

"And you couldn't think to *ask* him?"

"He might've said no, and my curiosity couldn't take that for an answer."

Spencer glared at her before pulling out his phone and hitting his home number.

"Hey, Gemmy, a little situation came up," he said. "Yeah, someone was after your brother's DNA again. Don't worry, Daniel's with me, and he's safe."

A slight pause.

"Well, it seems the Burke sisters turned him into a merman and threw him into the ocean. We're tracking him down now because they forgot to tag him. Heh, yes, I'll see what I can do about that. Love you too."

He disconnected, repocketing his phone.

Okay, so now the plan was to locate Travis and get a picture of him in his mer form, as Spencer's wife was rather curious about how her brother looked right now. To be honest, Spencer was also wondering about that. But he couldn't let Mara (or Lila, for that matter) know of his interest in seeing this.

As he prepared to resume the search, he could see a large shape in the distance. It was a little ways away, but he could tell it was a boat of some kind. Significantly larger than the one he was in, but that didn't take much.

"You see that?" he asked.

Mara leaned forward, her sister muttering at her pillow's sudden shift in position.

"Yeah...should we see about hitching a ride on that?" she asked.

"Couldn't hurt."

From there, they began the slow row toward this other boat, not knowing who or what occupied it as of yet.

Somewhere In The Atlantic Ocean

Travis, his two shark companions, and the orca (who he had found preferred to be called "Deb") had been moving forward and upward, looking for the first indication they could get of a boat. There was one small shape, but it seemed kind of little to be a boat. It did look like a decent snack, though, and so Requin made her way toward it with Roly in tow.

The merman paused as he saw them swim toward it.

"Hey, still gotta eat," Requin told him. "And that's probably a good source of food. So, gotta strike when I can. The little one's probably thinking the same."

"Yeah, I should get something to eat," said Roly. "And make sure she doesn't get it all first."

"Fair enough," he replied. "Welp, in case I don't see you guys again, thanks for sticking with me."

"Yep. Hope you get home safe," Roly told him before they and Requin made their way toward what they were sure was dinner.

Meanwhile, Trav rejoined Deb, the two of them continuing along in their search for a boat. It took a bit before they found a large shape at the surface. It was, presumably, a boat. At least, he hoped it was.

"I'll breach," Deb told him. "Just to make sure it's a boat."

"All right."

He watched as the orca swam upward at a faster rate than he'd seen yet. As she leapt from the water, he could feel something bump into his back. He turned to see that Roly had come back to them.

"How was the snack?" Travis asked.

"Kind of a bust," they replied. "It turned out it was just a ridiculously tiny boat with some humans in it. They had this glowing bubble around them."

Travis's eyes widened. A glowing bubble...like the shield spell Spencer used on occasion. Did this mean that Spencer was in the area? He wasn't surprised at the thought of him searching for him, of course. No, Travis knew how close he and Spence were. It'd shock him more if Spence *hadn't* been looking for him.

Deb returned soon enough. "Okay, it *is*, in fact, a boat," she said. "It's got a few people aboard. Not sure what they're all up to, but they're there."

Ooh...yes, he could get to the boat, get help, and ask them about locating Spencer and pulling him aboard! Then from there, they could head home together. He saw nothing wrong with this plan.

He thanked Deb for her help and shot upward through the water as fast as his tail could possibly propel him. He was so much closer to returning home now...!

As he breached the surface, he could see the glowing ball in the distance. But it wasn't quite close enough for his voice to carry if he called out. Plus, if he just headed over to Spence, he felt the mage might be exhausted and unable to teleport them home. And so, it was the boat for now.

The craft was rather large, now that he was next to it. He slapped the side of the ship a few times (first with his hands, then with his tail), hoping to get someone's attention.

That didn't work.

Oh, sure, they did notice him in the water, but it was more by chance. One of the young men aboard had been walking across the deck when he noticed the merman beside the ship. He pulled down his sunglasses (why he was wearing the things this late in the day was beyond Travis, but he wasn't going to judge right now) and called down to him.

"The hell?!"

"Hey, I need a ride! Mind helping me out?!" Travis called. His tail fin poked out of the water. "And yeah, that's my tail, so...I might need some water on that boat!"

The next thing he knew, there was a net being lowered into the water. He let it pick him up, figuring that to be the best possible way to get aboard in this form. He could explain his situation up there, anyway.

Though along the way up, he could faintly hear them chatting.

"You sure?"

"Yeah, man. He said it's his actual tail! How much you think we can get for a merman?"

"Well, let me get a look at him first..."

Travis slapped his forehead and groaned. Yes, this would be his luck, wouldn't it... He hitches a ride on a boat, only to find that they're willing to try selling him. To be honest, he was surprised this hadn't happened to him earlier.

They had hauled the net aboard, and he could get a clear look at these people. The guy with the sunglasses, apparently the ringleader of this group, looked like something right out of an 80s college movie, with his short blond hair and clean white polo shirt. There was a baby blue sweater tied around his neck, reminding him of the worst super-hero's cape imaginable. Khaki shorts and overly clean tennis shoes completed the look.

The other three guys were dressed similarly, one having brown hair, another black, and one was a redhead. Though Travis was sure the redhead's hair was a dye job, as he could see the brown roots. It was as though their captain had wanted each of them to have a different hair color.

"Hey, Kyle, is the tank still empty?" the leader asked.

The redhead, Kyle, shrugged, going to check that. The tank, it seemed, was below deck. While he went to take care of that, the leader poked at Travis's tail, marveling at it.

"Y'know, we'd normally be hijacking some fishers or collecting exotic fish to sell on the black market," he said. "But an actual freaking *merman*?! Oh, the haul we could get for that from the scientists in Hell Bent alone!"

Travis crossed his arms, holding back a laugh. Did he want to inform this guy that the scientists there had been getting to his genetic material for no charge for years by now? He considered it--deeply considered it--but ultimately decided it'd be funnier if he found out for himself.

"...Hey, what the hell?"

Travis looked at the leader, who was looking at Trav's tail. Or rather, his legs as the scales retreated, giving way to skin. The single limb was now back to its initial three: right leg, left leg, and his monkey-like tail. He twitched the tail a bit, glancing toward it. Well, as much as he could, given the net he was still trapped in.

"Heh...missed you," he told it, managing to poke at the tail with one of his toes.

"What are you?!" the crew's leader demanded, glaring.

"Right now?" Travis asked with a grin. "Naked and stuck in a net. Anyone got a knife?"

Atlantic Ocean

Near The Wreckage Of A Tiny Boat

The initial bump from below was enough to rouse both Lila and Daniel from their sleep. The second bump was all it took to bring their sad little craft to pieces. Spencer was relieved that all of them had the lifejackets, but he had noticed a couple of shark fins poking out of the water.

And that was what spurred him to create the bubble shield around the group. He was still annoyed with Lila and Mara for causing this situation in the first place, of course, but he didn't want to let either of them be hurt. Not on his watch. What they got into without him and Daniel around was their problem, but it wasn't an option right now.

He got a good look at the sharks as they chewed on the boat's remains. One was a great white with a bunch of scars. The other was a tiny hammerhead...perhaps of the bonnethead variety if one was to be precise. He took the time to tell his son about both types. Spencer's expertise may have been more in the vein of medicine, but he still knew enough to be able to identify the sharks to his kid and let him know that despite how scary they might seem, they didn't really mean any harm.

When the sharks returned to the depths, it was on to the next issue: transportation. Shields like this took effort to keep up for long periods of time, they still had a Travis to locate, and teleportation was rough enough with just one or two people, let alone all of them after finding him. Their best bet was to do as Mara had suggested earlier and try to get a ride on the ship.

It took a few moments to get the shield to transport them closer to the ship. As they got closer, it looked like it belonged to some rich sailor. Hopefully, this sailor would be an understanding type that would let them use his ship to pick up Trav.

More focus was needed to levitate the shield to the ship's deck. Spencer had his hand over his water vial's general location, channeling his energy into this whole task. And soon enough, they were aboard the ship.

Spencer let the shield down, taking a few breaths.

"...Is that Uncle Trav?" Daniel asked, holding onto his father's leg with one hand, pointing ahead with the other.

Spencer looked up. Ahead of them, currently being held face-down by three guys that had sort of an obnoxious rich guy vibe about them, was Travis. And from what he could gather, he was no longer in mer form. The fourth of the group seemed to be struggling with some rope, muttering to himself about why knots had to be so hard.

"...You wanna take this, or should I?" Lila asked.

"I got it," Spencer replied. "Could you two keep an eye on Daniel and not lose him?"

"We'll do our best," said Mara.

Not the most confidence-inducing phrase one could hear, but Spencer would take it for now as he strode forward. How best to deal with those four... He was taller than any of them, albeit much slimmer. However, he also knew that he was likely a more skilled mage than any of them could ever hope to be.

He focused on each of the four, thinking of a good spell to use. No matter what he did, he probably couldn't intimidate them. And so, he elected the sleep spell. It would render them fully unconscious for a good twenty-four hours. Plenty of time to get back home.

None had time to register what happened before the spell took effect. The four went down quickly, dropping around a rather perplexed Travis.

"...Okay, either I'm surrounded by narcoleptics, or...Spence?" he asked, craning his neck to look behind him.

Upon seeing the tall doctor standing there, Travis pushed himself upright, rushing over and hugging him. Spencer returned the hug, somewhat wishing that the half-monkey had pants right now or some means of covering himself. But mostly, he was just relieved to have him back. That said, he focused on using one more spell for now: a conjuring one. A blanket appeared in his hand, and he gave that to Travis.

Lila would be the one to steer them home, Mara serving as her navigator. The trip to shore would take a few hours, during which time Travis and Spencer (along with Daniel) would chat.

"So...what was it like?" Spencer asked. "Being a merman, living in the water for part of a day?"

The half-monkey sighed. "Well, getting food was kind of a pain. Sure, there was a lot around, but it kept being eaten by others. I got bitten or almost bitten a few times...weirdly, I felt a little *safer* than on land, if that makes sense."

Spence nodded. "Yeah, I can see that..."

"But I made friends with a couple sharks. One's this great white named Requin...she got attacked by an orca at some point. And she said a few of her other scars were from, like, sex, I guess. There was a little one named Roly that thought I was just a big fish at first. This one orca named Deb helped me find a boat...not sure she knew about its occupants, though."

The doctor leaned closer, pushing up his glasses. "Wait, so when you were a merman, you could communicate with the sea life?"

Travis nodded, crossing his arms somewhat smugly. "Damn right! Really, if it weren't for the fact that I'd feel lost without you and the rest of the family, I probably could've gotten used to it down there. But yep, I would've missed you too much."

"So, when'd you turn back into..."

Spencer gestured to his legs.

"I dried off enough after I got pulled out that they turned back," Travis said. "Best as I can figure, that's what happened."

The sound was faint, but the guys could hear Mara and Lila

laughing together as they steered the ship toward a dock. Some light-hearted bickering could also be heard.

"Finding you would have taken a lot less time if they remembered to tag you," Spencer said.

"Somehow, that doesn't surprise me," Trav sighed. "Them forgetting, and all...Here's hoping we don't have to deal with them again after we get home."

"Agreed."

From that point on, Travis wouldn't turn into a merman again, nor really have to deal with more experimentation from the Burkes. The closest he ever got to the merman form was when he would dip a toe into the water at the beach to see scales form on his skin or running into either of the sisters at the grocery store. But other than that, he managed to find other problems to run into.

FIN

K. Matt is both an author and illustrator living in a rural part of New York state. When she's not drawing comics, she's writing stuff that may eventually become a comic. Sometimes, she's been known to procrastinate (her favorite procrastination activity being baking). Fairly often, she's known to be better communicating through text as opposed to verbally.

Find out more: KaylaMatt.wordpress.com

facebook.com/HellBentBookSeries
twitter.com/MarieTwixie
instagram.com/kmatt666

SEA START

BY EMMA SHELFORD

A cloud of blood blossomed in the cave's still water. It was as black as squid ink and threatened to billow into my face in the same way. I needed to move, but I was transfixed in horror by what had happened.

By what I'd done.

The rich man's sightless gray eyes saw nothing as he floated past me. His white hair appeared gray with blood half-obscuring the deep gash I'd inflicted across his temple with a bone knife. Rich sirens sometimes commissioned mer folk to fashion weapons in their signature sharp-edged style. The blade I'd snatched from a wall-sconce of the rich man's cave in the upper reaches of the Seamount was the finest I'd ever seen. Not that I'd encountered many of the expensive blades before. Siren-human hybrids weren't invited to mingle with the likes of this man.

Water currents tingled on my skin, and the movement finally jerked me out of my mesmerized dread. Someone was coming. Three someones, if my skin sense could be believed.

I couldn't stay here. Half-siren scum didn't get fair trials. I'd never been caught during a theft, but I'd witnessed others endure severe punishments for stealing. But stealing coupled with murder, even accidental? I bit my lip until it throbbed in pain.

My long white hair whipped around my face as I kicked my powerful legs in a frenzy to escape. My kelp dress fluttered against my thighs as I fought to disappear through the cave's back entrance before the others saw me. If I could avoid being seen, I might survive long enough to blend into the half-human ghetto. If they saw me...

"Stop!"

A strident hum and click of command vibrated through my body. My head turned with an involuntary motion, and I cursed when the woman who'd burst into the cave got a full view of my face. Her pale gray eyes widened at the sight of the dead man, then she focused on me.

"You," she snarled, her humming, gestures, and clicks clearly communicating her intent through Seamount-speak. "I know you, scum. Lune Seafields, the thief they never catch. You did this."

"I didn't," I replied, my answering gesture trembling with fear. "I didn't mean to. He attacked me. I was defending myself."

The woman was an upper echelon siren, as near to the top as I was to the bottom. Her graceful legs were half-covered by a flowing dress of delicate red seaweeds, exquisitely—and expensively—prepared to hold together as a garment. My own serviceable dress was made from simple kelp, which was hardwearing and easy to design with. The darkness of the red seaweed—black at this depth, since red light didn't travel far into the water—contrasted strikingly against the woman's white hair and pale skin.

"You murdered him," she said flatly, her hands expressing herself with grim finality. Two men appeared behind her in the mouth of the cave, but she needed no support. As a powerful full-blooded female siren, she had us all in her power if she wanted. She continued, "And you will pay for your crimes. Excommunication followed by death."

My heart shriveled in my chest at this pronouncement. I didn't want to die. I'd only seen twenty-four sunsweeps, and life so far had been hard. I wanted more.

But excommunication, that was worse. If I were cut off from the goddess Ramu's love and grace, I would never return to her endless sea, even upon death. I would be less than nothing, doomed to swim forever sundered from my goddess.

This couldn't be the end. I wasn't ready for that.

I wasn't powerful enough to overpower the other woman, but surprise was a formidable ally. I opened my mouth and screamed a compulsion of defiance and disorientation. While the other three rubbed their eyes and twisted their bodies to rid themselves of the sensation, I darted out the back entrance and away from my accidental crime.

The cave opened into a communal area, lit only by phosphorescent algae lining the cave walls. Sleeping animals floated in midwater, their squashed faces peaceful in repose. Yatulls were water-breathing seals that lived only at the Seamount, and they were the perfect size to serve as mounts. The upper echelon always kept a few for that purpose. This cave served as a gathering place for tamed yatulls favored by nearby sirens.

A wild thought chased across my mind, and each notion stabbed me like the sharp end of a bone blade. I'd been seen. The upper echelon woman knew my name. I had to run, and the quicker, the better. If I stole a yatull, I could hide myself in the city far more quickly than by swimming myself.

Water paused in my throat with my caught breath, but I didn't have time to consider the matter further. The others would burst into this cave within moments—my disorientation blast wouldn't hold them back for long—and I needed to escape from this place soon. Where I went afterward, I would have to decide later.

I approached the nearest sleeping yatull and ran a hand gently over her head, humming a tone of soft control as I did so. She blinked and yawned, but I didn't have time to let her wake up slowly. I floated on top and swung my leg over her back. At the familiar gesture, she stiffened and readied her flippers.

Away, I hummed, and she didn't need telling twice. With a powerful thrust of her back fins, she propelled her long body through the wide entrance and into open water.

The yatull streaked over a rocky outcrop covered in swaying green anemones and dived deeper. The Seamount was a massive underwater mountain that didn't break through surface waves far above. One side disappeared into inky black depths, far deeper than I'd ever explored, but the other plateaued for a short time at the lower limits of light.

Between that point and the summit, the Seamount's inhabitants lived. The mountain was arranged with upper echelon folk of all types residing nearer the light. People became progressively worse off the further down one descended until reaching the half-siren ghetto near the plateau's edge. That was my home.

Or it had been. The ghetto wouldn't be safe for me, not now that the woman knew my name. My too-small feet and gold-tinged skin clearly revealed my human heritage. She would know exactly where to look for me.

I swallowed and directed my yatull in the direction of the plateau. I had to hide somewhere. Now, before the others caught up with me. I didn't have time to visit Eelway, my foster father, nor Fin and Spray, my best friends. If I stopped to tell them what had happened, my actions would only put them in danger.

The yatull sped over a slope of rough stone tufted with anemones, sponges, and sea stars. Underneath, a warren of tunnels and caves riddled the landscape and provided homes for inhabitants of the ghetto. My eyes grew warm, and I turned my head away from the familiar sight.

Past the ghetto, the light was dim, and I relied on my skin sense to visualize the world around me. Rocky outcrops housed soft corals and glass sponges, and occasional sea cucumbers wriggled in the silty seafloor between rocks. A crevasse yawned below my swimming yatull, and I recalled that even these flats hid caves and tunnels. Maybe I could eke out a living among them. The thought gave me no comfort.

A wash of sensation pulsed over my skin. My head whipped around, but I already knew what I would see.

A brigar jetted toward me, its gigantic fleshy body and angry-looking eyes at the forefront, extensive tentacles streaming behind. Brigars were octopuses, but their sheer size—larger than twenty of me stretched end on end—and long, grasping tentacles made them a formidable weapon used by sirens and mer folk alike. Add in their intelligence, and escaping a brigar was rarely done.

Mer folk protected the Seamount from discovery by dry folk, and one of their favorite ways to do so was by directing a brigar in the direction of a hapless boat. These creatures rarely responded to the siren call of pale folk like me, but mer folk were brave—or foolhardy—enough to force their will on the giant cephalopods, usually at weapon-point.

This was bad. The octopus was heading straight toward me. Clearly, the upper echelon folk chasing me had used their privileged status to direct a brigar my way. I had only seconds before its suction cups wrapped around my body and dragged me back to the Seamount to meet my fate. Assuming it wasn't hungry, of course.

My yatull bucked under my legs. I glanced around wildly, but the seafloor was too featureless to hide me. My roving eyes picked out a dark chasm below. The cave system. It was my only chance.

Pressure from the brigar's massive body assaulted my skin sense. I hummed a command to the yatull, and she dived straight down, twisting her sinuous body to squeeze into the narrow gap. I slid back until my hands gripped the yatull's tail to ease our passage.

The tip of a tentacle wrapped around my ankle. Its grip was forceful, despite the squishy bonelessness of the arm. Suction cups attached themselves to my smooth skin.

I kicked wildly, but the arm held on. My other foot scraped at my leg, trying to dislodge the tentacle, but it was relentless. With an inexorable force, it yanked me backward. My hands gripped the yatull's tail with a frantic death-grip, and the yatull yelped in pain.

I couldn't hold on for much longer. In desperation, I kicked my leg against the rough rock wall of the crevasse. Pain shot through my limb as the jagged stone sliced my skin, but the tentacle relaxed its grip.

"Go!" I shouted at the yatull, putting all my siren abilities behind the word. The yatull didn't have to be told twice. We shot through the tunnel, me banging against the sides of the crevasse in our haste.

The bleeding tentacle reached deep into the crack after us, seeking its quarry, but the panicked yatull was faster than the massive predator. My skin sense tracked the arm's movements, and my heart hammered like a crashing wave in my chest. Even though its arms were long, and octopuses were excellent at squeezing in tight spaces, the enormous brigar didn't have a chance at following us.

"Slow," I said to the yatull, and she stopped in a widening of the tunnel long enough for me to glide onto her back again. The tunnel was as dark as a moonless night, but I didn't need eyes. My skin sense filled in for my vision.

The tunnel was as wide as my outstretched arms and devoid of life in its blackness. A lone fish swam lazily at the edge of my sensing. Otherwise, the yatull and I were alone.

My grip on the yatull tightened. We weren't alone. For a moment of panic, I imagined the brigar jetted toward us. Then logic prevailed. The tunnels were far too tight for that monster. Instead, an octopus with a body no larger than my two fists put together stopped in front of me.

It gave a happy click and a hum, and my shoulders relaxed.

"It's fine," I said out loud to the yatull and myself. "Let's keep going, get past the brigar."

The yatull flicked her tail and glided silently forward. To my surprise, the tiny octopus followed us, clicking its interest. I ignored it. The little guy was cute, but I had bigger eight-armed problems to deal with.

We traveled through the network of tunnels in an easterly direction. I had no idea where they led, but my body could orient itself without conscious thought. I avoided tunnels with stagnant water, so I knew that the ones we followed would eventually lead us to open ocean.

At one point, I heard hums and clicks from a gap in the rock. I silently swam closer to listen.

"Keep the brigar searching," a voice said. I peeked out and recognized the two siren men who had been with the pale woman at the rich man's cave. They spoke with a male mer. "I want her found. We'll get our companion and some mounts and ready ourselves for pursuit if she escapes."

"She won't escape," the mer said. He flicked his fused legs contemptuously and swam away. The other two undulated their bodies in the direction of the city.

I floated, stunned, for a long moment. The sirens wouldn't stop until they'd found and punished me. I had no chance. My fate was sealed.

Unless I escaped the Seamount. Something expanded in my chest. It wasn't hope so much as grim determination. I was tired of being trapped in this city and tired of being ground into nothing by the upper echelon. They would never stop looking for me while I lived here. Soon enough, I would be found and punished. The narrow confines of the Seamount closed in, trapping me in their sickening grasp. Here, I was powerless to change anything or be more than I was. I would never be innocent in the eyes of those who ruled this city.

I couldn't be excommunicated and killed. It was unthinkable. But what could I do?

I had to leave.

My stomach clenched. Was I seriously considering leaving the Seamount? As far as I knew, there were no other settlements of pale or mer folk in this ocean, so leaving meant going to land. My lips pressed together. Why not? My own mother had made the dangerous trip on a youthful whim. If she could do it, why couldn't I? I snorted quietly. I only had to escape the brigar and find my way through the barrier surrounding the city.

But escaping was my only shot at living. I had to try.

I squeezed my legs, and the yatull continued forward. Finally, light glimmered at the end of our path. I took a deep breath and gripped my yatull more securely. We had to make a swim for it. Hopefully, the brigar was far enough away that it couldn't sense us, and it was occupied with searching the tunnels we'd disappeared into.

We emerged, blinking, and I concentrated with my skin sense while my eyes were still adjusting. With a sinking heart, I sensed the brigar behind us. It hadn't noticed us yet, busy as it was systematically searching every crevasse with its questing tentacles, but it would see us soon enough.

Before I could force the yatull back into our tunnel, the little octopus jetted in front of me.

Help, it said. Its knobby skin fluttered and changed hues. One arm ended in a smooth flattened region different from the others. The small creature must be a male. He wiggled his body with excitement. *Distract.*

I didn't have time to clarify the octopus' meaning before he squirted toward the brigar. Had he meant that he would help distract the larger cephalopod while we escaped? The offer seemed too good to be true, but I didn't have a lot of options. I had to take a chance on the little guy.

"Forward," I whispered to the yatull with a hum of command. She slinked toward the east. My heart thundered in my chest, and I waited for a rush of water that would precede the brigar's arrival, but it never came.

Had the little octopus successfully distracted the brigar? I turned my head, but both cephalopods were too far away for either my eyes to see or my skin to sense. I would have to trust my new ally, whatever his reasons were for helping me.

The rest of our journey over the plateau was uneventful, and my heart rate had returned to normal by the time the ground sloped downward again. I gripped the yatull more firmly between my legs. If I wanted to leave the Seamount, I had to pass the barrier.

No one was supposed to leave the Seamount. We were told it was dangerous out there. Dry folk would sooner slaughter us than speak with us. Strange creatures roamed the seas, more terrifying than a brigar or even the vast, serpentine ligan.

Mer folk were our protectors and wardens, and they guarded the outskirts of the Seamount in a patrol so tight that we called it the barrier, although no physical object impeded us.

But management of the barrier grew faulty when power in the Seamount switched hands. Every few decades, a political shakeup would rattle hierarchies and destabilize chains of command, and the barrier grew weak during these periods. We were living through such a time of turmoil, and I prayed to Ramu that my luck would allow me to pass through. I knew it was possible—my own mother had done it as a reckless act of rebellion during an earlier period of political instability—but I wasn't sure how.

A figure swam ahead, and I cursed. The sinuous form of a male mer materialized in my skin sense. Flowing lines of his elongated fused legs, the color of fresh kelp, contrasted with his flat features and harsh, angular face.

I forced the yatull behind a rock. Luckily for me, the skin sense of mer folk was underdeveloped. If he didn't see me, chances were, he wouldn't sense me another way.

"Over here."

The hum of greeting made me squeak with fright. I whirled around, my white hair floating past my face. A male siren beckoned from the mouth of a nearby tunnel. I dithered, but with the specter of the mer behind me, my decision was easy. I directed the yatull to dive after the pale man, hoping that I wasn't making a big mistake.

When we entered a spacious cavern lined with soft sponges, the man turned to me.

"Heading for land?" he said with a sympathetic gesture. "It's the only reason people come out here."

"How often do others come this way?" I'd thought commands to stay within the Seamount kept most inhabitants inside the barrier. Was this new generation of upper echelon youth braving the open ocean to explore foreign shores?

"More often than you think." The man shrugged. "The uppers like to vacation on land. It's different, exotic. I'm well-known as the one to come to if you want to seamlessly pass the barrier without the guards knowing. For a fee. I know the secret path, you see."

My heart surfaced then sank to the abyss. Passing the barrier was the largest snag in my ill-conceived plan. Even with political upheaval, the mer guard was a formidable obstacle.

But I had nothing to barter with. The upper echelon could afford to throw whatever they had at this strange man in the outposts, but I'd run away with nothing but my clothes and a pouch around my waist with a few odds and ends. Not that I had much else at home.

I only had one option. I took a deep breath and prepared to hum the man into compliance. Half-siren through I was, my feminine compulsion abilities outstripped the skills of a full-siren male. He wouldn't stand a chance against me.

My intentions must have shown in my expression because he held up his hand.

"Wait." He looked me over intently. "You're not a tourist, I can tell."

"What gave it away?" Fear sharpened my tone. "The tiny feet or the coarse kelp dress?"

"The fact that you didn't know the penalty of sirening me," he said calmly. "I have my own methods of protection, you know."

Although I doubted he had a brigar tucked in his sleeping cave, I still shuddered. If he felt protected against the might of the upper echelon, he had something powerful enough to stop me.

"I need to leave." I couldn't help the despair coloring my voice. "They'll kill me if I stay."

"A fugitive, hey?" The man stared intently at me. Then he smiled. "Lucky for you, I've always had a soft spot for half-sirens. My niece is one, she's a lovely girl. I'll let you go through just this once, for her sake."

"Thank you," I whispered, my eyes warm again. Finally, something was going right today. I needed every lucky break I could get.

My skin sense alerted me to the tiny octopus' presence before he tickled my elbow. I turned and hummed a tune of gratitude to the creature. By distracting the brigar, he'd saved my life and my place in Ramu's endless sea.

Come with you, he said.

Why? I asked. The Seamount was a lush habitat for creatures.

Big, he said. *Trapped. Forced.*

I frowned. What was he saying?

"Brigars are forced to defend the Seamount," the man explained. "Sounds like your little friend here isn't looking forward to his adult fate."

My heart squeezed. I'd never given brigars a second thought, except to dwell on their horrifying bulk. Would this sweet cephalopod be trapped in a life he didn't want once he was large enough to be of use?

Come, I said to the octopus.

He flowed toward me and wrapped a tentacle around my ear in a gentle gesture that nearly undid me. I'd been trying so hard not to think of the loved ones I was leaving behind. Bringing a friendly reminder of home wouldn't heal the pain, but it would salve it.

"If that's settled," the man said, waving us toward a dark tunnel mouth. "Follow me."

We swam through endless black tunnels. I lost track of time, although never of direction. Although the tunnels twisted, our path led us eastward. Sometimes the octopus—I'd started calling him "Squirter" in my head after he'd shot me with a playful jet to the face—fluttered beside me, sometimes he clung to my shoulder, and we rode the yatull together. The man swam steadily before us, leading us unerringly on a path that only he knew, and the yatull matched his pace with patience. Occasional light filtered down on us from gaps in the seafloor above, then we were plunged into blackness again.

Finally, our path lightened ahead instead of above, and the tunnel spat us into open water. My eyes widened at the deep abyss of darkness below. Our tunnel entrance was one hole of many that riddled this cliff like a sponge.

The man turned to me.

"This is where we part ways." He pointed to the east. "Head directly toward the morning light. After a half-day as the yatull swims, you will find a smaller, uninhabited seamount with a signpost. It will guide you to land."

"Thank you." I gestured to the man with a heartfelt sweep of my arms. "I can never repay you."

"Use this opportunity to be more than what you were forced to be," he said with a crinkling of his eyes. "The Seamount never gives half-sirens much of a chance. The ocean is bigger than you've been led to believe. Just use your siren ability wisely. That's how the upper echelon stay in control, by forcing their will on others. Be better than them."

With that, the man disappeared into the tunnel, leaving me with only Squirter and the yatull in the immensity of the open sea. I took a deep breath, rubbed Squirter on his mantle between his eyes, and squeezed the yatull with my legs.

"Let's go," I murmured to them, and we ventured eastward into the great unknown.

The featureless open ocean was eerie and too quiet. My only points of reference were the shimmering waves above and my constant sense of direction. The yatull swam unceasingly except when we sensed a school of herring in the distance. We dived into the herring ball that formed upon our arrival, and the three of us grabbed as many of the slippery silver fish as we could shove in our mouths. Once satiated, we continued our way eastward.

As the man at the barrier had predicted, I sensed a seamount by the time the light dimmed in the vast hazy blueness. It was nowhere near as large as the Seamount, my home.

My former home, I thought with a gulp of terror. My stomach twisted with homesickness at the memory of Eelway and the others.

They would be wondering where I was by now. Spray would be preparing our evening meal, and Fin would be chatting with our neighbors instead of helping. Unless news of the murder and my subsequent escape had already spread...

I shook my head violently to dislodge the pointless musings. I would never know what my friends thought. They would live out their lives at the Seamount, and I would swim to a new life on land.

The thought made me equal parts sick and fascinated. My mother had taken this journey once, although story time wasn't exactly in our repertoire after she'd dumped me in the ghetto as a small child. The shame of raising a half-human child had proved too much for her to bear. I knew some of the upper echelon youth saw journeying to land as a rite of passage, despite official censure and the difficulties of getting there. My mother had been one of them.

I had little curiosity for the man to whom she'd sung her siren's song. Land held exactly one draw for me: an escape from my pursuers.

I directed my yatull to the tip of the Seamount. As clear as southern waters was a large, flat rock covered with a thin layer of algae that didn't obscure scratches on its surface. With practiced eyes, I read directions in Seamount-script.

"Good," I said to Squirter, who clung to my shoulder with a sleepy look in his eye. "Now we know where to go."

He gave a happy click at my smile and curled his tentacles around my neck. I looked down at my slowing yatull. It had been a long journey, and the creature needed a break.

"My turn," I said. I slipped further down the yatull's back and gripped the seal's lower torso in a firm embrace with my arms so that my legs were free. Squirter nestled himself more securely against my neck, and the yatull relaxed. She wouldn't fall fully asleep—yatulls never did, instead using part of their brain to continue to swim slowly —so she would point her body in the direction we needed to go while I powered our motion. I wasn't nearly as quick as a yatull, especially with the bruising and scrapes from my fight with the brigar, but we would make waves while she rested.

Blackness enclosed us as night fell, but phosphorescent plankton lit the darkness with a display of glittering light. Trails of sparkling green followed my kicking legs and glimmered over our skins as I pushed our little group through the water.

It was beautiful, but the light made us a target for any watching predators. A shiver ran down my spine at the thought of the endless water below us. I'd lived my entire life on the reef of the Seamount, contained within the barrier. Predators were strictly controlled within the city's confines.

Out here, I was on my own. Squirter was cute but no match for anyone's teeth. The yatull could take care of herself, but the only loyalty she had for me was whatever I could force out of her. That might be enough, but I didn't like to count on the seal.

The yatull and I took turns propelling our group through the long night while little Squirter clung to my neck and slept. When the pull of the setting moon lessened, I knew that only a short time remained before the sea lightened with a new day. The thought invigorated my weary body. Surely, we were getting close to land. If I could make it to shore before my pursuers caught up with me, it was my best chance to escape punishment.

We'd been traveling through the vastness of the open ocean for so long without encountering much that I'd stopped paying attention to my skin sense. My first indication that something was wrong was the yatull's snort of unease.

I stopped undulating my body, and we hung in position while I tuned into my skin sense. My stomach dropped as five large, sleek bodies floated our way. What were these creatures? Were they a threat?

They swam closer, drawn by our presence. Light brightened the waters, changing the night's glittering illumination into daylight sunbeams. The five bodies grew clearer, and their strange black and white coloration made my eyes widen. They were clearly whales but of a variety I'd never seen before. Their white eyepatches gave the impression of staring blank eyes, but their real sight organs gleamed with intelligence at the base of the pale spot. They were at least five times my length, and they moved with the grace and speed of predators.

The yatull huffed in fear, and I hummed a tone of calming, despite my own panic. Squirter clung to my neck and matched his skin color to mine to escape notice.

We couldn't outrun them, not after traveling all day and night. We would have to fend them off and hope they didn't tear us to pieces. A stab of terror jolted my chest. I didn't want to die out here—what a waste of my escape, my life. At least I would have the chance to join Ramu when I died, but I'd really hoped it wouldn't be this soon.

I straightened my shoulders and slipped off the yatull. There was nothing else to do. I would have to fight.

"Sorry," I whispered to Squirter and the yatull. "I didn't mean for you to get caught up in this."

They didn't understand the finer details of my words, but Squirter stroked my cheek and peeled himself off me to float on his own. He flushed a brilliant yellow, visible in the shallows of these clear waters, and I couldn't help smiling at his aggressive color.

I had nothing, no bone blade, not even a rock to defend myself with. All I had was my song. It would have to be enough.

The five whales parted their pod and surrounded our little group in ever-decreasing circles. I drew in a deep breath, closed my eyes, and hummed a song of distaste. With any luck, it would make us appear unpalatable, and the whales would swim away to find tastier prey.

For a moment, I thought it had worked. Three of the whales peeled away from their circling and headed north. Two, however, paused for only a moment then resumed their paths. We must be the first prey they'd seen for a while.

Without warning, one of the whales darted in and snapped at the yatull with a mouthful of sharp teeth. If I survived this ordeal, I would have nightmares about that mouth.

The yatull gave a cry of distress and bolted away. The whale gave chase. I sent a call of return to the yatull, but she ignored me and disappeared.

That left Squirter and me against the last whale. Its beady eye sized me up as it passed. I felt as trapped and helpless as I'd ever had at the Seamount. I had nowhere to run, nowhere to turn, nothing to do but stay where I was and await my fate.

The whale darted toward me with that terrible mouth open. I kicked furiously to the side, but those pointed teeth grabbed my leg and pierced the skin.

I screamed, then instinct took over. Before the whale could shake me into submission, I bent at the stomach to pull my body closer to the creature. My leg, clamped in the whale's mouth, sent stabs of shooting pain through my calf, but I aimed my fingernails and jabbed at its black eye.

The whale released my leg with a mournful cry and turned away. I kicked with my good leg, then glanced at my injured one with hot eyes. Blood streamed from the puncture wounds in clouds of inky darkness. My heart plummeted. Even if the whale were done with me, which I doubted, the blood would attract every shark in the region. I was no longer Lune Seafields. I was now a piece of swimming bait.

The whale circled back, determination in its shiny eyes. Distaste wasn't enough. I needed to distract the whale. But how?

Slowly, building my idea as I went, I hummed a complex command. I had no idea if it would work, especially on an untested non-Seamount creature, but I had to try. I blasted a tone of deliciousness but with a westerly direction. If the whale took my bait, it would swim straight to my pursuers.

The whale passed me again, and I tweaked my tune with frantic hums. Surely, this frequency would be the right one. Would it work on one of these strange whales?

The massive creature passed again, and Squirter darted out. In a move both brave and extremely foolish, he jetted in front of the whale's nose, released a cloud of ink, then darted back to my side.

I gasped but didn't stop my humming. When the ink cleared, the whale's attention on me was broken. Instead, it glanced to the west.

After one more pass, it turned and swam back the way I'd come, hopefully to harass my pursuers.

Once the whale disappeared from my skin sense, my entire body wilted in relief. Then I tensed again. Blood still streamed from my wounded leg, and it wouldn't be long before the sharks began circling, even in these empty waters.

I called helplessly for the yatull, projecting my song as loudly as I could. I would have to swim by myself to land if the yatull had deserted me, but I didn't relish the journey. It would be far slower without a ride, and my pursuers would be mounted on yatulls of their own. How close was I to shore? Could I make it before I was captured by sirens or eaten by a shark?

Squirter landed on my knee then crawled to my wound. I watched in fascination and a little trepidation. Squirter was most likely a juvenile brigar, and while he appeared friendly, adult brigars were bloodthirsty and cranky. Would the taste of my blood alter his friendliness toward me? Even the beak of an octopus as small as him could leave a mark.

Squirter gently placed a suction cup on one of the bleeding tooth punctures, then another. Within a moment, every wound was covered by his tentacles, and the cloud of blood drifted away.

Thank you, I hummed to the little cephalopod, touched beyond words. He clicked happily and flattened himself against my leg in a streamlined position.

I undulated my body gently to avoid dislodging my tiny friend, and we carried on toward the east. I despaired of reaching the shore before my pursuers, but I had to try. Occasionally, as the sea grew brighter with daylight, I called for the yatull. I didn't expect a response. She was probably halfway to the Seamount by now.

My skin sensed a sleek body approaching, and I braced myself. Squirter's tentacles had sealed my wounds decently, but some blood escaped every now and again. Had a shark finally caught up with us?

The body resolved into the familiar shape of my yatull, and I relaxed. With a hum of greeting, I held my arms open. The yatull slid between them, and together, we swam east far faster than I could hope to manage by myself.

The featureless ocean was just as monotonous by day as it was by night but without the pretty distractions of bioluminescence. Sea jellies floated by on occasion, and a school of tuna swam past the edge of my skin sense, but we were otherwise undisturbed. Once, a sunfish drifted into view, and I snorted at its ridiculous fins, one at the top of its giant, disc-like body, the other at the bottom. Its undersized mouth opened and closed, and it looked like it grinned at me as it passed. I waved, feeling a little less alone.

When the sea was as bright as it ever got during the day, two bodies hovered at the edge of my skin sense. My stomach clenched. They were unmistakable—two sirens riding yatulls—and I clicked to my yatull to swim faster.

If I could sense them, they could sense me, and it was only a matter of time before they overtook us. I was tired and injured, and they'd somehow caught up to my desperate flight.

Wait, hadn't three of the pale folk pursued me? My mouth twitched in a smile of satisfaction. The whale I'd compelled had done its job, after all. One pursuer must have turned back to the Seamount with his injuries.

That still left two formidable opponents, and the shore was who-knew-how-far away. I needed a plan, but my tired brain only buzzed with panic. Escaping my fate was as hopeless as I'd always believed. I was trapped, no matter how far I swam. The Seamount's upper echelon ruled my life, and when these two caught me, they would rule my death.

Bitter resentment welled up. I'd never had a chance, and when I'd taken my only way out, they still dragged me back with tentacles as long as the sea was wide. Unfairness didn't begin to cover it.

Something large loomed on the surface ahead. I frowned and concentrated on deciphering the confused signals my skin sense was showing me. Waves lapped against the edges of the long, oval shape. It was rigid with no fins or flippers.

My eyes widened with recognition. It was a boat of the dry folk. I'd never encountered one before, but I'd heard stories.

My first instinct was to shy away and make sure the dry folk didn't see me. My next thought was more calculated. Why would I run from dry folk? I planned to live among them. Maybe this boat was a sign. Maybe I could use it to escape my pursuers.

The yatull grunted in protest when I pointed her head at the boat's hull, but she complied, used to following directions. When we were directly underneath, I gave her a swift hug, hummed *home* at her, and released my arms and legs. The yatull blew a gentle jet of water in my face, then twisted her sinuous body and disappeared into the distance.

The other yatulls bearing riders were fast approaching. If I were serious about boarding the boat, I needed to act now.

Hold on, I gestured to Squirter, and his arms tightened around my leg. I kicked upward, wincing at the shooting pain in my wounded limb.

Wave action pushed me around with unexpected force as I neared the surface. I'd rarely visited open air at the Seamount, and motion in the water was new for me. Currents were one thing, but this slop was disorienting.

My head burst from the surface, and foreign noises assaulted my ears. Everything was harsher, sharper, and louder than below. Shrieking calls of seagulls pierced my skull with unpleasant force. Wind passing my ears made a whooshing noise. It was odd and hard to ignore.

Deep-voiced shouting drew my attention to the boat's deck. Two men hung over the railing and pointed at me with wild gestures. I couldn't understand their words, but their meaning was clear.

One of them threw an orange ring overboard. Its garish color jarred my eyes. Nothing was that vibrant in the ocean, at least not in the depths of the Seamount where I usually resided. The ring flew toward me, attached to the boat by a rope. Good. They were trying to help me onto the boat. This would be easier than I'd imagined. As long as they weren't so helpful to my pursuers, this crazy plan might work.

I kicked toward the ring and clung to its hard smoothness. With jerky heaves, the man who'd thrown the ring hauled on the rope to pull me closer. Another flung two gray poles with hard lines between them over the edge.

I eyed it warily as I approached. Could I use it to get aboard? From the gestures and shouts of the men above, that was the structure's purpose. I let go of the ring and wrapped my fingers around the hard gray lines. With one hand after another, I hauled myself upward until my feet touched the bottom line. I winced as the rough surface grated against my tender soles.

The boat swayed alarmingly as I climbed, but the thought of my pursuers quickened my motions. When I was within reach, strong hands grabbed me under my arms and pulled me onto the boat. My unsteady legs folded, and I sank to the deck.

My eyes met my rescuer's, and his were an astonishing brown amid warm dusky skin. Only Fin in the ghetto had eyes that came close. The man's gaze traveled over me then stopped at my leg. He shouted something to his fellows.

I looked down. Squirter's pupils were narrowed, and he'd squashed himself as flat against my leg as he could manage. The man reached toward him as if to peel him off.

I shook my head violently and jerked my leg away. The man paused with a bewildered frown, and my eyes searched the deck frantically.

There. A cylindrical vessel made of a similar material to the smooth ring looked like it would hold water. I dragged myself over the deck and grabbed the vessel. How would I fill it with water for Squirter?

If I were going to live with dry folk, I needed to start acting like them, which meant breathing air. I'd heard stories of how our lungs worked in air as well as water—those tales were inherently fascinating to residents of the ghetto, since our parents had visited land in the past —but I'd never tried expelling water from my lungs.

But it was now or never. Squirter needed water, and I needed to live on land. I could hold my breath for a while, but not forever. I grasped the vessel with trembling hands, placed my head over the edge, and breathed out.

Water gushed out of my lungs, and at first, it was a normal breath out. Then I tried to draw in air, and that was when the coughing started. My diaphragm heaved, and water forced itself up my throat and into the bucket. Again and again, I coughed and spluttered, harsh air entering my lungs for the first time.

Finally, the coughing stopped, and I could control my breathing. I drew in ragged breaths of the harsh, dry air. The vessel was only a third full, but it would be enough for Squirter to stay wet until I figured out how to get more water for him. I peeled him off my leg and gently placed him in the vessel.

The man with the brown eyes gasped and pointed at my leg. The bleeding had mostly stopped, but purple bruising surrounded my puncture wounds. It was clearly a bite, and the horror in the man's eyes gave me hope that I'd earned more sympathy points.

A knock on the boat's hull nearly made my heart stop. My pursuers were here. One of the men shouted and pointed to the ocean below the climbing structure.

I clutched the brown-eyed man's forearm and pulled him down. He squatted to my level. How could I make him understand that I needed protection from the pale folk coming aboard? I didn't know his language, and he didn't know mine. The only way I knew how to communicate was to siren him.

I hummed a tone of pleading, then a warning of danger. Would my song work on a land-dweller? I bit my lip and hummed louder with my hand firmly clutching his arm.

His eyes narrowed, and he glanced toward the side of the boat. He stood and shouted something to the other men, then grabbed a pole with a sharp hook at the end. Wielding it like a weapon, he approached the boat's edge.

The remaining male siren's head appeared. The brown-eyed man jabbed at him, but the siren swatted the hook away and leaped into the boat with far more grace than I'd done. He took sure steps toward my rescuer and wrenched the hook out of his hands. They grappled, the male siren's face twisted with concentration.

Two other men rushed forward to help their fellow, but the female siren emerged above the boat's edge. She leaped toward the nearest man and wrapped strong fingers around his bicep.

The man immediately stopped, and his eyes glazed over. His fellow looked wildly between him and their new opponent. The female siren smiled and reached for him.

I would never win against a female full siren. She would compel every man on this boat to do her will, and her will was to capture me and drag me back to the Seamount for excommunication and death. No matter how far I swam, I was still trapped in the pincer-squeeze of the upper echelon. Was my capture inevitable? Maybe I shouldn't fight it anymore. Swimming away hadn't worked, and sirening the dry folk for help hadn't worked. I wasn't powerful enough to fight this woman.

My searching eyes landed on a hole in the deck, which was full of flopping silver bodies. An idea ballooned in my mind like a threatened pufferfish. Maybe I was going about this the wrong way. It was true—I would never win against this woman by using force or compulsion— but were they the only options? Maybe there was a smarter way. I'd lived for years on the strength of my smarts and sneaky abilities—in ghetto life, stealing for survival was a necessity—so why stop now?

A sharp-looking knife made of the same gray material as the climbing structure lay on a chair near the square hole full of twitching fish. I rose on my hands and knees and awkwardly crawled toward the chair, then grabbed the knife and a silver body from the hole.

One of the men who hadn't been in the fight ran up to me. I grabbed his arm and hummed a request for distraction. With a nod, he darted toward the woman.

I had only moments to act before the woman saw what I was doing. With a pulse of humming to soothe the dying fish in my hand, I plunged the gray knife into its stomach and drew it along its under- side. The fish twitched then fell still. Blood dripped onto my hand.

I couldn't waste it, so I brought the little body to my neck and smeared its red lifeblood across my throat, then I tossed the fish back into the hole. With the knife, I sliced the nape of my neck, grimacing with pain. The cut would make my subterfuge realistic, and the fish blood would convince others that I was bleeding out.

With a dramatic gasp, I dropped to the ground and flung out my arm with the knife until the blade clanged against the deck. Eyes flashed to me in shock, but I allowed my own to roll. Was my distress realistic enough? I twitched my limbs as if in my final moments. With one hand, I feebly made the sign for Ramu. Would the pale folk see it and accept that I would rather die than be excommunicated?

A man shouted in dismay, and I released all tension in my body. My eyes half-closed, and I stared glassily across the deck. My heart thundered in my chest. The beating would give my subterfuge away if I didn't control it.

I held my breath and willed my heartbeat to slow. This was a skill pale folk were capable of, and I pushed the time between heartbeats into longer and longer intervals to pretend my death was imminent.

The brown-eyed man skidded to his knees before me and grabbed my hand. He placed his fingers on my wrist and felt for a heartbeat. I forced my heart to slow beyond detection, and my vision tunneled as my senses shut down.

The man shook his head in despair and shouted something to the others. My fading sight brought me a vision of the siren woman shaking her head in disgust, gesturing "it's over" to her companion, and the two of them diving over the edge.

Two splashes ended the threat to my life and my eternal soul. With a gasp, I brought my heartbeat back to normal and sat up. The brown-eyed man stared at me with wide eyes. He pointed at my throat and said something.

I wiped the fish blood off my neck and smiled at him. He shook his head, bewildered, then his eyes crinkled, and he laughed. The laughter was tinged with wildness, but it still lightened the mood of the men aboard. I grinned wider and took his face in my hands in a gesture of thanks. I had no idea how dry folk did that, but his eyes searched mine with a recognition of my meaning.

"William," he said, pointing at his chest.

I had no idea how to say my own name in a way William would understand, so I simply pointed at his chest and repeated his name to show I understood him.

"William."

The words felt strange, vibrating in my throat. I coughed to clear the sensation.

He gestured to another man who brought a large square of material and draped it over my shoulders.

"We'll go to shore now," William said to me. I didn't understand his words and told him so with a frown. He pointed to the east and repeated one word. "Shore."

"Shore," I whispered. My eyes followed William's pointing finger. I'd escaped the Seamount, escaped my punishment, escaped the upper echelon's grasping hold on my existence. Now, I could do whatever I wanted with my life. A new way of existing spread out before me, vaster and more unknown than the open ocean.

I couldn't wait to greet it.

Join Lune on land in *Sea Fire* (Depths of Magic #1).

<u>Sign up today</u> to be the first to know when *Sea Fire* launches!

ABOUT EMMA SHELFORD

Emma Shelford feels that life is only complete with healthy doses of magic, history, and science. Since these aren't often found in the same place, she created her own worlds where they happily coexist. If you catch her in person, she will eagerly discuss Lord of the Rings ad nauseam, why the ancient Sumerians are so cool, and the important role of phytoplankton in the ocean.

Emma is the author of urban fantasy series, including Depths of Magic, Nautilus Legends, Magical Morgan, Immortal Merlin, and the Breenan Series.

Find out more: EmmaShelford.com

facebook.com/emmashelfordauthor
twitter.com/emmashelford
instagram.com/emma.shelford

BLACK'S LAIR
BY ROSA MARCHISELLA

CHAPTER 1

Captain Black loomed over Young Gilroy Vance, pressing his attack. He winked at the lovely Miss Miranda Danesbury, who watched in wide-eyed terror. Just the way he liked his women. And she was his. Young Vance would never see his dreams of love come true.

The cold light of the moon glinted in his hard eyes, raced along the edge of his blade, and gilded the slick edges of the Bloody Mary. It accented Miss Danesbury's lithe frame and the Bloody Mary's sleek build with equal vigor. It caressed both brown curls and cannons.

Built for speed and agility, the Bloody Mary spent years ruthlessly hunting other ships and out-maneuvering them. Tonight, she was cheek-and-jowl with the plump merchant ship, Lady Sparrow. Her deck rang with the shouts and metal clash of desperate men fighting for their lives.

Black's mistake had been sending the majority of his crew aboard the Lady Sparrow, though one could argue his mistake started earlier. He made so many bad choices since he boarded the rich vessel. Somewhere in the back of his mind, Black suspected this one may be the last.

Chaos swept across the Lady Sparrow. His crew screamed and scrambled to return to the Bloody Mary. Most either plunged into the cold waters or swung back to the Lady Sparrow. The ships were too far apart.

Black's attention flickered from the Lady Sparrow to his surroundings. His crew on the Bloody Mary was outnumbered, and their force dwindled quickly. He needed to extinguish brash Vance quickly and restore order. Then, he'd settle his score with Miss Danesbury.

With his attention diverted, Vance's cutlass struck his ribs. Black cried out in surprise and stumbled to the railing.

A high-pitched shriek sounded. Miss Danesbury raced toward him to slam her slight body into him like a rugby player. She bounced off his chest and skittered away. Black pitched off-balance. He reached for her, fingertips sliding across the soft ribbon of her dress before he toppled over the rail.

The sound of his body hitting water was lost in the roar of the Lady Sparrow exploding.

The fighting stopped as the stunned crew of the Blood Mary stared at the burning wreckage off their starboard.

Gilroy Vance raised his cutlass and gave a victorious cry. The Lady Sparrow's crew cheered and moved to disarm their defeated opponents.

Miss Danesbury raced into Vance's arms, and they kissed, passionately.

"You make it sound like our lives ended after that," Miranda groused. She pulled a shirt from the clothesline and folded it with quick, precise movements. Her once lithe body had rounded out with age, and grey streaks peppered her curls.

"Well . . ." Gill buried his ax in the chopping block and wiped his brow. "Things haven't exactly been exciting since."

Miranda shooed a chicken away from her basket of clean clothes. "Exciting? Who has time for 'exciting' between raising children and housekeeping?"

Gregory rolled his eyes and continued to stack split against the side of the house. Nearly the same age his parents were when they faced Captain Black, he'd heard this argument a hundred times or more with never a winner. It never stopped his parents from playing their parts, though.

"It's not like it's a big house," Gill grumbled. Their modest house had seen better days, and the repairs had been made by someone who lacked skill, but it was a good home.

Miranda put a hand on her hip. "Don't you get started on that! You're the one who had to do the honorable thing and leave all the treasure behind! We could have had a big fancy house, and servants, but no!"

Gregory mouthed, "but no," in time with Miranda. She turned her fiery glare on him.

"Don't you give me any sass, young man."

Gregory blushed. "Sorry, Mum. It's just that you two always argue about not going back for the treasure, and I don't understand why not."

Gill's frown deepened the wrinkles around his eyes and mouth. "There's blood on it. That's why not. Good and honest people died because of it. If we were to take it and live rich off their deaths, it would be like we helped kill them."

"That's ridiculous," Gregory snorted. "So long as their deaths were avenged, why should all that treasure go to waste?"

Miranda snapped a sheet she folded, narrowly missing Gregory's nose. He jerked back, startled.

"It's the honor of the thing." Miranda dropped the folded sheet into her basket. "The dead don't rest easy when someone profits from their demise."

Gregory dropped the last piece of wood on the pile and dusted his hands. "Where's the honor in living like dogs when the treasure could be doing good for people?"

Gill adjusted the cuff of his worn shirt, fingering the embroidered ivy pattern. "Better a living dog than a dead lion."

"How about a new library? Or feeding orphans? Would the dead rest easy then?"

Miranda and Gill exchanged a concerned glance. "You're an odd boy, Gregory. I don't know where you get such ideas."

Gregory frowned and crossed his muscular arms. "I'm not a boy anymore, Mum, and I get my ideas from you and Da. You wish you could've done more with your lives. Well, there is. You're the only one who knows where the treasure is now that Black is dead. Why don't you go claim it? Put it to good use."

Gill smoothed his fingers over the embroidered pattern again and exchanged another uneasy look with Miranda.

Gregory frowned, confused by their silent communication. "What?"

Gill cleared his throat and pulled the ax from the chopping block. "Our adventuring days are long behind us." His tone lacked conviction. He stared at the pile of wood, hands flexing on the handle. "Besides, the key to Black's Lair went to Dave Jones's locker, along with the rest of that rabble. It doesn't do any good to waste time dreaming about what can never be."

Gregory gave a disappointed shrug and watched the chickens peck in the shade of the shed. It was the same answer his parents always gave: *No key, no treasure.* His parents were both stubborn when they put their minds to a task. Why would they let the lack of a key stop them? There must be a way . . . He sighed. Arguing never changed their minds. *Stubborn.*

Gill blinked at the ax in his hand as if seeing it for the first time. "I think that'll be it for me today. I'm not as durable as I once was."

"Nor as dashing," Miranda muttered, shuffling further down the clothesline. "That never stopped you from flashing your smile around when you want something."

She winked to soften the impact of her words. Gill smiled faintly.

"I'll finish up, Da."

Gill handed over the ax. "All right, then." His eyes wandered over the matching ivy pattern on Gregory's cuff, and the far-away look returned. "I'll just toddle off to Murray's for a bit."

Miranda frowned. "Be back before supper, or you'll eat it cold."

Gill dropped a kiss on her shoulder. "I won't be late, sweet lady."

"I've heard that before," she muttered as Gill left the yard.

Gregory split his log with one smooth motion. "You're too hard on him, Mum."

Miranda *tsk*'ed in annoyance. "What do you know of it?"

Gregory shrugged loosely. "I know he regrets not doing better by you."

He started a steady rhythm: place the wood, swing, and split . . . *Thump, whoosh, crack!*

"When he's in his cups at Murray's, he goes on about how you're too good for him."

Thump, whoosh, crack!

"How he should have let you marry the man your uncle picked for you."

Thump, whoosh, crack!

"So you'd have all the fine and fancy things you deserve."

Thump, whoosh, crack!

Miranda froze. "He says that?"

"And more." *Thump, whoosh, crack!* "To hear him speak, one would think you're still the 'sweet lady' he fell in love with."

Miranda bowed her head to hide the tears in her eyes.

Thump, whoosh, crack!

"He loves you so much, Mum. It breaks his heart that things are hard for you."

Thump, whoosh, crack!

Miranda turned away, shoulders shaking in silent sobs.

Gregory stopped. "Are you okay, Mum?"

"Of course." The crackle in her voice belied her claim, and she wiped the tears from her face roughly.

Miranda yanked the remaining items off the clothesline and dropped them into the basket without folding them. "I have to start supper if it's going to be ready by the time your da gets back. Be a good boy and make sure the ax gets put away proper."

She snatched the basket and hurried to the house. If she ever existed outside Gill's love-fevered mind, his sweet lady was long dead. It was best to forget those days.

CHAPTER 2: THE PAST

Excitement sizzled through Gilroy Vance as he stood between his father and Captain Moore. He was nervous enough to vomit as he watched the crew load the Lady Sparrow for his first adventure with Vance & Font Trade Co.

Captain Moore checked his pocket watch as Mister Vance alternated between wiping the unnatural sweat from his pale brow and coughing into his brightly colored handkerchief.

"Now Gill, you mind Captain Moore. He doesn't need you underfoot. You're just a representative, nothing more. Font's already taken care of all the details in Port Royale. You just smile, nod, and flirt with the pretty girls."

The swirl of a skirt caught young Vance's attention. Mister Vance followed his gaze toward the dock, where a pretty lass smiled at something her elderly chaperone said.

Mister Vance stiffened. "Except her." He thumped Gill on the head with a forefinger, then waggled it under his son's nose. "Mind me on this, Gilroy. You're taking Miss Danesbury to the Caribbean to wed a friend of her uncle's with whom we're trading. No mischief!"

Young Vance blushed and returned his attention to his father. "I'm not a wally, Da. I'll be a perfect gentleman."

"I'll make sure of it," Moore assured. Ignoring young Vance's withering look, the captain stepped forward with a friendly smile to offer his hand. "Miss Danesbury."

The younger lady smiled sweetly, placing her gloved hand in his. "Good morning, Captain."

"You look resplendent this morning, Miss Danesbury." Moore bowed over her hand.

"Thank you, Captain. This is my companion, Miss Abigail Pennybuckle."

Captain Moore nodded cordially to Miss Pennybuckle. "Welcome to the Lady Sparrow, Miss Pennybuckle."

Miss Pennybuckle's thin lips stretched into a smile, wrinkling the weathered skin of her cheeks. "Thank you, Captain Moore."

Mister Vance shoved his handkerchief into a pocket and stepped forward. "Miss Danesbury. Miss Pennybuckle."

The ladies turned to him with a smile. He extended a hand in greeting.

Miss Pennybuckle ran a critical glaze over him and put a restraining hand on Miss Danesbury's arm.

"Mister Vance. How nice to see you up and about." Her reed-thin voice cut the air between them.

Mister Vance's smile faltered as he withdrew his hand. "All our hopes and aspirations for the future sail out with this ship. Nothing could keep me home today."

Miranda glanced at her companion before offering a kind smile. "Of course."

Young Vance cleared his throat. His father's lips curled in a sardonic smile. "Forgive me, ladies. My son, Gilroy."

Gill stepped forward and bowed over each lady's hand. "Miss Danesbury. Miss Pennybuckle. It will be a pleasure accompanying you to the Caribbean."

He flashed Miss Danesbury an extra charming smile. She threw an amused look to Miss Pennybuckle. The elder lady arched an eyebrow and looked down her nose at him in a bird-like stare. "How kind. Make yourself useful and bring our bags, if you would."

Vance's smile faltered.

CHAPTER 3

Groans and rough muttering echoed around the empty common room of Murray's Tavern as Gill laid his cards. "Another one for me, boys."

Murray, the tavern's namesake, and owner threw his cards down in disgust. "Every bleedin' time!"

Gill reached for the small pile of coins, looking at his companions for confirmation. Shep shook his balding head with a sigh. Neville clicked his tongue and sent his cards spinning across the table. Gill raked the pot with a grin.

Neville stretched his tall frame and rubbed his paunch. "You got anything to eat, Murray?"

Murray puckered his thick lips. "Naught but leftover stew the Widow Harris brought by."

The men shuddered, and Shep made a retching sound.

Neville slumped back in his seat and looked forlorn to the door. "Too bad Miranda's not here. She'd whip us up some nice grub." He nudged Gill with his elbow. "Fancy yourself some company for supper, Gill?

Gill's eyebrows rose. "What makes you think my sweet lady wants to see your ugly mug at her table?"

Neville blushed. The others laughed and thumped his back, good-natured.

Shep's laughter turned into a cough, and he took a swig of his drink. "Where is Miranda? Surely she's not having to watch over your boy."

"Nah. I just wanted a few rounds tonight. It's no fun when she always wins."

Murray grunted in agreement. "She's got the devil's luck."

Gill's smile lit up his eyes, and color filled his cheeks. "I remember the look she got the first time I saw her roll the dice."

Miranda loved to dice with the Lady Sparrow's crew. Her eyes twinkled, and a wild pixie grin flashed. Oh, how that look made his heart race.

"She blew on the dice and . . ."

Miss Danesbury whopped as the sailors shook their heads in disbelief. She'd beat them with their own dice. Again.

Then that stuffed hen of a chaperone called for her.

. . .

His companions waited for him to continue, but Gill was lost in memory.

The sun sparkled on her upswept hair and kissed her delicate shoulders. She gathered her winnings and stuffed it down her bodice.

"Until tomorrow's nap, gents," she promised.

Every eye watched her with admiration as she dashed off. She won a lot of coins that day, along with a few hearts, including his.

Gill smiled and shook the memories away. "She beats me fair and square every time. Problem is, she's a bloody jinx. Even when she's not playing, I can't win a cursed thing so long as she's in the room."

Shep pushed his cards away. "Well, you're doing fine enough now. I'm out. I need every copper I have left to pay the blacksmith."

"Yuh." Murray shoved away from the table and shuffled to the bar to refill his drink. "I'm out, too."

Neville tucked his large hands under his arms. "Me too."

Gill sighed. "Ah, well. I suppose I should get home before Miranda has reason to blister my ears."

He pocketed his winnings and headed to the door. "G'night, boys."

"'Night, then," Neville grunted. Murray waved his drink in way of farewell.

"Hold up, Gill." Shep stood, leaning heavily on his gaff pole. I'll walk with you a ways." He hobbled around the table, wooden leg thumping against the floor in steady beat.

CHAPTER 4

Miranda stirred the bubbling stew with her long-handled spoon. She loved this spoon. Gill made it for her so she stopped burning her wrists and singeing her hem when shorter spoons forced her too close to the fire.

Mother said she could sew her way to heaven, but cooking would always be hell for her. Mother was right. She could make her food taste good, but cooking never got easier.

THUMP.

"You all done outside?" Miranda glanced over her shoulder, looking for Gregory.

He didn't reply. Miranda shook her head. *Typical boy. They only hear when you say something they like.*

Movement in the corner of her eye warned her a heartbeat before someone grabbed her from behind. Hands closed around her arms, and a body pressed against her. She could tell from the stench it was neither Gregory nor Gill having fun with her.

She stabbed over her shoulder with the steaming hot spoon, making contact with something solid.

A shriek blasted her ear, followed by a wave of fetid breath. Her attacker released her. She spun to confront an alarmingly thin man hunched over with both hands over his right eye. Greasy dun-colored hair swung around his face as he glared at her with his good eye. "You stupid slag! You nearly put my bloody eye out!"

Miranda lunged to go around him. He grabbed her arm. "Oh no, you don't!"

She pulled her arm. Too light to resist, the man stumbled forward. Hoping she was strong enough to jerk free of his grasp, she bolted. The intruder had a two-handed grip on her forearm and dug his heels in, dropping his bottom like a child pulling on the lead of a donkey. The wrench on her arm catapulted Miranda back toward him. He fell completely on his behind, still gripping Miranda for all he was worth.

She tripped over him and slammed into the table, which, in turn, smashed into the fireplace with a splintering crash. Flames gnawed the overturned table hungrily as the pair grappled on the stone floor. Miranda kicked her attacker and scrambled away from him.

Eel quick, he pounced on her back and snaked an arm around her neck. She jabbed desperately over her shoulder with the spoon again. This time, he caught the spoon and yanked it from her grip.

"Not this time."

Miranda threw herself backward and landed hard atop him, willing herself to be heavy as an elephant. The man wheezed, and his arm loosened. Miranda rolled away and stood.

The table was ablaze, and flames licked the rafters.

Miranda dashed for the door and jerked to stop as a hand snagged her ankle. She pivoted and kicked her captor in the face with her free foot. The man yowled and released her.

CHAPTER 5

Ax still in hand, Gregory bolted toward the front door. The high-pitched scream frightened a decade off his life. He'd never heard a cry like that before. It was not something he wished to repeat.

A tall bald man stepped from the shadows to block his path. Gregory stopped short.

"Nice ax." The stranger's face split into an alarmingly wide grin, showing a set of jagged teeth. "Mine's nicer."

He hefted an ax with a blade as jagged as his teeth. Gregory took an involuntary step backward. The bald man laughed and swung at him. Gregory jumped back to avoid the savage blade. The ax bit into the side of the house, gouging a chunk from the wooden frame. Gregory gaped at the damage, then turned his stunned gaze to the bald man.

The man gave a satisfied grunt and advanced with another swing. Gregory parried. The impact jarred his arm, and he grunted.

The memory of the scream echoed in his ears, and the smoke eking from the house made his heart clench. *Ma's in serious trouble.*

Gregory clamped his jaw in determination and attacked.

CHAPTER 6

Greasy smoke and flames reached greedily for Miranda's hem. Breath rasping, her captor gripped the spoon in a white-knuckled grasp and dragged her into the living room by her hair.

Miranda knew she could outlast him if she kept fighting. Her hopes of escape dashed when she saw two men tearing her home apart.

The redhead with rat braids cussed. "Not one bit of jewelry, Quinn! Not a candlestick or even bloody hatpin in the whole place!"

The sound of her captor's gasping made Rat Braids and his heavily tattooed companion, Quinn, turn. They spied her captor and burst into laughter.

Her captor stiffened and swiped at his bloodshot eye. "What's funny, eh?"

"You, mate!" Rat Braids crowed. "You look like you got worked over by the blacksmith!"

He did. Besides the eye, his face was swollen where she kicked him, soot-covered his clothing, and his hair was smoldering in several places. By comparison, Miranda was mildly disheveled and with soot-smudged hands.

Her captor snarled and jerked Miranda's hair until she squawked. "She's stronger than she looks."

His companions laughed harder. Quinn motioned to the spoon. "What do you intend to do with that thing, Jelly? Paddle her bum if she gets out of line?"

Jelly snarled. "She nearly put my bloody eye out with it!" He pressed his mouth to her ear and growled, "I intend to return the favor."

Convinced of his sincerity, Miranda slammed her elbow into Jelly's gut. He released her with a grunt.

Miranda raced toward the kitchen. A solid object slammed into the back of her head, and she pitched forward into darkness.

CHAPTER 7

Sweat dripped into Gregory's eyes. Heat from the blaze at the back of the house washed over him, but it wasn't the only reason for the sweat. The bald man's ax skill required every ounce of Gregory's attention, strength, and speed. The longer he held off his attacker, the more aggressive and wild the man's fighting became. He obviously hadn't expected resistance. He was glad to ruin the man's plans, but he needed to end things quickly before the other man overpowered him or his mother burned to death.

Gregory feigned a lunge. The bald man jerked back and swung his ax to block. Without Gregory's ax to stop his momentum, the man went wide, giving him an opening to hook behind the ax head and jerk the weapon from his attacker's hand.

The bald man stared at him in opened-mouth disbelief.

Gregory smiled, pleased. "Viking Combat Reenactment Club."

The bald man's eyes flickered over Gregory's shoulder. Something slammed into the back of his head. His limbs unlocked, and Gregory fell to the ground, head reeling.

A tattooed man stepped over him with a belaying pin in hand. "I have to do everything myself."

The bald man snarled and snagged his ax.

The tattooed man tucked the belaying pin into his waistband as two more men arrived. One wore his red hair in matted locks like a Viking. The other looked like he'd been at the losing end of a boxing match and carried his mother over a shoulder. "Can we go now? She's heavy."

The one with Viking braids crossed his arms. "I ain't leaving without some loot."

The tattooed man rolled his eyes. "Quit your mewling, you pair of sods." He motioned to the bald man. "Ripper, take the woman."

The ax man hoisted his mother effortlessly.

Gregory struggled to stand. The tattooed man turned to him. "Nah, son. You stay put."

He tried to move out of the belaying pin's path, but his reflexes were too slow. The sound of the wood connecting with his skull reverberated in his ears.

CHAPTER 8

Shep drifted to a stop, eyes wide, and pointed to the horizon with the tip of his pole. "Ain't that where your house should be?"

The night sky glowed orange above the treetops. The moon played hide-and-go-seek through heavy clouds. Gill squinted. "Yes, but what—?"

Fire! Not clouds. Smoke.

Shep forgotten, Gill raced home.

The house was engulfed in flames, and the toppled woodpile turned the yard into an inferno. Gasping for breath and gripping his side, he staggered to the front door. "Miranda!"

The heat of the fire pushed him back and sucked the moisture from his skin.

Gill circled the house, looking for a safe entry. "Miranda! Gregory! Oh, God! Oh, God-have-mercy! *Miranda!*"

He choked back a sob. *Useless.* Flames lashed out every window and door.

Shep arrived. Grimacing in pain, he leaned heavily on his pole to catch his breath.

Gill looked at him with a haunted expression. "She's gone. My sweet lady is gone."

Shep's face crumpled, tears in his eyes. "Oh, Gill—"

A groan from the shed's shadow startled them. Gregory struggled to his knees. He touched his head and retched.

"Gregory!" Gill ran to his son and wrapped an arm around his waist. Gregory stared at the blazing house. Orange, yellow, and red danced in his glassy eyes.

Gill shook him to get his attention. "What happened, son?"

Gregory struggled to focus his eyes. "Men came."

Gill's grip tightened. "Men? How many? What did they want?"

Shep dragged the chopping block over, and they helped Gregory sit.

"I - I don't know. Three . . . No. At least four. One snuck up behind me and cracked me over the head. One had jagged teeth and an ax . . . One with Viking braids in his hair and another . . . The other one had . . ." The haze vanished from his eyes, and he sat straighter. "They took Mum!"

Delirious from heat and euphoria, an eerie titter of relief escaped Gill. "She's alive?"

Gregory touched his head gingerly. "I-I think so. I don't know. She wasn't moving."

"They wouldn't have taken her if she was dead," Shep offered.

"Why take her at all?" Gregory asked. "What did they want? We haven't anything worth stealing. All they took was Mum." He looked around. "And the chickens."

Gill looked at the burning house. "I don't understand."

"I think I do."Shep shuffled, his wooden leg scratching in the dirt. They look at him in expectation. He refused to meet their eyes.

A hard knot formed in the pit of Gill's gut. "What is it?"

Shep's fingers knitted together. "Your boy said one of them had braids in his hair. That tickled me memory." His eyes flickered to Gregory. "Was one of them covered in tattoos? Mermaids and the like?"

Gregory nodded, and Gill's eyes narrowed. "Why?"

Shep shifted, fingers weaving invisible yarn. "'Member a few days back when I went up the coast to get Merry Belle repaired?"

"Yes."

"Well, I was enjoying a cup or two of ale at Sanders."

Gregory dropped his head in his hands.

Gill groaned. "Aw hell, Shep. What did you do?"

Shep held out his hands like a shield. "Nothing. Just talked, that's all . . . Though I guess it was enough." Shep resumed his agitated shifting. "There was these gents hanging around. One with braids like Medusa's cursed shadow and the other covered in tattoos. They was talking about pirates and . . ."

Gill rubbed his face. "Heaven protect me from a blundering friend!"

Shep wrung his hands together. "I-I didn't think nothing of it at the time. You've told that story a hundred times, yourself!"

Gill put a hand on Shep's shoulder. "Peace, Shep. You couldn't have known."

"I still don't understand, Da. What do they want with Mum?"

The corners of Gill's mouth dragged deep. He looked grievous ill. "The location of Black's Lair."

CHAPTER 9: THE PAST

Alone in Captain Black's cabin, young Miranda Danesbury rummaged through the papers atop the desk. "Come on! Come on!"

She yanked open the drawer and rifled through its contents. Frustrated, she slammed her hand against the top of the desk. "There must be some kind of weapon in here!"

She spied a plain, clear glass decanter. "Ah-ha! This'll do nicely."

Grabbing the decanter, she hefted it to test its weight. Satisfied, she pulled off the stopper and raised the decanter to an imaginary crowd. "Here's to fortitude and a quick rescue."

Up-ending the decanter for a swig, she froze. There was something on the bottom of the decanter. She put the stopper back in and turned the decanter upside down to inspect the tiny markings. "What the devil?"

She moved closer to the lamp and held the decanter up, peering through the body. The markings loomed larger, refracted through the liquid, and magnified by the round glass.

"Well, well. If it isn't Pandora with her hand on the box."

Captain Black stood in the doorway, arms crossed.

Miss Danesbury fumbled the decanter. "I-I was just having a drink."

Black closed the door. "And found the only map to my secret lair."

She cringed. "I-it was a mistake."

Black pulled his dagger and held it between them. It was a beautiful weapon, delicately inlaid with silver. If its razor edge didn't gleam so wickedly or hover so close to her throat, she might have marveled at its elegance.

"There is no salve for mistakes, Miss Danesbury."

Black spun and threw his dagger in a fluid motion. It struck the far wall and buried into the wood, millimeters from a familiar face, partly bandaged and pale.

"Come to feel my peaches before they're ripe, Mister Lynch?"

A young man cowering in the shadow forced his wide-eyed gaze away from the blade to Captain Black. "I . . . came to see if you wanted refreshments."

Lynch's eyes strayed to the decanter.

Captain Black scoffed. "Is that so? Your fine Captain Moore used to let you wander into his cabin unannounced, did he?"

Lynch shrunk further against the wall he was pressed against. "I-I don't know nothing, sir." His gaze flicked to the decanter again. "I-I swear."

A crooked smile twisted Black's lips. "Survival instinct makes blind men and mutes of us all, does it?"

Lynch swallowed heavily. "Y-yes, sir."

Black made a disgusted noise in the back of his throat. "Get out."

Lynch hesitated.

"NOW!"

The boy jumped as if physically struck and bolted from the cabin, slamming the door behind himself. Black stared at the door thoughtfully, stroking his beard.

Miss Danesbury struggled for breath. "H-how did you know he was there?"

Black crossed to his dagger and pulled it out of the wall. "The question is, how did you not? His smell should have warned you he was here long before I arrived."

Black sheathed his dagger. "There's an old Scottish toast. Perhaps you know it." He took the decanter from her and held it aloft. "'*Here's to you, as good as you are; And here's to me, as bad as I am; But as good as you are, and as bad as I am, I am as good as you are, as bad as I am.*'"

She struggled to understand the toast while Black yanked the stopper off the decanter and took a deep drink. Instead of handing it back, he threw the bottle against the wall. It smashed with a wet explosion. Shards of glass shot in every direction.

Black crushed the pieces of glass under his boot to make sure they were too small to put back together.

Miss Danesbury licked her lips nervously. "Aren't you worried I might have memorized it? I might tell someone once you've ransomed me back to my family."

Black crossed to her with a dark grin. "'*When I was a child, I spake as a child, I understood as a child, I thought as a child.*'" He put a hand on her cheek. "It's time to put away childish things, Miss Danesbury."

CHAPTER 10

Gill sat with head in hands. Shep patted his shoulder while Murray watched Gregory pace the floor of the tavern, ax in hand.

Neville leaned back in his seat, rubbing his face. "It's not just a story? She really is a lady. I thought it was just a pet name you gave her. Like apple-cheeks or somewhat."

"No." Gill sighed. "She really is a lady."

Murray licked his lips. "Then what the devil are you two doing living in a hovel out here with us?"

Gill barked a dry laugh. "Hiding."

Gregory growled. "Not very well."

Gill sighed. "I'll start by going down to Sanders. Maybe I can find a trace of the bog-lickers who took my Miranda."

Shep straightened. "I'm coming with you."

"That's not necessary, Shep."

"Yes, it is. I'll never be able to live with myself if anything happens to your missus because I couldn't hold my liquor. I'm not much good in a fight, but I can sail a ship for you."

Gill glanced at his son, reluctance tugging the corner of his mouth. Finally, he nodded.

Neville shot forward in his seat. "Me too! I'm coming, too."

Neville looked at Murray expectantly. Murray held his hands in front of his chest and shook his head. "Don't look at me. I have a tavern to run."

"All right, then." Gregory headed for the door. "Let's go!"

Gill grabbed his arm. "Slow down, son!"

Gregory turned on him, wild-eyed. "Those villains have Mum! We have to hurry!"

"I don't know about you, but I'm knackered, and Shep needs to stare at the insides of his eyelids for a bit before he can set sail."

Shep nodded. "Sanders is only up the coast a bit. If we leave at first light, we'll have time to see if anything survived the fire before we set sail."

Gregory ground his teeth. Gill patted his shoulder. "She's been in worse scrapes than this. She'll be all right 'til we get to her. Besides, your mother can be charming when she wants. She probably has that rabble eating out of her hand."

CHAPTER 11

Tied hand and foot, Miranda dangled over the bald man's shoulder. She raised her head and squinted to make out her surroundings in the dark.

She glimpsed a harrowing figurehead and gold lettering, Endeavor. Sleek and, by the number of cannon ports, heavily armed. This was a true pirate ship.

Why did it have to be pirates?

They climbed the gangplank.

Miranda thrashed. "Let go of me, you naffer!"

Baldy tightened his grip, and the one called Jelly wagged her spoon threateningly. Tattoos and Rat Braids, who carried the carcasses of her best laying hens, ignored her.

Baldy dropped Miranda at the base of the mast. She landed heavily on her shoulder.

"OW! You bloody ponce! Untie me ri—"

Tattoos shoved a skunky rag in her mouth, but Miranda continued to rant. Disinterested in her flow of garbled venom, he tied her to the mast while Rat Braids disappeared.

Jelly glared at her from behind Tattoos and pointed to his bruised eye with the spoon.

Tugging the knots tight, Tattoos flashed a mouthful of shark teeth and patted her head. "Night-night, pet."

Then she was alone in the dark.

CHAPTER 12

Face twisted into a rictus of torment, Gregory stroked the ax tucked into his belt absently while Shep and Neville rooted through the smoldering rubble. Fueled by the woodpile, the fire had raged all night, destroying everything except the shed at the end of the yard.

Gill emerged from the shed wearing a ratty pack slung across his chest. "Well, this is it. Everything we own fits in this sorry bag."

"OW!" Neville sucked his finger.

Shep eyed him with amusement. "Burn yourself?"

Neville shook his head and held out a sewing needle. "Pricked myself."

Gill gave a strained laugh. "Leave it to you to find something that shouldn't be possible." He took the needle with a bemused smile. "Things can't be all bad, then. It's Miranda's lucky sewing needle. Mayhap it'll save us again."

Gill threaded the needle through the seam of his underwear and looked around one last time. "Off we go. My sweet lady hates it when I'm tardy."

CHAPTER 13

Cold saltwater shocked Miranda from sleep with a harpy shriek. She blinked stinging water from her eyes. Jelly loomed over her with a bucket in his hand. Her spoon was tucked into his belt.

I'm going to shove that spoon right up his —

Quinn yanked the gag out of her mouth, and both men stepped aside. An imposing man with a patchwork of ancient scars puckering his face crouched in front of her. Her lungs forgot how to work. White streaks peppered his sandy hair, and the parts of his face not scarred were sea-scoured, making his age impossible to gauge.

The unadulterated hatred in his dark eyes terrified her in ways his scars didn't. Enmity radiated across the distance and pressed her against the mast.

"Welcome aboard the Endeavor." His voice chilled as fiercely as his animosity burned.

"W-what do you want with me? I'm not worth anything."

"You are to me. Remember this, Miss Danesbury?"

The man held up a dagger.

The blood drained from Miranda's face. She shook her head. *No*. It wasn't possible. This wasn't just any dagger he held. The silver inlay haunted her dreams—*Black's dagger*.

"I-It can't be."

A cold smile slithered across his face as he purred, "But it is."

Miranda shrank away. "He's dead. I saw him die."

The man's smile widened, pulling at the chords of scar tissue. His hard marble eyes glinted. An icy lick of fear caressed her spine.

"No, my dear. You saw him fall. Only I saw Captain Black die. 'Twas nearly the last thing I saw as I took the key from him. His fingers were buried in my flesh as we sank into the brine. I had to hack his fingers off to be free of him. Even then, it was nearly too late for me."

Miranda searched the humorless faces of the men around her.

The scarred man twirled a lock of Miranda's hair around his finger with unnerving intimacy. How did this wretched man know her?

"I've spent twenty years looking for you, Miss Danesbury. Twenty years visiting your lovely kin, hoping one of them knew where to find you. Starting with your fat uncle in Port Royale."

Releasing her hair, he dragged his forefinger across his throat.

"No!" She'd walked away from her relations to protect them. How many died? What cruel fate had this twisted man bestowed upon them?

He considered her soberly, fingers unconsciously tracing the scars on his face. "Not all my endeavors were as satisfying."

"Rot in Hell!" Miranda sobbed.

His lips pressed together thoughtfully. "Perhaps I will, but first, you're going to lead me to Black's hidden treasure."

He stood and motioned for Quinn to untie Miranda. She stared at the mermaid tattoo on his forearm while he worked.

"I don't remember where it is."

The scarred man raked her with those terrible eyes. "I don't believe you. You're far too clever to have forgotten something so important."

He turned, and Quinn dragged Miranda after him. Jelly whacked her behind with the wooden spoon. She squawked in indignation. Mocking laughter followed her below deck.

CHAPTER 14

The men followed Shep as he hobbled across the street. Thick fog blanketed the port, muffling the scuff and tap of his wooden leg and gaff pole.

"Bloody fog," Gregory muttered. Neville grunted in agreement.

"Don't curse it too loudly," Gill admonished. "Right now, it's our only ally against them what took your Mum."

Gregory scoffed.

"If they're traveling by sea, they'll have to weigh anchor 'til the fog lifts," Shep explained. "It buys us time to catch up."

Gregory grumbled and shoved his hands into his pockets. Gill shook his head. *Was I so childish at that age?*

"Here it is." Shep motioned to a dingy building with salt-crusted windows. The sign above the door read "Sanders Tavern".

He held the door open for them, and Gill got his first look at the infamous tavern while the others crowded in behind him.

Cleaner than its exterior, Sanders Tavern bustled with grounded sailors and chatty locals. Flickering shadow hid the face of a hooded figure in the corner. Gill dismissed them. He was looking for a group of men, not a lone traveler.

"Oi!" the burly man behind the bar shouted. "Leave that thing by the door!"

"Aye." Shep stopped to prop his pole next to the door while the others headed for a table.

"Bloody fog," someone grumbled. He caught a glimpse of matted locks from the corner of his eye. *Viking braids* Gregory called them. A bloody mess is what they were.

"Another couple hours won't make no never-mind," his companion replied.

Shep turned as the second man reached for the door. Mermaid tattoo! He clamped a hand on the man's wrist. "It's you!"

The men turned to him, confused.

"Gill!" Shep shouted over the din. "It's them!"

The tattooed one cussed. "Let go of me!"

The man tried to pull from his grasp. Shep held on with both hands. "Gill! Gill!"

The one with the matted hair shoved him. Shep stumbled backward, tottering for balance on his wooden leg.

Gill, Gregory, and Neville raced to his side, scattering alarmed patrons. Neville caught him before he hit the floor.

Shep pointed. "Them's the ones!"

The pirates reached for the door.

Gill grabbed the tattooed one by the arm. "What did you do with my wife?"

Tattoos turned on him with a belaying pin in hand, and Gill dodged, barely avoiding being clobbered.

Gregory snagged the other man by the ends of his Viking braids and caught a blow to the gut in exchange. He doubled over with a grunt of pain.

"Didn't have enough last night, boy?"

"I'm . . ." Gregory wheezed for air. "Not. A. Boy!"

He straightened to deliver a punch of his own while Gill dodged another swing of the belaying pin.

"Here!" Gill's head jerked toward the speaker. The hooded stranger tossed a bar stool at him. He caught it by the leg and swung at Tattoos, knocking his arm wide. The man howled and dropped his weapon. Gill used the opportunity to smash him in the face. Tattoos went down, and Gill pinned him to the floor with the barstool.

"Where's Miranda?" he bellowed.

While he was fixated on the tattooed man struggling to get free of the stool, the redhead knocked Gregory and turned toward him, knife flashing. Shep's gaff hook snagged the knife from the man's hand, nearly taking a few fingers with it. A few vicious jabs of the hook tore the man's cheek open and sent him reeling.

"What did you do with my wife, you bas—?"

The redhead staggered into Gill. Both men tumbled over the stool, shouting and howling.

Tattoos scrambled to his feet and looked around for options.

Shep blocked the front door with his gaff pole. Neville picked up the fallen knife and brandished it with incompetence and determination. Gregory and Gill struggled to stand. The redhead curled around his injured hand, yowling in pain.

Tattoos grabbed the nearest tankard of ale and tossed it in Shep's face. Shep threw his arm up. Snagging his companion by the collar, Tattoos bullied his way past the sharp hook and disappeared into the fog with the redhead stumbling behind.

Gill raked the cowering patrons with a dangerous look. The hooded stranger had disappeared, but the rest of them . . . "Tell me what you know about those men."

The patrons exchanged nervous looks.

Gill hefted the bar stool by the leg. "SPEAK!"

Everyone burst into babbling at once.

CHAPTER 15

Miranda slumped wearily on the bed. Her head still ached, and the smell of the roast which filled the captain's quarters made her stomach uneasy.

"I never thought you two would run back to England." The scarred man shoved a slice of beef in his mouth. "Especially when you could have stayed in the Caribbean and gotten rich off coffee, tobacco, and spices."

Miranda grimaced. He sounded like Gregory.

An urgent hammering rattled the door. The captain put down his fork. "Come."

The door slammed open, and Quinn dragged Rat Braids. The redhead had a blood-soaked rag wrapped around his hand and held another to his face.

"Her old man tracked us down. Nearly tore Fitch's fingers clean off."

Hope surged through Miranda. Her brave Gilroy never let her down.

The captain stood to inspect Fitch's face. "So. The dog still has teeth."

A sinister grin crept across his face. A worm of fear writhed in her belly, and Miranda was relieved when he turned his awful gaze to Quinn. "Rouse the men. I want to weigh anchor the moment the fog starts to thin."

Quinn glanced at his companion and swallowed furiously. "Aye, Captain."

She watched the pirate's swift retreat with envy.

"What about me?" Fitch whined.

The captain grabbed his wrapped hand. Fitch squawked in pain as the captain peeled off the bandaging to reveal a pulpy mess of blood-crusted flesh.

"You'll never shit a seaman's turd, now."

The flat finality in his tone stole the warmth from her body. Miranda wrapped her arms around herself.

Fitch held his mangled hand to his chest and trembled. His voice took a pleading tone. "I-it'll heal."

"Not fast enough." The Scarred Captain pulled the pistol from his waistband and shot him in the chest. Fitch's limbs drummed a gruesome death beat as he hit the floor. Shock contorted his face. Miranda tore her eyes away.

"Jelly!"

Miranda flinched and watched the door to avoid the horror at her feet.

Jelly stopped cold in the doorway and stared at Fitch for a moment before forcing himself to meet the captain's hard gaze.

"A-aye, Captain?"

"Feed him to the fishes."

Jelly's eye twitched. "Aye, Captain."

She couldn't watch. No matter how many animals she'd butchered over the years for meals, she couldn't bear to watch Jelly drag the body across the room. She wanted to cover her ears to block out the wet sound of Fitch's seeping blood and the incessant scrape of his belt across the wood.

"Jelly."

Miranda cringed and risked a peek.

Jelly froze in the doorway, eyes wide and fingers white-knuckled around Fitch's ankles. "Captain?"

"Close the door behind yourself."

Jelly's shoulders sagged in relief. "Yes, Captain."

He hauled the body over the threshold and closed the door.

Alone.

The captain placed his pistol on his table. The malice bubbling beneath his skin radiated through the room. It caressed her. Probed her. Smothered her.

Miranda scrubbed her sweaty palms across her skirt and summoned the pluck of her youth. She'd faced wicked men before, pirates and landlords alike. They fed on fear, and she needed to starve this bastard. It was easier to find your spine when you had facts, though.

"Are you going to rape me?"

"Rape you?" The captain barked a dry laugh and raked a critical gaze across her body. She fought back a shudder, feeling naked and vulnerable. "That thought has brought me pleasure for many a year, but no. I don't want you too traumatized. At least, not until we reach Black's Lair."

He crouched next to the bed, voice soft. "Then, I'm going to take back the last twenty years of my life from you. One way or another."

CHAPTER 16

The men made their way through the heavy fog, shoulders curled under the oppressive ambiance.

"We could try to sneak aboard and make off with Miranda in the fog," Neville offered.

"Four men against a shipload of pirates?" Shep scoffed. "Are you daft?"

"Just a suggestion," Neville replied sullenly.

Gill's sigh seemed wrenched from his very marrow. "I'm going alone."

His companions protested, Gregory louder than the others. Gill stopped and turned on them. They fell silent.

"If all they want is the map to Black's Lair, Miranda can draw it for them, and we'll be on our way."

Gregory crossed his arms. "And if it isn't? Then what? We let a bunch of pirates spill your puddings?"

Gill rubbed the back of his neck. "We don't know they're pirates."

"Well, we know they're not law-abiding folk," Neville rumbled.

Gill scowled. "I'm going alone, under a parlay. If I don't come back in two hours, go to the magistrate."

Gregory opened his mouth. Gill shot him a hard look. His jaw snapped shut, and muttered a reluctant agreement.

Gill gave a satisfied nod and resumed walking. Neville and Shep exchanged a concerned glance and followed.

A movement in the shadow caught Gregory's eye. Seeing nothing amiss, he hurried to join the others.

CHAPTER 17

Gill grunted as he hauled himself over the railing of the Endeavor. The years of Miranda's cooking and the damp of the fog made the task harder than he imagined.

A group of men waited for him. He recognized the tattooed man from the tavern. The man's clenched fists and murderous glare unnerved him. Gill searched the group for his redhead companion until an imposing man with a horribly scarred face stepped forward.

"Out for a tour of the bay?" The question elicited snickers.

Gill stiffened his spine and pointed to the white handkerchief tied around his arm. "I'm here to discuss the release of my wife."

"Are you, now?" The scarred man's eyebrow arched. "What gave you the impression I'm willing to negotiate?"

Captain. Gill flashed his most charming smile. "Well, you didn't open fire on me."

The captain's brows lowered. "Don't let that lull you into a false sense of security."

His stomach sank.

A towering man leaned in and snapped viciously serrated teeth at him.

"Uh-oh," someone giggled. "Ripper's hungry."

Gill blanched. *Time to change tactics.* "I know why you took Miranda. If you let me talk to her, I can get her to draw the map for you. Then you won't have need of us, and we'll be on our way."

"Now, why would I do that? 'Tis true, your missus ain't much to look at anymore, but 'any port in a storm', as they say."

Gill flushed a violent shade of red, and his fingers curled into fists. The crew around him reached for their weapons. He forced himself to relax.

"Knowing the location won't do you any good without the key," he reasoned. "The lair is impenetrable."

"I know," the captain replied. "I have the key."

Gill's mouth gaped, mind racing to comprehend.

"As you see," he continued. "I hold all the dice."

Dice! Yes!

"I'll gamble for her release!"

The captain scoffed. "You've got nothing to offer me."

"If I win, Miranda will tell you all she knows about Black's Lair, and you let us leave peacefully. If I lose, you keep Miranda and . . ." He forced the words out. "I'll join your crew."

The cruel edge of the captain's laugh gutted him. "What would I want with you? The row out here nearly did you in! Look at you. You couldn't lift your arm to scratch your arse if your life depended on it."

The crew mocked him with fake crying and flapping of arms.

Gill grit his teeth and held his pride in check. "I'm a hard worker, and I won't expect a share of the treasure. My babes are grown, and your men burned my home to the ground. Without Miranda, I've nothing. I'd rather rot in your crow's nest than go home without her."

The captain eyed him thoughtfully.

"Very well," the captain finally replied. Gill's hope rose for the first time since he saw the fateful smoke on the horizon. "But I have no interest in your services. If you lose and I keep your sweet Miranda, you've no reason to live. I'll slit your throat and consider it an honest day's work."

No! Gill opened his mouth to protest.

"Swag, some dice if you please."

A roly-poly fellow with beads in his hair dropped dice into the captain's waiting hand.

"Quinn, have Jelly bring our guest out for a bit of fresh air."

"Aye, Captain.

Gill's heart leaped to his throat in panic. He was dead for sure if Miranda got anywhere near those dice. "No!"

Every eye turned to him, and a nervous laugh escaped. "I mean. No need to fetch her just yet. You know how women are about gambling."

The captain's smug smile stretched wider. "I certainly know how your sweet Miranda is about gambling."

Baffled by the comment, Gill watched Quinn hurry away.

CHAPTER 18

Gregory paced, hands in his pockets. His shoes thumped against the worn planks of the dock like a second-hand tracking time. "This is taking too long."

"Patience, lad," Shep replied, making himself comfortable on a stack of crates.

"We should never have let him go alone."

Shep rubbed his leg with a grimace. "Your da's managed to keep his skin this long."

Neville grunted in agreement, rubbing the back of his head.

Gregory made a disgusted noise. "By hiding like a criminal for half his life!"

"Your da's a good man!"

"Even good men can be cowards," Gregory grumbled.

Shep bristled and shook a finger. "You watch what you say about your da! By the time he was your age, he'd already had his share of danger! You say it makes him a coward. I say it makes him a wise man. Even the devil knows when not to push his luck. May you never have to learn the lessons your da has!"

Gregory dropped his gaze in shame. Neville rubbed the back of his head again.

"What the devil is wrong with you?" Gregory grouched.

Neville shrugged. "Don't know. Something's itchin' at the back at my head."

Shep rolled his eyes. "Don't mind, Neville. He gets like that. Last time he had this problem . . ."

Both men stiffened, instantly alert.

"We were being watched," Neville whispered.

Gregory looked around. "Where?"

They scanned the shrouded dock, peering into the shadows of the barrels and crates around them. *Empty*.

Neville clicked his tongue. "Guess I was wrong."

Shep clumped back against a crate, and it toppled over with a clatter.

"*Ow!*"

A hooded figure bolted from behind the crates.

"Get him!" Gregory shouted.

The men lunged. The figure dodged past them, only to be tackled by Gregory. They struggled, but Gregory was stronger. He pinned the stranger to the ground and yanked the hood off.

A stout woman in her early twenties snarled at him.

"Who are you?" Gregory demanded. "Why are you following us?"

The young woman brushed a strand of dark hair from her face. "My name is Alice. I'm hunting the man who killed my father."

She pushed him off roughly and climbed to her feet while the men exchanged uneasy looks. Alice was dressed like a man!

CHAPTER 19

The dice clattered as the Captain rolled them in his hand. *Clakity-clakity-clakity.* Gill resisted the urge to slap them from his hand.

"Gill!"

At last!

Quinn and a reed-thin man – *Jelly?* – escorted Miranda toward them. Exhaustion dragged at her face, but she bounded toward him like an excited kitten. The pirates jerked her back. She glowered at them. Jelly patted a wooden spoon at his waist menacingly.

"Isn't that—?"

Miranda shook her head in warning, and Gill stifled his curiosity.

"Thank heaven you're all right."

"What took you so long?"

Gill flinched at her petulant tone.

"How touching." The captain gave him a conspiratorial wink. "There's still time to reconsider."

"Reconsider what?" Miranda looked around for an answer. "What's going on?"

"Just a friendly little wager on the toss of the dice," the captain replied.

"Oh, Gill." Miranda groaned. "What have you done?"

The pirates chuckled and ribbed each other.

"One toss each," the captain announced. "Highest score wins."

Gill pressed his lips into a grim line.

"I'll just wait over there." Miranda turned to leave. Jelly jerked her back to his side.

The captain shook the dice and tossed them on the deck. Everyone leaned in to look.

"Nine."

The crew cheered, stomped, and whistled their approval. The captain bowed and motioned for Gill to take his turn.

Gill gathered the dice with a concerned look to Miranda.

"Please, God!" she whispered, lacing her fingers together. "Just once. Please."

Gill tossed the dice and watched breathlessly as they tumbled across the planks.

"Three."

Gill and Miranda groaned in unison. The crew hooted and jeered.

The captain clapped Gill on the shoulder. "You never could win when she was around, Vance."

Gill squinted at him, willing his brain to make the connection. "Do I know you?"

"Don't you recognize me, Gill?"

"Should I?" Gill and Miranda exchanged an uncertain look and peered closer. Under the age and the scars . . . something familiar about the eyes and the way the corner of his mouth hooked in contempt.

The captain placed a hand over his heart and feigned a wounded expression. "I'm hurt. After all, you both swore you'd always remember my unique *cologne*."

Young Vance and Miss Danesbury leaned on the Lady Sparrow's rail, gazing at the waves.

"You've never met this man?" Vance asked.

"Never," she confessed.

"What if you don't like him enough to marry?"

The breeze assaulted them with a rancid scent like spoiled milk, and they gagged. Miss Danesbury pressed the back of her hand to her nose. "What is that wretched stench?"

Vance looked around and laughed.

"There's your culprit," he pointed.

Miss Danesbury turned to find a young crewman glaring at them, face scarlet with humiliation. Her mouth dropped open in surprise and embarrassed. She knew him, but what was his name . . .?

Miranda and Gill look at each other in horror. "Lynch!"

The scarred man grinned, venom dripping from his voice. "Yes, Lynch."

Gill shook his head. "How?"

Lynch sneered with utter contempt. "How, indeed."

CHAPTER 20: THE PAST

Lady Sparrow bobbed as she cut through the waves, forcing Miss Danesbury to aim her next stitch careful. The sun was hot, and the crate she sat on numbed her bottom, but she was bored, and embroidering would land her in less trouble with Miss Pennybuckle than gambling.

"Oh, cor!" someone muttered. "Oh, blimey!"

Cook appeared, wringing the cap in his hands. "The Captain'll have me 'ead for sure this time!"

"Lose something, Cook?"

Cook gave a startled yelp, then sighed in relief when he saw her. "Oh, Miss Danesbury. I thought you was the Captain."

"Indeed?"A smile played on the corner of her mouth.

"I've lost the key to the brig again," Cook whispered.

"Well, as long as the crew stays in line, we have no need of it."

Cook twisted his cap again. "It's not that, Miss. We keep the water rations and good wine there, so's we don't run out afore we reach the Caribbean. You see?"

Her smile withered. "I'm afraid I do. I don't suppose Captain Moore has a spare?"

Cook's Adam apple bobbed nervously. "Aye, but 'e'll have me keel-'auled if 'e finds out I've misplaced it again."

"Well, we can't have that." She put her embroidery aside. "Where's the last place you remember having it?"

"I was . . ." Cook's brows lowered, and he tugged the cap. Hope lit his face. "I was with the Captain at the 'elm."

"Then let's check there first."

She led the way to the bridge. Farley stood at the helm and watched from under bushy brows while they searched.

"This is mighty decent of you," Cook whispered.

Captain Moore's heavy footfalls approached. They turned with guilty expressions before Miss Danesbury smiled sweetly. "Good afternoon, Captain."

Moore tipped his hat. "Good afternoon, Miss Danesbury."

"Captain."

"Cook. All's well, I trust."

Cook strangled his cap and cast a worried glance at Miss Danesbury. "A-aye."

"Good." Moore nodded absently, turning to Farley. "A word, Mister Farley."

A metallic gleam from the rail caught Miss Danesbury's eye. She grabbed Cook's arm and motioned with her chin. Cook snagged the key on their way past, and they hurried back to her abandoned embroidery.

Cook clasped the key to his chest. "Cor! Thank the saints we've 'ad calm weather! I'd lose me 'ead if it weren't attached."

"Oh!" A sly grin crept across her face. "That gives me a splendid idea!"

She pulled the needle from her pattern and measured a new length of thread. "Key."

"But, Miss—"

"Faith, Cook."

He reluctantly placed the key in the outstretched hand.

"Hat."

He handed over his cap and watched nervously while she sewed the key to the inside.

"Now, as long as you keep your head, you'll never lose the key."

She returned the cap to Cook.

He stared in wide-eyed reverence. "I-I don't know 'ow to thank you, Miss."

"*Sails to the port!*"

A sleek ship approached at an angle, riding high and sails full.

Miss Danesbury hurried back to the bridge and waited anxiously while Moore looked through a telescope.

Vance arrived, disheveled and gasping for breath. "Captain?"

Moore grunted. "I can't see her colors."

He passed the telescope to Vance.

"Another merchant ship?" Miss Danesbury searched his face for some clue to the situation.

Moore's face was impassive. "Perhaps."

"They've a lot of cannons," Vance noted.

Moore scowled and snatched the telescope from him. "Go below, Miss Danesbury."

She cast a concerned look to Farley. His weathered face remained indecipherable. *Blast it.* The sea scoured all useful emotions from them.

"I'm fine where I am, Captain."

Moore snapped the telescope closed with more force than necessary. "That was not a request."

His forbidding tone sent a chill through her. She cast a glance at the approaching ship. *A lot of cannons.*

Miss Danesbury grabbed her skirts and fled.

CHAPTER 21: THE PAST

The other ship was upon them by the time Vance armed himself with a cutlass. He could just make out the words "Bloody Mary" on the bow, and they hoisted the Jolly Roger. *Pirates.* His heart sank.

"Prepare to be boarded!" Captain Moore shouted. "Repelling poles!" The crew scrambled to obey. "Stand ready the cannons!"

The crew of the Bloody Mary stood at her rails, weapons drawn and grappling irons at the ready.

A bearded man's voice floated to them on the wind.

"'Twas fear that first made gods in the world, Mister Tupper." His ruddy face flushed with excitement.

"Aye, Captain," a broad black man replied.

"Let's make ourselves gods to these poor souls!"

"Fire!" Moore commanded as the ships drew even.

Cannons boomed, shaking the ship beneath their feet. The crew jabbed with repelling poles to deter the crew of the Bloody Mary. Others rushed forward to meet those who boarded.

Vance joined the melee, fighting shoulder-to-shoulder with Lynch.

A woman's scream cut through the cacophonous brabble of combat. Vance turned toward the sound of her cry, leaving Lynch vulnerable. "Miranda!"

Attention focused on the pirate in front of him. Lynch was unprepared to block a second attack. He dodged, but not far enough. The blade slashed his face, nicking the edge of his eye. Lynch shrieked and dropped his weapon, grabbing for his wound.

Vance jerked back to the fight, too late. Lynch was down, half-blinded by his own blood. Vance stared in horror, and something slammed into the back of his head.

Darkness.

Sharp pain throbbed through his skull. Vance groaned. He struggled to open his eyes and groaned again. The battle was over. His side had lost. Moore and what remained of his crew were gathered around the main mast. Most were injured but remained upright. He and Farley lay at their feet. Gill climbed to his knees and inspected Farley. The helmsman had a serious wound in his belly. He wasn't going to make it.

Using the mast to support himself, Gill stood and came face-to-face with Lynch, who held a bundled shirt to his face. Blood soaked the cloth. Gill winced an apologetic look. Lynch answered with a hate-filled glare. Gill dropped his gaze in shame.

Bloody Mary's crew surrounded them with a fence of sword tips, cudgels, and axes. The bearded man who'd shouted about being gods approached, pistol in hand. He grinned as if they'd gathered for a friendly picnic.

"Well, now! What was a good bit of fun! Those who don't know me, I am Captain Black."

The large dark-skinned man escorted Miss Danesbury and Miss Pennybuckle by their arms.

"Unhand me!" Pennybuckle demanded. "I am a lady."

"Sirreverence!" Black gasped, throwing a hand to his mouth in mockery. "However did that escape our notice? Why, Mister Tupper, we must let this dear lady fly free! 'Tis not decent to cage such a fine old bird."

"Aye, Captain." The dark man scooped Miss Pennybuckle into his arms and carried her to the rail. The elder woman flailed in protest.

"Stop!" Miss Danesbury pleaded, pulling his arm. "Stop it!"

The men of Moore's crew moved to help, only to be held back at weapon-point.

"Fly free, old bird." Black waved farewell. Tupper tossed Miss Pennybuckle overboard.

SPLASH!

Miss Danesbury shoved past cheering the pirates and lunged for Black, pummeling his chest in a flurry. "She can't swim!"

Amused, Black snagged her wrist and yanked her against his chest. Miss Danesbury gaped wide-eyed at him, mouth in a surprise "o".

Black grinned. "She can't fly either."

Her chin quivered, and hot tears leaked down her face. "Y-you bastard!"

"Such unsavory language." Black clucked, taking a deep whiff of her hair. "But a fine diversion."

He shoved Miss Danesbury toward Tupper, who caught her in his arms. Miss Danesbury curled into herself, trying to block out the last of Miss Pennybuckle's gurgled cries for help.

"Well, now." Black turned to Moore's crew. "We're all businessmen. Whether we can ransom her back to her family or not, this fine young miss has value to me and mine."

Black's crew murmured in agreement. Vance lunged forward. Black kicked him in the face, knocking him back. Cradling the side of his face, Vance glared murderously.

"The question is," Black continued smoothly, "do any of you bletherskates have anything to offer? If you can be ransomed to your families, you'll earn yourself a few more days of living. Anyone?"

Moore's crew shook their heads.

Black shrugged. "I've got a few men I'll need to be replacing. I'll show mercy to any one of you who'll swear on to my crew. Except you."

He pulled his pistol and shot Moore between the eyes. Miss Danesbury screamed as Moore fell dead atop poor Farley.

Black scrutinized his captives while they looked among themselves, frightened and hopeful. They wanted to live, but none wanted to be the first to betray their mates.

"I'll swear." Lynch shoved past Vance to Black.

"What's your name?"

"James Lynch, sir."

Black pulled the shirt from his face to inspect the gash. "Well, Mister Lynch. You won't lose the eye."

Black returned his attention to the captives. "Anyone else?"

Four other men timidly crossed to stand with Lynch.

Cook spat at their feet in contempt as they shuffled further into the shelter of their new crewmates.

"Do you swear to forsake all former vows, answering only to Captain Black as your captain?" Mister Tupper asked.

"Aye," the five turncoats agreed.

Black looked each in the eye to judge their sincerity. Satisfied, he smiled. "Welcome to my crew. As mates of the Bloody Mary, you're each entitled to an equal share of all plunder, including whatever's aboard this wreck."

The turncoats sighed in relief. Lynch's gaze strayed to Miss Danesbury.

"As I said before, we're businessmen. Piracy is not a way of life for us. It is an investment in our future. Fifty percent of all goods captured gets shared among the crew when we return to port. The other half gets sacked away in a secret lair which I have the only map and key to."

The newcomers exchanged apprehensive looks while Lynch continued to stare hungrily at Miss Danesbury.

"At the end of each year, anyone who wants to retire gets his proper share and is free to go as he pleases. Anyone willing to stay on keeps adding to the pot for another year. How long you stay on is up to you. Mister Tupper here has been with me for five years. When he retires, he'll have enough booty to make him a prince."

The turncoats looked at Tupper, eyes shining with admiration, and he grinned in pride.

"Any one of you have a problem with that?"

The other turncoats shook their heads.

"What about you, Mister Lynch?"

He dragged his attention away from Miss Danesbury. "You're a shrewd businessman, Captain. But . . . What about her?" He motioned to Miss Danesbury. "Do we get an equal share of Miss Danesbury?"

All eyes turned to Miss Danesbury. She crossed her arms over her chest, cringing from their attention.

"Fair question. Mister Tupper?"

Tupper leaned into her ear. "Yes."

Miss Danesbury whimpered as Lynch grinned in triumph.

"And, no," Tupper continued.

Lynch scowled. "What's that supposed to mean?"

"It means we each get an equal share of the ransom money her family pays. If her virtue stays intact, they'll pay handsomely, but for some reason, the upper-crust don't like to pay for plucked birds."

Miss Danesbury released a shaky sigh.

Frustrated, Lynch turned his wrathful gaze on Vance. "And them?"

"Kill them."

Lynch snatched a sword from the nearest pirate.

"NO!" Miss Danesbury shouted. "Captain Black, please! A barter!"

Intrigued. Black held up a hand. Tupper grabbed Lynch's arm.

"Spare Mister Vance and the crew," she begged. "Lock them in the brig and sell them for slaves. They're strong men. They'll get you good money."

"Slave-trading?" Black's nose wrinkled. "Not my style."

"Please!" she insisted. "I-I'll make it worth your while."

Black cocked an eyebrow and turned his full attention to her. "Just what do you think you have to barter with?"

Miss Danesbury glanced at Vance. He shook his head.

"You can have me." Miss Danesbury replied.

"No!" Vance objected.

Black's eyes sparkled with amusement. "In case you haven't noticed, Miss Danesbury; I already have you."

"*All* of me," she clarified. "I'll make sure my family pays full ransom. Whatever you want, I'll do willingly."

Hungry hope lit Lynch's face, and she hastened to add, "Just you, Captain."

Black looks at Vance's tortured expression with a smile. "Very well. Throw them in the brig!"

"NO!" Vance struggled against the men who hauled him away. "Touch her, and I'll kill you, Black!"

CHAPTER 22: THE PAST

Face bandaged, Lynch was put straight to work, swabbing the deck with an older fellow named Loris. Chewing his lip, he glanced at the bridge where Black manned the helm. Something about what Black said, enough booty to live like a prince. That's what they all said to make their crew fall in line. Right?

"Oi, Loris."

Loris looked at him from the corner of his eye. "Keep working while you gab. The Captain don't suffer slackers."

Lynch ran his mop along the boards absently. "What's this bunk about a secret lair?"

"T'aint bumf, mate. Captain's taking us there now. Why else do you think he'd be manning the helm with a pretty piece to warm his bed?"

"No one knows where it is?"

Loris dunked his mop. "None but the Captain. I heard he has a map in his cabin somewhere. Never seen it, though. Don't know anyone who has. The key neither."

Lynch huffed. "Why all the parlor games?"

"So no one takes it in his head to steal the key and make off with the hoard." Loris's tone said it should have been obvious. "Captain Black's been saving for ten years so's he can retire with his own empire. If you got enough coin, they'll make you Governor of one of these dunny piles."

Lynch chewed his lip again. "What's it like?"

Loris shrugged. "T'aint even a real island. Just a big rock with a tiny little hole in it. Looks like Poseidon's arse sticking out of the brine. We load everything in the longboats and row into the cave."

"Where does it go?"

Loris chuckled. "Nowhere, mate. It's nothing but rock and more rock. That's the trick. See, there's a gate in the rock . . . Under the water. It's bloody brilliant. Can't hold your breath long enough to pick the lock. Can't use explosives to blow the gate open. Captain Black dives down to unlock the gate."

Lynch stopped and gaped at Loris.

"We sink the goods and dive down after it. Gotta be quick and have good lungs, though. The gate's in a tunnel near ten feet. We got to drag all that loot through the tunnel to the other side."

"What's on the other side?"

"Keep working," Loris reminded him.

Lynch resumed swabbing. "What's on the other side?"

"Heaven, mate." Loris grinned." A cave in the middle of all that rock. So big you could entertain the king of Merry Old England and his hoity-toity suckholes in it."

Imagination took over, and a smile spread slowly across Lynch's face.

CHAPTER 23: THE PAST

Vance paced their small cell, stumbling over someone's foot.

"Give it a rest, boy," Cullyn, an older sailor with red hair grumbled. "You're not doing any good this way."

Cook mumbled in agreement, pulling his feet out of the way. Again.

"I can't just sit here, Cullyn."

Cook perked up. "You could tell them your family will ransom you."

"All my family's wealth is on this ship."

Cook deflated. "Oh."

"If only we had some way out of here!" Gill ranted. "We could take the ship back. Black left only a skeleton crew on board."

Cullyn nudged Cook, "Don't you have a key to the brig?"

Vance spun on him, excited. Cook cringed and shook his head. "I've lost it again."

Vance swore and slammed his hand against the wall.

"I'd lose me 'ead if it weren't—" He grinned. "Wait!"

Cook pulled off his cap, and Cullyn cocked his head. "You finally trained your fleas to pick locks?"

"No. Look!" Cook held his cap out to show the brig key nestled in its interior. "Miss Danesbury stitched it into me cap so I wouldn't lose it anymore."

Vance shook his head in wonder. "Clever girl!"

"Doubly clever for getting us put in the brig instead of turned into chum." Cullyn grinned. "Let's get out of here."

"And, quickly," Vance urged. "Our stinking hides aren't worth Miss Danesbury virtue."

CHAPTER 24: THE PAST

Lynch picked the lock to the captain's cabin. Miss Danesbury rummaged through papers on the desk, muttering to herself.

Perfect. He slipped inside with one eye on her.

"There must be some kind of weapon in here!" she complained.

Keeping to the shadows against the wall, he crept further into the room.

"Ah-ha!"

Lynch froze.

"This'll do nicely." She held a decanter, testing its weight.

Lynch bumped his head against a sconce and came to his senses. He was here for a reason. He quickly searched the sconce and then whatever furniture he could reach without leaving the shadows.

"What the devil?"

Lynch froze again. Miss Danesbury peered intently at the decanter, then held the bottom to the candlelight.

"Well, well. If it isn't Pandora with her hand on the box."

Young Lynch's bladder nearly released from fright at the sound of Captain Black's voice.

"I-I was just having a drink."

Black closed the door, cutting off his escape. "And, found the only map to my secret lair."

The decanter? Lynch's heart leapt with joy.

"I-it was a mistake."

Lynch crept toward the door, determined to return for the bottle at a safer time.

"There is no salve for mistakes, Miss Danesbury."

A dagger with silver inlay buried itself in the wall close enough to his nose to show him the whites of his own eyes.

"Come to feel my peaches before they're ripe, Mister Lynch?"

Heart pounding and limbs petrified from terror, Lynch barely knew what he was saying. He must have said the right thing because Black mercifully let him leave.

Lynch raced from the cabin like the hounds of hell snapped at his heels, and slammed the door behind himself.

Safe at last, he collapsed in the shadows, fighting off hysteria. He ignored the murmur of Black's voice from his cabin, taking deep breaths to calm down. His composure slowly returned. A triumphant giggle slipped from him.

"Here's to you, as good as you are, And here's to me, as bad as I am; But as good as you are, and as bad as I am, I am as good as you are, as bad as I am."

SMASH!

Lynch stiffened in horror. "No!" He pulled at his hair. "No, no, no!"

The alarm bell clanged aboard Lady Sparrow, and Lynch sobbed. *Now what?*

"They've retaken the Lady Sparrow!"

"I'll deal with you later," Black promised, exiting his cabin.

Black stood outside his cabin while his crew assembled.

The alarm bell fell silent. An eerie hush settled over them. The crew looked to Black nervously.

"Well?" Black barked. "What are you waiting for? Go deal with them once and for all, you fools!"

The crew scrambled into action.

Black snatched Lynch by the collar and dragged him out of the shadow. "You, too, Mister Lynch."

Black shoved him toward the railing. Lynch, he joined his new crew. With a glare at Black, he swung across to the Lady Sparrow.

The deck was empty.

Tupper motioned to the four new crewmen. "You four, check below deck. You . . ." he pointed to Lynch. "Check the captain's cabin."

"Aye." Lynch headed for Moore's suite.

CHAPTER 25: THE PAST

Black watched his crew cautiously spread out on the Lady Sparrow and frowned. "What skullduggery is this?"

"The kind which works against you, Black!"

Black spun around. Vance and the Lady Sparrow's crew stood behind him with weapons drawn. He looked around. Most of his men were on the other ship. A red-haired man had taken control of Bloody Mary's helm, steering away from the Lady Sparrow.

Black drew his cutlass and shouted, "To me!"

His remaining crew scrambled toward him.

Miss Danesbury poked her head out of his cabin. Black didn't have time to worry about that troublesome pixie or the combat around him.

"It's a trap!" someone shouted from the Lady Sparrow. *"She's going to blow!"*

Vance lunged at him.

"Back to the ship!" The cry spread. *"Back to the ship!"*

Men swung across, but the Bloody Mary had pulled too far away, and only a few made the gap.

From the corner of his eye, Black noticed Lynch clamber over the rail of the other ship and leap into the inky water.

Vance scored a hit. Black yelped in surprise, stumbling to the rail. The pain was minimal, the wound shallow. He'd survive, but he needed to keep his attention focused on—

Miss Danesbury flew at him, screeching like a Valkyrie, and plowed him with enough force to knock him backward over the rail.

The last thing he heard before hitting the frigid water was the ear-splitting explosion of the Lady Sparrow. Then the concussion of the blast slammed him into the sea.

CHAPTER 26: THE PAST

Burning debris rained down on Lynch. Waves buffeted him, slamming him down into its icy grip. Taking a deep breath, he dove below the turbulence until his lungs ached and his body rebelled.

He surfaced to calmer water and the smoldering flotsam of the Lady Sparrow. The Bloody Mary raced for the horizon, leaving him to live or die by his own wits.

Lynch swam to the largest bit of flotsam. It was already occupied. The other man didn't stir as he clawed his way onto it. He rolled the man onto his back, and an incredulous laugh erupted from him. *Captain Black!*

His luck had finally changed.

Lynch fumbled for Black's dagger with stiff fingers. The captain's glacial hand closed around his wrist, and he screamed in fright.

Black grimaced in pain, eyes ablaze with fury. "So, the green-eyed monster has come for me at last."

He wrapped his other hand around Lynch's throat and squeezed.

Hissing for air, Lynch struggled to free himself. He flailed at Black with his free hand, but Black's arms were longer. Lynch punched at Black's arm, trying to break his crushing hold.

His thrashing jarred them from their perch, and both men tumbled back into the water.

Lynch bunched his legs between them and planted his feet against Black's chest. Heaving with his whole body, he slid from Black's grip, earning himself deep gouges along the side of his neck.

Gasping for air, Lynch snatched the dagger from his captured hand and stabbed Black. The captain cried out and squeezed tighter, grinding his wrist bones.

Black sank beneath the waves, dragging Lynch with him. Lynch lashed out, stabbing Black over and over in wild panic until he noticed the captain's eyes were staring unblinkingly toward the surface.

Lynch tugged to free himself of Black's death grip. No use.

They sank steadily deeper. The edges of his vision dimmed. Lynch hacked at Black's fingers and made one last desperate effort to pull free.

Black's fingers gave. Lynch surfaced, gasping and wheezing. He stabbed the dagger deep into the wood he'd evicted Black from and hauled himself onto it. His eyes rolled, and consciousness fled.

CHAPTER 27

Captain Lynch fingered the long scar which ran the length of his face. "You're the one who earned me my first scar."

Gill grimaced as the old guilt returned.

"But it's thanks to you," Lynch said to Miranda, "I figured out where Black kept his key. I never got to repay you proper."

Miranda's chin came up. "You can repay me by letting us go."

"As settlement, I'll let him keep breathing for a while longer." Lynch turned to Gill. "Sorry, mate. Looks like you'll just have to find yourself another wife."

"I'm not done with this one yet," Gill snarled.

Lynch threw his head back and shouted, "Man overboard!"

Hands grabbed Gill by the arms and legs. He struggled against them as the pirates swung and tossed him overboard.

SPLASH!

Captain Lynch smirked at Miranda. "You've no manner of luck with companions, m'lady."

"At least this one can swim," she growled through clenched teeth.

He shrugged. "For all the good it'll do him. Mister Quinn?"

"Aye, Captain?"

Captain Lynch held Miranda's gaze with a smile, savoring her silent rage. "Set sail."

"But, Captain! The fog—"

"Is lifting!" Lynch's eyes blazed. "If you can't find your way out of this bay by now, I'll find another First Mate."

Quinn paled. "A-aye, Captain."

CHAPTER 28

Gregory and Alice eyed each other suspiciously.

"Why follow us?" he asked.

"You were leading me to my father's killer."

"And, how exactly did you plan to avenge your father? Did you think a brutal murderer was going to let you slit his throat?"

Alice drew her cloak around her. "That's my concern."

Gregory rolled his eyes. "Did you give this any serious thought before you went on this rampage of madness?"

Alice quivered with barely suppressed outrage. "I've been thinking of naught else for most of my life. It haunted my dreams and consumed my every waking moment from the time I could comprehend the evil of having my father stolen from me. I made plans and discarded them so many times, I scarce recall them all. In the end, it came down to this; I let fate lead me. When the time is right, I will make my move, and the man who murdered my father will die by my hand."

The men exchange nervous looks.

"There is more to life than revenge, lass," Shep said.

Alice's eyes narrow. "I'll have my revenge first. *Then*, I will reckon with the rest of my life."

"There's Gill!" Neville pointed with a relieved smile.

Gill approached through the thinning fog, soaked and rowing wearily.

Gregory's hopeful smile faded as the men moved to meet Gill at the end of the dock.

"Where's Mum?"

Gill pulled the oars in and lifted his arms. "A little help, if you please. My arms feel like hot iron."

Shep hooked the edge of the boat with his gaff and pulled it against the dock while Gregory and Neville hoisted Gill onto the dock.

"Where's Mum?" Gregory insisted.

Gill leaned heavily on Neville for support, shivering. "It's a long story. I'll need something warm in my belly and dry on my back first."

"I know a place."

Gill turned toward the new voice. A young woman stood behind them. Her cloak looked familiar. From Sanders?

"Who's she?"

"Another long story," Gregory replied.

"Abbreviate it for me."

Alice crossed her arms. "My name is Alice. I followed you in hopes you'd lead me to the man who murdered my father, so I can kill him."

Gill digested the information. "Right."

"Listen," Alice closed the gap between them. "The magistrate here won't help. He's paid well to look the other way. You want your wife? We'll have to go after them."

Gill shook his head. "How are we supposed to do that? They have a real ship, and no offense Shep, but Merry Belle will never catch them."

Shep flinched, shoulders drooping. "I know she ain't much, but—"

"She has no hope of matching the Endeavor for speed."

Neville clicked his tongue and tucked his hand under his arms. "Other than the general direction of the Caribbean, we don't even know where they're going."

"I do."

The men look at Alice, surprised. She rolled her eyes at them. "I've been hunting my father's killer half my life. I've learned to listen when men don't know they're being heard. Besides," she sniffed, "a pretty face and pitcher of ale will loosen any man's tongue."

Gregory ran a hand through his hair in frustration. "That still doesn't put a ship under our feet!"

"Don't get your whirligigs in a knot," Gill grumbled. "I know someone who might help."

"Might?" Gregory frowned.

Gill rubbed his eyes. "I don't think he'll be happy to see me. But food first. Please."

Alice beckoned and headed back to town without waiting to see if they followed.

CHAPTER 29

Font scrutinized Gill from behind his rickety table. His nose wrinkled as if he smelled something rotten. Gill struggled to keep his face neutral. They needed this man's help.

The cellar was cramped with Gill, his companions, the tubby old man, and his quartet of cutthroats. The groups eyed each other, dank air abuzz with tension.

"Well, well," Font finally tutted. "If it isn't Gilroy Vance. I thought ye were dead."

"My name is Gill Webster now."

Font laughed. "Webster? Ye named yerself after the cemetery where we buried yer da? Always were an odd boy. Never knew where ye got those crazy ideas, Vance."

Gill's teeth ground together. "Gilroy Vance is dead and buried."

"It seems like he's been dug up to give me indigestion," Font grumbled, leaning back in his chair. "None of us can outrun our past."

Gill tsked in annoyance. "I'm not here for philosophy lessons, Font."

Font glanced at Alice, who looked around in boredom, then at Gregory, who was near bursting with the desire to interject.

"What are ye here for? Not for a piece of the business. That went to the bottom of the sea with the Lady Sparrow."

"She wasn't your only ship," Gill replied evenly. "There was one other you used to outrun trouble."

Font's eyebrows crept toward his receding hairline. "And ye want to use her to catch up to trouble? I've been dodgin' creditors and livin' off dirt for two decades because of ye. With yer da dead and the Lady Sparrow decoratin' Neptune's bedroom, I had no way to pay back all those investors. Now, ye've come to rob me of the Specter, too? Ye can go to the devil, Gilroy Vance, or Webster, or whatever ye wants to be callin' yerself."

"They've taken my wife and burned our home."

Font spread his hands. "And I might put a blade between yer ribs for spite."

"He who is down needs fear no fall."

"And he who is low knows no pride," Font responded.

"Miranda is all we have left now."

Font stiffened. "Miranda? Danesbury's niece?"

"Yes."

Font's withered lips thinned, and he shrank into his seat. "I ain't interested. Hades grins at me from over your shoulder."

He motioned to the cutthroats. They stepped forward.

Patience snapping, Gregory shouted, "We can pay!"

The cutthroats stopped and looked to Font for direction.

Gill scowled.

"There's still the treasure, Da," Gregory pleaded.

The room became preternaturally silent. Gill's scowl deepened.

"There is no treasure," he replied, words heavy with meaning.

"There's no *key*," Gregory countered, "but there *is* treasure."

Gill looked at Font, then back at Gregory, torn.

"*Please*, Da."

Gill relented with a defeated sigh. "All right, boy. You win."

He rubbed his eyes wearily and returned his attention to Font. "When Miranda was held captive by Black, she saw the map to his hidden lair."

Font leaned forward with an excited grin. "So, there is a secret lair! I thought 'twas just a yarn."

"It's real enough. If you can get to it."

"After ye disappeared, some of the surviving crew returned. Found out about yer run-in with Black and his devil's bargain. Got a tally of who stayed true and who didn't. Those who turned yet lived, I sent a special thank-ye."

The old man ran a finger across his throat, and Gill paled.

"Well, you missed one," Gregory grumbled. "Lynch is the one who has Mum. Help us get her back, and we'll split the treasure with you. You can send a token of your appreciation to those who remained loyal, pay off the creditors, and live the rest of your days in luxury."

"Gregory!"

"Lynch, is it? Why didn't ye say so earlier? Seventy-thirty."

"Fifty-fifty," Gregory countered.

"Sixty-forty. I'm yer Mum's only hope."

"Fifty-fifty. Mum's the only one who knows where the treasure is."

Font tugged his lower lip, debating. "Fifty-fifty, but I'm comin' with ye. By Neptune's beard; we'll be makin' sure yer da doesn't sink another one of me ships and disappear again."

"Gregory!" Gill grabbed his son's arm. Gregory shook free, eyes still fixed on Font.

"Done!"

"Done!" Font slammed a hand on the tabletop, sounding like a gunshot. Gill shivered and prayed it wasn't a warning of events to come.

CHAPTER 30

The Specter was a thing of beauty. Designed for speed and stealth, her shallow draw made her perfect for smuggling ventures. Now, she was their only hope of catching Lynch.

Gill put a hand on Gregory's shoulder and led him away from the bustle of loading the ship. "I want you to stay with your sister."

"Bollocks to that!" Gregory snorted.

Gill stood taller. "Mind me in this, son."

Gregory shook his head. "I made a deal with Font—"

"And, I'll make sure it's honored as best we can."

Gregory's chin jutted. *So much like his mother.* "It's not your place. The man who strikes the deal must make it real."

"You're still a boy. You have your whole life—"

"I'm a man," Gregory insisted, arms crossed. "If I don't have my honor, what is my life worth? Besides, you need every pair of fighting hands you can find to get Mum back."

"He's right."

Gill and Gregory startled as Font materialized next to them. For a fat man, he moved like a ghost.

"I'm an old man, Gill. And so are ye. No one sane would be willing to go after a bunch of pirates for the sake of yer missus. My crew is loyal to me, but they'll not risk their necks for some bedtime story about hidden treasure. Bring the boy. You'll have need of him."

Gill hesitated, looking to Shep and Neville, who watched Font's crew work. The dim light of the hidden cove accented their age, and the mist highlighted the gray in their hair. *Out of options*. Gill sagged in defeat and nodded.

Gregory grinned in victory. Font raised an eyebrow. "Report to Captain Hammerfield. He'll find good use for your eager hands."

Gregory's smile faltered, and he looked to Gill.

"Go on," Gill shooed. "Enjoy the fruits of your desires."

Gregory set his jaw and stalked toward the Specter.

"Now, about this lassie yer thinkin' about bringin'."

"Not just thinking about," Alice declared, approaching.

Font frowned. "The men don't hold with having women aboard. We're not a passenger ship."

Alice placed a fist on her hip. "I don't care what the men hold or how long they hang on it to. Either I'm coming, or you'll never find Lynch and his crew."

Font glared at Gill, who shook his head. "Make it possible. Please. She refuses to tell us where to find Lynch until we're in the Caribbean."

"That way, you can't sail off without me."

Font growled. "I can't protect ye if the men want a taste of ye."

In a blur of flashing metal, Alice pulled a dagger, cut off the top button of his shirt, and sheathed it again. Font jerked away belatedly, groping at his missing button.

"I can protect myself. And I can pull my own weight."

"The devil you will!" Font fumed. "Find a dress and put it on. I'd rather the men lookin' at that and knowin' they can't touch than have them workin' side-by-side with ye, hot and sweaty like, starin' at yer legs and forgettin' their place.

"But—"

"No! I won't be budged for all the gold in the Spanish treasury." Font's voice swelled. "I'll not have people sayin' I let a woman trim me sails."

He stared at Alice, unwavering until she nodded.

CHAPTER 31

Alice smoothed her skirt. It was too long, too heavy, and too ridiculous, but she knew better than to trifle with Font.

She spied Gregory and headed toward him, passing Captain Hammerfield.

"Miss," the captain greeted.

"Captain."

The crewman splicing rope snarled at her and adjusted the bandage on his hand.

Alice ignored him.

"Mister Skive," Hammerfield barked. "What happened to your hand?"

Skive glared at Alice.

Hammerfield followed his gaze. "Well, I hope you learned to take 'no' for an answer."

Alice smirked as she continued on her way.

Gregory noticed her and straightened. "Good day, Miss Alice."

Alice laughed.

"What's funny?"

"I've never been called Miss Alice before. It's strange."

"Well, you never did tell me your last name."

"No. I like it. You say it in such a respectful manner. It . . . It makes me feel like I could be a decent person."

"You are."

"Not yet."Alice gazed out at the ocean. "Did you mean what you said before? About your father being a coward?"

Gregory blanched. "You heard that? No. I was frightened and impatient."

Alice looked at him from the corner of her eye. "And now?"

Gregory lowered his face. "Now, I'm embarrassed to have uttered such a horrible thing about my Da."

Alice returned her gaze to the waves. "I never knew my own."

"I'm sorry."

"What's he like, your father?"

A smile lifted the corner of his mouth. "He's an honest, hard-working man. He loves my Mum and never once looked at another woman. He always made sure we had enough to eat and had clothes on our backs before he ever spent a copper on himself. I used to think he was too strict. I see now he was that way out of love. He only wanted us to grow up to be honest and hardworking folk, too."

Gregory chuckled.

Alice looked at him over her shoulder. "What?"

He shrugged. "I used to think all those stories about being captured by Captain Black were make-believe to make us think he'd done something exciting in his life. It's hard to believe something so terrible actually happened to him – to both of them. They're honorable people, my mum, and da, and they were nearly done in before they could experience life. I didn't know how much I loved them until now."

Gregory stared out at the ocean to avoid her gaze.

Alice studied his profile. "Bermuda."

"What?"

Alice shrugged self-consciously. "Captain Lynch. He'll stop at Bermuda for supplies. There's no fort and limited military presence to contend with."

Gregory smiled, grateful. She smiled back shyly.

"It's like looking back in time," Gill sighed, watching Gregory and Alice bonding.

Font glowered. "By the powers, I hope not. Yer not sinkin' another one of my ships for a lass with a pretty twitch to her skirt. She knows too much, Gilroy. Mark my words; that gel is trouble."

Gill sobered.

CHAPTER 32

Night fell before they crept into the bay where Endeavor weighed anchor.

Captain Hammerfield peered through the telescope, ignoring Font's close proximity. "No movement. The boats are gone. It looks like they've gone to shore. There will be a minimal crew onboard."

"We can deal with them," Gregory muttered.

Hammerfield closed the telescope and turned to the waiting men. "We'll put anchor here and wait until dawn. If you're not back by then, we'll make for Antigua to restock and return to England. We want no encounters with the trouble you pursue."

"Fair enough," Gill acknowledged. "Thank you, Captain."

Gregory scowled but held his tongue.

Shep and Neville waited by the rope ladder.

"We'll be back quick as a whip," Gill assured them.

Shep's fingers tightened on his pole. "You don't mean to leave us behind?"

Gill put a hand on his shoulder. "Shep."

Shep scowled and lowered his head. "Bloody peg leg."

"It's not that. The fewer of us gallivanting around, the less likelihood of drawing attention." Gill placed his other hand on Neville's shoulder and looked from one to the other.

Reluctantly, the men agreed.

"You're good friends." Gill squeezed their shoulders and climbed onto the rope ladder. Gregory gave them a grim smile and followed his father down to the rowboat where Alice waited, once again in men's clothing.

"What are you doing here?" Gregory demanded as Gill settled in the boat.

Alice looked at Gregory like he'd gone mad. "I'm coming to avenge my father."

Gregory frowned. "It's too dangerous!"

Alice laughed. "I'm not some fair maiden to protect. Now shut up and get in, or I swear on my father's soul, I'll shove off without you!"

Muttering under his breath, Gregory dropped into the boat.

They closed the distance between ships in silence. The men quietly boarded Endeavor ahead of Alice to clear the way.

"Well, well. If it isn't the old dog and his mangy pup."

They gawked as Lynch as his crew drifted from the shadows. Ripper with the jagged teeth and Jelly with the spoon dragged Miranda on deck.

"How did you know?" Gregory demanded.

"I told you," Alice replied from behind him. "I'm hunting the man who killed my father."

She sauntered to Lynch's side and favored Gill with a look of contempt. "And that man is you."

"My da never killed anyone!"

Gill squinted at Alice, Font's words ringing in his mind. "You planned this all along. Who are you?"

A sly smile hooked the corner of her mouth. "Alice Black. I was six months old when you killed my father. He was making one last trip to get his treasure from the lair, and then he was going to retire.

"Instead of a life of comfort and a decent education, I ended up slinging ale in a filthy tavern while my mother earned our keep on her back. The only reason I was spared that fate is because my mother saved enough money to buy me passage out of that hole. She gave me every coin she had and told me to find the man who murdered my father. Take back the treasure and life he stole from us.

"That's what I intend to do. You stole my father from me, and my mother died because of the life you forced us to live. I had no one until James found me."

Gregory flinched, face wrinkled in disgust.

Lynch snaked an arm around Alice's waist. She smiled at him fondly. "He told me how you murdered my father. How he found my father and held him as he lay dying. And how my father entrusted the key to him. Now, I can have my revenge and reclaim what's rightfully mine."

Gregory snarled at Lynch. "You lying sack of—"

Quinn backhanded Gregory, sending him staggering backward. He glared at the man but spoke to Alice. "It's not true, Alice. You've traveled with us. You know my da."

Doubt flickered across her face and disappeared behind a cold mask.

"Do you really think Lynch is going to share the treasure with you?" Gill asked. "He's the one that killed your father."

Alice took a threatening step toward Gill. "Liar!"

"It's true, child," Miranda confirmed sadly. "Lynch told us how he endeavored to steal the key. When your father tried to stop him, Lynch stabbed him over and over again to get it."

"It's not true! James would never!" She looked to Lynch for reassurance.

Contempt twisted his scars. "All I had to do was spin a yarn or two, and you couldn't wait to do what I wanted. A kind word, a sympathetic remark, and you were on your back faster than the turn of the tide. You stupid slag. You truly are your mother's daughter."

Alice shook her head, stepping away. Lynch jerked her back by the elbow and kissed her crudely while his crew laughed and whistled lewdly.

Lynch shoved Alice toward Gregory, who caught her.

"You bastard," she sobbed.

"Well, it takes one to know one, dearie." Lynch turned on Miranda. "Now, you're going to tell me where Black's Lair is."

"I already told you, I don't remember."

"And, I already told you, I don't believe you. You'd better start remembering quickly, or I'm going to put holes in the people you love. Not big ones, mind. Just a lot of painful little ones until they've got nothing left in them to bleed out."

Miranda hesitated.

In a cold and quiet voice, Lynch spoke one word. "Quinn."

The tattooed pirate's dagger was out with a snick and a flash, pressed against Gregory's throat.

"Stop!" Miranda threw her hands out. "All right! I'll tell you."

She speared Lynch with a violent glare. "Gill, take your shirt off."

"What?"

Miranda snarled in frustration. "For once in your life, do what I ask without arguing!"

Gill flinched and pulled his shirt off with a wounded expression.

Everyone watched Miranda in fascination. She laid the shirt on the deck with the cuffs together and pointed to the embroidered ivy. "Here's your map."

Lynch scoffed. "Slit his throat."

"Look!" Miranda insisted.

Lynch knelt for a closer look.

"The ivy here. See the dark green thread? It's the map. These leaves in the lighter green, that's the coordinates." She ran her finger along the carefully stitched vines and leaves. "The number of leaves on the right cuff is the longitude. The leaves on the left, latitude. I knew I'd never remember, so I sewed it on Gill's shirts the first year we were married."

Lynch shook his head, impressed. "You always were clever." He turned to Quinn. "Strip them down. Make sure they don't have anything sewn into their unmentionables and put them in the brig. Except for her."

He pointed to Alice. "Her, you can have her for a bit of sport first."

"No!" Gregory wrapped his arms around Alice and hauled her over the railing. They disappeared into the darkness.

SPLASH!

Lynch huffed wearily. "Young love."

Quinn shifted uneasily. "Do we go after them, Captain?"

The captain raised an eyebrow. "How badly do you want her?"

The crew looked amongst themselves with a collection of frowns, and head shakes.

"That's what I thought." Lynch scoffed. "Get on with it."

CHAPTER 33

Shep and Neville hauled Gregory and Alice onboard, grunting and straining.

"What happened?" Shep asked.

Alice wrapped her arms around herself, shivering and staring at the water pooling at her feet.

Gregory pushed wet hair out of his face as Font and Hammerfield arrived.

"We weren't sure what to do when they sailed past." Hammerfield motioned to the empty bay.

"It was a trap," Gregory replied flatly. "Lynch knew we were coming."

Neville tucked his hands under his arms. "How is that possible?"

Font squinted at Alice. She blushed and ducked her head to avoid his gaze.

"It doesn't matter," Gregory answered. "I can't save them alone. I need men who are willing to fight."

Font shook his head. "I already told ye—"

"That was before I knew I had a map to the Black's Lair."

The men gawked at Gregory.

"Now, if you want your share of the treasure, you'll fight for it like honest men, or I'll go ashore and find a crew who will."

Font and Hammerfield looked at each other.

"Very well," Font agreed. "We're in this with you, but ye better not be foolin' with us, lad."

"I'm dead serious."

"I'll have some men go ashore for provisions," Hammerfield said. "We can set sail in a couple of hours."

The men headed off to make ready. Alice touched Gregory's arm tentatively. "I—"

He gave her a cold, hard stare.

"Thank you for—"

"Save it. I didn't do it because I have any fond feelings. I did it because it was the right thing to do. My father taught me that."

She flinched from the harsh words and watched him walk away, miserable.

CHAPTER 34

Gill held Miranda and stroked her hair. "My sweet, sweet lady. I am sorry."

Miranda peered at him, confused. "Whatever for?"

"I'm sorry I couldn't give you all the nice things in life you wanted."

Miranda smiled and stroked his cheek. "Silly goose. I never wanted those things for me. I wanted them for you. I knew the life I was choosing when I married you, and I haven't regretted a single day. I still love you more than life itself."

"Then I have everything I could ever want." Gill kissed her tenderly and smirked. "I have a present for you."

"Oh?"

Gill fumbled with the seam of his underwear and pulled out the sewing needle.

"It's your lucky needle. From the last time we were being held prisoner by pirates."

Miranda laughed and took it from him. "You always knew how to pick the perfect gift."

She threaded it into the seam on the sleeve of her slip and snuggled against him.

CHAPTER 35

Gregory spread his shirt on the captain's table and laid the cuffs together. Font and Hammerfield stared at the embroidered pattern in amazement.

"Well, I'll be," Font whispered.

Hammerfield counted the leaves and pulled out his map to make calculations.

"Nothing there." He pointed to an empty spot on the map.

"It'll be there," Gregory assured, gathering his shirt.

"One more thing, lad." Font cleared his throat with a look to the captain. Gregory stiffened in apprehension.

"The gel. She's one of them, ain't she?"

Gregory grimaced. "Not anymore."

"But, she ain't one of us, either."

Gregory sighed. "No, I don't suppose she is."

"There ain't a man aboard willing to follow ye if that turn-tail is running loose."

Gregory shrugged. "Stick her in the brig."

CHAPTER 36

The sun disappeared as the rowboats slid into the cave on the northern face of the rock island. Bundled on the bottom of the lead boat, Miranda and Gill blinked to adjust their eyes as the pirates lit lanterns to allow the boats to penetrate deeper.

They rowed until they came to a dead end.

"What's going on?" Jelly craned his neck to look around. "Where's the treasure?"

"Patience, Mister Jelly," Lynch advised. He quickly removed his coat, hat, and pistol. Black's dagger glinted from his belt. "I'll be back before you know it."

He dove into the water and disappeared.

Gill kissed Miranda's forehead, and they leaned back to wait.

The minutes stretched out. The crew shifted, uneasy.

"He's coming back, yeah?" someone asked.

"Of course, he's coming back," Quinn assured them.

"Unless he drowned," Jelly muttered.

Quinn cuffed him.

"Ow!" Jelly rubbed his head.

"You think the Captain spent twenty years getting here just to drown now?"

"Well—"

Lynch surfaced with a gasp. Everyone looked at him expectantly.

"Come in, boys," he grinned. "It's a fine day for a swim."

Darkness pressed in on them. Someone struck a match and lit a torch. The darkness retreated a few feet. More torches flared to life, and Black's Lair glowed with warm amber light. Gold, silver, and jewels glimmered and glinted in the torchlight in every direction.

Dripping and chilled, Lynch and his crew gawked around in awe. Even Gill and Miranda stared in wonder. Black hadn't exaggerated. The lair contained enough treasure for each one of them to live in comfort until the end of their days.

Someone tittered an unsteady laugh, and they slowly came to their senses.

"The ship'll be bulging at the seams with all this loot!" Jelly laughed.

"We'll all be kings!" The crew cheered and hugged each other while Lynch beamed like a proud father.

"Start loading the boats, men."

CHAPTER 37

Skive leaned against the wall outside Alice's reach. She gripped the cell bars, white-knuckled.

"Let me out of here! I have to avenge my father!"

"Captain's orders," Skive leered. "Nobody wants your pretty little blade between their shoulders."

Alice lunged, her bellow of frustration drowning out his laughter.

Skive dangled the keys from his finger. "They've all gone on their fool's errand. It's just you and me now, Pet, and you owe me a little recompense for my hand."

He unlocked the cell, and Alice scurried to the back wall.

"Bet you wish you had your little blade now, don't you?"

Skive cornered her and leaned in for a kiss. Alice punched him in the groin. He wheezed and doubled over. She brought her knee up to crack him in the face and Skive fell to the floor.

"Idiot."

Alice snatched the keys from his hand and spat on him.

CHAPTER 38

Miranda leaned wearily against Gill under the watchful gaze of Jelly and Ripper.

The beautiful golden light had dimmed to regular torchlight without the cavern's riches. Lynch sat like a king on his throne, watching the last load disappear into the water.

"The last of it is on its way, Captain," Quinn reported. "We can go whenever you're ready."

"Very good, Mister Quinn." Lynch stood with a leisurely stretch and strolled over to Gill and Miranda.

The couple craned their necks to look at him in resignation.

"You're going to kill us now?" Gill asked.

"After all the trouble you've given me? You've been the proverbial thorn in my side. Killing you quickly wouldn't be satisfying at all. No, mate," Lynch assured him. "I'm not going to kill you. I'm going to leave you here to contemplate the choices you've made for the rest of your life. Which ought to be three days unless you can find fresh water in this hole."

Gill straightened his spine. "At least we'll die with honor."

Lynch laughed. "If you call wallowing in your filth while wasting away to nothing, 'honor', then, yes. Ole Gilroy Vance will die with honor."

He turned a gleaming eye to Miranda. "As for you, m'lady. You're not as pretty to look at as my plump Alice, but twenty years dreaming of this day will make it just as sweet."

Gill's arms tightened around Miranda. She buried her face in Gill's chest with a sob.

Lynch thumped Jelly on the shoulder. "Don't worry, faithful Jelly. I'm not forgetting your poor eye."

Jelly giggled and stroked the wooden spoon.

CHAPTER 39

Distracted by the struggling woman, Quinn and Jelly carried Miranda by the arms while Ripper kept her legs locked together while they trailed behind the captain.

Lynch pushed the door to his cabin open and came face-to-point with a cutlass. He took a step back, and Gregory followed him onto the deck. "Surprise."

"Hardly," Lynch snorted. "I'm evil, not stupid. I've been expecting some pathetic rescue attempt from you, but this is plain stupid. You're surrounded, boy."

Gregory smirked. "I may be young, but I'm not stupid."

He motioned with his sword. The crew around them drew their weapons. The familiar faces of his crew had been replaced. Friends of the boy, no doubt.

The men dropped Miranda to reach for their weapons, and she wobbled toward her son.

Lynch pulled the dagger from his belt, stepped behind Miranda, and pressed the blade to her throat. "Drop your weapons or bathe in your mother's blood."

"I don't think so." Miranda pulled a sewing needle from her sleeve and stabbed Lynch's hand. He screamed and jerked away enough for her to duck out from his grasp.

Lynch drew his sword and lunged at Gregory, both blades aimed to kill.

Quinn, Ripper, and Jelly retreated to the rope ladder. Outnumbered and surrounded, Quinn and Ripper were killed quickly. With no one to hide behind, Jelly dropped his weapon and raised his hands. Miranda snatched her wooden spoon back from him and turned to find Gregory outmatched by Lynch.

The captain drove his sword toward Gregory's chest.

"No!" Alice appeared with a sword of her own, knocking Lynch's cutlass wide. "This dance is mine!"

She squared off against Lynch. He grinned, tucking Black's dagger back into his belt.

"Name your tune, dearie."

"*Alas, my love, you do me wrong,*" she hissed.

"Greensleeves it is, then."

Alice swung with a snarl, putting all her weight into the blow. Lynch sidestepped and disarmed her in one swift move. Grabbing her by the throat, he lifted her onto her toes. "I must admit, you're much better in bed than you are with a sword."

Lynch shoved his sword through her belly with a grin. "Your father had the same look on his face when I killed him."

"Y-you," Alice shuddered. "You mean this one?

She yanked the dagger from his belt and drove it into his heart. Lynch looked down at the dagger, mouth agape. His knees released, and he crumpled to her feet.

Alice struggled to remain upright. Gregory rushed to her side and carefully lowered her to the deck. She grabbed his shirt, panting against the pain. "F-forgive me?"

"Everything is going to be fine," he promised.

Alice smiled weakly. "Liar."

Her smile twisted into a grimace, and her eyes fluttered closed.

Gregory lowered his head and gently pried Alice's fingers from his shirt. "Search Lynch for the key."

"Wait," Miranda said. "It must have something to do with Black's dagger. It's the only thing that makes sense."

Gregory pulled the dagger from Lynch's chest and wiped the blade clean.

They examined the dagger. "You sure, Mum?"

Neville pointed to the silver inlay. "Look here."

Gregory frowned. "Yes, it's very nice craftsmanship, Neville, but I don't see—"

"It's not just decoration. *Look*."

Neville fiddled with the dagger. A section of the silver inlay popped in*to his hand. The key!*

Gregory laughed and patted Neville on the back. "Leave it to you to find something that shouldn't be possible."

Neville grinned and stood taller.

CHAPTER 40

Hands free, Gill hurried to untie his feet. The torch flickered. He only had a few more minutes before it guttered and plunged him into darkness. The rope gave, and Gill raced to the water, diving in.

He followed the underwater tunnel to the gate and tried to force it open. It didn't budge. The torchlight wavered. *No time!*

He reached through the bars to feel the lock in desperate hope Lynch had left the key. *Empty*. He tried to retract his arm. It didn't move. He was stuck.

Pressure squeezed his lungs. He was nearly out of time. Gill pulled on his arm frantically while precious air leaked from him.

With a last sputter, the torch died, and Gill was left in – not darkness?

Light glowed from the opposite side of the gate. Gregory's beautiful face moved toward him with something glimmering in his hand. Gill fought the desperate need to breathe in. Gregory shoved his arm free. Consciousness eked away, and his eyes rolled.

Gregory unlocked the gate, and it opened. Grabbing Gill by the wrist, he swam back to the surface.

Hands pulled Gill into a rowboat. He coughed and gulped huge lungfuls of air while Miranda rained kisses on him. "I thought I'd lost you."

"You nearly did." He wrapped his arms around her weakly.

Neville leaned over him with a grin. "Good to have you back, Gill."

Gill and Miranda lay on the bottom of the boat, holding each other, while Gregory rowed.

"I'll have none of your 'honor prevents us' nonsense," he scolded as they passed out of the cave. "You'll take your share of the treasure. I'm not listening to another twenty years of your bickering."

They looked at each other and laughed.

"We've raised a smart boy," Miranda said.

"No, sweet lady," Gill corrected gently. "We've raised a smart man."

"Uh." Neville looked past them, alarmed.

"What's wrong?" Miranda helped Gill sit up. "Sweet Mother of Mercy!"

"What?" Gregory stopped rowing and turned to look.

The Endeavor sped awa from them.

"They abandoned us!"

"Ahoy, the rowboat!"

The Specter appeared from behind the island with Font and Shep at the railing. The hook of Shep's gaff pole hovered suspiciously close to Font's throat. The old man gingerly pushed it aside.

"Ye didn't think I'd be leavin' ye behind?" Font shouted with a strained smile. "I'm a smuggler, Gilroy Vance. Not a thief."

They exchanged nervous glances and laughed. "Never crossed our minds."

ABOUT ROSA MARCHISELLA

Rosa Marchisella is the author of the gripping **Touch of Insanity** series and bone-chilling novella, **The Greatest of Books**. Her stories focus on fantasy, paranormal, and thrilling adventures, however Rosa also writes romance under the alias *Ramona Mainstrom*. A dynamic and prolific story-teller, Rosa has earned critical praise as a writer, stage actress, vocalist, public speaker, and artist. Her hobbies include gardening, playing games with her kids, and dancing around the house while singing made-up lyrics to vaguely known songs.

Find out more: RosaMarchisella.com

facebook.com/iamrosa.fanpage
twitter.com/RosaMarchisella
amazon.com/-/e/B071WDYYS7

A BREAKING AND CRUSHING OF YOUR BONES

BY LISAH JAYNE WALDEN

A writer is nothing more than a daydreamer. Do not take this as some form of judgment. It is the truth. Without the dreams of writers, we would not have such wonderful stories to read, and it is those stories that whisk us away from our boring and mundane lives. One must agree that a writer is, in fact, an artist. The writer creates characters, sets a scene, unfolds a story, which will, hopefully, ensnare the reader into that beautiful mind, making that reader want more and more. However, every artist needs a muse, something or someone to inspire the art. Oftentimes writers base their craft on events they have experienced.

Other times, it is a person or a thing that inspires. With this tale, it is the latter. Not a person. Not a thing, but rather the muse of the ocean. What should a writer do with such an entity, this muse, this gift? Some would even argue that such a muse is not a gift but instead a curse. An argument can be made that this is true of any muse for any artist; that voice, that image which will not dissipate until said artist has exhausted themselves to the brink of death to bring said art to you —at times left mad by the experience. These things happen, but what happens when the artist pushes back, seeking to control his muse rather than allowing the muse to enslave him? Our tale takes place in the seaside town of Tramore, where a young American writer and his bride bask in the fruits of his labor.

LeeAnne sat in her favorite wooden rocking chair in the living room of their new house, her hands pressed against the barred window as she looked at the crashing waves of the sea. All the windows were barred here. All the doors were locked. She did not question it, not anymore. It was commonplace for her now, this prison that kept her soul from what she truly wanted—the ocean on her skin. As much as she yearned for those waves to envelop her, LeeAnne's mind was too numb to fight or even question her present situation. Every day was the same, to be repeated yet another day: wake up, bathe, dress, break-fast of fruit and tea, sit by the window, lunch with her husband with more tea, sit by the window, dinner with her husband, and then… It was the *then* which was foggy.

As much as she tried, LeeAnne could not remember what happened after dinner. She never remembered going to bed. She always awoke in her room alone. Her husband, Jonathan, always slept in his own bed-chamber. If there was any tenderness, any marital union, she did not recall it. All she knew was the routine. All she waited for was this window, with its strong iron bars that kept her from ever feeling the sea.

LeeAnne felt a hand on her shoulder, a woman's hand.

"Ma'am, it's time for lunch."

LeeAnne remembered her voice. She smiled at the knowledge that she could remember anyone, a moment, a soft touch, a voice.

"Brianna," LeeAnne said as she smiled.

"No, ma'am. It's me, Katie."

LeeAnne turned from the window and looked at the older woman. She began to shake her head in defiance at the sight. This was not the woman who should be with her. Where was Brianna? Tears welled in her eyes. The older woman, Katie, knelt in front of her. She pulled a kerchief from her blouse and dried LeeAnne's eyes.

"You're not Brianna," LeeAnne whimpered.

"No, ma'am, but it is good that you remember her. Let's keep this memory between us, hmm? My name is Katie."

"Katie," LeeAnne said. Her brow furrowed as she pushed her foggy mind to remember. Slowly, her brow relaxed, and a smile spread across her face. Then she said, "Katie Cat. Katie Cat, who loves to catch fish."

"Yes, now you are remembering even more."

"Brianna is your daughter," LeeAnne stopped and brought her hands to her mouth. "Was your daughter. She was your daughter until Jonathan… I'm so sorry, Katie."

"No more words on this, ma'am. Jonathan is waiting for you to join him for lunch. You need to have another sip of tea."

"I don't want it. It makes me feel funny."

"Just a sip, ma'am. Just a sip to ease your mind."

LeeAnne begrudgingly accepted the teacup and took a sip.

"That's good," Katie said. "It won't be much longer now, I swear it."

With that sip of tea, LeeAnne's memories dwindled once again. She moved through the day like an automaton, existing in the same routine for just as she had every day prior.

Jonathan sat at his desk in a rather good humor. He had bedded his wife and had her put to bed for the night. And, as with every night he lay with her, the inspiration began to fill his head. He opened his laptop, his hands shaking as the power of his lovemaking, or rather taking, was ready to explode through his fingers onto the keyboard. What luck it had been to encounter such a creature.

He first met his wife on the eastern seaboard. He decided to leave Rochester, New York, and travel to Ireland for inspiration. He rented a small cottage to work on his first novel. It was do or die for him. Write and get discovered or fail and return to the mill. But the words would not come to him. He stared blankly at his laptop, drowned his lack of inspiration with more cheap whiskey until he gave up and walked along the sea.

At first, he thought he'd consumed too much whiskey. He blinked at the image coming towards him, a woman walking out of the sea. Her long white gown was somehow dry and billowing behind her, restless as the waves of the sea. Jet black hair and eyes even darker were a stark contrast to her pale, almost translucent skin.

"Love me," was all she said as she grabbed his face and kissed him.

A force surged within him. His skin tingled, and his words slowed, more than a drunken slur, rather like time was being slowed down. Even the images around him slackened. He could see the water spray dwindle, then crash onto their entangled bodies. As much as he was lost in that moment, in her, his mind raced, and words filled him until he shook. Those words needed to come out. He was torn. Stay with this beauty or write? She made the decision for him. She led him back to his rented cottage and laid on his bed.

"Write for me, my love. Show me your pain and joy in words. Your love and loss."

"My soul," he said.

She laughed. It was then Jonathan realized who she was and what she could do. He had heard tales of her before, but that was just a story, a myth told to him by his grandmother. Yet here she was—Leanan Sidhe, here to inspire and take his soul. Burn him out before his time. He would reach fame. She would return to the sea, and he would waste away or commit suicide from the lack of her touch.

You want to be a great writer, huh? Bet you stay at the mill. Everyone needs flour to live. Words on paper, your little stories are just that, stories. Be careful, lest the Leanan Sidhe come to you.

Those words of his grandmother filled Jonathan's head as the woman before him stripped off her gown and lay on his bed.

"Write for me," she said again. He wrote for her, and in doing so, he wrote for himself. His novel became a bestseller. He waited for his mystery woman to leave. She did not.

"Two more novels," she said. Jonathan agreed and accepted her kisses. His body was afire from her touch. He could already feel the pang of yearning, knowing that soon she would leave him. The loneliness would consume him. The madness would set in. The sea would call to him. He had two more novels before he was dead—two more novels to figure this out.

He researched fairy lore. He rather wished to talk to his grandmother, but his guest would not leave his side. She had no interest in his laptop. She hated it. Complained that he did not put pen to paper. He humored her, but as she slept, he continued his research.

Jonathan discovered he needed yarrow to combat her power, but not too much. He needed her inspiration. He also needed to render her powerless against him. He came up with a concoction of rue and crushed Xanax. Just a touch put into her tea until she began to forget. Forget who she was.

Now he could have her inspiration and put her destructive vampiric tendencies to bed. She became his girlfriend and his muse, then she became his wife. Jonathan was ecstatic. How many more creatures of the sea were out there? He had three best sellers. Hired a staff to watch after her and provide her *tea*. At first, he felt guilty about it. She was a creature of habit who feeds and lives, but he needed to live, and he wanted to also feed, feed off her inspiration. He would never let her go. She was here, twelve bestsellers later. She was a creature of habit, as was he. What other creatures were out there in the deep, blue sea?

Jonathan did not just become a bestseller; he became a collector. He became the ultimate fisherman of fae. Undines to cook his food. Selkies to serve as maids and serve as something else when the occasion arose. But his ultimate prize, his ultimate trophy, was his wife. He claimed her. She would not wander from his side.

Unfortunately, they needed to move back to the Eastern Sea. Her skin had begun to flake up. She was throwing up in the middle of the night. He bought a beautiful house by the sea. Windows were barred, and all the doors leading outdoors locked. She was not allowed on the grounds. However, Jonathan had the seawater brought in. A beautiful tub was fashioned for her and filled with seawater. He couldn't watch her nightly baths. Blood filled the tub as she screamed. Her lovely legs split apart until there were eight tentacles that became fluid with suckers basking in the seawater. At first, Jonathan was mesmerized by this transformation, but now he couldn't stomach it. This was his wife, his muse, his kidnapped sea fairy.

Those eight tentacles would gladly hold him under the deep and drain what was left of his soul. But why was he thinking about this? He should be writing. He looked at his drink. Maybe not enough yarrow. Jonathan poured another dram of scotch and put the yarrow powder in it. Her magic was stronger than normal. He would have to talk to Katie about the tea.

He looked back to his laptop, but nothing came to him. What was happening? The inspiration should just come now, as it always did, but instead, he was filled with these memories. Maybe another shot. Maybe some music. Everyone was asleep. Perhaps he could blast music to be inspired. No, this was not right.

I should be inspired now! I just had sex with her. It should happen right now. Nothing.

Jonathan looked around his study. Everything was in its place. Everything was also silent. Eardrum-pounding silent. He stood up and felt the keys of his house in his right pant leg. He shook the keys. No one can come in or get out without these keys.

Jonathan went to sit down when he heard the doorbell go off. He looked at the clock. It was two-thirty in the morning. Who would be here at this hour? He needed to write. Some kids playing pranks. He sat back down. The doorbell rang again. Jonathan shot up from his chair. He drank the last of the dram of his scotch. He stomped towards the door. He didn't open it but rather glared at the door. Then the doorbell rang again. This time Katie came to the head of the upstairs.

"Sir?"

"Go back to bed," Jonathan said.

The doorbell rang again.

"I'm sorry, sir, but who would be ringing at this hour?"

"Go back to bed."

"Yes, sir."

Jonathan walked back to his study and grabbed his revolver. He then approached the door. He peered through the peephole. "Who is it? And Why are you ringing my door at such an hour?"

He heard someone coughing, no hacking on the other side of the door. He looked through the peephole and saw a disheveled man in rags holding onto a walking stick.

"I just need to use your phone. Car broke down, and I need to call my sister," the man said as he coughed.

"Uh-huh," Jonathan returned. "No cellie? I don't have a landline?"

"Please, sir. Just need a phone and a towel. It's raining, and I'm drenched."

Jonathan became enraged at this intruder. He opened the door just so he could look at him. "You need a phone?"

"Yes, Sir, if you don't mind, and maybe a towel to dry off, if it pleases you."

Jonathan looked at the man. He was short. His shoulders hunched. He wore rags, worse than rags. Holes in all his clothes and the stench, the stench from this man reminded Jonathan of the subways in New York City, infestations of rats and cockroaches. But there was one thing about this man that did not fit—the gold necklace around his neck and the jewel. A single black pearl hung from that necklace. It was beautiful the way it glimmered.

He remembered seeing a similar necklace around LeeAnne. He, of course, took it from her and hid it away with other trophies from those he conquered from the deep. He looked at this stranger and his necklace. His stomach filled with bile, not with a sickness, but rather a want. "I will give you shelter if you give me that necklace."

"My necklace, sir?"

"Yes."

"I cannot do that, sir."

Jonathan attempted to shut the door, but the smelly man put his foot in the door. "I will do what you wish, assist you in your house for a time if that is what it takes for me to make one call and warm myself in your home." The man pulled his rags closer to his body. "But this necklace is not part of the deal."

All Jonathan could think of was that necklace. The darkness of it, the way it hung around his wife's neck. Now this stranger was here begging for his help wearing the same necklace. Was he one of them? Jonathan had to have that necklace. He couldn't stop staring at it. He felt the rising of his temperature, his sweat beading on his forehead.

He lurched forward and grabbed the necklace. He ripped it from the stranger and slammed the door shut. He heard the little man screaming on the other side. Jonathan felt drunk as he held the necklace. He heard the man screaming some utterance—something he didn't recognize.

"Briseadh agus bru ar do chanamha! I am Ian Murray, and I come for her! I come for all of them, Collector!"

Jonathan slid down the wooden frame of the door. He held the necklace in his hands. He heard three shrill screams from the man outside, that weird man who looked like a rat. He felt the man's pressure against the door as he sat there holding his necklace. That necklace, the same necklace as his wife, that damn necklace she refused to part with. This was a crazed drunkard. The necklace meant nothing. Commonplace for these parts, but in the back of his mind, he heard that strange man's words. Collector. Collector.

He had become one, as much as he didn't want to admit it. It started off with his encounter with the Leanan Sidhe. He became drunk with the power of writing she had bestowed on him and the riches that followed. Once he had figured out how to erase her memories and bind him to her, he wondered what other creatures he could use to his advantage. The more books he wrote, the more money he made. The more money he made, the more prestige he gained.

This newfound advancement needed to be visually seen. Nice truck, big fancy house, beautiful wife, and attractive staff. The selkies were easier to catch than he thought they would be. Pelts tucked away; they were now in servitude to him forever. Everything was progressing so well until the younger of the two selkies, the daughter, got the bright idea of diluting his wife's tea. LeeAnne began to regain her memories, who she truly was. He couldn't risk the rest of his staff acting out in disobedience. An example had to be made of her. He waited for his wife to be secured in his bedroom and called a meeting in the courtyard. A fire was set in the firepit. He held a bag in his hand.

"I will not tolerate disobedience on any scale. You all belong to me now, to this household, and as such, will abide by my rules. Should you not, you will suffer the consequences. He pulled Brianna's pelt out of his bag. The selkie screamed. Her mother, Katie, fell to her knees.

"Please, sir. She's but a headstrong child. You destroy that pelt; you'll destroy her soul."

"You creatures don't have souls." Jonathan held the pelt over the fire.

"We are not your slaves. We belong to the sea!"

"Used to belong to the sea," he said, tossing her pelt into the fire. "Now, you'll never return."

Brianna howled and screamed in a language he could not understand. It sent shivers down his spine. For the first time, he felt a sense of dread. Maybe he went too far, but he would never admit it.

"Let that be a lesson to all of you," he said as he walked away.

Brianna had gone mad. She didn't eat, didn't sleep, didn't bathe or change her clothes. She just walked in circles around the charred remains of her pelt in the firepit. Shortly after, she was dead—a mercy killing. Jonathan looked at the necklace in his hand. He had gone too far. Brianna must've called this man. He needed to figure out what he was and get rid of him fast.

Jonathan walked down the hall, and he saw Katie.

"Sir, can I be of some assistance?"

"No, Katie. All is well."

"Is it, sir? A breaking and crushing of your bones. That is what the gentleman screamed at you."

Jonathan turned and looked at her. She was smiling, a far too wide smile for someone who should be alarmed. Jonathan stopped walking. He looked at his maid. Then he began to laugh.

"You planned this," he said.

"Sir? Planned what?"

"This," Jonathan spat as he grabbed her by the forearm and twisted her to the ground. "Remember your daughter, my dear Katie. Remember her now." She was prone on the floor, him leaning over her.

"Aye, sir, I remember her. Do you?" Katie continued to laugh. "Aye, I remember her. Beautiful. Perfect. You caught us, you did, and kept our pelts. But my daughter didn't deserve what you did."

"Say her name."

"You say her name. You were the one who trapped her, caught her, and killed her."

"No, you killed her."

"I set her free."

"She could've been free with me."

Katie wrestled away from him and stood. "No one can be free with you," she said.

Jonathan struck her, sending her back to the floor. He straightened his shoulders, then his shirt. "Fetch my wife," he said.

Katie stood up again, holding her freshly bruised cheek. "Dunno where she's off to," she chuckled.

"Come again?"

"Wandered off, I'm afraid, that prisoner of yours."

"My wife better be in her room, as she is every night."

"Wives say 'I do' of their own accord. The lady whose memory has been erased every night cannot consent to such an arrangement, and therefore is nothing more than your slave."

"Your tongue won't wag as much when I burn your pelt as I burned your daughter's. You'll be reduced to a mind-numbed idiot walking the halls!"

"So many of my kind you have trapped and destroyed, but you won't trap me anymore, or her ladyship. You must possess my pelt to keep me. I'm afraid your late visitor has taken off with it." A loud crash could be heard from outside. Katie walked to the window, pulled back the curtain, and looked to the driveway. "Oh, my. It appears he is making some renovations to your Land Rover."

Jonathan pushed past her and rushed to the front door.

"Back in my youth, his kind would sicken the flock, but I guess your shiny truck will do!" Jonathan heard a low, ominous laughter erupt from her lips. It was as if a man was laughing through her, laughing at him. Before this night, there would have been strict repercussions, but there was time for that now. There were more pressing matters to attend to.

By the time he opened the door and rushed to his SUV, there was no sign of that strange man who called himself Ian. His handiwork was evident, though. Tires slashed, windows broken, even the engine was smoking. How was the engine smoking? The keys were still inside. Leather seats were slashed, and a weird viscous film covered everything as if a large slug had made its way with his vehicle. It was a complete ruin. Jonathan still had two vehicles in the garage. Perhaps they were still okay.

The garage was locked, but so was his Land Rover. Jonathan turned to run back into the house to grab the garage keys when he heard a shrill scream coming from above. Jonathan looked towards the source of the sound and saw Ian standing on his roof.

"Ay, Collector! Have I got your attention now? I come for what is mine, what you stole: my love and now my necklace!"

Jonathan shook at the sight of him, not out of fear but rather repulsion. How could his wife ever love such a hideous creature? The thought of her laying with him and then he with her churned his stomach. It not only made him nauseous, it made him enraged that a beauty as his wife would ever soil herself with such a thing. Jonathan would kill him, destroy his very existence. A new rage filled his heart. He would kill her as well, even if her destruction meant his own undoing.

The creature Ian screamed. Jonathan yelled back.

"Come join me by the sea wall, Collector. The sea will have what is hers!" Ian jumped from the roof, disappearing from his line of vision.

Jonathan yelled into the night air. He should go back into the house and collect his wife. He should grab the garage keys and get the hell out of there, but he could not think of such things. All he could think of was that vile, rat-like man who had touched his wife. Jonathan could have run through the house to reach the back. It was a shorter route, but his rage blinded him. He ran around the large expanse of the house. By the time he reached the sea wall, he was winded. He was flushed. He was full of jealousy. He was full of rage.

There before him was all his staff, creatures from the sea he turned into his slaves. They stood in two rows leading to Ian on the sea wall. The tide was high, sending the seawater over the stone. As the droplets of the sea hit his staff, the glamor of their human form began to fade. In the center were Ian and his wife, standing on the sea wall. Jonathan ignored the staff and ran towards them.

Ian kissed her, and she kissed him back. Jonathan could hear her moan, hear her say, "How do I know you? I know you."

"You know me, my love. I have traveled through the seas to find you, traversed into unknown and forbidden realms. I have been cursed for those travels, but I have found you now and will set you free."

"LeeAnne! Get away from him!"

"That is not her name. She is the Leanan Sidhe, a goddess and a muse from the sea!" Ian kissed her once again and threw her over the sea wall. He jumped down, laughing as Jonathan ran to the wall. "Go get her, Collector. She waits for you."

Jonathan saw her body crash on the rocks below. Her body smashed, blood flowing into the water. He ran around the wall and descended to the rocks, but her body was no longer there.

"LeeAnne! LEEANNE!" he wailed as he plunged into the sea, trying to find her.

There came a sharp sting on his right side, then his left. He felt similar stings in his legs and his arms. He cried out as he flailed in the water. He looked around and saw a small gathering of stingrays. Their tiny hooks entered his body. His skin felt tight as the poison of the stingrays entered his skin and burned its way through his veins, searching for his heart. He tasted the salty water of the sea enter his open mouth as he slowly became dizzy with toxins flooding his body. He began to descend into the depth of the sea. He felt his back cradled by a slippery, eel-like substance.

He looked to his side and saw the large tentacle of an octopus as it lifted him from the sea. The stingrays were still attached to him as he came out of the sea. He looked up the tentacle and saw that it was attached to his wife, to the goddess he enslaved. She was much larger now, the size of a small ship.

"Hello, my dear, husband. I remember everything. I gave you my words, but you got greedy."

"You would have killed me."

"Your kind is weak and always will die. I would send you to death with words from the sea, but your greed consumed you, and now you will be fed to my daughters of the sea."

The hooks from the stingrays pulled against his flesh as if his body were trapped by the hooks of fishermen, being pulled in different directions.

"Now you will die as nothing, body to never be found, your legacy burned to the ground. She brought her mouth to his ear. "Look now, as your slaves burn your prison to the ground."

Jonathan looked and saw his estate in flames. Everything he worked for, everything he stole, burning in front of his eyes. His bowels loosened as he defecated. He looked back at her, at his stolen bride.

"I love you," he mumbled.

The Leanan Sidhe did not answer him but rather ripped his head off with her sharp, shark-like teeth. She chewed on his head and swallowed it, then threw the rest of his body to the sea. The creatures of the sea went into a feeding frenzy on his bleeding corpse. The Leanan Sidhe returned to her more human form and walked out of the sea.

"You are all free now. Please forgive me for not protecting you sooner."

Katie fell to her knees, weeping. "My Lady, your forgiveness for the poisons I gave you."

The Leanan Sidhe knelt in front of the selkie. "Tsk, no. Stop that crying. You were a prisoner, as was I. No more harm shall fall upon your house. You protected me and aided in our escape from that vile human."

"It wasn't me who called the alarm. I was too afraid. No, it was my brave Brianna," Katie wept as she held her pelt to her.

"Brianna came from your loins, reared by you to become the bravest of us all. She paid for it dearly, but she is not lost. She is at peace with my sisters in the deep. There is a place reserved for you as well when your time comes to an end."

"Thank you, Mistress," Katie replied. She wiped away her tears as she once again adorned her pelt and swam off into the sea.

One by one, all the sea creatures paid their respects, and one by one, they disappeared into the sea. That left one creature on the banks. Ian.

"My love," the Leanan Sidhe said.

"My love," Ian replied. "I'm afraid I have lost it, the necklace you gave me.

"Not lost," the Leanan Sidhe replied. "All things of the sea return to the sea." She held out the necklace in her hand. "Let me place it around your neck once again?"

"If it pleases you."

"It pleases me very much," she said as she fastened the necklace back 'round his neck. She held his fat and sweaty cheeks. She looked at his hunched-over form and the tail that protruded from behind him. "Oh, my love, my sea poet. What have you done to find me?"

"I did what you bade me. I protected you. I wandered the seas into unchartered territories as a human, and being a human was my only crime. My love was my only virtue."

"You have suffered more than enough." The Leanan Sidhe kissed the top of Ian's forehead.

A bright light emanated from that kiss and encapsulated his body.

The hairs protruding from his skin fell away. The tail shriveled up and fell off his form. His bones cracked and grew. His form filled out the once saggy skin. Ian screamed from pain and excitement as he was returned to his former human shape.

"No longer a sewer rat, but my lover and protector." She placed one hand on his necklace and another on hers. "Call me, and I will come. If I beckon, you will answer. You are a part of the sea now, my love. You are a part of me forever."

Our tale is at an end, dear reader. It was a happy ending for Ian, for he truly loved his muse, even though it brought him to madness, diving him into the realm of sea fairies. He may have lost his human characteristics—transformed from a young and stunning seaman to a Fir Darrig. However, his heart remained true to his love and his true nature—a not-so-happy ending for Jonathan. One could argue that Jonathan was merely attempting to survive the powers of the Leanan Sidhe, that his human instincts of self-perseverance forced his hand. Others may surmise that the young, American author became consumed with greed and a desire for power over his muse and all the sea had to offer. In the end, the sea will claim what is rightfully hers. I'll end this tale with this question: How should a writer engage with their muse? Should engage the muse with love and adoration or inflict control. Either way, one thing is guaranteed as the outcome: madness and that insanity will have quite the story to tell you.

ABOUT LISAH JAYNE WALDEN

Lisah Jayne Walden resides in upstate New York with her two kids and three furbabies. She received a double BA in history and English from the University of Rochester and an MA in English from the College of Brockport. Her hobbies include reading and writing horror, watching movies with her kids, trying new cooking recipes, and gardening.

facebook.com/lisahwalden73

twitter.com/LisahZoe974

instagram.com/stillwritinglwalden

THE SEA KING'S DAUGHTER
BY ANTHEA SHARP

The surface of the North Sea rolled and ruffled quietly beneath the May wind. In the sky overhead, gulls caught the eddies, calling in high, lonely voices. The rocky shore of Eire rose on the horizon, a dark blur of land before the water stretched away for thousands of miles to the west.

Beneath the waters, the calm beauty of the day mattered little. Pale sunshine filtered down, and further down, to the very halls of the Sea King, where the matters of the world above meant very little. His palace rose from the seabed, whorls of shell and pearl glowing with iridescence. Four fanciful towers, one for each of his daughters, were decked with banners of woven seagrass that waved in the gentle eddies

The open, curved halls were traversed by fishes and merfolk alike on their way to the throne room for the birthday celebrations of the king's youngest daughter, Muireen.

This was not any birthday, however, but the coming-of-age Muireen had been waiting years for. Finally, she was turning seventeen and would be allowed to rise to the surface for her first glimpse of the mortal world.

Six years earlier, her eldest sister Aila had been the first of them to break the surface of the bright water and see what wonders the world above held.

"Tell us, tell us," her sisters had clamored when she returned, then listened, wide-eyed, to Aila's descriptions of the wheeling birds, the bright sun, the taste of air in her lungs instead of water.

She had even glimpsed a mortal ship riding majestic over the waves, all unaware of the kingdom they traveled over. Although her bodyguard had not allowed her to swim any closer, for fear of discovery, Aila had heard singing and a strange buzzing instrument not known beneath the sea.

The next sister to rise, Dagmar, had shaken her head dismissively upon her return.

"It's gray and cold," she'd said. "Water spits in cold drops from the sky, and the bones of fish float, rotting, in the waves. There is no reason to visit the world above."

"What of the mortals?" Muireen had asked.

"I saw no sign," Dagmar said, flat disinterest in her voice.

When the second-youngest sister made her trip to the surface, she proclaimed it "quiet and a bit boring."

Privately, Muireen vowed that she would swim toward shore. She would stay from dawn to dusk and do everything she could to catch a glimpse of the mortals who inhabited the world of air. Whether or not the guards that would accompany her would allow such a thing was a question she pushed away. Her determination was strong enough to succeed.

For years, Muireen and her sisters had scavenged the shipwrecks scattered on the ocean floor. But while her older siblings had lost interest, Muireen was still fascinated by the strange objects to be found in the detritus. She could not make heads nor tails of many of the items, but whether they were weapons or decorations or strange tools, they piqued her imagination.

"Why can we not visit the surface more than once a year?" she'd asked her father. "Surely we can learn things from the mortals above."

"No," the Sea King had said, his voice hard. "The only thing they may teach our kind is death and destruction. Our history is filled with tales of murder, the blood of our people staining the currents while they hunted us down without mercy. Once a year is danger enough."

Only the weight of law and custom kept her father from forbidding all merfolk from ever rising to the surface.

Today, though, was her day. Muireen's heart beat faster. Today, she would feel the mystery of the sun on her face, breathe the strangeness of air, hear the sounds of the birds.

And maybe, if luck was with her, she would set her eyes on a mortal.

***

Eiric Airgead set his carefully folded nets in his small boat, checked that it was not taking on water, then stepped in and pushed off from the stone jetty. The sky overhead cupped the pearly pre-dawn light, and the village's small harbor was busy with fishermen heading out to make the day's catch. Half the fleet was already gone, their boats patches of darkness over the pewter water.

The sea wind blew Eiric's dark hair about his face, the breeze strong enough for him to raise sail. Quickly, his boat flew out, rocking up and down when he hit the rougher water outside the sheltering curve of the harbor. Behind him, whitewashed cottages glowed softly with the dawn over their shoulders. The stone-walled fields and lanes climbed up the hillside, and he could see a half dozen villagers striding up to tend the fields and flocks.

He'd never had the heart of a farmer, himself. The sea always called to him, the waves whispering his name. The village lived by the sea and died by it, as well—as no doubt would be his own fate.

But while he lived, he'd ride his small boat over the waves, casting his nets beneath the surface to pull up silver shimmering wonders of fishes. He'd sing, and play the tin whistle tucked in his pocket to pass the time. Most of all, he'd know the freedom of the wind and water, the language of current and cloud.

Bright porpoises danced beside his boat, and seals watched him with their large, dark eyes. The huge *Ainmhí Sheoil* moved like a dark shadow below him, but he was wiser than to cast a line for the shark. His boat was too small, his arms too weak.

It took many men in a larger craft to ride out the death run of such a massive fish. Once, one of the village's boats was gone for nearly an entire moon. When they finally returned, they told a harrowing and heroic tale of being dragged far to the north by the basking shark, at last overcoming it and then making the long journey home. That winter, the village ate well.

Though Eiric fished alone, he contributed enough to the village's stores that he was considered a hard worker, and a good match for any of the lasses. Red-haired Biddy had made it plain she'd welcome him to come courting, but she had a hard edge that Eiric misliked. Perhaps he might instead woo Orla, who tended her flock of sheep, but she was a quiet girl. Too quiet, mayhap.

Eiric's mother was gone, and his father as well, leaving no one to push him toward a marriage he was not certain he wanted. And so, he fished, and played tunes up to the sky, and was content to live alone.

Muireen's sisters combed out her hair and braided it with pearls. They burnished the silver-blue scales of her tail until it glowed, and told her she was as beautiful as the sun slanting through the midsummer waves.

When she was finally ready, her sisters accompanied her to the curved-walled, iridescent throne room. There, the king and all the court had assembled to bid Muireen a safe journey to the surface. After an eternity of toasts and speeches, it was at last time for her departure. The currents swirled, tugging at Muireen's hair and slipping over her scales, whispering *come, come.*

"Don't do anything foolish," her eldest sister said as she embraced Muireen in farewell.

"Princess." An older warrior bowed before Muireen, her silver hair braided tightly against her head. "I am to be your bodyguard today. My name is Ceilp."

"Well met, Ceilp," Muireen said. "And thank you for your escort."

The Sea King beckoned, and she went obediently to float before him. *Soon. So soon.*

"Daughter." The king's strong voice sent ripples through the water surrounding them. "Today, you will breathe air for the first time and claim your birthright between the worlds. I call upon the blessing of the sun and moon to protect you. I command the tides and currents to carry you safely to the world above and back home to us. Go now, and see, but take care not to be seen in return. The safety of our people rests in concealment and caution. Do you understand?"

"Yes, Father." Muireen dipped her head in consent, but she could not contain the racing of her pulse.

Of course, she would be careful, but she would not return until she'd at least glimpsed a mortal. She'd waited her entire life to visit the surface.

The king lifted his scepter made of glimmering shells.

"Safe travels to you, Muireen, daughter of the sea," he said. "And to you, warrior Ceilp."

The merfolk and water creatures let out a liquid cheer. Muireen clasped her finned fingers together and bowed to her father. Her escort bowed even lower, and finally, they were free to go.

It took all Muireen's control to keep herself swimming at the sedate pace required by politeness. Although she wanted to give a mighty sweep of her tail to propel her through the pearly opening of the palace gates, the backwash would disrupt the onlookers. Only children and uncouth swimmers sent disruptive wakes when they swam inside the palace. Certainly, no princess of the sea would behave so rudely—even though her blood bubbled through her like air, seeking to rise.

Up, up to the brightness above the waves.

When the palace was a glowing shell behind them, Muireen glanced at her guard.

"Might we swim a bit faster?" she asked, trying to control the impatient twitch of her tailfins.

Ceilp frowned slightly. "Very well. I can see you won't settle until you take your first breath of air."

Muireen didn't hesitate. Stretching her arms ahead of her, fingers spread wide, she thrust her tail up, then down and surged forward. The sea pulled past, strands of kelp waving wildly behind them. Small silver fishes scattered before them, and Muireen laughed aloud.

Ceilp kept pace on her right, and though she was not smiling, some joy sparked in her eyes.

Far off and below them, the water shaded to indigo, marking the territory of the sea witch. Muireen glanced down and shivered. No one ventured into the witch's domain without a very good reason, and even then, such a journey was fraught with peril. She was an unsavory creature who wished nothing but ill upon the mer.

Legend held that once she had been the sea king's lover, but that her ill-humored nature had, at last, turned him against her. She'd been banished from court and left to dwell in the bitter shadows she preferred, stirring up mischief when she could.

Still, her magic was powerful, and sometimes merfolk in great need turned to her when all other hope was lost.

A shaft of sunlight sifted overhead, lightening the sea to a delicious greeny-blue, and Muireen banished all thought of the sea witch. Today there was no room for dark tales and darker waters. Not when the adventure of a lifetime awaited.

Eiric fished all morning, his nets yielding a fair catch. When the sun neared its zenith, he pulled out a hunk of brown bread and some dried fish to make a meal. As he finished brushing the crumbs overboard, the breeze freshened from the west.

He shaded his eyes with one hand and looked to the horizon. Clouds smudged the line between sea and sky, and he frowned. Might be a storm brewing, or mayhap just a squall, but a wise fisherman knew when it was time to head for shore.

Glancing back toward the sheltering bulk of Eire, he realized with a stab of dismay that he'd gone quite a distance from land. Sometimes the currents were tricky out of the north, pushing small boats such as his from their paths and out to sea.

He'd been careless, focused on the good fishing and the sparkle of sunlight on the water and paying little heed to the wind and waves carrying him away. Quickly, he stowed his nets, then wrestled with the sail. The wind was stubborn, changing direction as soon as he'd caught it. The sail luffed, sounding suspiciously like it was laughing at him.

"Hush now," he said, trying to soothe the coarse cloth as well as his own mounting unease. "We'll make it to shore soon enough."

At that, the wind died down entirely. Eiric let out a breath. Why did the elements mock him so?

He didn't want to cast his nets or line back out, in case the breeze freshened. To pass the time, he pulled out his tin whistle, the metal warm from where it had rested inside his coat and began to play.

Perhaps he could coax the wind to rise if he played something sprightly. Fingers flicking over the holes, Eiric spun the bright notes of a jig into the air. The slap of water against the boat kept an arrhythmic counterpoint but, alas, the sky remained still.

He played another jig, then a reel full of flurries and turns, and then a quieter tune, the melody of an old song about a lover lost at sea. He was not a singer, his voice too rough and low, but with the whistle, he could sing out, the notes pure and aching.

Something splashed in the waves behind him.

Eiric turned, halting the music, but there was nothing to be seen except a white froth like lace, already dissolving into the blue green waves. Likely it had been a fish leaping, or perhaps a curious seal, drawn by the sound of his music. Still, that didn't explain the prickling between his shoulder blades.

He waited for several breaths, but whatever it was had gone. Still, he resolved to keep a sharp eye on the water. Fishermen who ignored their instincts went soonest to the bottom of the sea.

"Halt," Ceilp said when Muireen was only a few lengths from the enticing glimmer of the surface.

Impatience surging through her, Muireen did as her escort asked. Overhead, the bottoms of the waves beckoned.

"Why?" she asked.

Ceilp gave her a serious look. "You have never breathed air before. And although our mer magic should make air no different than water, sometimes the transition can be awkward."

"I know," Muireen said. "We must take in a long sip of seawater, then let it out in three quick puffs, then rise to the surface and not breathe in for three heartbeats."

"Indeed," Ceilp said. "Remember it well. Also, it helps to be touching someone who has breathed both air and water. It aids the magic for some reason. Wait." She held out her hand to stay Muireen, who could not seem to keep herself from floating up.

"I will rise first to make sure it is safe," the guard said. "Stay two tail lengths below. Once I determine all is well, rise and take my hand. Then we will break the surface together."

Muireen nodded, her pulse racing like a high tide under the mysterious moon.

With a last, stern look, Ceilp swam up, her tail strokes leaving swirls in the current. After what felt an eon, she descended to where Muireen.

"It is safe," she said. "A storm brews in the distance, but that will not concern us."

She held out her hand, the webs between her fingers a pale orange that echoed the burnished hues of her tail. Muireen folded her fingers around Ceilp's, and, tails beating the water, they rose.

In her excitement, Muireen nearly forgot to suck in her seawater and let it out in three pulses. Still, she managed, releasing the last bit of liquid just before the top of her head touched that magical, permeable ceiling where water meets air.

Then her whole face emerged. Conscious of the change in her lungs, she held her breath. Her pulse thundered through her body. Once, twice, thrice. Then she opened her mouth and let the air come in, filling the places that had known only salt and the sea.

The world above the ocean was cool and bright. It felt strange to lose the comforting presence of the water against her skin. Her cheeks and lips and eyes felt bare in a way they never had before, as though something had been peeled away, leaving her exposed.

Her hair was stuck against her head, clinging to her shoulders instead of floating free. And the sounds! Everything was sharp and exciting: the hiss and rush of the water, a high whistling that must be the wind, a distant rumble of surf on stone. The cries of the gulls overhead cut through her.

"Ha!" She could not help her shout of laughter.

"Are you breathing correctly?" Ceilp asked, watching Muireen closely.

"Yes." The word trembled on Muireen's lips. Even her voice was different here, lower and husky-sounding.

"Good." Ceilp released her hand. "Welcome to the world above."

Muireen spun herself in a circle, taking it in. The birds overhead darted and wheeled like fish in the sky. Strange diaphanous whiteness floated higher in the blue. The sun was too strong to look at, the glossy, hard light on the waves enough to make her squint and blink.

"What is that?" She pointed in the direction the sun rose, where a long, dark shape lay low on the horizon.

"Land," Ceilp said. "The place where humans dwell."

Muireen's newfound breath hitched in excitement. "Can we—"

"No." The older mer's tone was forbidding. "No good comes from anything mortal."

"And what is over there?" Murieen nodded in the opposite direction, where a dark haze filled part of the sky.

"That is the look of a storm blowing in. Fear not; we will be safely below before it arrives."

Muireen frowned. "But I want to see the stars, and the moon, without lengths of water between me and the sky. Surely that is not too much to ask?"

"My duty is to keep you safe, princess." Ceilp emphasized the last word, reminding Muireen of her station and responsibilities. "For now, you ought to practice changing from breathing air to water so that your body may become used to the sensation. I will keep watch."

With a sigh, Muireen dove beneath the surface. The water wrapped about her like a blanket, comforting yet almost smothering. She longed to throw it off, to rise and feel the excitement of air about her once again.

What would it be like, to live as a human, wholly above the surface? To be unable to breathe water, to move about on two ungainly stalks, trapped against the ground?

She would never know.

Instead, she distracted herself with chasing a nearby school of porpoise in and out of the waves. Ceilp even joined in as they leaped and dove. Each time Murieen broke the barrier between water and air, she took in great breaths, tasting salt and cold and, once, a hint of something wild and green blown off the land.

"What is the land called?" she asked Celip, once the guard seemed in a better mood.

"I've heard it is called Eire," Ceilp said.

"Air?" Muireen laughed. "It is a fitting name."

Ceilp shook her head, but there was warmth in her eyes. "It has a different spelling and a different nuance on the tongue. It is the name for an ancient goddess of the land, and the mortals have called their home accordingly."

Once again, Muireen glanced at the dark length of the island and silently rolled the name on her tongue. Eire. It seemed a little closer than when she'd first glimpsed it upon the horizon, and she was determined to edge closer still.

After a time, the porpoises tired of playing, but under pretext of the chase Muireen had managed to maneuver herself and Ceilp nearer to the land. She sculled idly in the waves, letting the breeze explore her face. Then something tickled the edge of her hearing—a bright, breathy fall of melody that tugged her soul. Music?

"Do you hear that?" She lifted her head. "Oh, Ceilp, might we go a bit closer?"

The older mer set her hands on the two forked daggers belted about her waist as if to reassure herself of their presence. She glanced up at the sky.

"Music means humans," she said. "It is too dangerous."

"Please?" Muireen tried to keep her yearning from showing in her voice. "We'll be careful. Just—can't we see where it's coming from?"

This was her chance to see a human! She could not turn away from the opportunity.

"No." From Ceilp's tone, there would be no changing her mind.

Muireen shot a regretful glance at the receding porpoises. They would not provide cover any longer, which meant she must seize her opportunity now.

Before her guard could guess what she was about, Muireen dipped beneath the waves and sped in the direction the music had come from, using every trick of speed she knew. Behind her, Ceilp called for her to stop, but Muireen ignored the words.

Closer, closer, until she could hear the notes even beneath the waves, wavering and distorted, falling down like tarnished coins. She shivered with delight. Such a sound, made of breath and mystery, was never heard in the sea kingdom. Just ahead, she saw the curved bottom of a small boat, a promise of adventure riding the waves. Barely slowing, she shot up to the surface.

She rose above the waves long enough to glimpse a slender, dark-haired man leaning against the thin mast of his boat, a length of metal held to his lips.

Then Ceilp grabbed her tail and tugged her down with a splash.

"Foolish girl!" The guard glowered at her from the safety beneath the waves. "It's time I took you back to the palace."

"But—"

"No argument."

Under Ceilp's watchful eye, Muireen reluctantly turned her back on the bright glimmer of the world above. Her trick would not work a second time.

As they descended through the waters, the greeny-blue quality of the light seemed darker than before, the liquid murmur of the sea a poor echo of the dancing wind and calling gulls who owned the sky.

She closed her eyes, recalling the face and form of the human she'd seen. His cheeks were burnished bronze by the sun and wind, his dark hair worn short. He had seemed not much older than herself, and she wondered why he was all alone in a boat so far from shore.

"The storm's coming in," Ceilp said. "Feel it in the current? It's best we left the surface when we did."

Muireen did feel it, the first tremor of turmoil and churn, and her heart squeezed in fear for the fisherman playing his music far above. He was some distance from land, and his craft was so small. But there was no use in begging to return to the surface.

Too late, anyhow—the pearly turrets of the palace rose ahead, glowing with luminescence as the water darkened.

At the entrance to her tower, Muireen pulled a long strand of pearls from her hair and turned to Ceilp.

"Thank you for your escort," she said, handing the guard the pearls. "I will always remember my first journey to the surface."

"It was an honor," Ceilp said. "I am glad no trouble came of it."

"Of course not, with such a capable guard as yourself." Muireen smiled. "I truly am grateful for your service today." Most of all, she was glad of seeing the mortal man. But small fishes had big mouths, and she dared not speak of that encounter. Nothing but trouble would follow if the king knew of it.

"Muireen!" her sister Aila called from the near tower. "You've returned safely! Come and tell us about your first breath of air."

Ceilp made Muireen a formal bow. "I will inform your father that your birthday journey is complete, and you've returned safely. Good evening, princess."

"Fine swimming to you," Muireen replied.

As her guard departed, she glanced up and up. Barely at the edge of her vision, a faint turbulence roiled—the storm.

Her heart clenched at the thought of the fisherman—but her sisters were expecting her. No matter how much she wanted to surge back to the surface, she could not.

At least, not yet.

Eiric ducked his head as another wave crashed against the side of the boat, the harsh spray coating his face and hands. The wind pummeled him, and he reefed the small sail close, trying to control his craft in the face of the raging elements.

Most of the afternoon he'd spent frustratingly becalmed. When he'd tired of playing his whistle, he'd turned to mending the nets, though most of his supplies for such were back at his cottage. Still, it passed the time.

Finally, when the sun dipped low, racing its own reflection in the water, the breeze had sprung up. Brisk at first, then brisker still, until Eiric's boat ran before a fierce storm. No matter how nimbly he sailed, his heart clenched within him as the shadow of the clouds overtook the last pewter light shimmering on the sea.

All too soon, he'd been engulfed. Dark gray clouds matched the waves, and he lost all sight of the setting sun. Navigating by instinct, he prayed he was still headed east and not out over the open waters, where death awaited with outstretched arms.

It took all his skill to keep his boat running upon the backs of the waves and not directly into their hungry mouths. He did not always succeed. Fingers numb with cold, he fought the storm for what felt like hours. His ears were deafened by the rasp of the wind, his eyes stung nearly blind with salt.

Then he heard it—the crack and smash of waves breaking against stone.

He was near land, but not the sweet cove of the bay beside the village. No, he must have come in to the south where mighty cliffs rose, uncaring that a mortal life would be dashed to nothing against the rocks.

Aye, he'd wanted land. But not like this.

Forcing his hands steady, Eiric wove his boat through the water and wind, fighting to turn aside from the implacable cliffs. Hope strained his lungs as the sound of wave on stone began to fade.

Then he was pitched forward as the boat struck something in the water. Crying out, he grabbed for the side. Missed. A glimpse of black rock, splintered wood, and then the sea closed over his head, cold and relentless.

Muireen waited until indigo darkness filled the sea before slipping out of her tower room. The night guards were posted to keep watch for things coming into the palace, not sneaking out. Keeping to the shadows, she swam carefully until she was some distance from the pearly towers.

Then, with powerful sweeps of her tail, she drove herself up to the surface, angling for the place she'd seen the fisherman. The closer she rose to the ceiling of the sea, the more turbulent the water. The bottoms of the waves pulled at her hair and tried to unbalance her, the swirl of storm spinning her about.

Just before breaking into the air, she recalled her training and prepared her lungs for the transition.

Harsh wind battered her face and shoulders, so much spray in the air that for a dizzying moment her body did not respond. She choked on salt, on the horrible emptiness above the waves. Shuddering, she thrashed her tail, lifting her high enough that her lungs finally responded.

Gasping, Muireen swept her sticky hair from her face and searched desperately for the fisherman's boat. How could he survive such a rage of smacking water and tearing wind?

There was no sign of him.

Surely he'd made for land at the first sign of storm and was even now safely at home, far from the grasp of the sea. But even as the sensible part of herself argued that she ought to dive down to safety, something else pulled her on, toward the memory of where the island of Eire lay.

At length, a strange sound came to her ears, a rhythmic crash and crack. Before she understood it, the storm threw her forward, and she smacked against the side of a rock jutting from the water.

Pain flashed through her, and she ducked down, away from the greedy hands of the weather above. The power of the storm was blunted beneath the water, and she drew in a steadying gulp, searching for calm. She should not be here, where the rocks waited to tear her body.

A bit of wood brushed her arm, borne by the sucking current. Then another.

It took a moment to realize what it meant.

The debris was new and sharp-edged. Some craft had hit the rocks and wrecked. Panic flashing through her, she turned in a circle, every sense alert.

There! Overhead, she saw the remains of a boat smashing up against the stone. And there...

Time slowed.

Muireen's blood beat stronger than the surge of the waves in her ears. She dove, hands outstretched, for the form of the man sinking to his death. It was the fisherman, and for an instant she saw a silver thread stretching from her heart to his, a path of starlight, of fate.

Then she reached him and wrapped her arms about him, pulling them both up, up, driving through the rough water until she reached the harsh air again. He was heavy against her, and cold, his head lolling. The waves beat at them like fists.

Desperately, she swam, steering away from the terrifying crash of sea on stone. Surely the land held more than the hungry rocks. Breath heaving, she scanned the shoreline. There! A bare crescent of sand beckoned, barely wide enough for a single body, framed by jagged black stone. She forced herself forward, her timing and agility slowed by the body in her arms. The tide threw her up against the side of a rock. She twisted, and the stone left a long, painful scrape down her tail.

Then she was through the worst of the surf and felt the land rise up, pulling away from the sea. Teeth bared, she thrashed forward, for the first time cursing her tail. Ungainly against the rough grains of sand, she pushed the fisherman before her until he was out of reach of the waves.

He was not breathing.

Awkwardly, she turned him on his side and thumped his back.

"Come now, human," she cried. "Spit out the sea and live. Please."

As if hearing her, his body convulsed. A gush of water emitted from his mouth, and he shuddered. Muireen laid her hand between his shoulders and willed him to breathe.

Another shiver wracked him. He coughed again, and then she felt the blessed pull of air into his body.

"Yes," she sighed.

His dark hair hid his face, and she carefully pushed the sodden strands aside so that she might see his features. His cheeks were pale, but regaining color even as she watched. His lips were too soft for the rest of his face—the sharp nose and stern forehead, the black slashes of his brows.

As she hovered over him, his eyes opened. They were a wild, stormy blue. Muireen stared into those depths and felt the hook set deep inside her heart.

"You." His voice was a whispered croak. "Saved me."

"Shh," she said. "Rest."

He closed his eyes and lay his head back down on the sand, but still, he breathed. Beneath her hand, Muireen could feel his heart beating. Her fisherman would live.

But she refused to leave him alone through the night.

As the water pulled and pushed in and out of the little cove, she held him close and sang him the songs of the sea people in her low, husky voice. The storm quieted, and as the sky cleared, she was amazed to see a shimmer of tiny lights overhead—the luminescence of the night that mortals called stars.

After a time, she realized the blackness was fading, nibbled away at one side of the sky by the approaching dawn. She could not stay, could not risk discovery, though it tore her in two to leave her fisherman.

"Farewell," she whispered, bending to lay her lips against his.

Their breaths mingled, and a salty drop fell from her eye to splash against his cheek. He stirred, and in a sudden panic, Muireen thrashed herself back into the shelter of the sea. The water took her in, cool and welcoming, concealing the secret of her tail.

She hid behind one of the rocks that had battered her. Her body rocked up and down with the now-quiet waves as she peeked out and watched her fisherman lying upon the beach. Watched as he sat up and rubbed at his face, then looked about him like a man who had misplaced something important. Watched as he rose, and winced, and cast a regretful glance at the splintered boards that had washed ashore in the night.

Watched as he turned his back on the sea and trudged away from her into the light of dawn.

Currents of cold water wrapped about Muireen as she swam into the dusky waters of the Sea Witch's domain.

She should not be there, venturing into the clammy kelp beds in pursuit of a vain hope, but for the past week, she had been unable to think of anything except her fisherman. The sight of him walking away from her haunted her dreams, and her waking hours, until she could barely eat or carry on a conversation.

It will pass, Muireen told herself, but every day was worse than the one before. She could not help remembering the silver thread she'd glimpsed, tying them together. Was this the reason she could scarcely sleep?

A low moaning sound reached her ears, like the call of a whale, but full of menace, not melancholy. She shivered and swam on toward a blot of darkness visible ahead.

The blackness resolved to a cave mouth. Muireen halted, her hair drifting about her. It was not too late to turn back.

Oh, but it was. The moment she'd glimpsed the fisherman, it had been too late.

With a steadying gulp, she dove forward into the cave. It was even colder inside the black stone walls, and a faint greenish light emanated from the depths, a tunnel, leading her on. The sound grew louder, vibrating through Muireen's scales, until she could hardly think, let alone swim.

Then she emerged into a cavern, and the noise ceased. The green light illuminated pale fishes with bulbous eyes and a few sickly strands of waterweed growing from the cavern's sides.

But most of all, it showed the Sea Witch floating in the center of the space, her white eyes turned on Muireen. Hideous white eyes, white skin the color of dead things, suckered tentacles waving from her head instead of hair. Where her tail should have been was only a swirl of blackness, as though a squid had ejected its ink and fled.

I should not have come. Muireen's chest tightened, and she turned to flee. Rough stone greeted her, slimed with the secretions of moon snails. The tunnel she'd traveled down was gone. Panic racing through her, she pivoted to face the witch.

"Sea King's daughter," the witch said, her voice carrying the memory of a thousand shipwrecks, "I am so very pleased to see you. Tell me, why have you come?"

For a fleeting moment, Muireen was tempted to say it was all a mistake. Tempted to plead that the Sea Witch release her, unharmed, that it had been nothing more than a foolish dare.

But her heart ached where fate bound her to her mortal man. There could be no simple escape from that snare.

"There is a fisherman," she said.

The witch opened her mouth and let out a keening cry of laughter. "Oh yes, yes. One of those. Delicious. Shall I tell you the terms of the bargain?"

"But you don't know what I want," Muireen protested.

The Sea Witch's blank eyes stared at her. "Of course I do. You want to take on the semblance of a mortal girl so that you might seek out the fisherman you are so foolishly in love with."

"I'm not in love." Even as she spoke the words, though, a part of Muireen hummed in agreement. "How could I be in love with some ungainly human? I am a princess of the sea."

The witch held up a hand, black webs spread between her clawed fingers.

"I can see the strands of fate wrapped about your heart," she said. "You were wise to come to me, for I can give you what you desire. For a price."

"What is the price?" Muireen's lips felt numb, as though she'd swum through the poisoned strands of a jellyfish.

"You must give me your voice," the witch says. "In return, I will be able to transform you into human form—but only for a year and a day. At the end of that time, you will turn back into a mer and re-enter the sea forever."

A year and a day. It was not long enough—yet it was far better than nothing at all.

"I agr—"

"Wait." The Sea Witch smiled, showing rows of serrated teeth. "When you return to your form, you will come to me to reclaim your voice. And you will give me one more thing—the bitter tears of your desolation. For in such heart-wrenching sorrow lies great power."

Muireen glanced away from the witch's horrifying countenance and thought desperately, but she could see no alternative. Distasteful as the bargain might be, she must take it.

"It seems I have little choice," she said.

"That is truer than all the pearls in the sea," the witch said. "Now, open your mouth and sing your favorite lullaby."

From somewhere, she conjured a glass bottle and held it over her head.

"Sing," she commanded.

Muireen began, and she could almost see her voice disappearing into the bottle. Slowly, the glass turned a translucent silver-blue: the exact hue of her scales. When the song ended, she glanced down to see her tail leached to a sickly gray.

Her gasp of dismay was only a breath. When she tried to form words, nothing came out but little bursts of warm water.

"It is done." The witch tucked the bottle away. "Go now, daughter of the Sea King. Rise to the land, and when you exit the sea, your tail will disappear, and you will walk upon two legs. Or attempt to." She let out a harsh cackle. "I will look forward to your visit a year and a day hence."

The Sea Witch raised her hands and pushed, and a sudden dark current swept Muireen up. It bore her quickly through the tunnel and past the wavering kelp, through indigo waters to turquoise, and then pale blue.

With one final surge, it pushed her upon the shore—the same small beach where she'd taken her fisherman.

Muireen gasped and coughed, her lungs unprepared for the transition. Then fierce pain gripped her from the waist down. She opened her mouth but had no voice to scream. She could only watch in mute horror as her tail disappeared, leaving two spindly stalks in its place.

Legs.

That she must learn to walk upon.

For five days, Eiric rested in the bed he'd inherited from his parents. The white walls of the cottage wrapped around him. The breeze rustled the thatch overhead, reassuring him that he was safe.

The villagers brought him broth and helped him rise to use the chamber pot. Biddy was there more often than most, but Eiric did not have the energy to turn away. Fevers wrung him, and a thousand aches from being tumbled against the rocks below the cliffs.

"It's a miracle he survived," the people whispered. "He is truly blessed by the gods."

He did not feel blessed, but cursed. Whenever he closed his eyes to rest, which was often, nightmares of the crashing sea sucked him under.

Again and again, he fought to turn his boat, heard the sickening crack of the hull on stone, felt the hungry cold grasp of the waves. The only thing that made his dreams bearable was the memory of a young woman's face, looking down at him.

Her eyes were the warm blue of the sea at midday. Her long hair held brightness and shadow, tangled with seafoam. Her skin was pale, her hands upon his brow cool and welcome.

Each time he woke, Eiric was filled with a pang of loss. Had he imagined her, or had she rescued him from the storm's hunger?

A smaller, more urgent loss pained him as well, and that was the loss of his boat. He would have to go back to using the small leather coracle that had been his first vessel. No more venturing out into the deep, deep waters, where the catch was best. No more room to stow his finest nets. He feared it would be a lean winter.

Biddy would feed you, his thoughts offered up.

He could not think of it—not when the pearl-skinned girl haunted his dreams. And his wakings.

A week unspooled past, and Eiric finally woke feeling… not rested, exactly, but well enough to get out of bed and see if anything salvageable had washed ashore in the tiny cove that had saved him.

He took a hunk of bread stuffed with cheese, a skin of water, and a stout walking stick that had belonged to his Da, and set out over the headland. The sun warmed his shoulders and the top of his head, and he felt as though his life might be worth living, after all.

It took him some time to reach the narrow path cutting through the bracken that led to the tiny beach. He'd had to rest often and twice refilled his water skin from the small stream that crisscrossed his path.

His lunch called to him, but he'd be better off saving it for after he'd visited the shore. A reward for the hike back up the steep trail, which, in truth, he was not looking forward to.

For now, though, gravity aided him, and soon the crash of the waves against the cliffs filled the air. It took all his concentration to keep his feet under him as he made the last descent to the sliver of sand below.

His boots hit the sand and he stood a moment catching his balance and his breath. Then lost them both when he saw he was not alone.

She was there—the maiden who haunted his thoughts, sitting huddled against a rock, facing the sea. Her long hair covered her like a cloak, but she was naked, the pearly skin of her limbs shining in the sun.

Heartbeat thundering in his ears, Eiric glanced about the little cove, looking for her clothing, or her selkie skin, anything that would help him learn what kind of creature she was. For though she appeared mortal, he knew deep in his soul that she was a magical being.

Sensing his presence, she spun awkwardly about and fixed him with her blue, blue eyes.

"Don't be afraid," he said, his voice a hoarse whisper. "I won't harm you, I swear it."

He could not bear it if she fled back into the waves.

To his relief, she gave him a tentative smile and made no move toward the shining water.

"I'm Eiric," he said, little caring that he might be giving his name to a faerie. Even if she were a fey maiden, he feared he'd already lost his heart to her. Anything more was a trifle. "Do you understand me?"

She nodded, and the beauty in her face made him weak at the knees.

"Have you a name you go by?" he asked.

Again, she nodded. Then, with a stricken look, she brought her hand up to her throat and shook her head.

"You cannot speak?"

She opened her mouth, but no sound came out.

"Well then." Eiric settled on the sand. "Still, you and I might converse together in other ways."

A quick nod of her head.

"Where have you come from?"

She turned, hair slipping off one pale shoulder, and gestured at the sea. So, it was as he thought.

"Might I call you Muireann? It means 'sea fair' in my language. And you are very fair."

She blushed slightly and dropped her gaze to the sand. Eiric was hard-pressed not to stare openly at her nakedness. Instead, he pulled off his shirt and handed it to her.

"You might put this on, if you like."

Giving him a smile as quick as a silver fish, she held the garment up, studying it a moment before pulling it over her head. She had difficulty with the armholes, and he reached to help her, drawing one fine-boned hand through the sleeve, and then the other.

"You're not used to clothing, I take it."

He was rewarded with another of her darting smiles.

"I think…" He stared at the waves gnashing upon the rocks. "I think you saved me, sea-fair maiden. Was that you?"

In answer, she rose to her knees a bit unsteadily, then cupped his face between her hands. He held very still, as though she were a wild thing he did not want to frighten. Gods, but she was beautiful. And strong, and brave, by all indications.

Softly, she kissed him on the forehead.

Her touch was enough to undo him. Eiric gathered her into his arms and held her close. Her heart beat fast, and her skin was cool, but not cold.

Gently, quietly, they kissed, and his heart, at last, felt as though it had come home.

———

Muireen could scarce believe her luck. Her fisherman had come to seek her out! Joy surged through her in great waves, despite the awkward feel of her new body. And though she could not speak, they understood one another well enough.

She sat, nestled against his side, and marveled at the warmth of his human body. Together, they watched the waves come in until the tide nibbled at their toes. With a sigh, Eiric turned to look at her.

"The sun's soon to be setting. I suppose you must return to the sea now, fair maid, though my heart weeps at losing you."

She shook her head at him.

"No?" His eyes widened. "Is it possible you might come live with me and be my bride?"

She hesitated, but there was no way to explain that she must return to the sea in a year's time. That was a dim cloud on the horizon. After all, a year was a very long while.

She answered him with a kiss.

"Then, my love, we'd best away before dark. We can come another time to search for the wreckage of my boat—if any still remains."

She nodded and let him pull her to her feet. For a moment, she tottered, but with his help, found her balance. Walking was more difficult, though, and she let out a slight hiss of pain when she stubbed her toe on an outcropping.

"Sit here a moment." He guided her to a rock, then bent and took off his foot coverings.

They came in two parts, she was interested to observe. Mortal clothing was very strange.

"I fear my boots will be too large and trip you further, in any case. But my socks will give you some protection."

He held out the cloth wrappings, then helped her don them. They were warm from his body and smelled rather strongly, but she was glad of the layer between her tender new skin and the ground.

"Now, Muireann, we must climb to the top of the headland and walk a fair bit before reaching my village. Luckily, it will be dark, so we can avoid the worst of the questions until tomorrow. Are you ready?"

She nodded. No matter what difficulties lay ahead, and she was certain there would be many, it would be worth it with her fisherman by her side.

A moon passed, and though the villagers still treated Muireen with suspicion, they had come to accept she was there to stay. All except the flame-haired Biddy, who spat and made the sign of protection whenever their paths crossed.

Together, Muireen and Eiric had managed to pull his wrecked boat from the rocks. Paired with another ruined craft, they'd cobbled together an ugly but seaworthy boat that could take the two of them over the waves.

For though Eiric tried to protest, Muireen was determined to go out with him upon the sea. She'd let him fish alone in his small coracle and helped him gut and salt the fish he returned with, but she refused to waste their precious time by pining on land, waiting for him.

It was an advantage of not being able to speak, that she simply demonstrated her intent with actions. Though he pleaded, Muireen refused to leave her place at the prow of the boat, and so they set out together.

They worked well together, plying the nets and taking in the fish. And if, once or twice, Muireen spotted the trailing hair of a mer warrior beneath their boat, she was not alarmed.

No doubt her father had been full of wrath when he'd discovered her bargain with the Sea Witch—but such things could not be broken. Instead, it seemed he'd sent his guard to keep watch on her.

In the evenings, Eiric played his whistle as they sat before the fire in their little cottage. Muireen learned how to cook, though she was ever wary of the flames. She learned to sew, and to knit ungainly socks and sweaters that, while not lovely to behold, kept them warm as the night darkened.

After two moons, she was with child.

"Please jump the broom with me," Eiric said. "We should be hand-fasted. If not for your sake, then for the babe."

Muireen had refused each time he'd spoken of it before. She was far more comfortable going from cottage to sea and back, content in the simple life they'd woven for themselves. Putting herself on display before the villagers made the old fear rise that they'd see her as a mer creature and kill her on the spot.

But for him, and the little creature now swimming in her belly, she agreed.

The day of the ceremony dawned bright and clear. Eiric and Muireen broke their fast, and then he turned to her, smiling.

"My love, I'll leave you now to make ready. Orla has kindly agreed to come help you prepare."

They kissed, and then a knock came at the cottage door. Shy, dark-haired Orla stepped in, carrying a dress the color of seafoam at sunrise.

"I brought you this. It's been in my family for two generations. I thought I might be wed in it, but..." She glanced at Eiric, regret in her eyes. "Anyhow, I'd like you to wear it, Muireann."

Muireen brought her hands together and bowed in thanks. It was very generous. Perhaps—the thought stabbed her heart—perhaps in ten months, when she was gone, Orla might take her place.

Or perhaps not. The love between herself and Eiric was a strong, true bond. She feared he might go mad from losing her, which was part of why she'd refused to wed him. But now there was the babe.

Smiling, she set her hand over her belly. At least there would be some part of her remaining when she returned to the sea.

The ceremony was held on the headland, the bright ocean shining beneath. Eiric said the words, and Muireen emphatically nodded her agreement. Together they let the priestess tie a braided cord about their clasped hands, then jumped the broom while the villagers cheered.

That night they feasted on mutton and ale, and Muireen felt, for a small time, part of the human world.

Despite her insistence on going out in the boat with him, the time came when Muireen's belly was too large for her to be of much use. Too, a melancholy had settled in her soul. Only three months remained until she must leave Eiric forever and return to the sea. Ah, and the Sea Witch would reap well her harvest of tears, for already the sorrow of parting felt unbearable.

Eiric attributed her moods to the state of her body, and was ever patient and kind with her. If he feared that the babe growing within her was less than human, he never spoke a word.

She worried, though, with thoughts that kept her awake and fretting into the cold nights. What if the child was born with fins or a tail? What if she and the baby were cast out or killed?

Be well, she thought fiercely at the little life inside her. *Be human.*

From one day to the next, spring came upon the land. The days grew longer, and a warm wind blew over the sea.

And Muireen bore a baby girl, with no fins or tail, and her father's dark hair.

"We shall call her Brea," her father said, holding her up and smiling bright as the dawn.

Caught between great joy and great sorrow, Muireen smiled at him through her tears, and nodded. Now that her baby, her daughter, was born, she knew the pain of leaving would be doubled.

But for the month that remained to her upon the land, she could not let that shadow fall over her days. So, with great effort, she pushed it away. Instead, she concentrated on all the perfect moments: Eiric's smile and the scent of him, the soft skin of her daughter, the warmth the three of them made, curled up together in their bed.

The moon waned and went dark, and that night Muireen dreamed of the Sea Witch.

"Tomorrow," the witch said. "Tomorrow, you come back to the sea. If you are not in the water's embrace by sunset, your legs will disappear, and you will be revealed for what you truly are. And you will be killed for it."

Muireen woke, shivering, and knew the witch spoke truly. Even if Eiric tried to protect her, he would not be able to stand against the villagers. In her mer form, she would be too strange, too frightening. They would take her life, and little Brea's as well.

When Eiric woke and made ready to go out to his boat, she caught his arm and shook her head at him. *Don't go.*

"What's this, love?" He gazed down tenderly at her.

She touched her heart, then his, then glanced down at the babe sleeping in her arms. This was their last day together.

"Aye, I love you and our family with all my heart. But I must go out and fish."

She took his arm again, all her sorrow rising in her eyes, and he relented.

"Very well. But only for today."

She gave a small nod. Yes. Only that day—for tomorrow, she would be gone forever.

She packed a lunch, put Brea in her sling, and they roved out over the headland. Eiric collected a bouquet of wildflowers for her, and she kissed him, wishing that she could speak of what was to come.

They ate, drank cool water from the stream, and she led him to the path down to the tiny beach where they'd first met. The first shadows from the lowering sun began to fall across the land.

"Should we not be returning home?" he asked.

She shook her head and started down the path. How comfortable her legs had become in a year, how deftly she stepped around stones, feeling herself balance upright in the air. Even carrying the small weight of her baby, it seemed a simple thing, to stride across the land.

When they reached the sliver of sand, she sat, facing the ocean.

Eiric settled beside her, one strong arm around her shoulders as she fed Brea for the last time. When the baby finished, Muireen handed her to her father, her arms aching with loss.

The banners of the clouds were beginning to turn silvery orange. Heart aching, Muireen stood and stripped off her clothing: shawl, blouse, skirts, and shoes. She unbraided her hair until it fell loose about her shoulders, brushing her back and belly.

Eiric watched, his gaze solemn.

When she went to her knees before him, a single tear slipped from his eye.

"Ah, beloved." His voice was choked with sorrow. "Is this our end, then? Must you return to the sea and leave me cruelly alone?"

She set her hand on Brea's head, then looked deep into the eyes of her fisherman. *Be strong, for our daughter*, she thought, even as her heart was breaking.

Their lips met. The sun dipped lower, kissing the horizon.

Then Muireen pulled away and flung herself back, into the arms of the sea. Pain ripped through her as her legs cleaved together. She gasped, and in that moment, found her voice.

"Remember me, Eiric," she called. "You are my true love."

"As you are mine, sea-maid." He rose, cradling their child in his arms. "Will I ever see you again?"

"Look for me in the bright dance of the waves. In the foam upon the shore. Where you go, there, too, my heart goes."

Uncaring of the pain—what was one more stab when her soul was shattering?—she hooked her fingers beneath one of the scales of her newfound tail and ripped it free. Even as a dark current swirled in to bear her away to the Sea Witch, she flung the scale to shore.

The last thing she heard was the sobbing of her husband, the thin wail of their child.

"Oh, such bounty," crooned the Sea Witch as she captured Muireen's tears. "Not only mourning the loss of your love but of your baby. Such power."

At last, Muireen pulled away from the witch, shuddering, her grief drained dry.

"A pity that's the last of it." The Sea Witch held up the vial containing Muireen's sorrow. "Or is it? Tell me—where is your missing scale?" She pointed at the gap in Muireen's tail.

"I threw it to him," Muireen said defiantly.

"Ahh. Listen then, and I will offer you joy and despair in equal measure. Every year, upon this anniversary, I can use my magic to let you see the world of the mortals via the scale you left behind. I hope your husband keeps it safe and close by."

"He will."

"Then you will be able to gaze upon him, and your child, for a brief time. And when you say farewell, and once again the anguish falls upon you, I will take it for my own uses. Do you agree?"

"Will he be able to see me, too?"

"Of course, for that will make the pain all the greater." The witch gave her a horrible smile. "Since your pain prolongs my life, I welcome it."

Muireen did not like to think she was helping the Sea Witch in any way. And yet, to be able to see Eiric and her daughter once a year, however briefly, was a chance she could not refuse.

"Very well."

"Good! And luckily, you'll be out of the palace dungeons next year, just in time. Now go, back to your foolish father and worthless siblings, and give them my regards."

Again, the dark current bore Muireen through the reaches of the sea, depositing her where the indigo water faded into greeny-blue. Tiredly, she swam toward the pearly towers of the palace, ready to bear whatever punishment her father thought just.

Someday, though, she vowed she would make the Sea Witch reunite her and her mortal love.

The first time the silver scale lit with Muireen's image, Eiric thought he was dreaming. Gods knew, he dreamt of her constantly. But to his surprise, he could hear her, too.

"I have not much time, love," she said. "It is only through the magic of the Sea Witch that I may look upon you. Tell me, how do you fare? And our child?"

He showed her Brea, sleeping in her crib, told her all was well. Too soon, the light of the scale began to dim.

"When shall I see you again?" he cried.

"Next year." Her voice faded, and the cool silvery-blue scale reflected back the light of his candle.

Ah, the pain was worse after seeing her face. And yet, knowing that she still lived, that she cared for him and their child, was enough to soothe the worst of the ache.

Every year, for a brief time, magic imbued the scale, and Eiric was able to tell Muireann he loved her still. For he did, the flame of that love still burning fresh within him. He showed her how their daughter grew and shared her milestones—first steps, first words, first swim in the sea, which, thankfully, had not resulted in her sprouting fins or a tail.

"She is not a mer," Muireann said, "for never have our kind bred true with humans."

"I'm not certain she's entirely human, though," Eiric replied. "There is an odd touch of magic about her."

"Then perhaps she's a fey water creature of some kind. But she must find her own destiny."

Then the scale went quiet, and all other words must wait for another year.

It was not a pleasant thing, to bide so long, but it was enough. Eiric replayed their brief conversations in his head, traced her beloved features in memory, over and over. Their daughter grew into a lonely, quiet girl, and his heart ached within him for her solitude. He never spoke of her mother. That burden he would bear alone.

Many years passed until one day, while Eiric was out on his boat, the sky darkened with a sudden storm. He'd weathered storms aplenty, but this one felt different—full of menace. He quickly stowed his nets, the memory of the fierce gale that had nearly taken his life shivering through him.

This storm tasted the same, the air heavy and metallic with the rising wind.

Then it was upon him, waves churning, spray blinding his eyes. This time, he was too far from land, fishing over the deep waters. There would be no escape from the ocean's wrath.

Still, he tried, fighting to keep his boat upon the waves and not under them, bailing when he could. Although Brea was nearly grown, he did not want to leave her an orphan, both parents lost to the sea.

But he was given no choice in the matter. A great, black wave rose over his boat, then smashed down, punching him to the depths.

Eiric floated, blinking against the saltwater burning his eyes. Here, beneath the waves, it was strangely peaceful. The last of his breath left his body in a silver strand of bubbles, racing away toward the roiling surface. He let them go.

Then Muireann was there, floating before him. She pressed a bottle to his lips, and he drank, then gagged on the foul secretion.

"Swallow it," she said, tears in her voice. "I cannot you save you, otherwise."

Coldness all about him, Eiric swallowed. Then screamed as the cold burned away. Something terrible was happening to him, yet his sea maiden held him close.

Finally, shuddering, the pain passed. He looked up at his beloved.

"Are we dead?" he asked, amazed to find he could form the words.

"No, my love." She smiled at him. "You are no longer human, however. There is no return to the surface for you."

"As long as I might remain here, beneath the sea with you, I care not. Wherever you go—"

"There my heart also goes," she finished the words for him.

Together, webbed hands clasped, they swam, tails flashing through the water. Away from the storm and darkness, away from the cold, to an enchanted palace in the far south, made of shining coral.

There they rule to this day, wearing crowns of pearl and mantles of kelp, the Sea Queen and her once-mortal love.

~*~

END

Author's Note:

The Little Mermaid is my inspiration for this story. And while I wanted to incorporate some of the tragic elements from Hans Christian Andersen's original tale, I still wanted a fairytale happy ending for Muireen and her fisherman, no matter the sorrow it took them to get there.

To find out what happens to Brea, Muireen, and Eiric's daughter, pick up Brea's Tale and discover the magic of Feyland.

Want to make sure you hear about Anthea's new books? Join her newsletter, and get a *free* short story when you sign up! http://www.subscribepage.com/AntheaSharp

ABOUT ANTHEA SHARP

Growing up on fairy tales and computer games, *USA Today* bestselling author Anthea Sharp has melded the two in her award-winning Feyland series. She now makes her home in the Pacific Northwest, where she writes, hangs out in virtual worlds, plays the fiddle with her Celtic band Fiddlehead, and spends time with her small-but-good family.

Her books have won or placed in the PRISM, the Maggie, the National Reader's Choice Award, the Write Touch Reader's Award, the Heart of Excellence, and the Book Buyer's Best contests.

Contact her at antheasharp@hotmail[dot]com, and join her newsletter for all the news about upcoming releases, super sales, and reader perks!

http://www.subscribepage.com/AntheaSharp

facebook.com/AntheaSharp
twitter.com/antheasharp
instagram.com/anthea_sharp

THE ASTROLABE
BY JAMES RICKETT

I slid the loaf of bread into the oven and prayed it wouldn't turn into a dry, deflated mess this time. One of the first things I had learned about cooking in an airship is that foods bake differently when they are hundreds of feet above the ground, but after a few weeks, I was finally starting to get the hang of it.

Pulling my oven mitts off and dusting the flour off my apron, I went to the aft galley window and gazed out at the sky. Looking down at the land usually made me dizzy, so I looked up instead. The sky was clear blue with a few wispy clouds passing by. Sunlight gleamed off the polished wood and metal of the window frame. Despite my fear of heights, there was a certain excitement to living on an airship and traveling so far above the world.

As I stood wondering what I could see if the *Daybreaker* flew high enough, I caught a glimpse of something small flying toward the ship. The messenger hawk was coming! Maybe I would finally get a letter from home.

I grabbed a strip of dried meat, ran to the galley doors, and opened them. A blast of wind whipped my hair around my face and made my eyes water. I ran across the deck toward the fore of the airship, keeping my eyes locked ahead and not looking to port or starboard.

As I made my way to the quarterdeck, a dark-colored hawk flew down and alighted on a pole. I walked over to it and held out the dried meat, which it snapped up in its beak. I patted its head, and it cawed softly in response.

The quarterdeck door opened, and Tala rushed out. She and I had been friends since childhood, and we had been hired together for the crew of the *Daybreaker*. She was also the main reason I hadn't quit and gone back home weeks ago.

"Kayli, there you are!" Tala had to speak loudly to be heard over the wind. "What did we get?"

I unlatched the message tube from the hawk's leg and pulled out a roll of paper, holding it tightly so it wouldn't blow away. Tala leaned closer and tried to look at the paper, and her short purple hair blew in my face.

"I don't know," I said. "I can't read it with your big head in the way. Let's get inside, away from this stupid wind."

"I love the wind!" Tala said.

"Yeah, I know." I replaced the message tube, and the hawk flew off. We opened the door to the quarterdeck and stepped inside, where it was quiet.

I examined the paper and saw the words *To Captain Duncan Hawk-stone* on the outside. My heart sank.

"Never mind; it's just another dumb job." I handed the roll to Tala.

"Oh, were you hoping it was a letter from your parents?" Tala said. "Sorry, maybe you'll get something next time. If it makes you feel any better, I haven't gotten any letters from my family the whole time we've been on this ship."

"Yeah, but you enjoy being here and actually know something about airships, and you're not always mopey and useless and homesick like me."

"You're not useless. What would we eat without you to cook for us?"

"You'd starve, probably," I said.

"Exactly," Tala said. "And how do you know I don't get homesick, too?"

"You certainly don't show it," I said.

"You didn't have to take the job, you know," Tala said. "Even if I did beg you to."

"I know, but I just...oh, never mind."

"It's not so bad, is it?" Tala grinned and held up the roll of paper. "Maybe this will be an exciting new adventure, and you'll finally start having fun."

"You mean like our last exciting adventure when we transported five hundred chickens to Arcondis?" I said. "I'm still finding feathers in the hold."

"Well, maybe this job will be better than that one." Tala started to unroll the paper.

"Maybe you shouldn't open that," I said. "Captain Duncan might get angry."

Tala scoffed. "Right, can you imagine him getting angry about something like that?"

"What am I about to get angry about?" Duncan appeared behind us, making us both jump. He was a tall, handsome middle-aged man with dark hair and a perpetual carefree look on his face.

"Nothing, Captain." Tala smiled sheepishly and handed the roll to Duncan. "We're just, um, making sure all your correspondence is delivered to you in a timely manner."

"Ah, another thrilling quest, is it?" Duncan examined the paper.

"Exactly," Tala said. "That's what I told Kayli. I'm trying to cheer her up."

"Well, I suppose we don't all feel the call of adventure in the same way." Duncan unrolled the paper and looked at it. His eyebrows raised, and he began walking briskly down the corridor, with Tala and me almost jogging to keep up with his long strides.

"What? What is it?" Tala said.

"Have you ever been to the Sky Ocean?" Duncan said.

The door to the laboratory opened as we passed it on our way to the bridge, and Zaylen popped his head out. He was an older man with a gray beard who served as the ship's navigator, ancient technology researcher, and general source of obscure knowledge. "Did someone say, 'Sky Ocean'?"

"But, how do we get there?" Tala asked. "Has anyone ever done it before?"

"Yes, I've been there myself." Zaylen joined the procession now headed up the stairs to the bridge. "It's really quite simple. On occasion, natural portals to the Sky Ocean form inside storm clouds if they're big enough and if there's plenty of lightning. We simply find a large storm cloud and fly through it to the top."

"Really?" Tala said. "That sounds amazing!"

"Yes, that's how the cloud fishermen do it," Duncan said.

I started feeling queasy at the idea of flying through a storm cloud filled with lightning.

"Cloud fishermen?" Tala said. "Do they catch cloud fish, or do they just fish in the clouds? Or are they fishermen made out of clouds?"

"I'm pretty sure it's the first one," I said.

We ascended the stairs and walked onto the bridge. Flin sat at the helm reading a comic book which he quickly closed and put away. He sat up straight and adjusted his fancy leather jacket.

"Nothing to report, Captain," Flin said. "We're on course to dock at Skyport in three hours."

"Change of plans, Flin," Duncan said. "We're not going to Skyport yet. We're going to the Sky Ocean to find the wreckage of the *Nimbus*."

Flin pulled a lever on his console, and I steadied myself as the airship slowed down. He turned around, caught sight of Tala, and winked at her. She smiled in response.

"Why do we want to find the *Nimbus*?" Tala asked.

"Because that's where the Astrolabe is," Duncan said.

Tala, Flin, and I stared blankly at Duncan.

Zaylen laughed. "I don't believe these young people have heard of the Astrolabe. Well, it's an artifact created by the Ancient Ones, and it is said to have the power to find whatever treasure or item you're looking for. In other words, it's the ultimate navigational tool, assuming it works the way the stories say. A number of years ago, Captain Ordon of the *Nimbus* found it and used it to become one of the most prosperous airship captains in the Seven Realms. But the ship never returned from its last expedition, and the entire crew was presumed dead."

"That sounds great!" Flin said. "I'm in."

"I've been wanting to find the *Nimbus* for a while," Duncan said. "If we can get our hands on the Astrolabe, we could be fabulously wealthy. It's said the last place they explored was a lost city of the Ancient Ones. The cloud fishermen think they found its location." He held up the sheet of paper.

"Why don't the cloud fishermen try to find the Astrolabe for themselves?" Tala asked.

"They're probably too frightened to go near the place," Duncan said.

"Are there going to be...dead bodies?" I asked. This new adventure was sounding less appealing by the second.

"Well, I imagine they're all skeletons by now," Duncan said, "but you're welcome to stay on the *Daybreaker* while the rest of us go exploring."

"So, we're actually going underwater?" Tala said. "I didn't know the *Daybreaker* could go underwater."

My stomach churned at the thought of being underwater. I wished, not for the first time, that I had stayed home in Lindell.

"Well, it can," Duncan said. "We've done it a couple of times using a shield generator I conned somebody out of, long before you and Kayli came onboard, and Sierra attached it to the ship's systems. Don't worry; we'll be fine."

"Um, sir?" Tala said. "Doesn't it sound kind of dangerous to go to the same place where another ship met some horrible unknown fate?"

"That's a good point," Duncan said, "but we have an advantage."

He walked to a cabinet, opened a drawer, and pulled out a weathered, leather-bound booklet. "I got this journal from some Arcondian traders a few months ago. I don't know how they found it, but it contains journal entries written by one of the crew members from the *Nimbus*."

Duncan set the journal down on a table. "Here, take a look. Anyway, you all know serving on an airship can be dangerous work, but we'll watch each other's backs like we always do. If we can find the Astrolabe, then it will be easy sailing from now on. And even if we can't find it, or it turns out that it was just a myth, we should be able to scavenge some other valuable items the *Nimbus* was carrying around."

"But won't the heirs of the *Nimbus* want it back?" Flin said.

"I'm sure they will," Duncan said, "but according to the Admiralty Court of Dulain, if we claim salvage rights, there's nothing they can do about it since so much time has passed."

I picked up the journal and looked through its contents while the others continued discussing salvage rights, which didn't interest me. Most of it was routine log entries. There was a description of a giant hollow rock or mountain deep in the Sky Ocean that supposedly contained ruins of an ancient civilization. There were a few lines about an apparatus in a spherical chamber that was supposedly able to move an entire city. One passage on the last page caught my attention.

After much hardship, we finally discovered the fabled Astrolabe of Narvond. The captain keeps it in his quarters and will not suffer others to lay eyes upon it. There is rumor of mutiny among the crew, and I pray it does not come to that. We now prepare for another voyage to the Dark Rock, ever in search of more treasures from the Ancient Ones. I yearn for the day when I may retire from this life of scavenging.

That didn't sound very promising.

Duncan turned the sheet over and grimaced. "Dammit!"

"What is it?" Zaylen said.

"Anders and his crew might have gotten the same information,"

Duncan said. "We've got to get moving and find it before those bastards do!"

"We have the journal," Zaylen said. "That should be an advantage."

"And our ship is faster than the *Harrier*," Flin said.

While the others continued talking, Tala leaned over to me and whispered, "The *Harrier*? Didn't our crew get in a fight with those people last time we were at Skyport?"

"I have a feeling that happens every time they meet," I said.

"What course, Captain?" Flin said.

"Find some big storm clouds," Duncan said. "And fly to them."

"That's not very specific." Flin gestured toward the front window. "Look at the sky; it's completely clear. It could take days to find a storm."

"Great, we'll need a day to prepare anyway," Duncan said. "But we need to hurry if we want to beat the *Harrier*. Sierra needs to make sure the shield is operational. Zaylen, go down to the engine room and help her."

"I'll try, but you know how she is," Zaylen said.

"Yes, I know my daughter very well," Duncan said. "Tala, I want you to check the hull and make sure it's sound. And I'm going to find Jade and fill her in on our plans."

Duncan walked off the bridge and down the stairs, humming a sea shanty.

"He means, he's going to get Jade's approval, right?" Flin laughed.

"Well, she does own the ship," Zaylen said. "But I'm sure she'll agree. We need the money, and she's only slightly less reckless than he is. Oh, and I think I may be able to help you find a storm. I happen to possess an enchanted device that can sense weather patterns. I'll see if I can find it before I help Sierra."

"I just had an idea," Tala said. "We should catch a bunch of cloud fish while we're there and make money selling them to rich people. Kayli, you could cook the fish for them and invent some fancy new dishes."

Talking about cooking suddenly reminded me that I was in the middle of baking. "My bread!" I ran out of the bridge and back to the galley.

The next day, Tala and I checked the longitudinals and girders throughout the ship. Or, more accurately, I walked around carrying equipment for Tala while she did all the checking. The last area to inspect was the ship's hold. In the engine room, which was next door to the hold, Sierra was busy working on the shield generator that would allow us to travel underwater.

"So, what would you use the Astrolabe to find, if we ever get it?" Tala asked. "It's supposed to find whatever treasure your heart desires, right?"

"I don't know," I said. "If I tried to use it, it would probably just point me toward Lindell."

"You need to stop thinking about home all the time," Tala said. "There's got to be other things you want, too."

"There are," I said. *Like having my sister back, or at least knowing she's in a better place now. Or knowing that a better place even exists.*

"Besides, this is good for you," Tala continued. "I really miss your sister, too, but you needed to get out and see the world instead of staying at home being depressed all the time."

"I know," I said. "I've heard the lecture before; you sound like my mother."

"Look, if you really don't like it here, you can always quit and go back home," Tala said. "Don't worry about abandoning me; I'll be fine."

"That's only part of it," I said. "And I don't hate this ship. I just thought I could find answers up here."

"Up here in the sky?" Tala said.

"I know it sounds dumb, but haven't you ever felt like there's something wonderful up there, just beyond your reach? What if we could keep going higher and higher and actually get there?

"You mean, like the Upper Skies?" Tala said.

"Yeah, something like that. Do you think the people we've lost are up there?"

"Maybe." Tala tapped lightly on a beam with a small mallet.

I thought about my sister and how much she would liked to have been here. She had always been the more adventurous one. I remembered her, Tala, and myself going on expeditions to explore the forest around Lindell when we were younger. Tears started to form in my eyes, and a lump came to my throat, so I forced myself to think about something else.

"So, what would you use the Astrolabe for?" I asked.

"Hmm." Tala thought for a moment. "I don't really know. I don't like to think about the future much."

"Nothing wrong with that, I guess," I said.

"I know what the captain would use it for," Tala said. "Treasure, treasure, and more treasure."

We both laughed.

"Could you two keep it down in there?" Sierra's voice came from the engine room. "I'm trying to concentrate!"

"Sorry that we're trying to enjoy ourselves!" Tala said. She turned to me and muttered, "Is she ever happy about anything?"

Some swearing and crashing sounds came from the engine room. Sierra stormed out, carrying a long pole with a claw-like apparatus on the end. She was a slender young woman with dark hair like her father, Duncan. "I give up! There's no way this stupid thousand-year-old piece of shit is going to work!"

"But, I thought the Captain said it's been used before," Tala said.

"Yes, but that was before the stabilization matrix failed, and I had to reroute everything," Sierra said.

"Is there anything we can do?" I asked.

"Yeah, you could go bake a pie or something," Sierra snapped. "That ought to help."

Tala stepped toward Sierra and balled her hands into fists. "At least that would be more helpful than your constant bitching!"

Jade, the first mate, came down the stairs into the hold. She was strikingly beautiful, had long bright orange hair, and wore a dark green jacket with tails.

"We don't have time for drama, ladies," Jade said. "Your jobs are to make sure the *Daybreaker* is ready. Tala, what about the hull?"

"It looks good on the inside," Tala said, "but we should really be checking the strakes on the outside hull, too.

"You're probably right," Jade said, "but I doubt Duncan will want to stop and spend the time. Especially since he's in such a hurry to get there before the *Harrier*."

"It won't matter if I can't get the shield to work," Sierra said.

"Can't you just use auxiliary power?" Jade said.

"Yes, if your plan is for us all to drown when the shield fails," Sierra said.

"That might be a risk we have to take," Jade said.

Do we really? I wanted to say.

Tala rushed over to the starboard window. "Hey, guys! I think that's a big storm up ahead. Zaylen's weather-seeking tool really worked!"

I ran to the window. Huge gray thunderheads loomed in front of the ship, lit up by flashes of lightning. I took a deep breath and tried not to panic.

"Sierra, just get the shield working," Jade said. "Do what you have to do."

"Sure, I'll go sprinkle some magic pixie dust on it right now." Sierra strode back into the engine room.

Jade sighed. "And you two-" She pointed at Tala and me. "Go find Flin and tell him to report to the bridge." She turned around and walked up the stairs.

"Yes, ma'am." Tala turned to me and sighed. "I wish I could be half as awesome as Jade is."

"Don't we all?" I said. "Should we split up and look for Flin?"

"No need," Tala said. "I know exactly where he is—in the lounge. Come on." She grabbed my hand and dragged me up the spiral stairs in the aft section of the hold.

"Aren't we going the long way?" I asked.

"Yes, but I want to see the storm from the top deck!"

We went up another level until we reached the galley, then we exited out the galley doors and across the top deck. The air was humid and electric, and the wind was fiercer than usual. A towering bank of black clouds loomed over the ship. Lightning crisscrossed the sky.

"Isn't this exciting?" Tala yelled. Her purple hair was raised up on end.

"Yeah, but maybe we should get back inside," I said. "You know, before we get electrocuted."

"Right," Tala said. We entered the quarterdeck and made our way to the lounge. Flin lay asleep on one of the sofas, a comic book on his chest.

"Did he have too much rum last night?" I asked quietly.

"No, I think I wore him out when we—" Tala stopped herself and giggled. "Well, never mind that part."

She walked up to Flin, bent down, and kissed him. "Time to wake up, Flin. There's a ship that needs piloting."

"Um, are you two having a private moment?" I asked. "I can give you some space if you want."

Flin sat up and rubbed his eyes. "I didn't mean to fall asleep. Jade's not mad at me, is she?"

"No, but she will be if you don't get off your ass and report to the bridge," Tala said. "We found a storm!"

A loud thunderclap shook the *Daybreaker,* and Flin jumped off the sofa.

"Let's go!" Tala grabbed Flin's hand, then mine, and we left the room.

We ascended the two flights of stairs that led to the bridge. Duncan was at the helm piloting the ship.

"Never fear, your ace pilot has arrived," Flin said.

"Yeah, yeah, just get in the chair and do your thing, ace pilot." Duncan stood up, and Flin took his place.

A minute later, the ship plunged into the cloud, and the only thing visible outside the windows was a dark gray mist. Jade turned on the bridge glowlamps. A constant rumbling filled the air.

"Should I ascend now?" Flin asked.

"Not yet," Duncan said. "On my signal."

A huge web of lightning flickered right in front of us, followed by a deafening clap of thunder. Tala and I jumped.

"Okay, now!" Duncan commanded.

My stomach lurched as the ship began to ascend in a wide arc. I looked up at the ceiling viewport; it was covered with a thick haze which turned to rivulets of water splattering against the glass.

These people are absolutely mad, I thought. I imagined Zaylen in the lab below, looking out the window with glee.

Jade pushed the intercom button. "Sierra, activate the shield."

"Shield activated," Sierra's voice came over the intercom.

"Son of a bitch, I think it's working!" Duncan grinned.

Flin whooped with excitement as he gripped the controls tightly. There was a brief glow outside the windows, and then the dark gray mist was replaced by a bright greenish-blue expanse. The ship was completely underwater. Thousands of bubbles floated up through the water, and beams of golden light shone through it from some unknown source.

"We did it, Captain!" Tala said. "We're in the Sky Ocean! I can't believe it!"

"All right, let's find the *Nimbus*," Duncan said. "Everyone to your stations."

"Captain, I don't have a station," Tala said.

Duncan shrugged. "Then make something up."

I sat in the laboratory and looked out the window. I had been assigned to keep a lookout for the last place the *Nimbus* had explored. The *Daybreaker* floated through deep blue-green water, which seemed to go on indefinitely in all directions, even up and down. Millions of particles swirled through the currents, and schools of small fish occasionally swam past the ship. Glowing, translucent jellyfish swarmed and undulated, along with thousands of tiny, darting lifeforms. I felt like I could sit and look out the window for hours. Even my anxieties receded to the background for a while.

Zaylen sat at a table studying a chart and occasionally muttering incoherently to himself. Complicated cartographic instruments were strewn about the table. His wife Laurel studied a jellyfish floating in a tank she had just captured.

Tala entered the lab, walked over to me, and sat down. "Isn't this amazing? I can't believe we're actually in the Sky Ocean!"

"Yeah, it's great," I said.

"Your enthusiasm is overwhelming," Tala said. "You seem to be enjoying the view, at least."

"I'm on lookout," I said. "I'm supposed to let Zaylen know if I see a giant underwater island. That's what the journal says, anyway."

"If we had the Astrolabe already, we'd know exactly where to go," Tala said. "It would make Zaylen's job a lot easier."

Zaylen laughed. "If we find the Astrolabe, Laurel and I just might retire."

"What? You two can't leave," Tala said. "Who's going to do all our navigation and doctoring and ancient tech stuff?"

"Don't worry." Laurel gently prodded the jellyfish with a glass rod. "I'm sure you'll do fine without us. Zaylen and I love being here, but we also want to go back to Dulain and spend time with our grandchildren."

"Going back home sounds nice," I said quietly.

Tala rolled her eyes but said nothing.

Laurel looked at me and smiled. "Kayli, of course, you're free to go home if you're unhappy, but you might miss some good experiences. I believe you're on this ship for a reason."

"Do you really think so?" I asked.

"Yes, we're all here for a reason," Laurel said, "whether we know it or not."

"Look, is that a cloud fish?" Tala pointed out the window.

A large, semi-translucent fish with huge eyes and billowy fins swam past the ship.

"Yes, it is," Laurel said.

"And what's that thing?" Tala pointed at a great silvery serpentine shape in the distance.

"That would be a sea dragon," Laurel said.

"Oh, I hope it doesn't devour us," Tala said.

"It's most likely harmless," Zaylen said. "It's the krakens and leviathans you should fear."

"Oh, Zaylen, don't scare them too much," Laurel said.

"Krakens?" Tala said. "They have more than one kraken here?"

"Why can't we see this place when we look up at the sky?" I asked, wishing to move the subject away from giant deadly sea monsters.

"The Sky Ocean exists in a slightly different plane of reality, so it usually can't be perceived by normal human senses, unless you're in it," Zaylen said. "Which also explains why it doesn't come crashing down on the land dwellers. You see, the heavens are comprised of a great many layers, such as the Aether above the sky as we know it, but there are higher layers, many of which are hidden from us."

"So, what happens when you keep going up?" Tala asked. "Does the Sky Ocean have a top to it, like the normal ocean?"

"I knew an explorer who once tried to find out," Zaylen said. "He wanted to find the Upper Skies where some say departed souls go to dwell. He had studied the ways of the Ancient Ones, who were themselves obsessed with the secrets of what lies beyond the mortal realms of space and time. His ship traveled up and up until its shield failed, and he was forced to turn back."

I perked up at this story. "Do you know anything more about that explorer? Did he ever find anything?"

"Alas, I do not know," Zaylen said. "But he was convinced there was a place of unspeakable beauty and perfection up there somewhere."

"I wonder where that dragon went," Tala said.

I looked out the window on all sides, but all I could see were a few cloud fish. Then a massive, scaly maw appeared and swallowed one of the fish whole, scattering the others. Tala and I gasped as the massive body of the dragon swam past, making the ship rock from side to side.

"That's a sight you don't see every day," Laurel said.

"Amazing!" Tala said.

The dragon slowly disappeared into the murky distance, and only then was I able to relax.

"By the great gods, I figured it out!" Zaylen said. "We need to go that way!" He pointed slightly toward the port side.

"How can you tell?" Tala said. "We're surrounded by water on all sides, and it all looks exactly the same."

"Currents," Zaylen said. "These charts have the major currents of the Sky Ocean mapped out, and our ship's anemometers can detect them, and the journal explained which ones to follow. The waves from the sea dragon gave me the idea." He walked over to the intercom and spoke to the bridge, giving them an exact heading.

Tala left to carry out some duties, and the laboratory became quieter. After several more minutes of staring out the window, I began to see a small, round black object in the distance. I grabbed the telescope sitting beside me and looked into it. The object looked like a great craggy rock suspended in the endless ocean. As we approached, it gradually grew more distinct.

"I found something!" I said.

Zaylen rushed over, and I handed him the telescope and pointed.

"Interesting," Zaylen said.

"Is that the place the *Nimbus* found?" I asked. "The Dark Rock?"

"I think it is," Zaylen said. He turned on the intercom. "Bridge, we found the location. Do you see it? It's twenty-five degrees to port, minus five degrees altitude."

"Yes, I see it," Flin voice came over the intercom. "Adjusting course now."

A chill went through me as the sinister mountain-sized chunk of rock slowly grew closer.

It took another hour of traveling to actually reach the Dark Rock. As we moved closer, the water became darker and murkier, there were fewer fish, and the air inside the *Daybreaker* grew colder. I went to the galley to prepare a stew for lunch but ended up burning the roux because I was so distracted by the unnerving solitude and dark waters swirling past the galley windows. Instead, I put out some cold meats, cheeses, and bread on platters for the crew and left the galley. I resisted the urge to go to my room and hide under the blankets.

I went to the lounge to do some cleaning, but that turned out to be a bad idea since the lounge was in the fore of the ship, and its windows gave me a clear view of the Dark Rock. It was far more massive than I had imagined. It looked like a shapeless mountain that had been uprooted and sunk into the sea but remained suspended underwater instead of sinking. The sides were pockmarked with numerous craters and holes.

As the *Daybreaker* headed toward one of the holes, I turned away, too frightened to watch. Leaving the lounge, I headed down to the hold, keeping away from windows. When I got there, I found Tala, Zaylen, and Laurel standing at the windows and watching the smooth rock walls of the tunnel the *Daybreaker* was passing through. The glowlamps on the outside of the *Daybreaker* emitted a feeble light that barely revealed the sides of the tunnel. It was quiet, but at least there were other people around.

"Where are we?" I asked.

"Deep inside the Dark Rock," Zaylen said.

I walked over to Tala and looked out the window. The ship's glowlamps lit up the rock wall as we ascended. It was smoother now and covered with strange patterns and markings. The water grew lighter.

"I think we're about to surface," Tala said.

Waves splashed against the windows as the *Daybreaker* emerged from the water and floated up into an enormous cavern filled with towers, domes, odd-shaped architecture, and giant columns of rock. It appeared to be a subterranean city built inside the Dark Rock. It was a relief to finally be out of the water, even if we were in the center of a giant chunk of rock floating underwater in a vast ocean that was possibly in another dimension.

"This is amazing!" Tala said.

"That's not exactly the word I would use," I said.

"It appears the journal was accurate," Zaylen said. "The Ancient Ones built a city here. Quite remarkable! We may have a chance to study their ruins and technology. And Duncan will be pleased with the possibility of finding more ancient relics to sell."

"Did the Ancient Ones live underwater?" Tala asked.

"Not normally," Zaylen said. "I don't know how the Dark Rock got here, but I have a theory that it was originally a sky island that became trapped in the Sky Ocean because of one of the Ancient Ones' experiments gone wrong."

The engine room door opened, and Sierra stepped out, walked to the window next to ours, and looked out.

The *Daybreaker* floated over the water and stopped at the edge. Jade came down the stairs, walked to the ramp, and pressed the switch. It opened slowly and hit the stone floor of the chamber with a foreboding echo. Water dripped from the ship's hull across the opening.

We gathered at the open ramp and stared out at the ruins of the city. It was built mostly of dark green stone and looked remarkably well-preserved. The cavern was illuminated by great veins of some glowing mineral in the rock walls, and even the buildings of the city seemed to glow slightly. The most unusual thing about it was that the walls and ceiling of the cavern also had buildings on them as if the architects had been unaware of the concept of gravity. It was unpleasantly quiet.

"Is it safe to go out?" Tala asked.

"Probably, but 'safe' is a relative term in these kinds of places," Jade said.

Tala looked up. "Um, why are there upside-down towers hanging from the ceiling?"

Zaylen shrugged. "The Ancient Ones were a mysterious folk."

"This place creeps me out," Sierra said.

Duncan and Flin came down the stairs and joined us.

"Where's the wreckage of the *Nimbus*?" Flin said. "Shouldn't it be around here somewhere?"

"This is a big place," Zaylen said. "The *Nimbus* could be anywhere."

There was a low whooshing sound, and a sleek, shiny airship appeared from behind one of the ancient buildings and flew toward us. It looked similar to the *Daybreaker*, with a metal-reinforced wooden hull and a general shape like an ocean-going ship, but without the sails.

"Is that the *Nimbus*?" Tala said. "It's not a ghost ship, is it?"

"No, it's the *Harrier*," Duncan said. "That son of a bitch." He kicked a nearby barrel, knocking it over.

"So, Anders got here first," Jade said. "How the hell did that happen?"

"What now?" Flin said.

"I'm guessing they want to parley," Jade said. "Grab a weapon if you have one handy."

"A weapon?" I said in a tiny voice to no one in particular.

The others brought out various swords, staves, and other weapons from one of the hold's storage lockers. Tala approached me holding a crossbow and a foot-long metal rod, the latter of which she handed to me.

"I got your bo staff since you looked too scared to get it yourself," she said.

I took the rod with a trembling hand and flicked it with my wrist, making it telescope out from both ends into a five-foot-long staff. Then I pressed a switch to make it retract and attached it to my belt.

"Remember, we've both been trained," Tala said.

"Training is one thing, but I've never been in a real fight," I said.

"It'll be okay," Tala said. "Duncan and Jade will take care of us."

"What would I do without you?" I said.

"Probably crawl down into the bilge and hide," Tala said.

Jade walked by, brandishing a pair of throwing knives. "Don't worry, you two," she said. "Nobody is going to get hurt; the point of this meeting is to intimidate each other. We'll all walk out there, the two captains will posture and insult each other's manhood for a while, and then we'll go our separate ways. It'll be fine. Just try not to look so...cute and helpless."

"How do we do that?" Tala said.

"I don't know. Try scowling more," Jade said.

"Everyone ready?" Duncan put his sword in its sheath at his belt. "Let's go."

Duncan walked down the gangplank, and we all followed him out onto the smooth damp floor of the cavern. Our boots echoed ominously. Looking out at the grim, silent towers and walls of the ancient city, I felt a renewed sense of dread.

The *Harrier* slowly descended a hundred feet away from the *Daybreaker,* and its gangplank lowered. I kept behind Duncan and Jade and peeked out between their shoulders to see what was going on. A tall bald man I recognized as Anders emerged, flanked by several of his crew members.

The two groups walked toward each other. I wondered what would happen if it actually came to blows. I knew Duncan, Jade, and Sierra were excellent fighters, and possibly Flin, too. Zaylen was older, but I'd been told about the many adventures he and Laurel had been on, and he seemed like he was still in good shape.

We stopped a few paces from each other. Duncan's longcoat was loose and slightly tattered, while Anders wore a stiff pea coat with fancy embroidery.

I studied the faces of the *Harrier* crew. Besides Anders, there was a large, bearded man, a man with a long nose and a rat-like face, a young woman with dark green hair and tattoos, and several others. Overall, they looked meaner and tougher than us. They also slightly outnumbered us. A younger man with tousled blue hair and a nice-looking face stood among them. He didn't seem like he belonged in that crew of brigands.

"Anders, what a pleasant surprise," Duncan called out. "I didn't expect to see you venturing out into such a dangerous place. Shouldn't you be in your quarters, sipping herbal tea?"

"Hawkstone, I'm surprised you managed to find anybody still willing to take orders from you," Anders said.

"It must be my natural charisma," Duncan said. "I'm impressed that you managed to find this place."

In response, Anders pulled out a small leather-bound book and held it up.

"Son of a—," Duncan muttered.

"Of course," Anders said, "it was obvious this book was only a copy of the original, and therefore other parties would be privy to the same information. I simply had to be faster than everyone else. I've already claimed salvage rights on the *Nimbus*, so I'm afraid there's nothing for you to do here but go back the way you came."

"You know you can't claim salvage rights until you actually find the ship," Duncan said. "And I'm pretty sure you haven't found it yet."

The blue-haired man's eyes met mine, and he smiled. I got the impression he didn't want to be here anymore than I did.

"Very well," Anders said. "But when we do find it, be prepared to leave empty-handed."

"I'm hurt, Anders," Duncan said. "I thought you'd want to share, especially after all we've been through together."

Anders smiled grimly. "Indeed. Know that we are prepared to defend what is ours by force, if necessary."

"So are we," Duncan said.

Anders scoffed. "You're outnumbered, and your crew is mostly women. I wouldn't advise it."

"Care to find out for yourself?" Duncan said. "Looks can be deceiving."

A couple of Anders' men raised their weapons.

"I say we deal with 'em now, Captain," the rat-faced man snarled, brandishing an odd-looking hooked sword.

"I'm giving the orders here, Garon," Anders said.

"But there's more of us than them, Captain," Garon said.

"Gentlemen," Zaylen said. "And ladies. Must we resort to violence? This is a find of immense archaeological significance."

Then everyone started talking angrily at once, but they were interrupted by a deep booming sound that made the ground vibrate. Everyone stopped and looked around.

"Um, what was that?" one of Anders' crew members said.

There was a low, grinding rumble, and the ground started to move. The cavern, maybe the entire Dark Rock, was slowly tilting.

"Back to the ship!" Duncan yelled.

Anders shouted something at his crew, and they all sprinted toward their ship. As some of us tried to climb onboard, a wave of water knocked us to our knees.

I tried to get up but slipped on the wet ground that was becoming increasingly tilted. Duncan grabbed my hand, but more water poured across the ground, and his grip slipped. I heard someone yell my name as I slid down, away from the ship and into the ancient city. I looked up and saw the *Daybreaker* floating up to avoid crashing into the rising ground.

I slid on a cascade of water down what seemed to be a street, passing various towers, fountains, and sculptures. The ground was now at a very steep angle that would have been difficult to walk on even if it wasn't covered with water. I slid to the edge of a chasm and fell into it, feeling like my stomach was coming up my throat. I splashed into frigid water, then fought my way to the surface, but more water continued to pour down all around me. Barely able to see anything, I swam toward what appeared to be an archway. It was tilting like the rest of the city, but it seemed to be going back in the opposite direction and righting itself.

Something brushed against my legs, and I swam faster, hoping it wasn't something alive. I reached a stone embankment and pulled myself onto it. It was level, and the movement of the city was ceasing.

Water still cascaded from above, but I was protected from it by the chamber I was in. My body ached from numerous bruises. My clothes were soaking wet, and I shivered from the cold. Worse, the water level was rising and already starting to spill onto the floor.

I glanced back and saw a large blob with multiple appendages moving under the water. I felt for my staff at my belt, although I wasn't sure how much good it would do against a sea monster. Maybe it was just a harmless octopus. Or a mini-kraken.

Glowlamps on the walls lit up the chamber with an eerie light. Huge stone statues of vaguely humanoid shapes lined the walls. They seemed to watch me as I walked past them. Out of the corner of my eye, I thought I saw one of them move slightly.

I waded through the rising water as fast as I could, crossing the chamber and ascending a set of stairs on the opposite side. They led up to another chamber, but this one only had one other exit, and it was blocked with rubble. I looked down the stairs and saw the water rising more rapidly, flooding one step at a time until it reached the top of the stairs and stopped. I was trapped.

As I started to wonder how long it would take me to starve to death, water began gushing in from the rubble-filled exit. Soon the water was up to my knees. I thought about trying to swim underwater down the stairs I had come from, but I was afraid I wouldn't be able to hold my breath long enough. And there was also that sea creature with the tentacles.

"Help!" I called out, although I knew nobody could hear me. "Help me!"

Serves you right for getting involved in this airship business when you should have just stayed home, I thought. *Creator, if you're out there, please get me out of this. Well, at least if I die, I'll know what happens next, and maybe I'll even see my sister again.*

The water was now up to my waist. My legs were becoming numb from the cold. I thought about Tala and my family and how they would respond to news of my demise. I imagined Tala sitting on a sofa in the ship's lounge, crying her eyes out. Then I wondered if everyone else had made it back to the *Daybreaker* safely. In all the confusion, I wasn't really sure. I thought about what my sister would have done in this situation. I knew she wouldn't have given up.

I can't let them down, I thought. *Still, if I make it out of here, I'm going to quit and go back home to my old job at the bakery. It's not like I'm going to find what I'm looking for here, anyway. I'm sure Tala will understand.*

Looking around the chamber, I spotted a small trapdoor in the ceiling with a broken ladder leading into it that started halfway up the wall. I had to wait until the chamber filled up with enough water so I could reach the bottom of the ladder.

I waded over to the wall and waited for the water to rise, hoping the octopus wasn't following me. In a minute, it was up to my neck, and before long, I was treading water. Grasping at protrusions in the wall, I floated upwards until I could reach the ladder. The glowlamps on the walls were now underwater, as were the statues.

I climbed up the ladder, but when I reached the trapdoor, there didn't appear to be any way to open it. Fighting down the urge to panic, I banged on the solid metal surface of the door. With a squeaking sound, it slid open a few inches. I reached up and tried to pull the door open with one hand but only succeeded in moving it an inch. The water now covered my legs. *Just don't look back*, I thought. I looked back anyway and saw something large slithering just under the water.

"Help!" I yelled.

A pair of hands appeared at the edge of the door and pulled on it. The opening slowly widened, and the knuckles on the hands whitened with the effort. I reached up and helped pull, and the door opened enough for me to climb through.

I looked up, and a familiar face looked down at me—the blue-haired man from the *Harrier*. I cried out in relief and astonishment. He reached down, and I grabbed his hands and climbed through the trapdoor.

"Are you okay?" he asked.

"Yeah, I'm just cold," I said. "And there might be a big octopus down there. Or maybe it's a small kraken."

"A kraken?" His hand moved to the hilt of the sword strapped to his belt. His left sleeve was torn and had blood on it.

"What about you? Are you hurt?" I asked.

"It's nothing," he said. "I just got hurt when I was falling down here. We're both lucky to be alive. I'm Jerad, by the way."

"I'm Kayli." I brushed strands of wet hair out of my face.

"Nice to meet you," he said. "It looks like we both got separated from our ships. That was crazy, wasn't it? I had no idea this whole place was going to start spinning around."

"Thank you for saving me," I said.

"No problem." Jerad gave me a goofy grin. "It's a good thing I happened to end up in the same place as you. This ancient city is gigantic. We should probably keep moving." He pointed to the trapdoor where water was starting to bubble out and spread over the floor.

"This whole city isn't filling up with water, is it?" I said.

"I don't know, but we need to try and get to someplace higher," Jerad said.

We walked through the room and ascended yet another staircase. My clothes were still dripping and uncomfortable, and I shivered a little. The walls were covered with complex patterns of foreboding runes that seemed to change when I wasn't focusing on them.

"I think this place is haunted," I said.

"Maybe," Jerad said. "I like your hair. It's very pretty; I don't see that shade of pink very often."

"Thank you." I blushed. "It's magenta."

"So, how long have you been on your airship?" Jerad asked.

"About three months." I appreciated his efforts to keep my mind off our frightening surroundings.

"Oh, that's not very long. What do you do?"

"I'm the ship's cook."

"Really? Your crew is lucky. Our cook quit a few weeks ago, and we've been taking turns cooking, except the captain, of course. Some of those guys burn everything."

"What do you do, besides burning the food?" I asked.

Jerad laughed. "I'm the ancient technology expert."

"Oh, that explains why you look different from the rest of your crew," I said. "You're a scholar, not a pirate."

"Are you saying I don't look tough enough?" he said.

"Well, compared to some of those other guys, maybe a little."

"You don't really look like pirate material, either."

"Is that so?" I said.

"Well, you just look too...nice."

"Is that a compliment?"

Jerad laughed. "Well, it's supposed to be. Anyway, they might look rough, but my crewmates are decent people. Mostly. There may be one or two exceptions, like Garon. He's an asshole; you have to watch out for him."

"What about your captain, Anders? I've heard some not-so-good things about him."

"He's all right, most of the time," Jerad said. "And I've heard things about your captain, too."

"Well, they obviously don't like each other very much," I said.

"Hmm, should we even be talking to each other?" Jerad said. "I mean, we are supposed to be enemies, after all."

"We're terrible pirates, aren't we?" I said. We both laughed.

The staircase finally ended, and we found ourselves in front of a closed door with no handles or visible means of opening.

"Finally." I took deep breaths. "I thought those stairs would never end."

"How do we get this door open?" Jerad muttered.

"I thought you were an ancient tech expert," I said.

"Nobody is really an expert in this stuff," Jerad said. "We've barely figured anything out about how it works, even the tech we're already using. And I don't have a lot of experience in the field, either."

"So, what you're saying is you don't have any idea how to open it." I grinned at Jerad to let him know I was teasing, but the stairwell was so dark he probably couldn't tell. "I bet Zaylen could open it. He's our expert. Of course, he's a lot older than you, and he's been everywhere and done everything."

"Well, I guess you're stuck with an inexperienced doofus like me," Jerad said.

"I'm sorry," I said. "I didn't mean it that way. I'm just babbling to keep myself from panicking."

"It's okay." Jerad slid his hands over the door and the adjacent wall and rapped on it. "I wish I could meet this Zaylen guy and talk to him. It's too bad we can't all just work together for a change."

"Yeah, wouldn't that be nice?" I said.

"I think I found something." Jerad pushed on a section of wall, and the door slid open with a harsh grinding sound.

We walked through the door and onto an open platform. We were much higher than before, and the ancient city spread out before us. A high walkway leading to another tower branched off the platform, and many other walkways joined towers together in the distance. The glowing veins of rock on the cavern walls dimly lit the city around us, but the airships were nowhere to be seen. Below us, the submerged parts of the city gave off a ghostly glow.

"I hope they're looking for us," I said.

"I'm sure they are," Jerad said. "I mean, what would they do without us?"

"Your job sounds important, but I'm just a cook," I said. "They don't really need me." I knew deep down they wouldn't abandon me, least of all Tala, but that didn't stop me from doubting.

"Don't say that," Jerad said. "I know they'd miss you if you were gone. And I'm sure you're there for a reason. Anyway, we should probably try to get to a place where we have a good chance of being found."

"What if we look for that shipwreck that we came here to find?" I said. "Our captains will probably both want to get their hands on the Astrolabe first, and then go look for us next. I remember reading in that journal that they were planning on exploring the center of the city, and there was something about a really big round building."

"Your captain let you read the journal?" Jerad asked.

I put my hands on my hips. "What, you think just because I'm the ship's cook that I'm not important enough for things like that?"

"No, I didn't mean that." Jerad raised his hands. "It's just that, Captain Anders can be very secretive. Anyway, what about that thing?" He pointed at a round edifice in the middle of the city, some distance away. "Do you think that could be our spherical structure?"

"It's the biggest spherical structure around here that I can see," I said.

We started across the walkway, and I stayed in the center, trying not to look down. I felt a little queasy and stopped walking. Jerad turned and looked at me.

"Are you all right?" he asked.

"I'm...kind of afraid of high places," I said.

"And you work on an airship?" Jerad laughed.

"Yeah, I know. It's pretty dumb, isn't it?"

"No, I didn't mean that. I'm sure you have your reasons."

"I do," I said, "it's just that...well, let's keep going before I lose my nerve." I wanted to explain my reasons, but he might think I was being foolish.

"Here, take my hand, and I'll guide you across." Jerad held out his hand to me. "You can keep your eyes on the floor or on me if you want."

"Thank you." I accepted his hand gratefully and took comfort in his touch. He was shaking slightly, too.

An hour later, Jerad and I were walking through a series of chambers and corridors, trying to stay moving in the same direction. Our footsteps echoed eerily, but we kept up a constant conversation. I was grateful I wasn't alone, and even more grateful my companion happened to be a kind, good-looking guy. I kept seeing shadowy things just at the edge of my vision, but I was afraid to mention them.

"I wonder why everything here is so bare," I said. "Hardly any furniture or tapestries or anything personal at all."

Jerad shrugged. "Maybe the Ancient Ones took everything with them when they left this place."

"I wonder why they left," I said.

Jerad stopped. "Did you hear that?"

We listened for a moment. A faint metallic scraping sound came from behind us.

"I heard that," I whispered. A chill went down my spine.

"I don't like the sound of that, whatever it is," Jerad said. "Let's get out of here."

We walked briskly toward the end of the corridor. A sound like the skittering of hundreds of metallic roaches came from behind, and I turned around. A tall, vaguely cylindrical metal creature lumbered toward us, shambling on a huge number of spindly jointed legs like a particularly hideous giant spider. It had a single large glowing red eye.

I screamed. Jerad grabbed my hand, and we both started running. I could hear the monster coming after us, but I didn't dare look back. We reached the end of the corridor and found ourselves in an enormous hall. We ran until we reached a dais with a few ornate chairs lying on their sides.

The metallic beast stopped a few yards away from us. A small cannon-like apparatus on top of it swiveled and pointed at us. Jerad stood in front of me, and I braced myself for something deadly to fire from it, but the cannon only sparked and hissed. The monster raised several of its tentacle-like legs and approached. Some of the tentacles had spiky blades at their ends.

Jerad drew his sword and slashed at the creature. He cut off one tentacle, but several more tentacles wrapped around his blade, wrenching it from his hands and snapping it in two. I backed away until I was against the wall of the chamber, my heart pounding. Jerad picked up one of the chairs and held it in front of the monster. It waved its tentacles at him as he tried to strike it.

Come on, Kayli, get out your staff. You're not going to let Jerad die while you do nothing, are you? I took the staff off my belt, extended it, and forced my legs to move forward. I swung the staff at the monster. The staff hit a tentacle and broke it in half. Another tentacle snaked out at me, but Jerad grabbed it before its blade could slice me.

Several more tentacles aimed themselves at Jerad, poised to slice him to ribbons. I thrust my staff at the monster's red eye. The staff shattered the eye and pierced through its mechanical body. It hissed and sizzled and stopped moving.

"That was amazing, Kayli!" Jerad unwrapped a limp tentacle from his arm. "I hate that my sword broke, though."

"I'm sorry about your sword." I retracted the staff and tried to hook it to my belt. My hands trembled so badly that I dropped it. "What is that thing?"

"My guess is it's a sentinel created by the Ancient Ones to guard their city," Jerad said. "I wish I could spend a few hours studying it, but we need to hurry and find our ships."

"Yeah, it might not be dead." I bent over to pick up my staff. "Or another one might show up."

I looked at Jerad's hands and saw he was shaking as much as I was. We started walking toward an exit at the other end of the great hall. As scary as the sentinel was, I found myself dreading the shadows even more.

"It's funny," Jerad said. "I've been looking forward to exploring an ancient sky city like this, but I guess I was expecting something less depressing. This place is so dead and empty. I thought I could find something amazing if I traveled high enough into the sky."

"You feel that way, too?" I said. "That's what I've always wanted. That's why I joined an airship crew. Well, it was also because my friend Tala talked me into it. But I just want to know what's beyond, you know? I...I lost someone."

"I know what you mean," Jerad said. "That's how I felt when my father died."

"It was my sister, Kimberlyn," I said. Tears came to my eyes again, but I let them. "She died two years ago. And I've just wanted to know that she's not really gone."

"I know that feeling," Jerad said. "There has to be a place where everything is perfect. And you just want to find it and know for sure."

"That's what I thought, too," I said. "Only I'm not so sure anymore. Maybe there's nothing at all."

"Maybe not," Jerad said. "But we can keep looking, can't we?"

"Yeah," I said.

We stepped out onto a wide stone bridge that crossed over a reservoir of dark water. On the other side was a series of pyramid-shaped structures. Beyond that was the spherical shape we had been trying to reach.

"Look, there's the thing." I pointed. "We're almost there."

We walked across the bridge and entered one of the pyramids. Inside was a massive chamber filled with equipment, pipes, and conduits. A few broken-down mechanical beings lay on the floor. They looked like they had served as caretakers rather than guards like the hideous creature we had fought earlier.

"It's warm in here," I said.

"I think this was the power generator for the city," Jerad said.

We reached an area where a gust of hot wind blew out from a grate in the floor.

"Nice, maybe we can finally dry off our clothes," Jerad said.

He carefully stepped out onto the grate. "It seems sturdy enough," he said.

I joined him, feeling warm for the first time since we had arrived on the Dark Rock. I looked down and saw an orange glow far below.

"There must be some kind of energy source down there," Jerad said. "It must be what powered their bigger technology, like making the island spin around."

As Jerad continued talking about ancient technology, he unbuttoned his vest and took it off, letting his shirt air out more. I followed his example and took my vest off, and the draft promptly blew my untucked shirt up. I squeaked, grabbed the hem of my shirt, and pulled it down. Jerad laughed.

Our clothes were mostly dry after a few minutes, so we stepped off the grate. It felt wonderful.

"Your hair is a mess!" I laughed and pointed at Jerad's frazzled hair.

"Ha, you should look in a mirror," Jerad said.

I quickly ran my fingers through my tangled hair, trying to comb it into something less chaotic.

"Don't worry; you look beautiful." Jerad said. Then he blushed and looked away.

I looked down at my curvy, slightly chubby figure. *Does he really think I look beautiful? I wonder if he fancies me. I wonder if I fancy him.*

Jerad and I continued through the power plant until we reached an exit. It opened out onto another walkway that led to the spherical structure. We walked inside it. It was large enough that the *Daybreaker* probably could have fit inside it. The inside walls were covered with strange lines and glyphs. At the center was a shiny orb floating inside a sphere of glass and metal, with numerous rods extending from the sphere to the walls of the chamber. The walkway we stood on went through the center of the chamber and connected to a platform below the shiny orb.

"Interesting," Jerad said quietly.

"I think I know what this is," I said. "I read about it in the journal. It's the thing that makes the Dark Rock tilt back and forth."

"Shh," Jerad said. "If that's true, that means something already triggered it when we first got here."

"You mean there's somebody or something else here?" I whispered. A disturbing image popped into my head of metallic sentinels or undead *Nimbus* crew members shambling around.

Jerad shrugged. "Not necessarily. Maybe the mechanics are just failing, and it sometimes gets set off by random vibrations or something. It is ancient, after all."

"Oh, I thought it might be monsters."

"There's always that possibility, too. We should be quiet when we go past it, just in case."

"Why would they even build something like this?" I asked. "Who wants to live in a city that spins around?"

"Who knows?" Jerad said. "Maybe they were able to control gravity, so they could live on all sides at once?"

We started walking across the bridge that led to the center of the chamber. It was narrow and had no railings, like most walkways in the ancient city. When we got to the platform, Jerad spent a moment studying the orb floating inside the glass and metal sphere. It rotated and pulsated with light.

Satisfied with his examination, Jerad motioned to me and continued across the bridge to the other side of the chamber.

My boot struck an upturned piece of metal on the walkway, and I stumbled, making a loud thump as my other foot hit the walkway. A low grinding noise came from below. I turned around and saw the orb in the center glow red. Jerad and I froze. There was a slight tremor, and then everything was silent, and the orb dimmed.

"That was close," Jerad whispered.

"Sorry," I hissed.

We exited the chamber and found ourselves in a huge open space surrounded by high walls and towers, some of which were horizontal to us. The area appeared to have been a garden or courtyard, but it was now filled with dead trees and empty fountains. Pieces of timber and chunks of masonry littered the area.

On the far side of the courtyard was the husk of an airship wedged between two towers. It was falling apart and looked like a vessel from an older era. There were the remains of great wings on its port and starboard sides and a gilded mermaid figurehead on its prow.

"That's got to be the *Nimbus,*" Jerad said.

"I hope our people find this place soon," I said.

"So, who gets to claim salvage rights?" Jerad asked. "We got here at the same time."

I shrugged.

"I've got an idea," Jerad said. "Let's go in there and look for the Astrolabe while we're waiting for the others to show up."

The thought of going inside that ghost ship filled me with dread, but I didn't want to let Jerad know how afraid I was. We walked across the courtyard and found a large hole in the side of the ship's hull six feet off the ground.

"I'll give you a boost," Jerad said. "Step on my hands." He knelt down, laced his fingers together, and put his hands out.

"Are you sure?" I said. "I'm not very light."

"I can do it," he said.

I stepped onto his hands, and he lifted me up as I grabbed the top of the ledge and pulled myself up. A sensation of vague hostility flowed from the ship's dark interior, and I stayed as close to the edge as possible. I helped him as he clambered up after me.

We walked into the bowels of the *Nimbus*. It was darker inside, but some of the ship's glowlamps still worked. It was more ornate and antiquated than the *Daybreaker*. The wooden floors creaked as Jerad and I stepped carefully over them. Two skeletons with dried skin and tattered sailor outfits still clinging to them lay in the middle of a corridor. Both grasped swords in their bony hands.

"It looks like they died fighting each other," I whispered.

"So, there was a mutiny," Jerad said. "Just like the journal predicted."

Jerad casually stepped around the skeletons. I darted past them quickly, afraid a skeletal arm might suddenly come to life and grab my leg. I looked down a dark corridor and thought I saw a faint shadowy shape moving at the end of it.

"Um, let's not go that way," Jerad said.

"Oh, you can see them, too?" I said.

"Yes, and they're probably best avoided."

We walked up a spiral staircase and entered the bridge. All the equipment was smashed, and several more skeletons lay strewn about. From the windows, we could see the courtyard below.

"I wonder if this guy was the captain." Jerad stood in front of a skeleton wearing the remains of a bright red longcoat, sitting in an ornate chair, with a sword sticking through his rib cage.

I stepped over to where Jerad stood. The skeleton grinned at us. I stared into its empty sockets, unable to look away. I suddenly felt angry at Jerad for dragging me into this place. *This ship is clearly haunted, and all he cares about is exploring. Doesn't he care how I feel?*

I was about to speak my mind when a low whooshing sound came from outside. My anger faded away as quickly as it had appeared. Jerad and I looked out the window.

"Kayli, my ship is here!" Jerad pointed out the window at the *Harrier* flying down to the courtyard. "And so is yours! They got here at the same time."

I sighed with relief as I saw the *Daybreaker* descending on the opposite side of the courtyard. I wanted nothing more than to get back on board and away from this horrible place.

"Let's get out of here," Jerad said. "I don't think this ship likes us." He walked quickly out of the bridge, almost running.

"I couldn't agree more," I said.

I started to run after him, but a gleam of light on the skeleton captain caught my eye. Something was hidden just below its coat. Taking a deep breath, I reached out and moved the coat lapel. A flat, oval-shaped metallic device hung from the skeleton's neck. It was covered with smaller concentric circles and strange etchings. I knew it must be the Astrolabe.

Bracing myself, I grabbed it quickly and tried to pull the chain over the skeleton's head, but the chain caught on the skull and sent it tumbling off the neck and onto the floor in front of me. I let out a little scream.

"Kayli?" Jerad stepped back onto the bridge.

I stuffed the Astrolabe in my pants pocket and turned around. It barely fit, and I glanced enviously at the much bigger pockets on Jerad's pants.

"I'm okay," I said. "It's the skeleton. It's just...really creepy."

Jerad and I quickly retraced our steps. I felt bad lying to him, but it would be better this way. I would go tell Duncan I found the Astrolabe, and we would get out of there before Anders and his crew could figure out what happened.

"Well, I guess we should get back to our ships," I said as we made our way out of the *Nimbus.*

"I almost wish we didn't have to. It's been fun adventuring with you, Kayli."

"Yeah, it has," I said. "We should, you know, keep in touch." *Will he even want to after he finds out I lied to him?*

"I'll write to you," Jerad said. "But what are we going to tell the others? I mean, they'll probably want to know which of us got to this area first, so they can claim salvage rights or whatever."

"We should just tell the truth, right?" I said. "We got here at the same time."

When we reached the opening in the hull of the *Nimbus*, Jerad jumped down to the ground. He caught me around my waist as I half-jumped, half-slipped down. I threw my arms around his neck to steady myself. We looked at each other awkwardly, then let go of each other.

I turned and saw, to my dismay, Duncan and Anders in the middle of the courtyard, standing a few feet apart and flanked by some of their crew members. *So much for getting out of here without a confrontation,* I thought.

Duncan and Anders stopped talking, and everyone turned and watched Jerad and me as we walked toward them.

"Well, this is awkward," Jerad said quietly.

We separated and walked toward our respective crews. Tala ran toward me and hugged me with one arm; the other hand grasped her crossbow.

"I'm so glad we found you," Tala said. "We were looking all over the place for you. We also found some valuable stuff." Then she lowered her voice. "Who's the cute guy?"

I turned around and saw Jerad reuniting with his crew. The girl with the dark green hair and tattoos was talking to him.

"His name is Jerad," I said. "I'll tell you all about it later."

"I can't wait." Tala's eyebrows raised.

Duncan put his hand on my arm. "It's good to have you back, Kayli."

"So, Jerad," Anders said, "I assume you discovered the *Nimbus* first, did you not?"

Jerad pointed at me. "I'm sorry, Captain. She got here first."

Jerad must be trying to avoid a fight, I thought. *He's letting us have the treasure.*

"So, you let a girl beat you here," Anders said. "I must say, that is very disappointing."

Jerad remained silent and stared at Anders. I suddenly had a strong desire to kiss him. Jerad, that is, not Anders.

Everyone was silent for a few seconds. Anders clenched his fists, then spoke again. "We all know the law. Captain Hawkstone has salvage rights." He started to turn around.

"Wait! We've been tricked!" It was Garon, the man whose face reminded me of a rat. "They're lying! I think Jerad and that girl already found the Astrolabe together, and they've made a pact to keep it for themselves! You all saw the way they were acting together."

"Hmm, that's an interesting theory, Garon," Anders said. "Perhaps they should both be searched?"

"We didn't find it," Jerad held up his arms. "Search me if you want."

Everyone turned to face me.

"I don't have it either." I hoped nobody would notice the bulge in my pocket.

"That's not good enough," Garon said. "They could both be lying. I demand they be searched!"

"I agree," Anders said.

Duncan shrugged. "All right, fine."

Knowing it would be better to admit I had the Astrolabe rather than face the indignity of having someone feel all over me, I pulled it out of my pocket and held it up. It glistened in the dull light of the ancient city's glowlamps.

"I have it!" I said. "But Jerad is innocent; he didn't know anything about it!"

Everyone stared at me wordlessly for a couple of seconds. Jerad's mouth hung open. Then they all snapped out of it and started drawing their weapons.

"Sorry to disappoint you, Anders, but we'll be taking our leave now." Duncan held up his sword. "Everyone back to the ship."

We all slowly backed away, not wanting to let our guard down. Duncan and Jade positioned themselves in front of me. Jade sighed as she whipped out a pair of katana blades.

"This isn't over yet!" Garon yelled.

Two *Harrier* men grabbed Jerad from behind and held his arms. Garon pulled out a dagger and held it to Jerad's throat.

"Give us the Astrolabe, or he dies!" Garon said. "Sorry, Jerad; no hard feelings, I hope?"

"What are you doing, Garon?" Anders snapped. "Are you mad?"

"Sorry, Captain, but we didn't come all the way out here for nothing," Garon said. "I think Jerad fancies the girl. We'll see if she cares for him as well." He moved the dagger closer.

"Don't worry, Kayli," Duncan said, still backing away. "They won't kill their own crew member."

"Won't I?" Garon pressed the dagger blade closer to Jerad's throat.

"Don't hurt him," I pleaded, but my choice was clear. Even though I would be betraying my crew, I couldn't let Jerad die.

"Enough waiting!" Garon said. "He dies."

He moved the dagger to cut Jerad's throat. I pushed between Duncan and Jade, clutching the Astrolabe and running toward him, yelling, "Stop!"

There was a twanging sound, and Garon dropped his dagger and slid to the ground, a crossbow bolt protruding from his eye. I turned around. Tala was holding her crossbow up, her face frozen in shock at what she had just done.

"Oh crap," Duncan muttered.

Most of the *Harrier* crew yelled, brandished their weapons, and came at us. Jerad elbowed one of the men holding him in the stomach, making him double over, then wrenched himself free of the other man's grip. I made my way toward the rear of my group, putting the Astrolabe back in my pocket. Anders looked unsure whether to go along with his mutinous crew or not, but he joined the fray as well.

The next minute was complete chaos. Duncan and Anders were

locked in combat, their swords clanging together. Jade fought three opponents at once, weaving among them and swinging her blades with unbelievable speed. I took my bo staff off my belt and extended it to its full length.

A man with dark blue hair ran toward me, swinging a flail. Resisting the urge to go hide in the ship, I stood my ground. The man swung his flail at me, and I blocked him, then I swung my staff at him, and he blocked me.

"Give me the Astrolabe, girl," he snarled.

Another man showed up and swung a scimitar at me, but Zaylen appeared behind him and cracked him in the head with his nunchucks, making him crumple to the ground. The other man was taken by surprise, and I swept his legs, knocking him to the ground.

Close to the dome structure, the big guy from the *Harrier* picked up a chunk of a statue and hurled it toward Flin. Flin ducked, and the projectile struck the side of the dome. There was a loud echoing crash, and the ground began to tremble. Everyone stopped fighting.

"Gods, could this get any worse?" Flin said.

There was a loud grinding sound as the ground slowly began to tilt again. Everyone stopped fighting and ran back toward their ships. Pieces of masonry and rock started rolling in the direction of the tilting.

A tremendous crack sounded behind me. I looked back to see a section of a tower break off and fall down. It smashed into the *Harrier*, completely destroying it. Their crew scattered, trying to avoid falling debris.

I reached the gangplank of the *Daybreaker* and hesitated. Duncan and the others arrived a few seconds later.

"Captain, we have to help them." I pointed at the *Harrier* crew.

"Kayli's right," Tala said. "We can't just let them die."

Duncan grimaced. "We don't have time. We've got to get out of here before we get pulverized, too. Better them than us."

I stepped onto the gangplank and hesitated, looking for Jerad. I caught sight of him as he stumbled and was hit by a falling rock.

Without thinking, I ran off the gangplank and rushed out into the courtyard toward him.

"Kayli, wait!" Duncan yelled behind me.

The ground was so sloped now that walking was difficult, and I slid several times before I reached Jerad. He lay on the ground as blood seeped from a gash on his forehead.

"Jerad!" I bent down and shook him.

His eyes opened, and he tried to sit up. "Kayli, get back to your ship. Save yourself."

"No, it's my turn to save you." I put my hands under his arms and helped him stand up. I was afraid I would see the *Daybreaker* flying away when I turned around.

"Anders!" Duncan yelled.

I looked back. The *Daybreaker* was still there, but Flin was piloting it, tilting it at the same angle as the ground to avoid being damaged.

"Over here!" Duncan yelled. "Get your crew on board!"

Anders and his crew ran across the courtyard toward the *Daybreaker*. I thought the ground would stop moving and go back to normal like it did the last time, but it continued to tilt more precariously. With Jerad's arm around my shoulder, we somehow stumbled back to the airship. Duncan and Anders helped us climb onto the steeply tilted gangplank.

We were the last ones to make it in. The gangplank closed, and the ship rose into the air and leveled itself.

"Thank you, Captain," I said.

"Don't mention it," Duncan said. As he rushed toward the stairs, he muttered, "I'm going to regret this."

Jerad collapsed to the floor, and I held on to him and tried to slow his fall. I sat down on the floor and cradled his head in my lap. Blood trickled down the side of his face. A few other people had also been injured, either by falling debris or during the fighting.

Laurel came down the stairs with her medical bag and began examining Jerad first.

"Is he going to be okay?" I asked.

"I think so." Laurel took out a piece of cloth and pressed it to Jerad's wound. "But that's a deep cut, and he might have a concussion. Hold this against him while I check on the others. I'll be back in a minute, dear."

I looked out the starboard window. The ship was still moving, and bits of falling rubble flew past. The rumbling sound continued, and the ship lurched back and forth, no doubt swerving to avoid falling obstacles. A few feet away, a man from the *Harrier* put his arm around a fellow crew member who was weeping.

Tala ran by holding a wooden box. She stopped when she saw me and looked down at Jerad.

"Is he all right?" she asked.

"I think so," I said. "What's going on?"

"The Dark Rock is still spinning; it won't stop," Tala said. "Both captains are up in the bridge. They've agreed that we need to get out of here before the whole place destroys itself."

The ship tilted hard to port, and Tala almost fell over. A large unsecured crate slid across the floor of the hold, and Laurel deftly moved aside to avoid being hit by it as she tended to a wounded man.

"Sorry, I have to get these tools to the bridge," Tala said.

She ran toward the stairs. I felt my pocket for the reassuring shape of the Astrolabe. It was strangely warm. I wanted to go find Duncan and hand it over to him before some of the *Harrier* crew decided to take matters into their own hands again but taking care of Jerad was more important. Hopefully, the others would realize starting another fight would be a very bad idea.

A minute later, the ship flew into a water-filled tunnel like the one we had traveled through on our way to the center of the island. I tried not to think about how difficult it must be for Flin to pilot the *Daybreaker* while the island was still rotating.

Jerad opened his eyes and looked up at me. "Oh, hey, Kayli. What's happening?"

"The Dark Rock is still spinning," I said. "We're trying to get out. I'm sorry about the *Harrier*."

"At least I get to spend more time with you."

"And I'm sorry I didn't tell you about the Astrolabe."

"That's all right. You did save my life, so that makes up for it."

The view from the window became brighter. The deep blue waters of the Sky Ocean were now visible.

"It looks like we made it out of the Dark Rock," Jerad said.

"Now, all we have to do is find a way out of the Sky Ocean," I said.

Zaylen rushed down the stairs and headed toward the engine room.

"Zaylen, what's wrong?" I said as he walked by me.

"The shield mechanism is failing," he said quietly. "If we don't get out of the Sky Ocean in the next few minutes, the ship will flood. I'm on my way to the engine room to help Sierra however I may."

"I can help." Jerad groaned and tried to sit up.

"This is Jerad," I said to Zaylen. "He's the tech expert for the *Harrier*."

"Is that so?" Zaylen said. "Then we welcome your assistance if you're not injured too grievously. But I must hasten to the engine room."

I stood up and started to help Jerad to his feet as Zaylen continued into the engine room.

The woman with dark green hair walked toward us. "Let me help," she said.

We helped him up and walked slowly toward the engine room with Jerad's arms around our necks.

"Hi, I'm Kris," the woman said.

"I'm Kayli."

"So, you're the girl who found the Astrolabe," Kris said. "Do you still have it with you? Don't worry; I'm not going to try and steal it or anything."

"Yes, I still have it," I said.

"I wonder if it was all worth it," Kris said. "We lost our ship and a crew member, and we might all die anyway."

"I wonder if everyone is wrong about the Astrolabe." Jerad breathed heavily as he struggled to walk. "Does it even find treasure at all, or does it do something else? Think about it. If the *Nimbus* crew really became as wealthy as the legends say, why would they need to keep coming back here to this dangerous place? Shouldn't they have all retired in luxury?"

"Maybe that's why the *Nimbus* crew mutinied," I said. "According to the journal, the captain wouldn't let anyone else use it; maybe it's because he didn't want anyone to know it didn't work the way he expected."

"What does it find, then?" Kris said.

I remembered what Zaylen had said about the Ancient Ones. They were obsessed with what came after death, and they had made the Astrolabe. *What is it that I want? I want to find home. Not Lindell, not the Daybreaker, but my true home. Can the Astrolabe show me that? Can it take us there and get us out of here?*

The Astrolabe grew warm against my body. Was it responding to my thoughts?

I'm here for a reason.

"Kris, can you get Jerad to the engine room?" I said.

"Sure," Kris said.

"What are you going to do?" Jerad removed his arm from around my neck.

"I'm going to use the Astrolabe." I ran up three flights of stairs and various corridors to reach the bridge. I was completely out of breath when I got there.

The bridge was a chaotic scene, with Duncan standing in the center of the room barking orders at everyone and Flin, Jade, Anders, and Tala operating various stations.

"We have two minutes left until the shields fail," Jade said.

"That's not nearly enough time to get to a portal, is it?" Duncan said.

Jade shook her head.

I pulled the Astrolabe out of my pocket and held it in front of me, and it gleamed brightly. Everyone on the bridge stopped what they were doing and turned to look at me.

How does it work? Do I have to hold it and utter some sort of incantation? This is so embarrassing. What if nothing happens? Creator, please help me.

I held the Astrolabe up. "Show me the way home."

It grew hot in my hands, and its etched lines and circles glowed. A beam of intense white light burst from it and shot out of the bridge, shining through the window and piercing the murky waters of the Sky Ocean. The beam continued to emanate from the Astrolabe, curving up as it vanished into the distance.

Everyone stared in amazement.

"What the—?" Duncan said.

"Where is it pointing?" Jade said.

"I...I don't know," I said.

"Whatever it is, it's got to be better than drowning," Duncan said. "Flin, follow that beam!"

"Yes, sir!" Flin adjusted his course, guiding the ship up and toward the beam's terminus.

The ship sliced through the waters with incredible speed as if it were caught up in the stream of light from the Astrolabe. My hands trembled as I kept a tight grip on it. The water itself grew brighter as we continued traveling along the beam's course. A school of jellyfish shot past the starboard windows and out of sight below us. Something shimmered outside one of the windows, and there was a sound of glass cracking.

"The shield is failing." Jade pointed at the window.

A fine spray of water came from the crack and puddled on the floor of the bridge.

"Captain," Sierra's voice came over the intercom, "we managed to get another minute out of the shield. But wherever you're going, hurry up!"

"Thank you, Sierra," Duncan said.

We continued traveling upwards. The light grew stronger, and the *Daybreaker* burst out of the water. Brilliant light flooded through the windows on all sides.

"We made it out!" Tala yelled. "We're saved!"

"But where are we?" Flin said.

I went to the bridge doors and cautiously opened them. The others followed me as I stepped out into the light, shielding my eyes. The air was warm and breezy. Crew members from the *Daybreaker* and the *Harrier* emerged from other doors and hatches and slowly walked around the main deck, gazing out at the whiteness. They glowed from the light, making me think of angels.

I walked down the stairs to the main deck, went to the starboard taffrail, and looked out. We might have been a thousand miles above any ground, but for once, I felt no fear. As my eyes adjusted to the bright light, I could see more of our surroundings. The ship was surrounded by a foamy white expanse that might have been the surface of the Sky Ocean, but I wasn't sure if it was actually water. A pod of whale-like creatures frolicked nearby, jumping in and out of the white substance and scattering glowing droplets.

Tala giggled and tried to catch floating particles of light in her hands. Sierra stood on the deck with a look of wonder on her face. Jerad was there, looking around in amazement. Our eyes met, and he smiled. Nobody spoke; we were all too transfixed by the sights and sounds around us. Just as the Dark Rock had felt dreadful and hostile, the very air of this place exuded wholesomeness.

I looked out and saw a bright green land in the distance. It was too far away to make out any details, but I felt certain my sister was there, and many others. I felt a strong desire to leap from the ship and swim toward it.

Then the light gradually receded until it reached the level of a summer sun at early evening, and all the people and objects on the *Daybreaker* returned to normal. The far green land vanished. Streams of water dripped off the top of the quarterdeck, and puddles on the main deck reflected sunlight. A seagull flew overhead and perched on one of the ship's railings. Now a calm, dark-green ocean lay below us, lit up by rays from the setting sun, and several lush islands were visible in the distance. Everyone stood on the deck in a daze. The big, bearded man from the *Harrier* stared out at the horizon and wiped tears from his eyes.

"Um, did anyone else just see that, or am I going crazy?" Tala said.

"I saw it." I was relieved to know that whatever it was, it wasn't just in my head.

"Where are we?" Flin asked.

"I believe those are the Taramar Islands," Zaylen said. Laurel stood next to him, and his arm was around her. "We're not too far away from Dulain and the Skyport."

Jade approached us. "Kayli, you've more than proven your worth as a member of this crew."

"Thank you." My vision blurred from the tears in my eyes.

"And Tala," Jade continued, "I know killing a person isn't an easy thing to live with, but you did the right thing."

Tala nodded and looked much more somber than usual. Jade walked away, and I turned to Tala and hugged her.

"I'm glad you talked me into working here," I said.

"I knew you'd come around," Tala said. "Hey, that...vision, that place we all saw; was that what you've been looking for?"

"Yes, I think it was," I said. "I hope it was."

"So, are you content now?" Tala said. "You're not going to leave, are you?"

"I'm not leaving the *Daybreaker*," I said. "Not anytime soon, anyway."

Tala smiled. "What an adventure. I'm gonna go take a long shower."

Flin approached, and Tala rested her head on his shoulder while he put his arms around her. I looked for Duncan and found him talking to Sierra. He kissed her forehead, and she hugged him and walked away. I walked over to him, pulled the Astrolabe from my pocket, and handed it to him.

"Kayli Starbell, good job." Duncan smiled and put his hand on my shoulder. "I'm proud of you. You're the most resourceful ship's cook a captain could ask for."

Then he turned to Anders, who stood nearby. "Anders, I've been thinking, life is too short for us to be enemies. Going through this near-death experience, or whatever that was, has put me in a generous mood, and I'd like to compensate you for the loss of your ship."

"Is that so, Hawkstone?" Anders eyes narrowed.

"While we were looking for our missing crewmate, we happened upon a stash of ancient technological devices which could be quite valuable," Duncan said. "It was a lucky find; there wasn't much left in that ancient city worth taking. I want you to have them. And this, too." He handed Anders the Astrolabe.

Jerad stood a few feet away, also watching the conversation.

Anders raised his eyebrows and took the Astrolabe. He held it in his hands and closed his eyes. "Show me the Lost Fortune of Aquilath."

He remained motionless for a few seconds. Nothing happened.

Anders opened his eyes. "That's what I suspected. It's only good for spiritual enlightenment and that sort of nonsense, not practical things. You can keep it."

Duncan took the Astrolabe. "I'd say what just happened was pretty damn practical, but I won't argue with you."

"Something tells me what we just experienced was a once-in-a-lifetime event," Anders said. "I will take the rest of the treasure, though."

"You have my word," Duncan said. "It's down in the hold. You and your crew can take it when we drop you all off at Skyport. I trust your crew will behave themselves while they're on my ship, without me having to keep them in the brig?"

"They will," Anders said as he and Duncan walked toward the quarterdeck entrance. "And by the way, perhaps I underestimated your crew."

"I'm sure you did, Anders," Duncan said.

Jerad started to walk toward me.

"Jerad, come help me inventory this ancient tech," Anders called out.

Jerad hesitated, looked at me, then turned to Anders. "I'll just be a minute, Captain."

Anders nodded and followed Duncan into the quarterdeck. Jerad walked over to me.

"You should be resting." I reached up and touched his forehead. "Your injury; what happened?" There was now only a light scar there.

"It just...healed, somehow," Jerad said.

"I'm glad," I said. "Do you think we'll ever see that place again?"

"The Dark Rock?" Jerad grinned.

"No, silly, you know what I mean."

Jerad turned serious. "I think we all will."

"Me, too," I said. "You know, your captain could have taken the Astrolabe and sold it, even if he doesn't have any use for it himself."

"I'm sure he knows that," Jerad said. "That's probably his way of thanking your captain and making peace with him."

"So, what's going to happen with your crew?" I said.

"I don't know," Jerad said. "Maybe we'll be able to get another ship, or maybe we'll just go our separate ways."

"Our ancient technology expert might be retiring soon," I said. "Maybe you could...stay here with us." I blushed and looked down at the deck. "If you want to, that is."

"I'd like that," Jerad said. "Do you think they'd hire me?"

"I'll tell them that if they don't, I'll burn all their meals." I laughed. "Speaking of food, it's been hours since any of us have had anything to eat. I should probably go to the galley and fix something."

"And I should probably go help Anders with the ancient tech your captain is giving us," Jerad said.

We looked at each other, then looked down, then looked back up at each other.

"Okay, then," I said. "I'll...see you later."

"Yeah," Jerad said.

I looked at him, wondering if he was going to kiss me. He moved forward a little but then hesitated. I threw my arms around his neck and pressed my lips to his. He put his arms around my waist and held me as we kissed.

ABOUT JAMES RICKETT

James Rickett lives in Texarkana, Texas with his wife Catherine and their three children. He works as a software developer to pay the bills. In his spare time, he enjoys writing fantasy and sci-fi stories. His other hobbies include playing the piano, digital art, cooking, occasional stage acting, contemplating deep theological and existential issues, and video games.

His favorite writers are C.S. Lewis, J.R.R. Tolkien, and G.K. Chesterton. His favorite films and television include the Lord of the Rings trilogy, Firefly, Kimi no Na wa, and most Studio Ghibli movies.

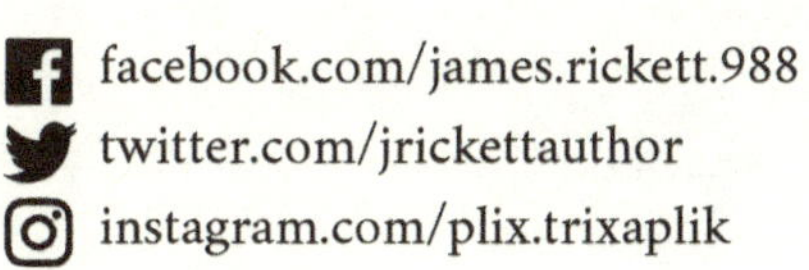

MORE BY FICTION-ATLAS PRESS

Fiction-Atlas Press releases two anthologies a year. We hope you'll check out some of our past anthologies or sign up to be notified about future ones on the next page!

Chasing Fireflies:

A Summer Romance Anthology

A Twist of Fate:

A Twisted Fairy Tale Anthology

Counterclockwise:

A Fiction-Atlas Time Travel Anthology

Beyond the Mask:

A Fiction-Atlas Superhero Anthology

Unknown Realms:

A Fiction-Atlas Press Anthology

The Devil You Know:

A Fiction-Atlas Press Anti-Hero Anthology

Bloodsport:

A Fiction-Atlas Vampire Anthology

THANK YOU

We hope you have enjoyed our anthology.
It would mean the world to us if you had the time to leave a review!
Reviews are what keep us writing!

FOLLOW FICTION-ATLAS PRESS FOR INFORMATION ON FUTURE PUBLICATIONS.

FICTION-ATLAS
PRESS LLC

http://fiction-atlas.com

facebook.com/fictionatlas
twitter.com/fabookbargains
instagram.com/cl_cannon
youtube.com/clcannonauthor